RESISTANCE

Daniel Kalla

TOR®

A TOM DOHERTY ASSOCIATES BOOK
NEW YORK

This is a work of fiction. All the characters and events portrayed in this book are either products of the author's imagination or are used fictitiously.

RESISTANCE

Copyright © 2006 by Daniel Kalla
Teaser copyright © 2006 by Daniel Kalla

A Tor Book
Published by Tom Doherty Associates, LLC
175 Fifth Avenue
New York, NY 10010

www.tor.com

Tor® is a registered trademark of Tom Doherty Associates, LLC.

ISBN 0-765-35439-X
EAN 978-0-765-35439-6

First edition: May 2006

Printed in the United States of America

0 9 8 7 6 5 4 3 2 1

For Mom and Dad

ACKNOWLEDGMENTS

I am so grateful for the feedback and encouragement of my loyal friends and family who read *Resistance* when it wasn't much more than a bulky stack of 8 × 11 pages. They include: Duncan Miller, Geoff Lyster, Brooke Wade, Alisa Weyman, Dave Allard, Peter Allard, Lisa and Rob King, Deedee and Kirk Hollohan, Jeff Jacobs and Deborah Rath, Dan Rath, Lissy Jarvik, Sonja Rath, John Ward, Maria Hugi, Jeremy Etherington, Janet Mutch, Susan Rhodes, Janine Mutch, Shannon Taylor and Lorne Folich, Alec and Theresa Walton, Sue Sutherland, Peter Olson, Steve Linville, and Glen Clark.

I want to thank my agent, Henry Morrison, whose level guidance and wisdom I've come to depend on. I'm grateful to Dr. Marc Romney for generously sharing his vast knowledge of microbiology. And a very special thanks goes to the wonderful and tireless Kit Schindell. As my first reader, her insight and feedback always improve my stories.

I am so fortunate to have Tor/Forge for a publisher. From Tom Doherty's considered involvement onward, Tor is run like a caring family. I want to thank Linda Quinton, Tom Espenchied, Seth Lerner, David Moench, Paul Stevens and copyeditor John Morrone. And of course, I have to single out my amazing editor, Natalia Aponte. Putting aside her substantial creative contributions, she is the best advocate and friend an author could hope for inside the publishing world. Thank you, Natalia.

And lastly, I would be nowhere without my family. Tim and Tammy, Tony and Becca, and of course, Mom and Dad, have been there for me since long before my writing endeavors. My two girls, Ashley and Chelsea, believe in their daddy even though they're not allowed to read his books. (Chelsea might be the best eight-year-old publicist in the world.) My wife Cheryl has managed to smooth out the road to publication, pulling me up from the lows and covering for the rest of my life when I'm immersed in a manuscript. Thanks, Cheryl.

1

Portland, Oregon

He eased the stolen black Ford Explorer to a stop behind the Dumpster in the dismal alley. When he switched off the ignition, the interior lights brightened and he caught a glimpse of his own reflection in the rearview mirror. There was nothing familiar about the face staring back. With three days' worth of stubble, spiked black hair and frosted tips, and the thick chain and heavy cross dangling from his neck, he could have been eyeing a total stranger. Someone he would have despised at first sight.

Dennis Lyndon Tyler—or at least that was who his out-of-state driver's license purported him to be—appreciated order in his life. Normally fastidiously clean-cut, he favored a dark jacket and tie for his assignments. Simple. Dignified. Nondescript. But now he dressed like a walking neon sign in a shiny blue track suit with reflective white Nikes and the gaudiest Rolex knockoff he could find. And he couldn't shake his low-grade nausea from the stench of his own cheap cologne.

Tyler peeled his eyes from the mirror. A job is a job, he repeated the familiar mantra in his head. The money is right. *Focus*.

He stepped out of the car. As he instinctively smoothed out the creases in his jacket, his hand brushed over the hard metal strapped under his right sleeve. The gun's contact brought a welcome sense of familiarity.

Walking the alleyway, he deliberately infused his normally crisp stride with the cocky spring he had noticed in the others he'd studied. After three weeks of posing, the gait had nearly become second nature. He could maintain it without trying.

This was the fifth alley he had covered tonight. Yet another of the many gathering spots for the lowest of Portland's lowlifes he'd visited in the past few days. They congregated here, huddling in the doorways and other nooks and crannies among and between the rundown buildings, preoccupied with their sole reason for existence. Drugs.

He'd chosen well this time. This alley writhed with junkies. Male. Female. Some alone, others clustered in groups. A number of them looked young enough to be in junior high school. A few lay on their sides or sat propped up by a wall, their glassy eyes open and pinpoint pupils staring out at nothing. Several fumbled at the tourniquets on their elbows or at their partners' necks, searching for that elusive vein to inject whatever chemicals they could force into their bloodstreams. Though Tyler had become accustomed to the activity, his guts still churned from the stench of the Dumpsters and the smothering sense of desperation and need.

As he passed by, he caught the eye of a number of junkies who recognized his unofficial uniform. A tall thin man with a ravaged face and matted hair swaggered up to him. He stopped directly in Tyler's path and, without a word, nodded to him.

Tyler eyeballed the addict up and down. His cheeks were hollow, and his scraggly pale arms bore telltale scabs crusted over. Still, Tyler decided that the man didn't quite fit his need. He shook his head. When that didn't budge the junkie, he narrowed his gaze and curled his lip into a slight sneer. That sent the man scuttling like a beetle back into the shadows of the nearby building.

He repeated the same silent dance with four or five other alley dwellers. He recognized a few potential candidates but passed them over too, remembering that he had been instructed to choose only the *absolutely* sickest-looking of the junkies.

Near the end of the alley, where the light of the main street glowed like the opening at the end of a tunnel, movement caught Tyler's eye. He turned to see an emaciated woman leaning against a Dumpster. She struggled to push herself upright before staggering out to meet him.

The woman was so gaunt that Tyler couldn't pinpoint her age closer than a range of twenty to forty. She had scruffy jet-black hair and thick chapped lips. Despite the drizzly spring night, she wore a torn black miniskirt and tank top, which exposed a bony sunken abdomen and legs so skinny that they didn't taper from thighs to ankles. The Aztec sun god tattooed on her shoulder appeared asymmetrical like a painting whose canvas had shrunken underneath it. A pink, rhinestone-studded handbag hung off the same shoulder. Studying her large gray eyes and delicate nose, Tyler imagined that once she might have been pretty. Now, with skeletal features and weeping sores on her chin and cheek, he found her repulsive.

Her lips parted into a forced, toothy smile that accentuated the broken incisor on the upper right side of her mouth. "You got anything for me, hon?" she asked in a throaty voice that was meant to sound seductive but struck Tyler as pathetic. He breathed in the scent of her nicotine-rich breath. It mingled with her stale, diseased aroma.

She was the one.

He tilted his head and smiled. "What you looking for, gorgeous?"

"Beggars can't be choosers," she said with a giggle and

swayed unsteadily on her feet, like a tree hit by a sudden gust. Then her smile vanished, and resolve hardened into the deep ridges of her face. "If you gotta know, I'm an old-fashioned girl. None of this crystal meth shit. I like eightballs."

An old-fashioned girl. Tyler suppressed a smirk. A month ago, he didn't know what eightballs were, but in the past few weeks he had dispensed several powdery packets of the cocaine and heroin used to concoct the cocktail, which seemed to be a favorite among the most hard-core users. Without a word, he fished in his track suit jacket pocket and pulled out two separate wads of silver foil. They looked as if they had been hastily packaged, but Tyler knew better. He had selected them earlier from the briefcase full of perfectly matching packets that had arrived along with his instructions. Then he had taken the time to grind them with a foot into the hotel bathroom's floor to produce an even more tattered and authentic looking result.

Tyler held the silver foil out in front of him in his open palm. When the woman reached for his hand, he closed it shut around the foil. She jerked her hand back as if it had been slapped. She stared up at Tyler with a look of sudden desperation. Her hand fumbled inside her purse but emerged empty. "I got jack right now for cash, but I got something else . . ." Tyler knew where she was heading but he kept his fist closed and watched her expressionlessly.

"We can get a room around the corner." She forced her eyes wider and slowly ran her tongue along her upper lip until it touched the crusting sore at the edge. "And I do everything there. *Everything.*" She pointed to his fist and gyrated her bony hips slightly, causing her to stumble a step. "Know what, baby? I'm going to give you the fuck of the century in trade, 'kay?"

The thought intensified Tyler's nausea, but he maintained his poker face. *Focus.* He opened his fist. "Tonight's your lucky night," he said. "Since I'm new to these parts, I'm offering samplers. This one's on me."

The woman's hand shot out and grabbed the packets with surprising deftness.

Tyler watched as she jammed the foil deep into her handbag. "You got your own rig?" he asked, referring to the syringe and needle she would require.

"Yeah, yeah, in here," she said distractedly, snapping up the purse as if he might revoke his offer at any moment.

"What's your name?"

"Carol," she sniffled. She shuffled on the spot, looking desperate to leave.

"Carol," he repeated, amused by the middle-class blandness of how it sounded under the circumstances. "Next time, you'll know who to see about buying your stuff, right?"

"Oh, absolutely, you're my new man, baby," she said, not bothering to ask his name. Then she swiveled on the spot and lurched on her pumps back to the Dumpster.

Tyler watched until she disappeared into a crack in the building behind the alleyway. He had no idea what was in the packets he had just given her, but he had little doubt that it was more than just heroin and cocaine. And from the substantial deposit to his numbered Grand Cayman account, he inferred that it was going to dramatically shorten what little was left of Carol's pointless life.

Running his hand along the sharp and ridiculous spikes of his highlighted hair, all traces of Carol vanished from his consciousness. He turned and headed back for his car.

A job is a job, he said to himself. The money is right. *Focus*.

2

Vancouver, Canada

Five more minutes and then I'm gone, Thomas Mallek promised himself for the third time since arriving. Feeling exposed in the flimsy blue hospital gown, the forty-year-old had sat on the same narrow stretcher for almost two hours without anyone paying him an iota of attention. Mallek figured his swollen knee could wait until he saw his family physician Monday morning; no doubt Dr. Ng would squeeze him in sometime. The busy lawyer, father of three, and dedicated marathoner did not have an evening to spare. Especially not at the emergency room of St. Michael's Hospital.

The place was a zoo, complete with sights, sounds, and smells foreign to Mallek. Drunks, street people, and various eccentrics filled the waiting room and paced the hallway; some looking bored, others menacing. The page for "security, stat" to this location or that seemed to crackle over the loudspeaker continuously. The antiseptic smell mingled unpleasantly with urine, vomit, and body odor that permeated the area.

Just as Mallek gingerly eased his leg over the side of the bed to leave, a voice spoke to him. "Mr. Mallek? I'm Dr. Gayle."

Mallek looked up at the young doctor who, with his hair tied back in a ponytail, wore green scrubs and a haggard expression. "Tom," Mallek said, stretching out a hand.

The doctor met Mallek's handshake, then waved a hand at the chaos around them. "Friday night," Gayle said by way of explaining all the problems in this corner of the world.

Mallek chuckled. "Don't know how you do it, Dr. Gayle."

"My fault. I wasn't smart enough to get into an ophthalmology residency." Gayle shrugged. A hint of a grin broke through his exasperated frown. "What's up with your knee?"

"I was out for a ten-K tune-up run earlier," Mallek said. "The toe of my shoe caught a crack in the pavement. About a block later I realized my foot was still stuck in the crack."

Gayle smiled. "Did you feel a pop?"

"Not only felt it, I heard it!" Mallek said. "My knee swelled right away. Now I'm having a hell of a time bending it."

Gayle nodded. "Can you lie back on the bed? I want to have a look."

Lifting his foot back onto the bed hurt Mallek even more than before. He expected Gayle to reach for his knee, but instead the doctor stood back a step and stared from the uninjured knee to the sore one. With a satisfied grunt, he bent over and gently rested the back of his hand on the knee, feeling, Mallek assumed, for warmth. Then the doctor put him through a series of mildly painful manipulations, the worst of which was when he held Mallek's thigh with one hand and tried to pull his calf forward with the other as if opening a drawer.

Gayle straightened up and folded his arms across his chest. "Hate to be the bearer of bad news, Tom, but I'm concerned you might have torn your ACL. That stands for—"

"Anterior cruciate ligament," Mallek finished the sentence with a heavy sigh. "I know. It's a big fear among runners."

"All athletes," Gayle said.

"Now what?"

"We should get an x-ray tonight," Gayle said. "Then we'll set you up with crutches—"

Before Gayle could finish, a series of unintelligible screams erupted from a flailing drunk in the waiting room, followed immediately by the familiar hiss of the loud-speaker: "Security, stat!"

Gayle smiled sympathetically at Mallek. "It won't take too long, Tom. Promise."

Mallek chuckled. "Any chance security could x-ray me? They seem pretty available."

Fifteen minutes later, Mallek had begun to doubt Gayle's word. No one had come to get him for an x-ray. Instead, the action had moved closer to him. In the stretcher beside his, the paramedics had unloaded a skinny teenage girl with dyed blue hair and wearing a tattered T-shirt, tartan skirt, and torn stockings. Though the curtain was drawn between their stretchers, one of the two flaps had peeled back giving Mallek a clear view of the girl. Her eyes were half shut and her words were garbled. Mallek assumed she was stoned, but from the way she moaned and thrashed on her bed, he recognized her agony. And the source of her pain—a swollen, fiery red thigh with a central bull's-eye-like white-head about the size of a dollar coin—stared back at him through the curtains' gap.

When the girl tried to bolt off the bed, the call for security broke again over the loudspeaker.

The team scrambled around her. The three burly security guards, looking like white-shirted cops, barked at her to stay still. The order struck Mallek as redundant because they pinned each of her arms to the bed while they secured thick black belted restraints around her wrists and ankles. A nurse fumbled with IV tubing at her arm. The girl's moans evolved into screams of indignant outrage.

Someone dressed from head to toe in mask and gown walked up to her bedside. Only when he spoke did Mallek recognize him as the ponytailed doctor. "Angie, we've got to drain your abscess," Gayle explained to the teenager but got only yelps in response.

Gayle instructed a similarly garbed nurse to inject two different drugs, which Mallek assumed were sedatives, because the patient stilled within a minute and only the odd groan emerged from her lips. Then Dr. Gayle prepared a surgical tray by the girl's knee.

None of the staff noticed the gap between the curtains. Mallek was too riveted by the unfolding drama to mention anything. When Gayle pulled a stool up to the girl's knee, Mallek realized he would have a bird's-eye view of the impending procedure on her thigh.

Forgetting all his earlier impatience, Mallek—a devout fan of the *Operation* show on The Health Network—watched transfixed as Dr. Gayle swabbed at the swollen thigh. Gently bending his painful knee, Mallek shuffled himself sideways on the stretcher and leaned forward for a better view.

Mallek flinched when Gayle buried the long needle into the top edge of the girl's abscess. The injection provoked a muted cry and a twitch from her before she fell back on the bed. Then the doctor reached for a gray scalpel that looked to Mallek like a box cutter. Holding the scalpel as if it were a pen, Gayle placed it against the skin over the center of the bull's-eye and pressed down.

The moment the blade sliced the skin, the abscess erupted. Yellow pus shot out from the wound and sprayed like a water fountain with a thumb pressed over its nozzle.

Mallek was so stunned by the unexpected jet of pus and the way the doctor jerked back and almost fell off his stool that he didn't immediately notice he'd been sprayed. It wasn't until he felt the wetness at his cheek that he realized a drop of pus was running down his face.

3

Philadelphia, Pennsylvania

From the forty-sixth floor of the forty-seven-story building, Dr. Ellen Horton stared out the floor-to-ceiling windows. Had she squinted, she might have been able to make out the figures of the rush-hour crowds scurrying along Walnut Street below. But her gaze never shifted from the tinted windows of the matching monstrosity across the street, as she forced herself to think of anything but her impending presentation to SeptoMed's board of directors.

I don't belong here, Horton thought as she smoothed the front of her pinstriped jacket and matching skirt. Fondly, she recalled the casualness of university meetings. At those functions, she would have been far more likely to see T-shirts and track pants than the ties and jackets that were the rule at SeptoMed. The indifference to fashion was only one of many things she missed about the academic world she had left behind.

Nothing felt the same since Horton had "jumped ship to the dark side" as her former colleagues had half-joked about her move to the pharmaceutical giant, SeptoMed. Despite their teasing, the exponential rise in her salary had nothing to do with her choice. Even after the six-figure checks began to roll in, Horton maintained the same lifestyle—an obliviousness to material comfort that bordered on the Spartan—with which her parents, both college professors, had raised her. She still showed up to work every day in her '92 brown Ford Taurus sedan, carrying a bag lunch and the same tattered briefcase she'd owned since her postgraduate days.

What Horton needed from SeptoMed was the state-of-the-art lab and the limitless resources that came with their generous offer. Without that support, she might never have had the chance to see her life's work come to fruition. And she had sacrificed too much—childless and single at forty, her closest companion was a temperamental eight-year-old cat—to tolerate failure. But the prize was close. She felt it. In spite of the setbacks of the past two months, her drug would come to market. "Just don't screw this up, Ellen!" she warned herself under her breath.

Horton heard the door to the boardroom swing open, and she turned from the window. Luc Martineau, SeptoMed's vice president of research and development, stepped into the reception area. He was dressed as impeccably as ever, in a gray three-button suit with a royal-blue textured silk tie. Horton couldn't help thinking that with his black hair styled in gel, chiseled cheekbones, and cleft chin, Martineau looked more like a male model from the pages of a European fashion magazine than the Ph.D. researcher he had once been.

Upon reaching her, he pulled her into a tight embrace. She was acutely aware of his designer cologne and the tautness of his chest and arms around her. Again she experienced the confused stirrings that his physical contact always seemed to bring.

Martineau stepped back and appraised her with eyes as blue as his tie. His lips broke into a welcoming smile. "You look wonderful, Ellen. Are you ready?"

Her anxiety dissipated in his confident presence. "As I

ever will be, I guess." She brushed a lock of hair off her forehead.

"Good." He winked. "Let's go convince the board. Then lunch maybe, yes?" he said with a trace of the French accent that he seemed to lapse into whenever he was at his most charming.

Martineau turned for the door, but Horton didn't budge. "Luc, what if they ask about the trials?"

He looked back over his shoulder with an unperturbed shrug. "So, you'll tell them."

Horton stiffened. "Tell them?"

"Of course, Ellen." His smile remained fixed, but the warmth drained from his eyes. "You'll tell them exactly what you have found in the human trials."

She felt the pressure welling in her chest again. "But not about the chimps?"

Martineau studied her for a moment without commenting. "Think of your audience, Ellen," he said evenly. "They are not academics. They don't care about chimpanzees."

Horton sensed his irritation; they had covered this ground already. But she couldn't ward off the rising doubt.

Martineau began to walk toward the door to the board-room. "They are waiting," he said without looking back.

She nodded half-heartedly at his back and followed him.

Inside the spacious boardroom, the shades had been drawn across the bank of windows but the soft fluorescent lighting provided almost a daylight feel to the room. On the large white screen against the far wall, the introductory slide of her Power Point presentation awaited.

Horton kept her eyes to the floor until she reached the head of the table where Luc Martineau stood. He beamed at her without a hint of the coolness of moments earlier. She allowed herself a quick scan of the forty or so people collected around the long conference table. The men outnumbered the women by at least two to one. Male or female, they all wore suits. As she had never made a presentation to the board in her eighteen months at SeptoMed, she recognized only a few faces. One of them belonged to SeptoMed's CEO, Harvey Abram. Sitting upright with bone-straight posture at the far end of the table, the bearded older man inspected her with disturbing intensity. He nodded to her once, but the gesture brought no reassurance. Out of reflex, Horton smoothed her jacket and skirt with another sweep of her sweaty palm. Then she reached for the remote control on the table.

Martineau cleared his throat loudly. "It's a huge honor for me to introduce our next guest." He clasped his hands in front of his chest. "Believe me, I dedicated six months of my life trying to convince Dr. Ellen Horton to join us at SeptoMed. It was the single most grueling project of my career." A few of the suits laughed politely. "But as you're about to see, without a doubt it is my greatest coup." He smiled at Horton, which only heightened her anxiety. "Dr. Horton holds both an M.D. and a Ph.D. She came to us from Temple University, where she was the youngest tenured professor ever in the faculty of pharmacology. Since joining us, Ellen has perfected a groundbreaking new antibiotic: *Oraloxin*. A name that I promise will become dear to you all in the very near future." He stepped away from the table and held out a hand magnanimously in her direction. "Without further ado, Dr. Ellen Horton."

"Thank you, Dr. Martineau," Horton said as the applause died down. She clicked a button. The room darkened. The screen filled with a large white circle covered in random splotches and streaks of purplish-blue consisting of innumerable discrete small dots, as if painted in the Impressionist style.

The room went quiet. "Staphylococcus aureus," Horton said. "One of the most ubiquitous bacteria in existence." She directed her laser point at the purplish-blue blotches. She circled one of the purple blobs. "There isn't a person in this room who doesn't have millions of these organisms growing on their skin as I speak."

With the lights dimmed and her slides behind her, she felt

herself begin to relax. A polished speaker from years of lecturing undergrads, Horton instinctively tailored the level of her talk to the nonscientific audience around her. "Normally, staph aureus is a commensal. In other words, it lives on the skin without causing infection." She clicked a button and an arm appeared on the screen. It was fire-engine red from the elbow down. In the center of the forearm, the skin rose into a huge whitehead that looked as if a golf ball had erupted through the skin. "But with any break in the skin it can become invasive. Staph aureus is responsible for most boils and abscesses." She ran the laser pointer over the fiery skin. "Along with group-A streptococcus, or G.A.S., it also causes the vast majority of the type of skin infection known as cellulitis."

She clicked the remote and the infected arm gave way to the picture of a man whose identity was protected by the black bar running across his eyes and mid-face. His complexion was ashen. A tube led from his mouth to the life-support system by his bed. Other tubes, lines, and wires crisscrossed his body, as if he lay under a power grid.

Horton deliberately paused to allow the deathly image to sink in. "Not uncommonly, staph aureus is responsible for more invasive forms of infection such as bone infections, meningitis, or pneumonia, as we see in this patient. And it can be rapidly fatal." She paused. "The man on the screen died within hours of this photo being taken."

She advanced the slide. A steadily climbing line graph popped up on the screen. "In the 1950s, the first penicillin-resistant strains of staph aureus emerged. In the seventies and eighties, resistance to another common antibiotic, methicillin, was first noted. This led to the genesis of the very first of the *superbugs,* methicillin-resistant Staphylococcus Aureus or MRSA." She pronounced the latter *mer-sa.*

Ice tumbled into a water glass and then the room fell into absolute silence. "Superbugs are forms of multiresistant bacteria that live, breed, and spread within *hospitals.*" Horton stressed the final word. "They are resistant to most classes of common antibiotics. And because of the intrahospital spread, they pose an enormous threat to health care delivery."

She pressed the remote, and the original slide with the circle of blue and purple streaks reappeared. "Today there are numerous other superbugs, but MRSA is the single most prevalent. Up until now, the only treatment available for MRSA involved expensive and potentially toxic intravenous medications, usually requiring hospital admission, thereby risking further spread." She shook her head. "Aside from the immeasurable human cost, the annual expense of dealing with MRSA is estimated to be from six to eight billion dollars in the U.S. alone."

Horton shifted from foot to foot, suddenly aware that all the eyes in the room were on her. "But SeptoMed might be able to forever alter that landscape," she said, flushing as she spoke the painfully rehearsed lines Martineau had insisted on. She pressed the button. An organic chemical formula filled the screen, complete with chains and dashes linking Cs, Os, and Hs. "Ladies and gentlemen, allow me to introduce Oraloxin.

"Oraloxin represents a brand-new class of antibiotics which we've termed membrocidals." She advanced to the next slide, which showed a spherical bacterium occupying most of the screen. "This is a single MRSA cell. Note the thickness of the cell wall, which is the bacterial equivalent of a coat of armor." From the side of the screen an animated V-shaped structure swooped toward the cell and dug into the cell wall like an angry hornet. "This model simulates what happens when a molecule of Oraloxin binds to the bacterial cell wall." As the "V" penetrated deeper, the cell began to fissure, like an egg cracking in slow motion. Then the two halves separated and the cell's contents spewed out. The rest of the cell suddenly deflated like a balloon popping.

"In clinical testing, Oraloxin has shown remarkable effectiveness in combating MRSA," Horton said, her tone somewhere between pride and self-consciousness. "With one-hundred-percent sensitivity. In other words, all MRSA infections have been susceptible to the medication thus far. And not *just* MRSA. Oraloxin performed equally well against other bacteria, even a multiresistant form of staph aureus that we genetically engineered in our lab."

Horton flushed again as she heard the grumbling of approval from around the table. She cleared her throat, forcing to herself to pause before delivering the punch line. "Unlike most other MRSA treatments, no blood testing is required with Oraloxin." She took a deep breath. "But I believe the most promising feature is the drug's mode of delivery. It can be given as a once-daily, five-hundred-milligram pill for ten to fourteen days. In other words, Oraloxin represents the *first* outpatient and oral treatment available for MRSA."

Horton clicked a button and the screen went white. She ran her prerehearsed closing line through her head before speaking it aloud. "Oraloxin is not only a powerful and brand-new weapon in the struggle against MRSA, but it will help keep the infection out of the hospital where it wreaks most of its havoc." She exhaled slowly. "Thank you for your attention."

The lights came up. Luc Martineau was the first to clap, but others around the table joined in until a chorus of applause had erupted. Harvey Abram smiled at her from the far end of the long table, but Horton read only conditional approval in his expression, as if his smile said: "Sure it looks impressive, Ellen, but you haven't accomplished anything yet."

A woman near the end of the table, two seats away from the CEO, spoke up. "Dr. Horton, first, congratulations on the brilliant discovery. Well done! But can you tell us about the medication's side effects?" she asked in a polite but insistent tone.

"Of course." Horton locked eyes briefly with the attractive middle-aged woman who had posed the question. "In our volunteers, we have noticed a predictable incidence of gastrointestinal side effects, including nausea and diarrhea, which is standard for all antibiotics. The other side effects are rare and comparable with the placebo groups."

Her answer led to another round of applause from the directors.

"But you've seen no worrisome or unexpected complications?" the same woman demanded, as she ran a hand through her short gray hair.

Horton glanced over to Luc Martineau. His blue eyes widened almost imperceptibly. She understood. *Don't mention the chimps!*

Horton looked down and focused on the conference table in front of her. "No person in any phase of the testing has demonstrated a major adverse outcome," she said quietly.

The comment was met by more applause, but Horton was immune to its effect.

She looked up. Abram was no longer smiling.

Horton inhaled and then exhaled a slow deep breath, but it didn't relieve the sudden heaviness in her chest. She felt her throat tightening as if it might close up at any moment.

There's no turning back now, Horton thought as she forced the saliva down the parched pinhole that was once her throat.

4

Seattle, Washington

Dr. Catalina Lopez sat at the table on the podium, struggling to keep the boredom off her face as she listened to the man at the microphone's rambling question about West Nile Virus. She had already decided she would allow her partner on the panel, Dr. David Warmack from the state Department of Health, field the convoluted question.

While she recognized that public awareness was an important component of her job, Lopez never imagined that these community public-health forums would consume so much of her time. When the thirty-two-year-old epidemiologist had landed the coveted job of officer at the EIS, the Pacific Northwest Epidemiological Intelligence Service, she had envisioned a life of exotic outbreak control and vital infectious-disease surveillance. She pictured herself managing an outbreak of the avian flu, SARS, or some brand-new, emerging pathogen that hit Seattle or one of the other urban centers under her watch. And Lopez knew she could manage such a crisis well—certainly well enough to earn her a job back at EIS's central command in Atlanta at the Centers for Disease Control. To Lopez the CDC represented the Vatican City of communicable-disease response, and EIS headquarters its Sistine Chapel.

Her frustration with her current assignment of West Nile Virus surveillance was that the bug had yet to reach the Pacific Northwest. As a result, she had nothing to track. She felt as if the only use she lately had for her thirteen years of postgraduate training—including medical school, a masters program, and an epidemiology residency—was in reassuring retirees and terrified mothers that the killer mosquitoes had not swooped down on them and their children.

"Dr. Lopez? Wouldn't you agree?" David Warmack's question jerked her out of her daydreaming.

Lopez could tell from the wry smile on Warmack's face that he knew she hadn't paid attention to the question or his answer. You old bastard, she thought affectionately. She had a soft spot for Warmack, whose looks and deep resonating voice, she thought, bore a striking resemblance to Gregory Peck. And though Lina had no tolerance for the male colleagues who eyed her with barely concealed desire, she never minded that the happily married old fox shamelessly flirted with her.

Lopez flashed him an "up yours" smile and playfully kicked his foot under the table. "Dr. Warmack, I don't think I could possibly agree more. After all, as you constantly point out to me, you're never wrong."

"Finally, we agree on something!" Warmack said.

The scattering of laughter allowed Lopez to duck the answer. Not wanting to risk a follow-up from the man at the mike, she quickly pointed to a woman waving her arm from the fourth row of the packed auditorium. "Yes. In the red sweater. Ma'am, you have a question?"

Without looking for a microphone, the woman belted out: "I'm still not clear. How do you know if you have West Nile Virus?"

"Most times you don't know," Lopez said. "For example,

after the first North American outbreak in 1999 in New York, there were only a few hundred cases reported, but a random sampling of the population in Queens suggested that roughly five hundred thousand had been infected."

"Oh my God!" the woman said, as if she were suddenly stricken with the virus.

"That's good news," Lopez reassured with a sweep of her palm. "It means that most people had such a mild illness they weren't even aware of it. With West Nile, most people don't get much more than a cold or mild flulike symptoms. Many have no symptoms at all. Very few develop the dreaded complication of encephalitis or brain infection." She bit her lip, weighing whether her next sentence would reassure or provoke anxiety among the jittery crowd. She decided to take a chance. "In fact, your risk of getting encephalitis from chicken pox is not much lower than with West Nile Virus," she said. "Does that answer your question?"

The woman in the red sweater nodded but looked as skeptical as ever.

"Hey, docs," a hulking man asked as he stooped over to speak into the standing microphone placed in the room's center. "How about mosquito netting? You think . . ."

Lopez's felt her Smartphone silently vibrate against her belt. In the few months she had owned the device, she had already become hooked on the combined phone, electronic organizer, and e-mail retriever. A self-admitted e-mail junkie, she couldn't resist the promise each new message held (but rarely delivered). She slid a hand down to free the phone from her belt. Cupping it in her hand, she discreetly brought it up to the table.

The "high priority" exclamation point caught her eye. And when she saw that the message—a lab report of bacteria growing in a patient's sputum—came from Harborcenter's microbiology lab, she knew it had to be significant. Hurriedly scrolling through the report, she saw that the lab had isolated group-A streptococcus from an ICU patient with pneumonia. The same infection had killed the Muppeteer, Jim Henson. And aside from severe pneumonia, Lopez knew the same dangerous bug caused necrotizing fasciitis, better known and rightfully feared by the public as flesh-eating disease. Lopez intended to follow up on the invasive G.A.S. result the moment the forum ended. But just as she was about to slip her Smartphone back onto her belt, something in the report popped out at her. The sensitivity list. She read through the list of antibiotics tested against the contagion in the lab and noted that beside each drug a fat *R* appeared. The letters implied the patient's group-A strep was *resistant* to every single antibiotic, meaning none of the standard drugs would fight off this strain of G.A.S.

Lopez's pulse quickened. There must be a mistake! she thought. No such multiresistant G.A.S. had ever been described in the world. Lopez scrolled down to the final line. In bold letters, a note read: "Sensitivities were confirmed on three separate cultures." This meant the lab had triple-checked the result.

Her mouth went dry. She felt her heart thud against her rib cage. The sound of Warmack's words faded into the back of her consciousness. If the lab was right, the world had just been introduced to a previously unseen pathogen.

A brand new and deadly superbug.

Don't get ahead of yourself, Lina, she thought. She took a deep breath and looked up to see Warmack eyeing her. From his furrowed brow, Lopez knew he had noticed her concern.

Aware of the eyes in the auditorium focusing on her, Lopez leaned closer to Warmack and whispered in his ear: "David, look at this result." With the smartphone trembling slightly in her hand, she held it up for him to read.

He scanned it in a flash. When he looked up at her, his gray eyes showed uncharacteristic fear. He said very quietly: "Cat, this is a problem."

5

Portland, Oregon

The man whose license identified him as Dennis Lyndon Tyler was itching to get out of Portland. He had come to loathe the city in the same way he had Seattle and Vancouver during his stays there. Even his memories of San Francisco, where he had once lived for a year, were clouded by the miserable assignment. During his nocturnal existence peddling unknown wares along the West Coast, Tyler had seen none of the famed beauty or charm of those cities. All he experienced were their seedy underbellies; human garbage seething in a live can.

Walking out of the alley, he realized with considerable satisfaction that the packet he had just unloaded on the cadaverous transvestite—who would likely not live to see the week's end—was the last one he needed to dispense. Tyler longed to return to his hotel and climb into the shower. He intended to spend hours under the its soapy, cleansing water, scrubbing away every infinitesimal trace of the last month from his body. Then he would pack up his disguise and sink it to the bottom of the Willamette River.

He was brought back to the moment when two men suddenly stepped out from behind either side of his SUV. Despite dressing similarly in black nylon windbreakers, black jeans, and tinted glasses, the two could not have looked less alike. The African American with the shaved head stood at least six-five and Tyler guessed that he weighed more than 300 pounds. His white companion was a head shorter and probably half as heavy. Tyler knew instantly that the littler man in the baseball cap was in charge, his companion the muscle. Tyler stifled a sigh. He'd seen the same stereotypical pairing so many times before.

The men sauntered up until they stood a couple of feet from Tyler, their aftershave overpowering his own. The small man folded his arms across his chest and cocked his head. "The fuck you doing, mister?" He sneered.

Tyler shrugged in feigned confusion. He pointed his key at his SUV. "Going to my car."

The man grunted a laugh and then turned to his huge companion. "Frigerator, this son o' bitch must just hate being alive!" he said, making the fat one laugh.

"I don't know what your problem is, but I got places to go . . ." Tyler took two steps to his right in an attempt to walk around the men.

The smaller man shot out his hand, which now held an open six-inch switchblade. "My *problem* is, you motherfucker, that you're working *my turf*." He waved the knife in front of him. "Tell me one reason why I shouldn't cut you up right here and fuckin' now."

Tyler moved his hand to his jacket pocket. The knife shot up to his face at eye level and hovered less than inches away. "Move again and you're finished!" the knife-holder snapped, cuting an *X* in the air so close to his face that Tyler felt a breeze from the blade. *"Finished!"*

Tyler's hand froze outside his pocket. He glanced over to

the huge enforcer, who now pointed what he recognized as a Glock 25 at the center of his chest.

Focus, Tyler thought. He smiled calmly. He gently patted his outside pocket. "The one reason you asked for? It's in here."

The smaller man pulled back his knife a few inches from Tyler's face. His shiny teeth flashed in a malicious grin. "You better not be shitting me, or I promise you . . . I'm going to fuck you up. Then I'm going find your bitch and do her the same," he snorted. "Then again, two to one, this cocksucker *is* someone else's bitch. Aren't you, queer boy?"

Tyler didn't answer. Rock steady, he languidly slipped his hand in his pocket and circled his fingers around the wad of bills. He eased the hand back out of his pocket and then turned it over to show the dealers.

The dealer's eyes lit up at the thick wad of hundred-dollar bills. "Toss it here!"

Tyler threw him the clipped bills. The dealer caught it with his free hand. The switchblade retracted as he slipped the handle back into his jeans. Then he began to flip through the stack of money.

"Can I go now?" Tyler asked.

The dealer kept his eyes on the counting. "I won't ever see you in Portland again, huh?" he grunted.

Tyler nodded. "Probably wouldn't be wise."

"Maybe the stupidest move of your shitty little life." The dealer said without taking his eyes off the money. "Now get the fuck out of here!"

Tyler stepped a few feet to his right. But without looking, he knew the gun was still trained on him.

Focus.

"Know what?" the dealer said. "My gut tells me this asshole doesn't listen too good. Frigerator, maybe he would get the message better with a couple rounds in his chest."

Tyler stood still except for his middle finger, which flexed until it grabbed the loop of wire dangling from his sleeve. He slid the loop forward and felt the click as the Jacob's-ladder mechanism sprung the NAA Black Widow revolver into his palm.

He took mental aim.

His arm swung to the right. The moment his hand stilled, he fired two shots.

The right lens of the enforcer's glasses exploded and a puff of blood and tissue sprayed from his forehead. After a momentary pause, the huge man toppled backwards, slamming into the pavement with an enormous thud.

The dealer's head snapped up from the money he was counting. His jaw fell open. "What the fuck . . ." he sputtered.

"You know what, friend?" Tyler smiled as he steadied his aim. "You swear a little too often. It's tiresome."

Then he shot him in the face.

6

Vancouver, Canada

"Crap!" Dr. Graham Kilburn muttered as he glanced at his watch and realized he was already running twenty minutes late for his office. Stepping into the elevator, he reached into the jacket's pocket, pulled out his cell phone, and hit the speed-dial key.

His receptionist Louise answered on the first ring. "You better be calling from our waiting room," she grumbled.

Kilburn chuckled. "Louise, are you sure you're not Sister Theresa from my third grade at St. Xavier's?"

"Believe me, Dr. Kilburn, if I had a ruler lying around this office I wouldn't think twice about rapping your knuckles with it," the sixty-three-year-old receptionist huffed in her whisky-and-cigarette-infused voice. "We've already bumped Mrs. Fitzsimmons twice. And the way she's looking at me right now . . ." she sighed. "How much longer?"

"I've got an urgent consult at St. Michael's," Kilburn said.

"Oh, Dr. Kilburn, not again!"

The infectious disease specialist still marveled at how his

receptionist had no qualms with treating him like a disobedient preschooler but insisted on addressing him only as 'doctor' despite his repeated requests to use his first name. "I've been asked to give an urgent second opinion," Kilburn said. "A young guy with pneumonia. Father of three. He's not doing well."

"Oh, I see," Louise said, her tone suddenly concerned. "Okay. I'll reschedule Mrs. Fitzsimmons. She'll have to understand. The next two appointments after her are followups anyway. I won't need you back until 3 P.M."

"Ah, Louise, did I call you Sister Theresa earlier?" Kilburn cooed. "What I meant to say was *Mother* Teresa!"

"At my age, it's not healthy to have smoke blown up my ass, Dr. Kilburn." Her deep chuckle turned into a cough. "Go help that young man. I'm off to find a sharp ruler."

Kilburn stepped out of the elevator onto the ninth floor, the respirology ward. After another busy night on call, punctuated by two more drunken phone calls from Kyra, Kilburn felt spent. But the ward's purposeful buzz energized him. The bright corridor bustled with people and outfits. Gowned patients pushed poles bearing IV bags up and down the hallway. Staff wearing scrubs, short and long white coats, and such a rainbow array of hospital uniforms rushed by that Kilburn had trouble distinguishing physicians from cleaners.

Reaching the nursing station, Kilburn pulled up a chair at the computer in the semiprivate nook at the back. On the temperamental electronic records system, he pulled up Thomas Mallek's chart. After scanning the admission history and lab work, Kilburn viewed the chest x-ray online. He studied the image, adjusting the contrast and brightness and zooming in and out on various zones of the chest. With a dense white patch occupying the normal blackness of the lung's right bases, he decided the x-ray was classic for an advanced lobar pneumonia.

Kilburn tapped the mouse, and the sputum culture report appeared. The preliminary results read "gram-positive cocci in chains." Must be invasive group-A strep, he thought. The antibiotic sensitivities were listed as "pending," but he knew that G.A.S. had a good response to most antibiotics, which made the patient's stormy hospital course even harder to explain.

He rose from the desk and walked halfway down the hall to Mallek's private room. Stepping inside, the first person Kilburn saw was a woman sitting in the bedside chair and clutching the patient's hand in hers. Her red eyes and drawn face suggested she hadn't slept in days. Despite her fatigue and lack of makeup, the fortyish woman was still attractive with short brunette hair and large hazel eyes.

Kilburn turned his attention to the patient. Thomas Mallek lay propped up on the bed against a pillow with a sheet drawn around his waist. Much of his face was covered by a clear plastic oxygen mask known as a *Star Wars* mask because of its similarity in shape to the one worn by Darth Vader. From the mask alone, Kilburn appreciated the severity of the pneumonia. If the *Star Wars* mask failed to help, a ventilator and life-support system would soon follow. His eyes were drawn to the patient's exposed chest where the gown had fallen open. Mallek had a lean runner's chest, but he was breathing far more quickly than expected. The muscles between his ribs sucked in with each breath. Without raising his stethoscope, Kilburn recognized the signs of severe respiratory distress.

He approached the patient with a smile. "Mr. Mallek, I'm Graham Kilburn, an infectious-disease specialist."

"Tom," the patient croaked over the hissing of the humidified oxygen that misted around his face, as if he was breathing outside on a cold winter's morning. "This is my wife—" he began to say but a coughing spasm cut off the words.

"Annie," the woman said with a forced smile and rose to shake hands.

Kilburn waved her back down. He rested a hand on the bed railing. "Listen, I know both of you have probably told Tom's story so far to seven hundred different people, from nursing aide students to the dean of medicine."

Mallek laughed weakly. "Maybe only four hundred," he said.

"Nature of the beast in a teaching hospital, I'm afraid," Kilburn said with an apologetic shrug. "I've read your chart, but I'd still like to hear in your own words how you ended up here."

"Four or five days ago . . ." Mallek puffed, "I began . . . to come down with . . . a sore throat . . . and then the cough . . ."

Seeing the deeper indrawings in the patient's chest wall, Kilburn laid a hand on his shoulder to interrupt. "Listen, why don't you let your wife tell me? You can cut in anytime she screws up."

Mallek nodded gratefully.

"Ten days ago Tom twisted his knee while running. Torn ligaments." Annie shook his head at her husband. "I told you it was a bad idea to run those kinds of distances in the dark."

"Annie . . ." Mallek puffed.

Annie rubbed her eyes. "Sorry, one sentence and I've already screwed up." She laughed self-consciously. "Tom was instructed to keep his leg up. It's not like him to stay still for a moment—busy lawyer and even busier dad, coaching two of our boys in hockey—but he actually took the doctor's advice and stayed off his leg for the first few days." She sighed. "Then he began to complain about a sore throat—"

"When?" Kilburn asked.

"Five days ago," she said. "The next morning he woke up burning with fever. Stayed in bed most of that day. He insisted he would be fine with a bit of rest, but the day after he looked even worse. He had trouble getting out of bed. And coughing! He was bringing up this awful green junk." She glanced at Kilburn desperately. "Dr. Kilburn, in eighteen years together, I've never seen Tom with so much as a head cold. He's the one who takes care of the rest of the family."

"That's me. Nurse Tom." Mallek squeezed her hand, but his attempt at humor sent him into a violent coughing spell that shook the bed and left him gasping.

"It's okay, Tom." Annie dabbed at his brow with the moist cloth in her free hand. Soon her husband's breathing settled back to its quieter but labored pattern.

"So you brought him to the emergency room?" Kilburn asked.

"Dragged him!" She sighed with a fond smile for her husband. "He was too weak to fight. But after his last experience with his knee, Tom didn't want to come back."

Kilburn cocked his head. "Tell me about that visit."

"Out of control . . ." Mallek gasped. "Never seen anything like . . ."

Annie stopped him with another dab of his brow. "He was here on the previous Friday evening. The place was just wild. Took three hours before the doctor saw him."

Mallek turned to his wife. "Hon, tell him . . . about the girl."

Annie nodded vehemently. "While Tom was waiting for his x-ray, they brought a girl into the stretcher beside his. A young drug user. She was in rough shape."

"Was she coughing?" Kilburn asked, trying to fit the pieces together.

Mallek shook his head.

"Tom said she had a big infection on her leg." Annie's face crumpled into a quizzical frown. "An abscess or something?"

"Sounds right," Kilburn said. "Go on."

"They had to open it up then and there." Her expression hardened with sudden indignation. "They didn't even move her away from Tom. They just stuck a knife in it right there. He saw the whole thing. Not only that, but he got sprayed by pus!"

"*Really?*" Kilburn asked, amazed.

"Could have been . . . partly my fault," Mallek said with obvious effort.

"It wasn't, Tom!" She looked to Kilburn. "Because he didn't say anything when they set up for the procedure, Tom thinks he was to blame for getting soaked with body fluids. It's outrageous."

Kilburn found himself nodding in agreement. The blatant breaches in infection control that he saw around the hospital aggravated him to no end. "Where did Tom get sprayed?"

"On the side of his face." Annie ran a finger down her own cheek and lip, and then shook her head. "Probably how he got this infection, right?"

"I'm not sure." Kilburn shook his head. "It would be an unusual way to get pneumonia, but the whole incident is bizarre." He made a mental note to track down the young drug user from the ER, hoping the staff had taken swabs from her wound so he could compare them to the bugs growing in Mallek's sputum.

"Okay, just a couple more questions." Kilburn led Annie and Mallek, who chimed in with a few choppy phrases of clarification, through a standard infectious-diseases interrogation. But he learned nothing that he hadn't already read in the chart. Then Kilburn plugged his stethoscope into his ears and put the patient through an equally unenlightening physical exam.

Annie turned to him, eyes hungry for news. "What do you think, Dr. Kilburn?"

Kilburn slung his stethoscope over his shoulders. "Tom has a progressive pneumonia that hasn't responded to two different antibiotics as well as I would have anticipated."

"What does that mean?" Annie demanded, her voice quivering.

"Could mean a few things," Kilburn said in his most soothing tone. "Antibiotics don't work instantly. Most of them kill the bacterial cells when they're dividing, which takes twenty-four to forty-eight hours minimum. Maybe the antibiotics simply have not had time to work yet. Or possibly, the bacteria growing in the sputum is not the cause. In other words, it might be a contaminant and the real source is a virus or fungus that can also cause this kind of pneumonia. Or . . ." He stopped himself.

"Or what?" Mallek asked, pulling at his oxygen mask.

"Or the bug in question—group-A streptococcus—is re-

sistant to the antibiotics you've been treated with thus far."
Kilburn dismissed the idea with a wave of his hand. "But
that's only a theoretical risk, because the bacteria is known
to be uniformly sensitive to both drugs."

"So, what do we do?" Annie asked, rising from her chair.

Kilburn smiled and pointed at Tom's chest. "We hit this
infection hard. Very hard! I'm going to add a third antibiotic
and antiviral medication, just to cover all bases. Meantime,
you two hang in there. We'll take it—"

He was interrupted by a knock. A tiny Asian woman in a
lab coat reaching past her knees stood in the open doorway.
"Sorry to interrupt, doctor," she said in a Filipino accent.
"I'm from the lab. The nurse told me to give you this." She
waved a single sheet of paper at him.

Kilburn walked over and took the page from her.
"Thanks," he said, closing the door behind her. Returning to
the bedside, he glanced at the final culture and sensitivity report. He read the sensitivity report a second time to ensure
he hadn't misread it.

What the hell? he thought.

Despite his lack of expression, Annie picked up on his
concern. "What is it?" she asked with a note of painful urgency. "Is it about Tom?"

"It's the report on the bug in Tom's sputum," Kilburn said
calmly.

"And?" she asked in a whisper.

He dropped his hand to his side. "I don't know whether
this is a lab mistake, but the group-A strep in the sample has
not responded to the antibiotics as usual."

"Oh my God!" Tears welled in Annie's eyes and flooded
over the rims. Her husband reached a shaky hand up to her
face to wipe them away.

"Listen to me," Kilburn said gently. He put his hand back
on Mallek's shoulder but stared into Annie's eyes. "Our lab
tests only a sampling of antibiotics. We have others to
choose from. In a way, this could be good news for Tom. We
might have found the reason that he hasn't responded to

standard antibiotics. Now we can bring out our biggest guns."

Annie sniffed and nodded. The stream of tears slowed. The panic on both their faces subsided.

But despite Kilburn's calm smile, his heart pounded and sweat collected under his arms. The lab report held repercussions far beyond the fate of the poor couple in front of him.

What the hell is brewing in your chest, Tom?

7

Portland, Oregon

Arms folded, Detective Seth Cohen stood motionless in the alley. A light dawn fog drifted by his feet, but his eyes were fixed a yard in front of him on Portland's twenty-second and twenty-third murder victims of the year. Jimmy Mitchum and Mack "Frigerator" Baxter—whose bloody shattered sunglasses still sat perched on his nose—lay in the center of the alley sprawled at right angles to one another. In his nine years with Homicide, Cohen had come to know these two drug dealers better than he'd wanted.

"Hey!" Detective Roman Leetch called out from where he stood beside the Crime Scene Investigation truck blocking the end of the alley. Leetch put a hand on his heart in mock sorrow. "Stare as long you want, but Jimmy and Frigerator ain't coming back, KC!"

Cohen didn't bother to look up from the corpses. The initials, which stood for "Kosher Cop," no longer registered with him. The nickname dated back to his days in the police academy when the others found out that he didn't eat pepperoni or ham on his pizza. He had tried to explain that he wasn't a kosher Jew, he just didn't like meat on pizza, but the moniker stuck the moment it passed his drunken friend's lips. Lately most people shortened it to KC.

Leetch lumbered up to Cohen's side and punched him playfully on the shoulder. "So, KC, what'cha think?"

Cohen pulled his eyes away from the murder victims and looked over to his partner. The youthful-looking, fifty-year-old detective carried at least fifty pounds too many on his tall frame. Cohen battled the opposite problem. At six feet, he had trouble maintaining his weight—an already lean 160 pounds—but he knew the distance running he did wouldn't help.

"I think it's a miracle, Rome," Cohen finally said.

Leetch's face creased slightly with confusion. "A miracle?"

Cohen nodded at the bodies. "That no one did this sooner."

Leetch broke into a slow chuckle that sounded like an engine catching. "No kidding," he said. "These boys had no shortage of enemies. Might as well open the Portland White Pages and call it our suspect list."

Cohen nodded. "Still . . ."

"Still what, KC?" The grin left Leetch's lips.

Cohen squatted down until his head was only two feet from Mitchum's. He pointed at the hole in the middle of his forehead. "A very good shot."

Leetch didn't bother to hunker down to Cohen's level. "Probably an execution," he said with a wave of his big hand.

Cohen shook his head. "Rome, they're a good six feet apart." He swung a finger from Mitchum's skinny form to Frigerator's mass. "And see how Frige's arm is bent at the elbow with his hand above his head?"

Leetch scratched his mop of curly black hair. "You think he was holding a gun?"

Cohen nodded.

"Maybe. Maybe not." Leetch eyed Cohen steadily. "Where are you going with this, KC?"

"There's no powder residue on either of them. These two weren't shot from close range, execution style." Cohen cocked his finger and fired an imaginary bullet into the site of Mitchum's wound. He glanced over to Leetch. "Rome, I think we're looking at the losing side in a gunfight."

"Okay, say we are," Leetch said. "What's the big deal? These guys go to war over pocket change."

"But this scene is too tidy for a war."

Recognition crept into Leetch's expression. "Yeah . . ."

Cohen straightened up to his full height. "Guys like these . . ." he sighed. "They unload their automatics like they're paid by the bullet. They may or may not hit the intended target, but you'd be hard pressed to find an intact window or an inflated tire for a couple blocks."

"True enough." Leetch chuckled. "And the CSI boys didn't find a single stray slug. This was the work of a very qualified hitter, wasn't it?"

Cohen tilted his head from side to side. "Makes you wonder."

"Who would waste money on such a pro for those two losers?" Leetch thumbed at the bodies.

"Don't know," Cohen answered distractedly. The shooting troubled him. With most pristine crime scenes, he could re-enact events as they unfolded in his mind's eye. This one was different. He had no feel for it. He wasn't even certain whether the two victims had walked into an ambush or initiated the fight that led to their deaths.

"Detectives," someone yelled.

Cohen looked over to see a uniformed cop hailing them from the other end of the lane.

"What you got?" Leetch called out to him.

"A witness," the cop called back and pointed to the building. "Maybe."

Still lost in his thoughts, Cohen followed Leetch to the other end of the alley. Littered with Dumpsters, parking stalls, and loading docks, in the brightening morning light it could have passed for any commercial lane. A far cry from the gathering point for addicts and drunks that Cohen knew it transformed into after sunset.

Cohen didn't see the woman until they reached the end of the alley. In the corner building's recessed parking lot, she sat on the ground with her back against a garbage bin. With her skinny legs akimbo, her short black skirt had pulled up and displayed the edges of her frayed, lurid-pink panties. Her greasy black hair was slicked against her head. And her torn, once-white T-shirt exposed a right arm that was red and swollen from elbow to fingers. She looked familiar to Cohen, but then most of the users did; he spent a disproportionate amount of his investigative time in this neighborhood.

"We'll take it from here. Thanks." Leetch nodded to the uniformed cop who, looking miffed at the dismissal, sauntered off without a word.

The woman looked up at the detectives with pinpoint pupils and glazed eyes. Cohen recognized the signs of a heroin high. "Morning officers," she mumbled and stared past them vacantly. "What's up?"

Cohen knelt down beside her. This time, Leetch labored to lower himself into a partial squat. "I'm Detective Leetch," he said. "This is Detective Cohen. What's your name?"

"Carol." Her eyelids drooped.

"You got a last name, Carol?"

"Wilson."

Leetch circled a finger in the air. "You around here last night, Carol?"

She yawned, exposing a front tooth broken near the root. "Most nights. Most days."

"Notice anything out of the ordinary?" Leetch asked.

"Nothing ordinary around here," she said.

"Okay." Leetch rolled his eyes. "How about Frigerator Baxter and Jimmy Mitchum, you know them?"

Carol didn't answer, but recognition registered on her gaunt face.

"Someone killed them last night."

She stared back at Leetch with utter apathy. "Occupational hazard," she said.

"Did you see them last night?" Leetch asked.

"Don't remember," she said.

"We're Homicide, honey." He pointed at her ratty pink handbag beside her. "We don't care what's in your bag." He heaved an exaggerated sigh. "But if you don't cooperate a bit more, we're going to have go through the hassle of busting you for whatever rig you got in there."

The threat had its desired effect. Her eyes widened. She struggled to sit up straighter, and she moved her legs closer together. "Yeah. I saw those pricks last night."

"What did they want?"

"What they always want," she snorted. "Money."

Cohen allowed Leetch to lead the interview while he absorbed the details. He couldn't help inhaling Carol's stale aroma, which brought back raw memories of his mother's final days wasting away from breast cancer. Carol exuded that same death smell.

Cohen shook off the painful memory and focused his attention on Carol's angry red arm, the skin stretched to the point of translucence and the fingers swollen into sausages. He noticed how she held it tightly against her body without moving it so much as a flicker.

Cohen wet his lips. "Carol, how did Jimmy and Frige seem to you last night?"

"Don't know what you mean," she said.

Cohen smiled. "I think you're sharper than you let on, Carol."

"Sharp enough to live in an alley, turn tricks, and inject crap into myself day and night," she grunted. Then she raised her head slightly. "You wouldn't know it, but I graduated college."

"I'm not surprised," Cohen said. In his work, he had come across doctors and lawyers who had ended up in the same alley, slaves to the same chemicals. "How were Jimmy and

Frige acting last night? Did they strike you as nervous? Pissed off? Looking for someone?"

Her mouth opened and she started to speak, but she stopped abruptly.

Leetch leaned forward as if he might grab her, but his hands stayed by his side. "What is it, Carol?"

"They wanted to know if I'd seen anyone new around," she said quietly and looked away.

"As in a new dealer?" Leetch asked with a raised eyebrow.

She nodded to the ground.

"What did you tell them?"

"No."

Cohen wagged a finger at her and smiled again. "But you had, Carol, hadn't you?"

Her head drifted forward and her eyes fell to the ground as if she might nod off. "Two, three nights ago, this guy came around. Offered me a free eightball. Called it a 'sample'. Told me he was setting up shop in the neighborhood."

"What did he look like?" Cohen asked.

"Like all of them." She shrugged. "Cheap. Flashy. Dangerous."

"You're not helping me with my sketch artist." Leetch held out his palms and wiggled his fingers. "Draw me a picture, Carol," he coaxed.

She looked up at Leetch but pointed to Cohen. "Kind of like him. Tall, thin, and good-looking in that dark way. But he wore this shiny track suit and a thick gold chain."

Leetch uttered a grumble of laughter and elbowed Cohen in the midsection. "You ought to get a load of Seth in *his* track suit and chains. Absolutely adorable." He turned back to Carol, his face all business again. "How old a guy, do you figure?"

"Thirties, maybe," she said. "Couldn't tell."

Cohen stared at her. "Did you see him again after he gave you the 'sample'?"

She nodded. "Last night."

"Did you talk to him?"

"No." She pointed out to the center of the alley. "But he walked right by."

"Did he see you?"

"Yeah," she said. "He stopped and looked me over. Didn't say a word. It was freaky. He had this weird look on his face. Like he was surprised to see me. And his eyes . . ."

"What about them?" Leetch grunted.

"They were black as night. They looked . . ." She hesitated. "Dead."

"What time was that, you figure?"

"One or two?" She held up her barren left wrist. "I don't have a watch."

"And how long after—" Leetch started.

"Maybe half an hour after Jimmy and Frige came by here," Carol answered before he finished the question. Then her eyelids drifted shut. She nodded to herself. "About five or ten minutes after the guy walked past me, I heard a couple of pops." She swallowed. "Pretty sure it was a gun."

Leetch glanced over to Cohen meaningfully. Cohen returned the gesture and then turned to Carol. He held his left hand out to her, offering to help her up. "Why don't you come with us, Carol?"

Her eyes popped open. She leaned away. "Whoa, whoa, you said if I cooperated . . ."

"You've been a big help." Cohen smiled and nodded at her arm. "I want to take you to the hospital. Get your arm looked at."

She shook her head. "I'll be okay. I've had worse."

"Have you?" Cohen asked, still holding his arm out to her.

She wavered a moment. Then she reached out with her left hand and grabbed his. Cohen pulled her to her feet, amazed at how little effort it took.

She let go of Cohen's grip and used her left hand to splint her other arm against her body. "You know, he did this to me," she said impassively.

"The new guy?" Cohen asked.

"Yeah." She swayed on her feet. "A day or two after shooting his eightball, my arm began to swell."

She lurched to the side and Cohen shot out a hand to her shoulder to steady her.

"Thanks," she said with a gulp.

"Carol, you okay?" Cohen asked.

When she looked up at him, her eyes misted over. "You know, I've shot a lot of crap into this arm, but it's never been near this bad before."

8

Vancouver, Canada

With Thomas Mallek's chart open in front of him, Dr. Kilburn sat amid the commotion of the ICU nursing station scratching a note in his barely legible scrawl. He fought the impulse to impale the chart with his pen and hurl it across the nursing station, for all the good his or anyone else's notes had done.

Twenty-four hours earlier, they had moved Mallek to an isolation room in St. Michael's ICU. None of the potent antibiotics infused into his system had alleviated his pneumonia. Mallek had slipped into a delirious state of semiconsciousness, mumbling nonsensically and unable to recognize his wife or children through the room's sealed windows. His respiratory status had deteriorated. His blood oxygen percentage—a vital measure of the lungs' ability to absorb oxygen from the air and transfer it into the bloodstream—hovered in the seventies, a critically low level. Kilburn knew Mallek would soon require life-support. Corroborating his theory, an open tray stood ominously at the head of the bed, fully prepped for a physician to intubate—slip a tube down Mallek's windpipe—and attach him to a ventilator.

Minutes earlier, Kilburn had tried to explain the patient's condition to his wife, Annie, in the ICU family conference room. Prepared to face her anger or blame, Kilburn saw neither. Legs crossed and a weak smile on her lips, Annie sat stoically and listened to his explanation. When he finished, the tears began to roll down her cheeks and fall onto her blouse. She tried to speak, but it took a few attempts before her voice cooperated. Finally, she reached out and touched his sleeve lightly. "Dr. Kilburn," she said between soft sobs. "There must be something . . ."

But there was nothing.

The mutated group-A strep that was multiplying unchecked in Mallek's chest had materialized out of nowhere. And it resisted everything Kilburn had thought to throw at it.

His thoughts drifted from Annie to his little sister Kyra. He remembered her similarly plaintive cries for help the day Social Services threatened to place Matt and Shayna in foster care. At the time, he was overwhelmed by the enormity of responsibility in assuming care of his then four-year-old nephew and two-year-old niece. But at least then he had the ability to intervene. Now, six years later, he felt utterly useless.

The loudspeaker's salvo jerked him from the memories. "Code Blue ICU! Code Blue ICU!" the voice repeated.

Kilburn was up and moving without waiting for a room number. He knew where to go.

His heart slammed against his ribcage as he sprinted the twenty yards to Mallek's room. But he knew better than to break infection control protocols. He grabbed a set of protective gear from the stack by the door. Wrestling himself into the gown, he hopped one-footed into each shoe covering, before slapping on a cap and surgical mask with clear eye shield. Hurriedly, he stuffed his hands into two pairs of latex gloves.

"Full body precautions!" he yelled to the other members of the Code Blue team who stormed the hall.

Bursting into the room first, Kilburn saw Mallek lying on the bed. His skin was gray and his chest still. His nurse, the only other person in the room, was a flurry at the head of the bed. She pinned a triangular bag-mask device over the patient's face, struggling to pump oxygen into his lungs. She glimpsed in Kilburn's direction without breaking the rhythm of her bag squeezing. "You a doctor?" she demanded.

"Yes," he said, trotting to the bedside. "Graham Kilburn. Infectious diseases."

She nodded. Her thumbs repositioned the mask while she pulled Mallek's jaw forward with her index and middle finger. "Stopped breathing two minutes ago," she said in a clipped but calm voice. She squeezed the bag so hard it looked as though she were trying to pop it. "Lungs are so full. He's almost impossible to bag."

Bright red numerals flashed 62 percent oxygen saturation on the bedside monitor. A warning light flickered like a strobe. The alarm bell blared nonstop. Even though Kilburn could also see the jerky heartbeat traced on the screen, he reached a gloved hand to the side of the patient's neck to convince himself there was still a faint pulse. Leaning closer, he heard a loud hiss with each pump of the bag and realized most of the oxygen was leaking around the face seal without reaching Mallek's desperately deprived lungs.

"Blood pressure is holding in the eighties," the nurse said. "But he needs to be intubated—stat!" She glanced at Kilburn, her eyes afire. "Can you?"

He hadn't attempted the technically demanding maneuver in three years. But he knew that Mallek couldn't wait an extra minute for the cardiac arrest team outside the door to struggle into their protective gear. Without a word, Kilburn pounced on the tray behind him and grabbed the scythe-shaped laryngoscope in one hand and the clear snorkel-like endotracheal tube in the other. The sweat began to roll into his eyes. Realizing how dangerous it might be to bring his already contaminated glove near his face, he resisted the temptation to dab at his forehead. Instead, he blinked the sweat away.

Kilburn looked over to the nurse and nodded. She returned the gesture and then yanked the bag-mask off Mallek's face. Thick green liquid pooled in Mallek's open mouth and dripped out over the corners of his lips. Kilburn heard a faint gurgling noise and saw small bubbles form and pop in the mouth's secretions. The decayed smell of pus wafted up to his nose.

Kilburn hunched forward until he hovered inches from Mallek's head. A bead of his own sweat trickled down from the inside of his visor and fell on the patient's face. He thrust Mallek's neck even further back with his free hand, and then slid the blade of the laryngoscope over the tongue. He pulled up and forward with the device's handle, lifting Mallek's jaw and opening the mouth wider. A gush of green flooded over the sides of his mouth and spattered Kilburn's face-mask. Instinctively jerking back, he prayed that he had secured his mask well enough.

Kilburn glanced at the nurse. "Suction!"

She slapped the foot-long curved suction catheter into the hand in which he already held the endotracheal tube. He stuck the catheter deep in Mallek's throat, but the small vacuum couldn't keep up to the lungs' massive production. The monitor's alarm shrieked in his ears, warning him the patient was dangerously underoxygenated. He already knew. Mallek's lips had turned dusky blue.

Kilburn needed to see the vocal cords to pass the endotracheal tube into the windpipe, but he couldn't even spot the blade of the laryngoscope through the secretions. His own chest thumped harder. "Got to do this blind!" he said to himself as he dropped the suction catheter and the laryngoscope on the bed.

He slid a finger along the tongue until it ran into the soft nub of tissue it sought: the epiglottis. With his trembling right hand, he snaked the endotracheal tube along his finger and beyond the epiglottis. First pass, he felt nothing but smoothness as the tube slipped into the esophagus. Wrong passage. He pulled back and tried again, forcing the tube even further forward. This time, his fingers met the welcoming resistance of the tracheal rings. The tube bumped down the windpipe. A geyser of green sputum erupted from the other end, forcing him to duck again.

When the flow slowed to a trickle, the nurse passed Kilburn the ambubag. He attached it to the end of the tube and squeezed the balloon-like pump, meeting fierce resistance. Sweat poured off him as he fought to squeeze breath after breath of oxygen into the fluid-filled lungs.

Kilburn felt a hand on his shoulder. He looked up to see that two more members of the ICU team had reached the bedside. "Good work, Graham. We'll take it from here," Robin James, the ICU attending physician, said as he gently pulled the bag from Kilburn's hands.

Kilburn nodded and backed away from the bed. There was nothing more for him to do.

Though it had seemed as if the nurse and he had been alone with the patient for hours, the intubation had taken less than two minutes. More gowned and masked members of the Code Blue team flooded into the room. Kilburn watched as they swarmed the patient. Nurses started new intravenous lines and piggybacked medications on top of existing ones. The respiratory technician hooked the endotracheal tube to the ventilator. Orders were voiced in even tones. Everyone moved with urgent, nearly choreographed, purpose. None of them showed a trace of panic, but their determination was palpable.

Despite the expert intervention, Mallek's color never lightened. And the vital-sign readings on the monitor steadily deteriorated. His oxygen saturation level dipped into the fifties. His blood pressure fell below sixty. The monitor's alarm screamed its unrelenting concern.

Then Mallek's pulse began to slow.

"Damn it!" Kilburn muttered under his breath. He turned and headed for the door. He didn't want to stay for the end.

9

Philadelphia, Pennsylvania

Once or twice a minute Horton's computer chimed to announce the arrival of another e-mail demanding urgent attention. The calls, faxes, and e-mail were coming in nonstop. With the FDA approval hearing for her brainchild Oraloxin only weeks away, it was now crunch time. But in spite of the looming deadlines, Horton had spent the past half hour staring beyond her screen saver—her cat lying upside down on the bed and scratching at the air—at the ominous gray skies. She imagined how it would feel to climb out the window of her eighteenth-floor office and simply let go. Would those last moments—her body tumbling and ears ringing—be peaceful? she wondered. Or would they be seconds of sheer terror, equal parts panic and regret?

The thoughts of bridges, buildings, and pills had resurfaced in the past days. But they weren't nearly as compelling as the time eight years earlier when she reached such a low that she had no choice but to overdose on tranquilizers, an act that landed her in an ICU, followed by a month in the psychiatric ward. No. Her mood was now stable enough. She had been diligently taking her anti-depressants. She decided that the morbid suicidal fantasies represented her brain's idiosyncratic way of facing the mounting stress. The fatigue didn't help, either. Ever since she heard about the two chimps in her lab, sleep had become elusive. And she remembered from her time in med school how much havoc poor sleep could wreak on the psyche.

Horton was thankful for the knock at her door that pulled her back into the moment. She looked up to see Dr. Neil Ryland standing in the doorway. The mere sight of him chased the dark musings from her mind.

"How you coping, El?" Ryland asked as he wandered into the room.

Horton smiled at the stocky microbiologist. They had worked together on the development of Oraloxin for more than five years, long before SeptoMed expressed interest. Ryland's steady presence had made Horton's jump from the university to private industry far less lonely. "Okay, Neil." She hit a button on the keyboard and her cat was replaced onscreen by the Oraloxin logo. "And you?"

"Fine. But I don't have all that celebrity stuff to deal with." He waved his hand in front of him. "Don't get me wrong, El. I'd rather have a bad case of the clap than all that bull you have to put up with. You can keep your Nobel Prize. I like my privacy."

"Nobel Prize. Right!" Horton shook her head and laughed. "But you can't stay out of the limelight that easily."

"Believe me, nobody wants to see me in bright lights." He shrugged, his eyes downcast and cheeks pink with boyish bashfulness.

Despite being a year older than Ryland, Horton saw him as the rock-steady big brother she never had. She knew that other women found him handsome. Though a few pounds overweight, his extra bulk suited his round face with its dark green eyes and fair-skinned complexion. His self-effacing humility and easygoing manner only accentuated his charm.

But despite their shared interests and closeness, she regarded Ryland in an asexual light. At times, she wondered if he had a life outside of the lab. Then she realized with a pang of embarrassment that he could just as easily think the same of her. And who could blame him?

Ryland plunked himself down in the chair across from hers. He rested his elbows on her desk and interlocked his fingers. His brow furrowed and he pointed at her with his index fingers. "El, you haven't seemed yourself this week."

"Just tired," she said. "I'm not sleeping well, Neil."

His frown persisted. "Why?"

She looked down at the desk. "Those chimps . . ." she said quietly.

Ryland shook his head. "El, we've been over this. Two chimps out of hundreds don't add up to any kind of statistical significance."

"I know but—"

"No buts." He swept the air with a dismissive palm. "In all those clinical trials we've been running, we haven't seen anything close in humans."

She fidgeted with the pages on the desk in front of her. "It's only been a year, Neil."

"That's eons for a drug that patients take for only one or two weeks. Even Vik concedes that," he said, referring to Dr. Viktor Leschuk, the third member of the triumvirate on the Oraloxin project. "And you know what a skeptic Vik is."

"I guess."

He fixed his eyes on hers. "Ellen, you've got to trust me on this one. It's going to be fine. I promise."

"Okay." She smiled and looked up to see that, as if on cue, the skies had cleared outside her window.

"El, have you talked to anyone outside the lab about the chimps?"

Feeling suddenly sheepish, she shuffled through her papers. "Only Luc Martineau."

"Oh. Pretty boy," he grunted disapprovingly. Horton again noticed the air of protectiveness Ryland displayed whenever Martineau's name arose. Even though she never discussed her feelings for the suave VP, Ryland seemed aware of her vulnerability to his magnetism. "And how did *Dr.* Martineau take it?" he said without hiding the contempt in his tone.

She shrugged. "Luc didn't seem too concerned."

Ryland's expression softened. He studied her with a mischievous smile. "See? If even the cover-your-ass guy isn't worried, you know it's no big deal."

Relieved at the break in the tension, she laughed heartily. "I guess."

But Ryland's eyes darkened again. "El, you have to be very careful who you talk to about this. There are extremely jealous people out there. And you know how gossip spreads in our circles."

She couldn't argue. The scientific community was worse than Hollywood when it came to airing dirty laundry; rather than sex scandals or weight problems, academic gossip focused on research failures, perceived plagiarism, or ethical breaches. And Horton knew too many colleagues who would delight in seeing a fellow scientist fall publicly on her face.

"I'll just vent to you, Neil," she said. "Promise."

"Consider me your exhaust pipe." With a smile, he rose from his seat. He headed for the door, but then stopped halfway and turned back.

She shook her head. "What, Neil?"

He stared at her with the look of a wounded puppy. "El, we . . . you have come way too far to be undermined by idle rumors now."

"I won't mention the chimps outside the lab again," she said. "Now go do something more useful than hassling me." She forced a smile, but she felt a familiar tightening behind her sternum. She took a few deep breaths and tried to swallow away the sudden constriction in her throat.

10

Vancouver, Canada

The moment Parminder Singh regained consciousness in the post-op assessment room of St. Michael's Hospital, she forced her head off the bed and focused her swirling vision on her left arm. She had a nightmarish flashback to the moment prior to going under when Dr. Wong had warned her that she might wake up missing part or all of her arm.

Parminder scanned the limb desperately. From the shoulder down it was swaddled in thick bandages. She felt no sensation in the entire arm. For a few panicky moments, she wasn't sure if she still had a hand. Then she glimpsed a trace of pink at the far end of the bulky dressing. Concentrating intensely, she wiggled the pink nubs poking out from the end of the gauze, and realized, with a flood of relief, she was looking at her own fingers.

"Thank you, God!" She moaned a prayer in Punjabi, and let her heavy head fall back on the bed.

She felt a hand on her forehead. "It's okay, Parminder,"

the nurse's voice cooed above her. "Everything went well. Your operation is over."

Parminder couldn't hold her eyes open. They drifted shut. She thought of her little six-month-old, Harjeet. He was the most wonderful blessing imaginable. She hoped Gurdev could manage Harjeet alone. Her husband loved their son— the boy they had both prayed for—but he was so new to fatherhood, he could barely change a diaper. Like Parminder, Gurdev was only twenty, but she had an advantage: She had helped look after her younger brothers ever since she was out of diapers.

She wanted so desperately to be home with her family. All this trouble over a breast infection that the doctor had told her was common among nursing mothers.

But her case had proved more serious. When pills failed to work and she spiked a fever, she was forced to go to the emergency room where the doctors prescribed once-daily intravenous injections for three days. Two days after completing her treatment and recovering from the infection, she noticed redness at the site where the intravenous had been. The pain soon followed, and it was unimaginable—even worse than childbirth. Soon her fever ran higher than ever. In the middle of the night, Gurdev rushed her back to the emergency room where she heard the doctors and nurses whispering a strange term, "nectrotizing fasciitis," that she couldn't even pronounce. Dr. Wong was the first person to call it *flesh-eating disease*. Even in her rudimentary English, Parminder understood the gravity behind the term.

She was too tired to remember the rest. She felt herself floating off to sleep.

"Please, God, don't let me die," she mumbled in Punjabi. "Not for me. Gurdev cannot care for Harjeet all alone. They need me. . . ."

11

Vancouver, Canada

As soon as Kilburn stepped into his office, Louise rose from the chair behind the reception desk. Her hair was its usual frizzy tangle of gray, and her blue eye shadow as thickly applied as ever. Limping over to meet him at the door, she threw her flabby arms around him and squeezed tightly. He hugged back, thankful for the embrace.

"Even you can't win them all, Dr. Kilburn," she said as she finally released him.

He sighed. "This one was tough."

"How's his wife?" Louise asked.

He shook his head and swallowed away the sudden lump in his throat.

"She'll be okay, you'll see," Louise said, though she had never met Annie Mallek. "She needs time to grieve. Believe me, I know."

He nodded. Louise's husband had died long before Kilburn met her, but he knew how much she still missed him.

"Louise, do you have any bottles of the good stuff buried around here?" he asked.

She let loose a throaty laugh. "Remember last year's Christmas luncheon? After that, I thought I was forbidden from bringing my friend Johnnie Walker to work any more."

"He's welcome here today." He forced a smile. "In fact, tell him to bring a couple of buddies."

Louise eyed him knowingly. "Speaking of, Kyra called twice this morning. Said it was important." She sighed. "Of course, the poor thing always says it's important."

Kilburn felt the anger surging. He rubbed his eyes aggressively with his palms. "Not today, Louise. I can't deal with her today," he grumbled.

"Fair enough." she said. "Besides, you're one popular doc. Seems like everyone wants a piece of you."

Calmer now, Kilburn pulled his hands away from his eyes. "Who else?"

"Let's go check the list." She turned and headed for her desk.

Following her, he noticed her limp was even more pronounced. "What are you doing about that hip, Louise? Have you seen Dr. Clement yet?"

"Yeah, I saw him," she said when she reached her desk. "He wants to operate. Give me a new hip."

"And?"

"I told him I'd think about it." Louise chuckled. "Nothing personal, Dr. Kilburn, but I don't particularly trust doctors. And I *really* don't like hospitals."

He didn't argue. Considering Tom Mallek's recent death, he understood her sentiments. Hospitals could be very dangerous places.

She sat down gingerly in her seat and then reached for the stack of neatly printed messages on her desk. She leafed through the papers, divided the pile in two, and placed the thicker stack on the corner of her desk. "These, you can worry about later. Nothing urgent here." Then she took the three remaining sheets in her hand and handed him the first page. "Okay, there's a Dr. Nelson Amar from the Centers for Disease Control looking for you."

"In Atlanta?" he said in surprise.

"That's the spot." She passed him another page. "But that's nothing. This call came from Switzerland. A Dr. Jean Nantal with the World Health Organization."

"Wow." Kilburn had never met the WHO's executive director of communicable diseases, but like most of his colleagues he knew Nantal by his all but legendary reputation. "I guess we've got some serious attention now."

"Is that good?" Louise asked.

"No." He sighed, turning from the desk. "It's not good at all."

"One more, Dr. Kilburn." Louise waved the final note at him. He reached out and took it from her hand. "A Dr. Melanie Wong. She's called three times this morning."

Kilburn felt a rush of foreboding as he glanced down at the number. "Did she say what it was about?" he asked.

"They don't tell the live voicemail much." Louise pointed at her chest with both thumbs, but her confident grin belied the self-effacing reference. "But she said it was urgent."

"Thanks, Louise." He forced a smile. "For everything." Then he turned and walked down the short corridor to his private office.

He slumped into his desk chair and placed the three notes in front of him. He viewed each, though there was no doubt which call he had to return first. Dr. Melanie Wong was not the type to leave three messages without urgent reason. He grabbed the phone and punched in Wong's pager number.

While waiting for her to call back, he again considered where Tom Mallek could have acquired his resistant group-A strep. Neither the police nor Social Services had tracked down Angelica "Angie" Fischer, the ER patient whose pus had sprayed Mallek. Unless they found the HIV-positive drug user, they would never be able to confirm the link to Mallek because the swabs from Angie's original wound were never sent to the lab. But even if Fischer were the source of his infection, where did she pick it up? He racked his brain. It made no sense.

The phone rang. He reached for it warily. "Graham, it's Melanie Wong," the plastic surgeon said in her rapid staccato tone.

"Hi, Melanie." Kilburn pictured the petite workaholic surgeon, dressed always in scrubs and usually rushing to the clinic, the ER, or the OR—often all three.

"I operated on a twenty-year-old yesterday with necrotizing fasciitis of her entire forearm," she said in a clipped clinical tone.

"An IV-drug user?" he asked.

"Not at all," Wong said. "A previously healthy East Indian woman. A new mom. Developed the flesh-eating disease at an IV site just above her wrist."

Kilburn's temples pounded. He felt a sinking feeling in his chest. "Did she get the original IV put in at St. Michael's?"

"Yeah," she said with surprise. "At our ER. She had come for three days of outpatient antibiotics for an unrelated breast abscess."

His temples beat like a drum. How many others? he thought without voicing it. "How bad is it, Melanie?"

"We got it early, Graham. We spared her limb, but she lost a lot of skin and muscle on the dorsum of her forearm."

Kilburn ran a hand down the back of his own arm as she described it. "But?" he said.

"She was doing well yesterday post-op. We have her on high-dose intravenous clindamycin, but this morning when I checked her preliminary culture results—"

"She was growing group-A streptococcus resistant to all antibiotics," he cut in.

"How did you know?"

"We had another case." He rubbed his temples with his free hand. The sense of defeat returned as strongly as those final moments in Mallek's ICU room.

"How did you treat it?" she demanded.

"That's the whole problem, Melanie. We couldn't. Nothing worked. He died with me standing by and watching."

"I see," she said stiffly.

"Your patient might have picked it up from the same ER patient who infected mine. It's an ultraresistant form of group-A strep. The latest superbug."

Wong took a long breath before speaking. "What do I do for her, Graham?"

"She needs to be isolated."

"Already done. Is my staff at risk?" Wong asked. Then added softly, "Am I?"

"Not as long you've been careful," Kilburn said. "Unless she has pneumonia, she doesn't require respiratory precautions. Group-A strep spreads only by direct contact. But your patient needs the strictest of contact precautions—gloves, gowns, and very thorough hand washing after any contact with her."

"Understood," Wong said. "But Graham, I can only cut out so much of her skin. How do I treat the rest of the infection?"

Kilburn swallowed. "Melanie . . . I don't know that you can."

12

Portland, Oregon

At the Oregon Health Sciences University Hospital's ER, Cohen and Carol Wilson had to squeeze into the last two available chairs in the corner of the waiting room. Cohen was thankful for the seats. Having watched Carol stumble out of his car and weave the short steps toward the ER doors, he realized she wouldn't manage standing up.

The waiting room teemed. Old people languished on stretchers. Children cried and shrieked in parents' arms. Patients with every assortment of sling, cast, and bandage—some bloody and others improvised with T-shirts and rags—sat in chairs or hobbled between them. Doctors, nurses, and other staff ducked in and out. The voices, moans, yells, and other hospital sounds blended into loud white noise that forced Cohen to raise his normally quiet voice so Carol could hear him.

They had been in the waiting room for over an hour. Cohen had intended to leave Carol under the staff's care, but no one had come for her since registering. Something in

Carol's face kept him from leaving. From her enlarging pupils alone, he knew that her last dose of heroin had begun to wear off. But she appeared even drowsier. She had lost more color, and had turned as pale as the off-white wall above her head. She slumped in her chair, looking as if the work of sitting upright consumed most of her energy. She never mentioned the pain in her swollen right arm, but she braced it rigidly against her with her other arm. The slightest nudge from passersby brought a wince to her face.

Searching for a distraction for both of them, Cohen asked, "Where did you grow up, Carol?"

"Northern California," she said. "Palo Alto."

To hear her better, he leaned closer. "What was that like?"

She shivered in the seat and wrapped the hospital blanket, which Cohen had scavenged, tighter around her shoulders with her usable hand. "White."

Cohen tilted his head. "White?"

Her lips parted in a shy smile, again revealing her broken tooth. "White bread. White picket fences. White people." She breathed the words in shallow short bursts. "My dad's an engineer with Hewlett-Packard. Lots of techie types in Palo Alto."

He cleared his throat. "So how did you end up in Portland?" he asked.

Carol stared back at him, her eyes glassy, but holding a glimmer of understanding. "You mean, how did I wind up in the gutter." She looked away. For a moment Cohen thought she might not answer, but then she began to speak softly. "I was a good kid, you know. Studious type. Wanted to be a teacher like my mom." She laughed weakly. "My kid sister Amy was the rebel. I was the goody-goody who never touched drugs or booze."

Cohen studied her without interrupting. He had seen the look before. It was the face of a witness or suspect who had been bottling up a story for a long time and was ready, anxious even, to unload.

"At college, I had this roommate who introduced me to

stuff." Her voice trembled as her shaking became more prominent. Cohen resisted the urge to wrap an arm around her shoulder. "She was real arty. Convinced it was the 'intellectual' thing to do. Nothing serious. We smoked some weed. Dropped a few hits of Ecstasy. And we drank a fair bit." She paused. "Too much, probably. But I got my degree and then got into a post-grad program at Berkeley in education." Her voice cracked and she swallowed. "My parents were very proud." She shrugged her arms and then grimaced in pain. She fell silent.

Cohen stared at her. He wanted to know more about this person whose complexity he had only begun to appreciate. "What happened in grad school, Carol?" he pressed.

"One day, a friend of mine dragged me to this party. I didn't even want to go." She breathed more rapidly and hugged her blanket tighter. "I was given this pipe to smoke. I was so fucking naïve, I just assumed it was hash." Her voice wavered. "You know? I was hooked from that very first puff."

"Heroin?"

She nodded and sniffled. Tears began to well in her eyes. "You wouldn't believe how fast you fall." She looked down and spoke to the floor. "I didn't lose my virginity until college. And by the time I went to grad school, I'd only ever slept with two guys. But by year's end I was turning five or six tricks a night to pay off that fucking habit." She swallowed. "I tested HIV-positive a couple years later."

"And your family?" Cohen asked, gently.

Carol shook in her seat. "They tried so hard . . . ," she choked out through her sobs. "For years, they tried. Mom, Dad, Amy—a teacher now, by the way—they just couldn't cope anymore. The last time I walked out on rehab, they gave up on me. I just couldn't give the shit up." Cohen handed her a wad of Kleenex and she used them all to wipe away the mucus and tears, but the effort seemed to exhaust her. "I don't blame them." She panted heavily. "I would've done the same thing."

Cohen mustered a smile.

Carol suddenly slumped lower in her chair. In a blink, her complexion switched from white to ashen. She lifted her good hand and indicated her swollen elbow. "I guess I should thank that prick for the sampler he gave me." Her eyes swam around the room. "Think he might've been doing me a favor by . . ." Her words trailed off.

Cohen shot a hand out to grab her, but it was too late. She toppled forward in a dead faint and hit her head on the ground, landing in front of the woman across from her who jumped onto her seat and screamed in disgust at the disheveled addict at her feet.

"Nurse! Doctor!" Cohen shouted, as he leapt to his feet. "Somebody!" he yelled, crouching to his knees beside Carol.

A pool of blood had formed around Carol's head. She wheezed loudly. And she trembled so violently, Cohen wondered if she was seizing.

Staff came running from two directions. They swarmed around her. Someone in the crowd yelled: "Gloves and masks, she could be H1V-positive."

Through the bodies, legs, and arms of the ER staff, Cohen saw that Carol had managed to roll herself over. Blood dripped out of the gash on her forehead, but her eyes were open. They searched the room until they locked onto his. She held out her shaky hand to him. "Detective," she gasped in more of a tremble than a voice. "Please don't leave me. . . ."

13

Seattle, Washington

When the Q&A at their public-health forum showed no sign of tailing off, Drs. Lopez and Warmack exchanged a glance and wordlessly decided to cut the session short with little explanation to the West Nile Virus–obsessed audience.

Having carpooled together from their offices, which were a block apart on Sixth Avenue, they hurried out to Lopez's black convertible, an Audi A4. An impulsive gift to herself upon landing her job with the EIS, the car payments regularly swallowed a huge chunk of her monthly paycheck, but she would have sooner parted with her condo than her convertible. As it was still twilight, Lopez considered lowering the top but realized she was too preoccupied by the news of the resistant group-A strep to enjoy the warm spring night.

Warmack and Lopez piled into the car. Out of reflex, she brushed back her unruly black hair—a constant frustration to her despite the compliments it provoked—from her eyes. She glanced over to her veteran colleague who hadn't said a word since leaving the building. Though deep in thought,

Warmack's placid face showed neither the concern nor the excitement that consumed Lopez since viewing the inexplicable culture and sensitivity result on her Smartphone.

As they pulled out of the parking lot, Lopez said, "David, if that lab report on the group-A strep came from another private lab I wouldn't believe it."

"I know." He pantomimed ripping a page up. "Into the shredder."

"But this is Harborcenter we're talking about." She downshifted, allowing the engine to rev higher. "They're the best. And they checked the results three times."

He nodded.

She tapped the steering wheel restlessly with her fingers. "There is no such thing as group-A streptococcus resistant to all common antibiotics."

"*Was* no such thing, Cat," Warmack said. "Was."

Since her father died, Catalina Lopez hadn't let anyone else get away with calling her Cat, not even her former fiancé. The nickname always conjured memories of Papa. It had been ten years but she could still picture him so clearly; from his broad shoulders, bushy moustache, and kind laughing eyes down to the faint scent of the cigars he swore up and down he never smoked. Though Warmack's use of the nickname stirred the same memories, somehow it felt okay to Lopez. He reminded her a little of Papa. And she liked that.

"David—" She cleared her throat. "I was in Zaire during an outbreak of Viral Hemorrhagic Fever. And I was in Atlanta at the CDC when SARS first broke." She felt herself flush, embarrassed to admit to her clinical inexperience. "But I've never been in the potential hot zone of a *new* emerging pathogen."

"This is what you've trained your whole life for." The lines around his mouth crinkled into a warm smile, but Lopez detected a trace of gentle mockery in his eyes. "We're epidemiologists, Cat. We live for this stuff, right?"

She nodded, willing the redness away from her face. "Tell me what it's like."

"I've never been there for the *first* case report either,"

Warmack said. "But I've witnessed my share of emerging pathogens. I saw one of the earliest outbreaks of legionnaire's disease. And I was doing this same job in the seventies when Herpes came along and scared the pants off everyone." He chuckled. "Technically, it scared the pants back *on*. For a while, people almost stopped screwing indiscriminately." His smile vanished. "Then hepatitis C and HIV showed up, and the smart ones really did stop having unprotected sex." He paused. "Funny thing is, Cat, it doesn't matter what the threat du jour is—HIV, toxic shock syndrome, legionnaire's, or SARS—there's always one common denominator."

"Fear?" she offered.

"Not just fear," he said wistfully. "It's healthy to fear what is dangerous. But emerging pathogens always bring out *irrational* fear. You understand?" He pointed at the roof of the car. "The sky-is-falling kind of stuff."

Lopez was struck again by Warmack's understated wisdom. He had such a youthful manner that she sometimes forgot he had been an epidemiologist for almost forty years. "It's a fine line between protecting the public and panicking them," she said, "isn't it?"

"You got that right, Cat." He shook his head and sighed heavily, showing more of his sixty-eight years than usual. "No matter what the threat, from tainted oysters to a meningitis scare, it always feels like we're walking the same tightrope." He shrugged slightly. "And sometimes, like in the case of the Toronto SARS outbreak, it's impossible to protect the public *without* inciting mass hysteria."

The remark deflated Lopez. She was relieved to see the turnoff to Harborcenter Hospital approaching. Slowing on Ninth Avenue, she turned into the staff parking lot and parked in one of the spots marked "Reserved for Physician on Emergency Callback." When Warmack shot her a doubtful glance, Lopez shrugged. "What? We're physicians. Can you imagine more of an emergency callback than this?"

They walked through the sprawling hospital complex, an

architectural joining of the original century-old structure with larger modern additions. Their first stop was the massive second-floor ICU where the staff had drawn the unusual sputum samples from Tonya Jackson.

After showing their identification at the desk, a clerk led Lopez and Warmack to a physicians' office in the back. With a small TV, a mini-fridge, sofas, and a coffee table cluttered with magazines and plates, it reminded Lopez of an oversized dorm room.

In a white coat and blue scrubs, Dr. Dean Peters lay back on a couch. Legs crossed, he rested his head and back against the armrest while staring blankly at the basketball game on the TV screen. The ICU's senior resident glanced at the two newcomers without acknowledging them.

"Dr. Peters?" Lopez asked the young man who had the kind of Ken-doll good looks that never did anything for her.

His eyes never left the ball game. "Yup."

"I'm Dr. Catalina Lopez with the CDC and this is Dr. David Warmack with the Department of Health." She nodded in Warmack's direction.

"Okaaay." Peters stretched out the word.

She took a step forward, deliberately standing between Peters and the TV. "You looked after Tonya Jackson?"

"Jackson . . . Jackson . . ." He searched aloud for a mental match.

"A twenty-two-year-old woman with pneumonia. She was in the ICU as of three days ago."

"Oh sure, yeah," Peters grunted. "She came from the medical ward. Barely lasted here long enough to get registered in our computer."

"She died?" Warmack asked.

"And in a hurry," Peters said, sounding almost grateful.

Lopez folded her arms across her chest. "Can you give us just a little more to go on?"

"I'm on my third night," Peters muttered, as if this piece of information automatically excused his rudeness. Leisurely, he adjusted himself from a prone position from to sitting up. "She was an HIV-positive junkie. An absolute mess. Took up our last bed," he snorted. "By the time she got here, she had double-sided pneumonia. Even on the ventilator, we couldn't keep her oxygen saturations up. She was on multiple antibiotics, but they had no chance to work." He craned his neck to look around Lopez at the TV. "I figure it must have been staph aureus or group-A strep that did her in so quick. The addicts are really susceptible to those skin bugs."

Lopez took another step to her right, further blocking the screen. "What do you know of her premorbid condition?"

"Doubt she ever was premorbid," Peters grunted. "The girl had full-blown AIDS and weighed about eighty pounds. She was covered in track marks and multiple skin ulcers from popping. Popping is when—"

"We know," Lopez snapped. "Necrotic ulcers from the vasoconstrictive effects of cocaine injected, or 'popped,' under the skin." She sighed. "Both Dr. Warmack and I are epidemiologists. We have a vague idea what drug users are susceptible to."

"My point is," Peters said, unperturbed, "she looked like someone looking for an excuse to die." He flashed a look somewhere between a smile and a sneer. "Know what I mean."

"And that just broke your heart, didn't it?" Lopez said.

Peters shrugged unapologetically. "Look around this ICU," he grumbled. "We never have space for the traumas, the hearts, and the other tax-payers who need our help, because most times we're wasting our resources on patients like her and the other addicts and drunks with their self-induced problems."

You judgmental prick, Lopez thought. Just as she opened her mouth to respond, she felt Warmack's hand gently pull at her elbow. "Dr. Peters," he spoke up. "Have you had any other similar cases come through the ICU in recent weeks?"

Peters stifled a yawn. "We always get our share of septic pneumonias, but none like her."

"And no new cases since?"

"No." Peters frowned, as if realizing for the first time that the visitors had not arrived merely to harass him. "Why is the CDC and State Health interested in this case, anyway?"

"I guess you never checked Jackson's sputum culture results, huh?" Lopez sighed.

Peters shrugged. "I don't have time to run around checking on dead people's lab results. Don't know about you, but it's not the best use of my time."

"Too bad," Lopez said evenly. She fought off the urge to demonstrate the right uppercut her cousin had taught her to throw when they were both eight. "The sputum cultures grew group-A strep."

Peters flashed a self-satisfied, told-you-so grin.

Lopez smiled back. "But this wasn't just any G.A.S. According to microbiology, it's resistant to all antibiotics."

Peters eyes widened. "*All* antibiotics?"

"Everything the lab has tested it against so far." Lopez turned for the door. "But that's not useful now that the patient is dead, right?"

Peters sprang off the couch and followed her. His look of self-assured indifference gave way to sudden concern. "Hold on! I was the one who intubated her." He pointed at her. "Remember with SARS? Intubation was a huge risk to the physician."

"I do remember, yes, Dr. Peters." Finding his panic easier to stomach than his arrogance, Lopez was tempted to walk away without responding but decided against it. "Did you wear precautions?" she asked.

He nodded vigorously. "The works. Gown, mask, gloves, and goggles."

"Provided you washed your hands well, you should be okay."

Peters nodded. The color came back to his face.

She fished in her purse and pulled out a card. "If you see any other cases even vaguely resembling Tonya Jackson's, you call me. Day or night, okay?"

Peters took the card from her hand and nodded.

"And Dean, doesn't matter how much you think you know." Her eyes met his contrite stare. "You'll never be a good physician until you develop a little more compassion for *all* your patients."

Lopez and Warmack left without another word. They took the first set of stairs they passed to the main floor and then followed the signs to Microbiology. A technician led them past the microscopes, centrifuges, and other machines resting on countertops or standing alone on the floor of the lab. From the other side of the room, a distinguished, gray-bearded African American man, in a navy jacket and dotted red bowtie, strode toward them. "David!" he said in a rich baritone as he extended his hand to Warmack. "It has been far too long."

Warmack met the handshake enthusiastically. "Thanks for meeting us so late, Phil." He turned to Lopez and placed a hand paternally on her shoulder. "Phil Alan, this is Catalina Lopez. She's the CDC's regional EIS officer. No doubt she will one day be either the director of CDC, the surgeon general, or the secretary of health. Likely all three."

"Honored," Alan said with an affable smile and slight bow of his head.

Lopez waved the comment away. "He's all talk. Thanks for meeting us, Phil."

"Dr. Phil is no slouch either." Warmack looked at her with a raised eyebrow. "He runs the show here at Harborcenter."

"David, you do have a gift for exaggeration. And I'm choosing very polite words for it." Alan turned to Lopez. "I'm the acting department head. I did the job years ago, but now I'm a figurehead while the hunt for a suitable—read younger—candidate continues."

Before either could comment, Alan spun and headed toward a long countertop against the near wall. "Come," he called over his shoulder. "I want to show you something."

They followed him to the counter. Alan held up a culture

plate, which looked like a flat brown dessert plate with a clear top. Lopez knew the sealed plate posed no risk to handlers.

Alan held the plate closer for his visitors. "This is typical group-A strep. Grown from a young man in the ER with strep throat." Several round grayish blobs appeared on the plate's brown surface. In the center of each blob, a tiny white disc sat surrounded by a ring of brown where the gray had receded.

Alan pointed to the gray areas. "These are colonies of G.A.S. The white discs are various antibiotic preparations— penicillin, erythromycin, and so on. As you can see by the gaps in the gray surrounding each disc, the bacteria are sensitive to all the antibiotics we tested it against. Very typical for G.A.S."

Alan put his hand in the top drawer and pulled out another similar looking plate. It had the same gray blobs and white discs, but on this plate, each of the gray blobs extended to the edges of the white discs without any brown gap between. "This is the Culture and Sensitivity plate grown from the sputum of Tonya Jackson." He held it out for the others to see. "As you can tell, the G.A.S. has not responded to any of the antibiotics we've tried against it."

Lopez took the plate from his hand. She held it up and tilted it back and forth, hoping against reason that she could alter the results with a different angle of light. Though the plate was physically light, she felt the metaphorical weight of its significance.

"No chance of a mistake, Phil?" Warmack asked.

Alan shook his head. "Not after three cultures."

Lopez's stomach churned. She tasted acid at the back of her throat. It was one thing to read a series of initials on her smartphone's screen, but to see the actual menace growing unchecked on the culture plate in her hand brought the reality home with a visceral pang.

She put the plate down on the countertop. "So, no antibiotic you know of is effective against this organism?" she asked.

Alan paused. "Essentially . . . yes."

They fell into silence. All eyes were fixed on the plate.

Alan slipped his hand back into the drawer. He pulled out a second culture plate and placed it beside the first. Lopez studied the plate, recognizing that the two were almost identical. "Is this one of the confirmation cultures?" she asked.

Alan shook his head slowly. "We plated this thirty-six hours ago," he paused. "It's from a different patient. An elderly man who has been in hospital for some time. He was staying in the room next to Tonya Jackson's."

"Oh, crap!" Lopez glanced from one veteran physician to the other and recognized the worry in both their eyes. "It's spreading. . . ."

14

Philadelphia, Pennsylvania

Ellen Horton sat at the small conference room table of her SeptoMed lab, staring at the tables and graphs until they seemed to float in front of her. She used to look forward to these early results from the multihospital trials of her drug Oraloxin, so much so that she could hardly stand to wait for them. But as she wearily scanned the pages from Chicago, the first center reporting, she prayed only that she wouldn't see any bone marrow side effects reported in the treatment group.

To her right, Neil Ryland leaned back with his fingers laced behind his head, casually viewing the tables and graphs as if reading the Sunday paper. On Horton's left, Viktor Leschuk, her other lieutenant on the Oraloxin project, hunched forward and pored over the pages intently.

Horton had long been aware that the two men were a study in contrasts. Though close friends, they reminded her of two cold war adversaries from an old spy movie. Ryland was the unflappable, upbeat young American right down to his rosy cheeks. Leschuk was the brilliant, brooding Eastern European. In his late fifties, the balding, compact veterinarian-cum-pharmacologist had defected from Kiev in the early 1980s. Like other Eastern European scientists she knew, Leschuk struck her as perpetually homesick. Even though he spoke English well, most of his personal conversations were in Ukrainian. And the times Horton had gone out for dinner with Viktor and his wife, Oksana, they always went to the same Ukrainian restaurant. Horton knew, however, that Leschuk had never gone back to Kiev since the Iron Curtain fell, and he'd never spoken to her of his former life there.

Ryland's face broke into a wide smile as he reached for a sheet in front of him. "Did you see this graph?" He beamed. "The response rate was quicker in the Oraloxin group than with intravenous vancomycin!"

"It's only two hundred patients, Neil," Leschuk cautioned with a wag of his finger.

Mouth agape, Ryland stared at his colleague. "You're kidding me, Vik, right?"

"What?" Leschuk frowned.

"Our *oral* antibiotic works faster against MRSA than the *best* intravenous preparation and all you have to say is"— Ryland dropped his voice an octave and assumed a Boris Badenov–like comic Russian accent—'It's only two hundred patients.'"

Horton bit her lip, unsuccessfully fighting back a smile.

Leschuk shrugged. "You vant I should get ze Champagne and caviar now?" he said, deliberately exaggerating his own accent.

Ryland laughed. "I just want a little grin, Vik. Even a smirk will do."

The right side of Leschuk's lip rose in a feigned smile. "Happy?"

"Ecstatic." Ryland chuckled. "Vik, we've toiled away in this lab for a long time." He pointed a finger around the windowless room. "Every once in a while I think it's a good idea to celebrate the little victories." He tapped the page in front of him. "Like this one."

"Neil has a point." Horton reached a hand toward Leschuk's wrist but stopped a few inches shy. "I never dreamed Oraloxin would work faster than an intravenous antibiotic."

"That is not the issue." Leschuk glanced from Ryland to Horton. "Ellen, we've had your drug in the lab for more than three years now."

"And?" Ryland frowned.

"We know what it can do against MRSA." Leschuk brought a hand up and rubbed the thick stubble on his chin. "I'm not worried about how well it works."

"Damn it," Ryland groaned and rolled his eyes. "Here we go again."

Leschuk covered his eyes with his hands. "Neil, can we really close our eyes and pretend it never happened?"

Ryland grabbed for the page in front of him. "It never *did* happen!" he said hotly, waving the sheet. "Look. Here's the list of side effects the investigators documented in Chicago. Nausea, diarrhea, hives, insomnia . . . I don't see anything about bone marrow problems."

Horton reached over and gently pushed the paper down to the table. "That's not Viktor's point."

"I know," Ryland said, his voice calmer. "But we've been over the primate findings so many times. We don't know what went on with their bone marrow. Two chimps out of hundreds, maybe a thousand, do not—" Ryland stopped in midsentence when he heard the knock at the open door.

Horton looked over to see Luc Martineau, debonair as ever in a four-button navy suit, standing in the open doorway beside a woman in a stylish gray jacket, slacks, and wide-collared cream blouse. Horton recognized the attractive middle-aged woman with short gray hair as the one who had asked the questions during her presentation to the board.

"I'm sorry to interrupt," Martineau gushed. He turned to the woman and spoke as if the others were not in the room.

"Our scientists! It's impossible to find a time when they're not buried in their work."

"Please join us," Horton said, feeling underdressed in her jeans and running shoes.

Martineau and the woman walked into the room and stopped at the table in front of them. "Ellen, Neil, Viktor," Martineau said warmly. "I would like you to meet one of our board members, Dr. Andrea Byington. Dr. Byington has—"

"Oh, please Luc, it's Andrea," she said affably and held out a hand to the scientists.

Horton was surprised by the powerful grip behind Byington's small, perfectly manicured hand. She recognized the last name immediately. It was synonymous with old money in Philadelphia. And she knew that Byington Pharmaceuticals was one of the principal companies in the merger that created SeptoMed.

After introductions, Horton asked her: "Are you a physician or a researcher?"

"Neither, really." Byington smiled warmly. "I'm a clinical psychologist." She quickly added, "But I haven't practiced in years."

Martineau held out his palms deferentially to Horton. "Ellen, after your presentation to the board, Andrea wanted to come meet you and—"

Byington interrupted him again by resting a hand on Martineau's shoulder. When her hand didn't leave his shoulder, Horton felt an unexpected twinge of jealousy. "I wanted to come to congratulate you," Byington said, "all of you, on your brilliant discovery."

"Yes, well, thank you." Horton cleared her throat. "It's still very early days, though."

"You'll never get El to accept a compliment, Andrea," Ryland piped up. "But Vik and I will." He grinned and glanced over to Leschuk who sat stone-faced. "Right?"

"Brilliant work. All of you," Byington repeated with a laugh, finally removing her hand from Martineau's shoulder. "I'm absolutely awed by the breadth of your accomplishment. I understand FDA approval is expected in the next week or two."

Ryland pointed to the papers in front of him. "And this will only help."

Byington glanced at the papers. "What is it?"

"We have several clinical studies going on concurrently," Horton explained. "One on the West Coast in hospitals from San Francisco to Vancouver. Another in Florida. And two in Europe. But these are the first—granted, early—results from a trial in Chicago involving two hundred patients with MRSA." She summarized the results, downplaying their significance.

Byington's eyes widened and her lips broke into a big smile. " 'More rapid and effective than the gold-standard intravenous treatment for MRSA?' That's astounding!"

"I thought so." Ryland nodded, beaming.

Byington pulled a chair up to the table. She sat down to join them and Martineau did the same. "You know my grandfather, Ezra Byington, founded the company very soon after Sir Alexander Fleming discovered penicillin," she said. "It was no coincidence, either. Granddad considered antibiotics *the* panacea." She smiled nostalgically. "He was a pigheaded idealist. He wanted to single-handedly wipe out all infectious diseases."

"There are worse things to be pigheaded about, *non*?" Martineau brushed at a few imagined flakes on his jacket.

"True enough, Luc." Byington pointed a finger at Martineau playfully. As her wrist shook, Horton noticed the diamond-studded tennis bracelet that slid up and down. "My grandfather died in 1978 believing his company and others had nearly wiped out all infectious diseases. In a way, I'm glad he never lived to see the surge in antibiotic resistance and emerging superbugs of the last twenty years." Her gray eyes drifted elsewhere. "Granddad hated to lose." She nodded to herself. "It's a Byington trait."

"Ah, but thanks to these three, maybe we're winning again." Martineau reached forward to pat Byington on the hand, causing Horton another jealous pang.

Ryland glared at Martineau. Horton saw that the disdain in Ryland's eyes bordered on hostility. But when he spoke, his tone was cordial. "There's no maybe about it, Luc."

"Your work is so important," Byington said emphatically. "Obviously, Oraloxin won't hurt SeptoMed's share prices, but it means much more than that."

"Yes," Horton said. "Having an oral antibiotic to treat MRSA will offer a whole—"

"Of course, Ellen, that's a vital breakthrough," Byington interrupted the pat speech with a slightly condescending smile. "But even more important, your drug could reinvigorate antibiotic research and development. Do you realize that in 2002, the FDA approved seventy-nine new drugs and not one of them was an antibiotic?"

Horton shook her head and Ryland shrugged, but Leschuk nodded to the table.

"And why would we drug companies throw money into antibiotic R-and-D?" She held her palms out in front of her. "It costs millions—sometimes billions—and for what? If you're lucky enough to succeed, you produce a drug that people might take for seven, maximum ten days, at a time. Whereas if we produce a new blood pressure or prostate medication, the patient is committed to a lifetime's worth of prescriptions."

Martineau placed both hands on the tabletop. "Not to mention the risks," he said gravely.

"Exactly, Luc!" Byington said. "Our last two antibiotics cost SeptoMed in the neighborhood of four hundred million dollars and neither made it to market. One didn't work and the other had intolerable side effects. Statistically, only one in seven new antibiotics ever do reach market." She stared at Horton. "Even then, there are no guarantees. You remember trovofloxacin? A terrific antibiotic that just happened to cause a rare complication of liver failure."

Horton's pulse sped up. She felt on edge. Byington was hitting too close to home in her comparison.

"No question trovofloxacin saved far more people than it

killed, but these days that's not acceptable," Byington sighed. "No. The standards the FDA sets are so rigorous. Most drugs older than twenty-five years would never be approved if they had to pass muster all over again."

Ryland folded his arms across his chest. "What's your point, Andrea?" he asked, sounding as defensive as Horton felt.

The heiress smiled benignly. "That we're fighting an uphill battle, but thanks to you the playing field has been leveled a little." Byington turned to Horton and looked deep into her eyes, her own gray irises dark to the point of opacity. "Ellen, we have an obligation way beyond SeptoMed and its employees and shareholders to ensure that Oraloxin succeeds." She paused. "Do you understand?"

A belt snapped tight against Horton's chest. She knows, Horton thought. *She knows about the chimps.*

15

Portland, Oregon

When Cohen walked back into Homicide's reception area, his partner Leetch stormed out of the back office to meet him.

"KC, I checked my e-mail twice," he said with a smile that didn't mask the edge in his voice. "But I never got the memo about you taking the day off."

"I was at the hospital," Cohen said quietly as he walked toward his office.

"Damn it!" Leetch said. "I was trying to reach you all day."

Cohen stopped. "Sorry. I had to turn my cell phone off in the hospital."

"You telling me you spent the whole day at the hospital with Carol from the alley?"

Cohen didn't respond.

"Look, I don't want to meddle or anything. And far be it from me to judge . . . but I think there's a potential problem in your latest relationship." He paused, but Cohen didn't bite. "I'm not talking about the fact that she's lives in a garbage bin and has a hundred-dollar-a-day coke and heroin habit. Those are just normal relationship bumps to work out." His voice took on a quiet conspiratorial tone. "But Seth, I don't think Carol is Jewish."

"She's dead," Cohen said flatly. He shook his head and strode into his office, closing the door behind him.

No sooner had Cohen sat down behind his desk before the door burst open. "What are you talking about?" Reaching the far edge of the desk, Leetch's round face crumpled into a grimace. "*Dead?* You just took her to the hospital this morning. It was only her arm!"

Cohen shrugged. "Septic shock."

"Which is?"

"Apparently, an overwhelming infection in the bloodstream," Cohen said.

"How did it happen?" Leetch asked quietly.

Cohen gave Leetch a brief rundown of what happened in the ER, but he left out the personal details Carol had shared with him.

"And you stayed with her the whole time?" Leetch asked, incredulous.

Cohen nodded.

"Why?"

"I don't know. She was alone." He didn't tell Leetch about Carol's last shaky words to him or anyone else: *"Please don't leave me."* The phrase had hit Cohen hard. His mother had spoken the same words to his father and him right before she slipped into a terminal coma.

Cohen shook off the memory. "They moved her into the resuscitation room," he said impassively. "They put her on a ventilator. Hung all these IVs. They worked on her for hours. Just as they were about to transfer her to the ICU, her heart stopped."

"Shit!" Leetch said. "I'm sorry."

Cohen shrugged again, deliberately disguising his deeper-than-expected sense of loss.

Leetch pulled up a chair and sat down across from Cohen. They sat together in silence for a few moments. Cohen cleared his throat. "Guess we should get on with finding out who killed Jimmy and Frige."

"Good idea." A mischievous grin broke across Leetch's lips. "Otherwise, what am I going to do with the trophy I got for the killer?"

Cohen chuckled. "Rome, don't you find the whole scenario with Carol and the two victims a bit unusual?"

Leetch drummed his fingers on the desktop. "You mean because the guy who gave the free drugs to Carol *might* be the hitter on Jimmy and Frige?"

"Exactly."

Leetch frowned. "We don't know that it is the same guy. Could have been a coincidence. Or, not to speak ill of the dead, but Carol might have been feeding us nothing but horseshit."

Cohen leaned back in his chair. "Why?"

"No offence, KC, but drug addicts have been known to lie now and again," Leetch said. "Maybe she wanted to get back at us for years of run-ins with the cops." He snapped his fingers. "Or could be she was involved in Jimmy and Frige's departure. And she was just covering her own ass."

"Good point." Cohen rolled his eyes. "Maybe the whole emaciated and dying drug addict shtick was just a world-class cover for a world-class assassin?"

"Smart ass!" Leetch grumbled with a half-smile. "Okay, maybe poor old wrist watchless Carol got her times confused. She might have seen her Johnny-come-lately dealer two hours before or after she chatted with our corpses. Or maybe it was just plain coincidence that this guy was even in the neighborhood at the same time." He sighed heavily. "There are a hundred plausible explanations that don't link him to the two stiffs."

Cohen nodded. "True, but let's just pretend for a moment he's the dealer *and* the killer."

Leetch snorted. "If we're playing 'Let's Pretend,' I prefer doing shopkeeper and-customer with my daughter, but if you insist, can I play the part of Jimmy?"

"You look more like Frigerator these days," Cohen said. And Leetch responded by flashing him a middle finger, but he couldn't pull it off with a straight face.

Cohen looked up at the fluorescent light above Leetch's head. He tapped his chin with his thumb. "What's Johnny-come-lately, as you call him, doing on skid row?"

"I thought we established that," Leetch sighed. "He's working. He's a dealer!"

Cohen squinted at his partner. "And why does he kill the two other dealers?"

"A turf war."

"*Riiight*," Cohen said slowly. "A turf war, even though the crime scene doesn't look like one either of us has ever seen."

"Remember your words?" Leetch said. "They just got 'outwitted' or 'outmatched' or one of your other fancy Ivy League terms."

Cohen knew his partner was playing dumb again—Leetch finished the *New York Times* crossword puzzle *in ink* four or five days a week—but he didn't call him on it. "The more I go over it in my head, the way Frige went down . . ." he said. "I think he had his gun out. I think the shooter might have got the draw on him."

"Wait a minute." Leetch stiffened in his seat. "Are you saying *they* accosted the killer?"

"Carol told us they were looking for him."

"Makes sense, I guess." Leetch scratched his forehead. "Those two would be more likely to put up with someone shit-kicking their grandmothers than allow another guy to work their territory."

Cohen sat forward in his chair and tapped the desktop with an index finger. "Rome, that's the part that bugs me most. This new guy, who was allegedly working the territory, gave out a free sample to Carol three days before the shooting." He held up three fingers to emphasize the point.

"But then he never tries to find her again."

"So?

"What kind of dealer is that?" Cohen wondered aloud.

"He gives her free samples and the next time he runs into her, three days later, instead of trying to sell her stuff, he looks 'surprised' to see that she's still standing."

Leetch nodded slowly. "If that's true—and all we have is Carol's word—I got to admit that's tougher to explain."

"At the hospital, Carol kept saying how it was the sample from the new guy that made her so sick. She was positive there was something in that eightball."

Leetch's eyes widened. "Hold on!" he snapped. "Are you suggesting we have some nutcase—mind you, a pro-hitter nutcase—going around trying to kill junkies with tainted eightballs?"

Cohen shrugged his shoulder slightly. "Just thinking aloud, Rome."

"No." Leetch shook his head. "I'm done with wild speculation. Sorry Carol died, but she's not the victim. Jimmy and Frige are." He glanced at his watch. "It's near quitting time. Tomorrow, we go find their killer. And if he's not too dirty, we give him a big hug."

"Works for me," Cohen said. "Except for the hug." He had every intention of tracking down the person who gunned down Jimmy and Frige. For him, all open homicides were like itches he couldn't scratch enough. But far more than solving the dealers' murders, Cohen wanted to know what the killer gave Carol. And why.

16

Seattle, Washington

Opening the door to her two-bedroom condo that overlooked Pike Place Market and Puget Sound, Lopez was almost bowled over by her eighteen-month old wheaten terrier that bounded straight into her arms.

"Careful, Rosa!" she said affectionately to the thirty-pound bulldozer, who looked like a cross between a poodle and Scottish terrier. She dropped the dog on the carpet, knelt down, and wrapped her arms around her. She allowed Rosa to cover her faces with licks, knowing that her colleagues at CDC would be horrified by the bacterial exposure. Finally, she broke off the hug. "C'mon, girl. Let's get your leash and go for a walk."

The word "walk" sent Rosa into another ecstatic, hopping frenzy. Lopez always told people she couldn't wait for her dog to outgrow the puppylike stage of hyperactivity, but secretly she got a kick out of Rosa's unflagging enthusiasm. And her dog's adoration was the perfect tonic for her bleak mood since viewing the ominous culture plates at Harborcenter's lab.

As she was leashing up Rosa, the phone on her belt vibrated. She brought it to her ear. "Lina, it's Nelson Amar," her boss said in his usual crisp voice.

She straightened. "Oh, Nelson, I was going to call you in the morning." She glanced at her watch and calculated that being 10:15 in Seattle meant it was after midnight in Atlanta. "I thought it was too late now."

" 'Late' is part of the job description at EIS, Lina," Amar said, and Lopez wondered if he meant to be condescending. "I wanted to talk to you about this resistant group-A strep."

"You've heard?" Lopez said. "I only got the results a couple of hours ago."

"I heard yesterday," Amar said.

"Yesterday?" her voice squeaked, causing her to flush. "I don't understand. . . ."

"Dr. Graham Kilburn called me," Amar said, his voice taking on an impatient edge. "They've known for days. In fact, Kilburn had already been in touch with the WHO."

The conversation kept getting murkier for Lopez. "I don't know a Dr. Kilburn."

Papers rattled in the background. "An infectious disease specialist at . . . St. Michael's Hospital."

"St. Michael's?" Then it hit her. "Nelson, you're not talking about Seattle, are you?"

"Kilburn works in Vancouver, Canada. You're the closest EIS officer I have in the region." Amar's voice assumed a suspicious edge. "Wait a minute. If you didn't know about the Vancouver cases, how did you know about the resistant G.A.S.?"

Lopez's mouth went dry. She dropped Rosa's leash. "We have at least two cases in Seattle," she said quietly.

"In *Seattle?*" There was a long pause. "Just when were you planning to tell me?" he said gravely.

"In the morning," she mumbled, too preoccupied to care about his reprimand.

"Lina, tell me about the Seattle cases—now."

Lopez told Amar what she knew of the dead HIV-positive

addict with pneumonia, Tonya Jackson, and the second case, Harry Wales, with the necrotizing fasciitis. "I've only known for less than three hours, but we've put the hospital on the strictest infection-control alert. And we've issued a warning throughout King County to report any case of streptococcal infection. I'm just about to draft an urgent e-mail memo for all public health officials and physicians in the region."

Lopez stopped and waited for Amar to elaborate on the Vancouver cases, but he remained silent. Amar had a reputation at the CDC for tightlipped evasiveness even with members of his own team, but she was determined not to be left out of the loop. "Nelson, what's going on in Vancouver?"

"There have been three cases with similar lab results to yours," he paused, as if weighing how much more to share. "A previously healthy man died of pneumonia. Another woman is being treated—if that's the right word—for a necrotizing fasciitis of her arm."

"And the source?" Lopez pressed.

"Dr. Kilburn thinks she's an HIV-infected intravenous drug user who had her abscess drained in the ER," he said. "She has since disappeared."

"Wow," Lopez said. "Two drug addicts develop the same never-before-seen infection nearly simultaneously in two different countries. What are the chances?"

"You make it sound it like they happened on either side of the globe," Amar countered. "How far apart are Vancouver and Seattle?"

"About a hundred and fifty miles," Lopez said, acknowledging to herself that his point was valid. She glanced down and saw that Rosa was staring at her with her leash in her mouth and her tail wagging frantically. "Still—" she said quietly.

"Still what, Lina?"

"Have you considered the possibility that this is not a random outbreak?" she said, regretting her phrasing the moment it left her mouth.

"Of course, I've considered it!" he snapped. "I *always*

consider it. But we're talking about a new superbug here, not anthrax or smallpox or some other bioterrorism weapon."

"Yes, but—"

Amar cut her off. "We know that the inner-city HIV population is the perfect breeding ground for spontaneous antibiotic resistance. It's happened with vancomycin-resistant enterococcus and multiresistant tuberculosis. It only makes sense that this resistant group-A strep would appear among the users."

"But in two places at once?" Lopez said.

"*Those* people are the most itinerant in the world," he said with a trace of scorn. "If it's taken hold in one group of urban addicts, you know how quickly it spreads to other cities. We've been through this before."

Not like this, Lopez thought, but she sensed it was pointless to argue with her boss. Instead, she said, "I'd better talk to Dr. Kilburn. Maybe even go to Vancouver."

"I was thinking the same," Amar agreed. "The sooner we track the source, the sooner we can control the spread." He sighed heavily. "Listen, Lina, I like Canadians. I do. But I have to warn you that they're so damn obsessed with personal rights and freedoms that they make it very hard to track people." He cleared his throat. "Just ask the homeland secretary."

"Might be a little early to blame Canada for our outbreak," Lopez said.

"I'm not blaming anyone. But we need to act quickly," Amar said in a lowered voice. "If this superbug claims a foothold in the hospitals like the ones before it already have. . . ."

He didn't finish the warning, nor did he need to. Since viewing that disastrous Culture and Sensitivity report, Lopez had trouble shedding the visions of hospital wards overrun with patients infected at the very place they had come to for help.

She looked down at Rosa whose tail was no longer wagging. The dog's ears were pinned back and her head was cocked; she was the mirror image of her owner's anxiety.

17

Seattle, Washington

Marilyn Wales Carlyle baked in the gown, gloves, face shield, and cap the nurses insisted she wear while visiting her father, Harry Wales, in the isolation room at Harborcenter. The fifty-two-year-old mother and grandmother had been warned not to lay a hand on her dad because of the risk of contagion, but Carlyle flatly refused to comply. And having glimpsed Carlyle's fierce determination, the nurses had given up trying to force her.

Carlyle's chair was pulled close to the bed, but she spent most of the time on her feet, leaning over the bed-rail, squeezing her father's hand and dabbing at his dripping brow. She sang the same songs that in her childhood he sang to her. When he was agitated at the nursing home, those Sinatra and Bennett standards used to always placate him. But her singing did nothing now to deter his moans and cries. Only morphine seemed to help, and that help was short-lived and incomplete.

At eighty, her dad suffered from moderately advanced Alzheimer's to the extent that he recognized his daughter only on his best days. She hadn't expected him to last much longer. At times, she had prayed for him to be freed from the misery of his wheelchair-bound dementia. *But not like this,* she thought. *No, never like this.*

The persistent bedsore on his leg, which had led to his most recent hospitalization four weeks earlier, had flared unexpectedly into an aggressive skin infection. The doctors feared it was flesh-eating disease. But everyone agreed that Harry was too frail for major surgery. With Carlyle's support, the doctors decided to treat him conservatively with only painkillers and IV fluids but no antibiotics.

After they had rushed her father into the cold isolation room, Carlyle learned that had they wanted to treat him, the doctors had no effective antibiotic available. She'd never heard of the mutated group-A streptococcus that was infecting her father's leg, but she overheard the nurses whispering that the bug was the same one that had claimed the life of the tragic girl who had stayed in the room next to Harry.

Typical of her father's tenacity, he refused to go quickly. Two days after the diagnosis, he continued to languish on the ward. His leg looked more like a burnt log than a human appendage. Why, Carlyle wondered for the umpteenth time, couldn't the nurse give him the whole syringe-full of morphine and end his agony? If they only left her alone for a minute with the syringe, she wouldn't hesitate to plunge it into his IV.

A drop of liquid fell on the bed and she realized she was crying. Carlyle reached her gloved hand up to her face. She slid it under her face shield, wiped away the tears, and then rubbed her nose with the back of her hand.

Her hand froze.

Oh my God! Carlyle thought. Her heart thudded in her ears. The nurse's warning reverberated in her skull: "The bacteria is spread most often via hand contact. Never, never, *never* touch anyone, including yourself, with your gloves still on!"

Her eyes fell on her father's gangrenous leg.

What have I just done?

18

Vancouver, Canada

Kilburn had just entered his car and closed the driver's-side door when his cell phone rang. He patted his pocket and looked under the seat. By the fourth ring, he narrowed down the source to the glove compartment of his '98 Jeep. He reached a hand in and dug through the papers, before his fingers wrapped around the phone's vinyl casing. He answered without looking at the call display.

"Graham," the voice chirped. "It's me."

He was tempted to fake cell signal failure and hang up. "Kyra," he sighed. "Today is not good."

His little sister giggled. "Oh, honey, you always got to make time for family."

"I'm on my way to the hospital."

"Like every single other day, huh?" she said with a slight slur.

His anger stirred. "You're drunk."

"I've had one lousy drink," she snapped.

"Damn it, Kyra—"

"Don't you judge me! You have no idea how hard it is to look after two kids when you're on your own."

He grunted a laugh. "That's precious, Kyra, coming from you."

"I know, honey," she said, her tone syrupy-sweet again. "You've been a big help with the kids. Given them a good male role model. Unlike that deadbeat son-of-a-bitch father of theirs. But Gray, it's different. You're not alone."

"You do remember that Michelle moved out, right?" he said, feeling the pressure build behind his temples.

"She'll be back," Kyra said happily.

"She's not coming back!" he said through gritted teeth. "She couldn't handle three kids that weren't her own."

"Two kids," Kyra said. "And that's a bit selfish—"

"Kyra, *you're* the third child! She loves Matt and Shayna. She was happy to have them with us. But you—"

"What about me?" she demanded, her voice quavering.

"Michelle said you drained so much of my emotion there was nothing left for her," Kilburn said evenly. He felt the pangs of guilt even before he heard his sister start to choke back sobs on the other end of line.

"Oh, Graham, I'm so sorry," she moaned. "I ruin everything for everyone, don't I?"

He inhaled a long, slow breath. "That's not true," he said in a gentler tone.

"I really am King Midas in reverse," she sputtered and dissolved into tears.

"No, Kyra, you're not," he said, slipping into autopilot. He could have this conversation in his sleep. Once the alcohol or drugs took hold, his lovely sister degenerated into a volatile wreck prone to fits of melodrama and self-pity. After fifteen years of suffering through the seesaw battle he still hadn't lost hope that one day she might emerge for good from the haze of addiction. But he knew his faith had been stretched closer than ever to the breaking point.

After a minute or two of listening to her rambling self-recriminations, Kilburn said in a firm tone: "Kyra, enough, okay?"

She was quiet in response.

"I'll pick up Matt and Shayna tonight on my way home from the hospital," he said. "They're going to have to hang with their uncle for a while. They'll be okay with that?"

"You kidding?" She sniffed, her voice steadying. "There's no place they'd rather be."

"You leave them with Corazón, okay?" Kilburn said of the Filipino nanny, who had bailed Kyra out as often as he had. "I'll pay her when I pick them up."

"Thanks, Gray," she said softly. "I'm sorry. . . ."

"I've got to go, Kyra—"

"Gray," she pleaded. "You know I never drink in front of them, right? You know that?"

"I know," he said and hung up the phone.

He hadn't seen his ten-year-old nephew and eight-year-old niece in more than a week. And they hadn't stayed with him since Michelle moved out two months earlier. Thinking of the kids, Kilburn broke into a grin. He marveled at how well they had turned out, considering their turbulent lives. Shayna was prone to occasional sullen moods and Matt got himself into trouble from time to time with his impulsiveness, but the kids were never the problem. Their mother was.

Involuntarily, Kilburn's memories drifted to the night a month before Michelle moved out, when Kyra, drunk to the point of incoherence, had woken them yet again with a three A.M. phone call. He eventually hung up on her and left the phone of the hook.

Rather than roll over and go back to sleep, Michelle yanked the covers off her and sprung out of bed. Flicking on her lamp, she stood by the bedside in the weak light wearing only a long T-shirt, arms crossed over her thin chest and a glare chiseled on her angular face. Kilburn had seldom seen her as angry.

"When will this end, Graham?" Michelle said slowly, her voice trembling.

"What can I do?" Kilburn sat up and rubbed his eyes. "You heard me chew her out."

"And you'll spend tomorrow picking up the pieces," Michelle snapped.

"She's my little sister," he said softly, avoiding her fiery eyes.

"Graham, you're just enabling her!" she said, unrelenting. "Besides, there's a limit to even what family can expect from you."

Kilburn exhaled slowly. "But, Michelle, you know it's more complicated than that."

"I don't want to hear about that ancient summer again!" Michelle shook her head wildly. A frown line cut deeply between her hazel eyes. "You didn't wreck her life, Graham. Kyra has managed that on her own."

"I was supposed to have protected her," Kilburn said distantly.

"How can you protect her from herself?" Her voice rose to nearly a shout.

He shrugged, defeated. "And Matt and Shayna?"

Michelle's expression softened. "Of course, those poor kids. . . ." She sighed with genuine affection. "They'll need to come stay with us again."

Kilburn nodded. They stared at one another for a short while. "I'm sorry, Michelle."

After a moment, Michelle smiled weakly. Then she climbed back into bed and turned off the light. She rolled toward him. Her hand reached for his arm in the darkness and squeezed it tenderly. "I know you're only trying to do what's right for Kyra. And I know you didn't ask for any of this." Her voice cracked. She was close enough that he picked up a whiff of her mint-flavored toothpaste. When she spoke again, her voice was steady. "Graham, Kyra takes so much out of you emotionally, I'm not sure there's enough left over for us."

As Kilburn pulled into the St. Michael's parking lot, he forced the memory from his mind, and refocused on the

medical crisis at hand. He climbed out of his car and headed
for the front door. Approaching the entrance, he stopped to
read one of the many large warning posters plastered on the
walls and doors. It spoke nebulously of an infectious outbreak in the hospital and warned visitors and staff to avoid
the hospital unless "absolutely necessary."

A sound drew Kilburn's attention. A block down from the
entrance, a reporter was facing the cameraman in front of
her and talking into a handheld microphone. Here we go,
Kilburn thought. The phone calls to his office from the media would soon follow.

Stepping through the front entrance, he almost bumped
into a tall thin woman scurrying past. It was Barbara Moyes,
St. Michael's infection-control nurse. She stopped short, her
worried gray eyes giving way to recognition. "Graham! Are
you coming to the task force meeting?" she asked.

"No, Barb, sorry," he shook his head. "I have to see a patient urgently."

In her early fifties, Moyes had a narrow, fretting face. She
nodded knowingly. "Parminder Singh, right?"

"Yeah," he said.

Moyes shook her head solemnly.

"Barb, are there any new cases today?"

"Not so far." She bit her lip. "Well, not at St. Michael's,
anyway."

His pulse quickened. "At another hospital?"

"There's a bad pneumonia at Vancouver Central Hospital.
Nothing is confirmed."

Kilburn rubbed his temples with one hand. "But if it *is* resistant G.A.S., there is no point contaminating *two* hospitals."

"They're considering transferring her over here."

"They shouldn't wait," he said. "Barb, the woman I'm
about to go see, you know she developed her necrotizing
fasciitis at an IV site, right?"

Her frown deepened.

"That means one of our ER nurses either used the same
pair of gloves more than once or did not wash hands between

patients before starting that IV," Kilburn said flatly. "There is no other explanation for the spread."

"I've put signs up everywhere about hand washing. I am trying to speak to every single staff member." She looked on the verge of tears. "I can't be pulled in any more directions."

Kilburn smiled reassuringly. "I know, Barb. You're wearing about twenty bull's-eyes right now."

She laughed halfheartedly.

"Just make sure people wash their damn thumbs, too." He sighed. "Never fails to amaze me how many staff don't include their thumbs when they wash."

"You're preaching to the converted, Graham."

He laughed. "Actually, I'm preaching to the preacher. I think you once caught me with my thumbs dangling in the breeze when I was a junior resident."

Moyes glanced at her watch. Her brow furrowed. "My meeting's starting."

Kilburn returned her wave and then headed straight for the ICU. Donning the head-to-toe body precautions, the sense of déjà vu was uncanny. Parminder Singh lay in the same room where Tom Mallek had died days earlier. Kilburn knew they were trying to limit the spread of the new superbug by physically clustering the cases. But he wondered if such measures had come too late.

He stepped through both sets of sealed doors and into the room. At Parminder's bedside, a male nurse in a face shield was busy removing the dressing on the patient's infected left arm. He stopped and looked up at Kilburn.

"I'm Dr. Graham Kilburn, with infectious diseases."

"Mel," the nurse grunted. "Mind if I finish this dressing change?"

Kilburn nodded. "Don't mind me."

The patient lay perfectly still on the bed during the painful-looking procedure, but Kilburn understood why. Singh was unconscious. And the endotracheal tube sticking out of her mouth meant she was connected to a ventilator.

Kilburn's eyes fell to Singh's swollen, deformed arm, as

Mel peeled off the dressings. From the elbow to the fingers, the skin had been surgically splayed along the back of her arm. Large chunks of skin were missing, exposing gobs of yellowish-gray fat and patches of brownish-red muscle. Singh's arm looked like the bloated body of a fish that had washed ashore, but it lacked the putrid smell. Instead, his nostrils filled with the strong antiseptic scent of iodine and alcohol.

"Look at this." Mel pointed to a thick fiery band of red that led from her elbow up to her shoulder. "It's spreading upward."

"Are they taking her back to the OR?"

"What's the point?" Mel shrugged.

"Where's her medication record?"

Mel jerked his thumb in the direction of the tabletop behind him. Kilburn walked over and scanned the list. He shook his head as he realized that every conceivable class of antibiotic had coursed through Parminder's veins. And yet the infection still marched up her arm unabated.

Once Mel had finished the dressing, Kilburn approached the bed and took a closer look at Parminder Singh. Though dark skinned, her complexion had turned sallow. Her swollen eyes were shut and the muscles around her mouth fasciculated in tiny spasms. Her other arm, though untouched by infection, had swollen as well, likely secondary to massive amounts of IV fluids. Kilburn knew the patient suffered from overwhelming sepsis or blood poisoning. She couldn't last much longer in this condition, but he saw few additional treatment options. "I'd like to give her intravenous gamma globulin," he said. "Also, I think we should try activated protein C."

Mel cocked his head. "Really?" he said in surprise.

"We're clutching at straws here," Kilburn sighed. "I'll go put the orders in the computer."

He had just finished removing his gown and scrubbing at the sink outside the room when a turbaned man carrying a baby approached. The baby cried and squirmed, but Gurdev

Singh's eyes showed far more distress than his son's. "You are the doctor of my wife?" he asked in a frantic Punjabi accent.

"One of them. I'm Dr. Kilburn."

"What can you tell me of her?"

Kilburn looked into his eyes. "She is extremely sick, Mr. Singh."

Gurdev nodded violently. "But she will get better soon?"

Kilburn shook his head slightly. "Mr. Singh, I don't know that she will."

Gurdev began to hyperventilate. His shoulders shook. His eyes went even wider. "But, doctor! Our baby, Harjeet." He pulled the boy off his shoulder and held him out to Kilburn. "Who will take care of him?"

Kilburn swallowed. "We're doing everything we can."

Gurdev slung the baby back over his shoulder and took a step closer. He reached out and grasped Kilburn's shoulder, applying slight pressure. "Doctor, you must make Parminder well again." His high-pitched voice cracked, and he squeezed harder. "You must. *You must.*"

The ICU clerk—a middle-aged woman with a kind, grandmotherly face—rushed over to join them in the hallway. "It's okay, Gurdev. Give me the baby."

As Gurdev let go of Kilburn's arm, the clerk reached up and took the baby from his arm. She put Harjeet over her shoulder and rocked him to quiet in a matter of seconds. "Come with me, Gurdev. Let's put the baby down for a nap."

Kilburn mouthed the words "thank you" to the heroic clerk as she led Gurdev off to the family conference room. He stood in the middle of the hall and watched them go. His heart sank. He never felt more useless in his life.

He mentally reviewed the list of antibiotics in his mind again, realizing the team had already tried everything. There were no other options.

Head down, he trod back to the nursing station. He pulled a consultant's note sheet off the shelf. He patted his pockets but came up empty in his search for a pen. At the back of the station, he scrounged around the desk until he found a discarded ballpoint pen. He sat down. When he brought the pen to paper, he noticed a red-and-white logo on the pen that read "SeptoMed." For a moment, flickers of recognition danced around his head without quite connecting. Then the idea hit him: Maybe there *was* one other dim hope.

Ignoring the no-cell-phone rule, he grabbed his phone out of his pocket, dialed directory assistance for toll free numbers, and remained on the line while his call went through. An automated answering machine picked up. He pressed the "0" button several times until a live voice came on the line.

"SeptoMed Pharmaceuticals. This is Amber. How may I direct your call?"

"I would like to speak to Dr. Ellen Horton."

19

Seattle, Washington

"Every new emerging pathogen crisis needs a catchy acronym. It's the Eleventh Commandment," Dr. Warmack had said to Dr. Lopez on their way home from Harborcenter. And overnight a new name and acronym had popped into CDC vernacular. By morning, people were calling the new bug 'Multi-resistant group-A streptococcus' and shortening it to MRGAS, which they pronounced as "mer-gas."

Lopez hardly slept a wink. E-mails and calls from Atlanta had continued nonstop, while an impromptu approach for limiting the spread was being hammered out by the CDC. Though MRGAS had not yet surfaced into public awareness, the buzz had already hit the infectious-diseases community. And though MRGAS was brand-new to the planet, the concept of a superbug resistant to all antibiotics had, like a prophesized apocalypse, been feared and expected for years by those on the inside. The day had arrived, and they even had a term for it: "the post-antibiotic era."

Lopez was running on pure adrenaline. And once the

shock and fear had subsided, her stomach fluttered. Like a surgeon facing the riskiest and potentially most rewarding operation of her life, she felt simultaneously scared and energized by the prospect of her role in the efforts to contain the MRGAS outbreak.

After a quick shower and cup of instant coffee, she scrawled a note for the dog sitter, gave Rosa a quick hug, and then headed for the door. Reaching for the doorknob, her smartphone rang for the fifth time that morning. She pulled it off her belt and answered.

"Dr. Lopez?" the man asked in a smooth French accent.

"Yup. Who's this?" she said, realizing her phone etiquette had begun to slip.

"Terribly rude of me, I apologize," he said warmly. "I am Jean Nantal, calling from Geneva. I am the—"

"Of course, Dr. Nantal with the WHO," she said, awestruck to be speaking to the WHO's executive director of communicable diseases. "As part of my thesis, I studied your legendary work on the global smallpox vaccination program," she gushed.

"You must have studied ancient history in school, then?" he laughed easily.

"Hardly!" she said. "What you and the others accomplished—"

"Was a long time ago, but thank you," he said graciously. "I hope I'm not calling too early. I get hopelessly confused by time zones. I think it should be about seven-thirty A.M. in Seattle, but I must confess it might be midnight or noon for all I know."

"No, that's the right time," Lopez laughed, realizing that Nantal's reputation as a world-class charmer was justified. "I'm just heading out the door to go back to the hospital to interview a patient with early MRGAS."

"Indeed," he said. "Dr. Lopez—"

"Lina."

"Of course. And please, I am Jean," he said. "I was hoping you might update me as to where your cases stand. I have spoken to Dr. Kilburn in Vancouver, but I only know what Nelson Amar told me of the Seattle cases. And I believe he relied on you for the information."

"Certainly." Lopez gave Nantal a concise update of the Seattle cluster, and then added, "Jean, there's another woman in isolation. Her father had nectrotizing fasciitis. And it seems she accidentally exposed herself with a contaminated glove. She's the one I am interviewing today. After that, I plan to drive to Vancouver to meet Dr. Kilburn."

"Very good," Nantal said.

"Jean, how involved is the WHO?" she asked.

"Thus far we're not, beyond acting as consultants. Nelson was confident that the CDC could lead the investigation." Nantal paused. "Lina, he told me you were very capable."

"He did?" she said without masking her surprise.

"Ah, Nelson." Nantal laughed again. "I believe the American expression is 'his bark is worse than his bite.' Yes?"

Lopez chuckled. "But it's a pretty impressive bark. Did Nelson mention our concern that the simultaneous outbreaks might not be random?" She neglected to clarify that it was far more her concern than his.

Nantal paused. "He did."

"What do you think, Jean?"

"In this day and age, it is always a concern," he said wistfully. "Lina, do you mind if I share a little of my personal experience?"

"Mind?" she said. "I'd be honored."

"Ah, I must one day read that thesis of yours. You have a wonderfully inflated sense of my importance." She imagined him wearing the same playful smile on his long but distinguished face that she had seen in old interview clips. "In my years of doing this work, the one mistake I've seen committed time and time again—and I'm as guilty as anyone— is to make assumptions about emerging pathogens. Whether the spread is random or not, it is vital to keep the possibility in mind, though not to the exclusion of other alternatives. Does that make sense?"

"Absolutely. I will try to keep my mind as open as possible." "But," she said with a laugh, "I'm Catholic *and* Hispanic. I think I'm genetically preprogrammed to always assume the worst."

"Which makes you the perfect epidemiologist." Nantal chuckled. "Lina, if I can be of any assistance to you with your investigation, please call me at any time."

"I might take you up on the offer, Jean."

"*Bien sûr,*" he said. "And if you have an extra copy of your thesis. . . ."

After hanging up, she headed straight down to her convertible in the underground parking. It was a cool drizzly morning, so putting the top down was not an option. She pulled out of the garage and headed for Harborcenter.

Her head ached from all the angles she considered and reconsidered about the MRGAS outbreak. Seeking distraction, she switched on the radio and turned up the volume when she heard Sugar Ray's "Every Morning" playing. The song, a favorite of Keith's, stirred up memories of her former fiancé. How did we screw it up? she wondered. But it was only nostalgia talking. She remembered the facts vividly.

Lopez had met Keith, an internist, during her first year in med school, the same year her father died. He had been sweet in supporting her through the bleakest period of her life, through daily phone calls, prepared meals, and a shoulder whenever she needed one. His empathy made it easy for her to fall in love with him. And yet, ironically, Keith claimed it was her father—or the memory of him—that kept getting in their way.

She clearly recalled their final night together, four years earlier. They had stayed up the whole night talking, crying, and even making bittersweet love on the sofa. The discussion lacked the shouts and recriminations of the previous heated ones, in part, she thought, because both of them were already resigned to the end of the relationship.

"Lina, it's impossible to compete with a ghost," Keith said

from where he sat, on the sofa where they had just made love, inches away but without touching.

"I never wanted you to compete," she said with downcast eyes.

"But that's how I feel. Like I'm living in your dad's shadow. And I can't ever measure up to him."

"That's ridiculous," Lopez muttered.

"Maybe," Keith said gently. "But I can't help how I feel. Maybe this is my issue, but I always sense that you'd rather have your old family back than start a new one with me."

"Not true." But even at the time, she knew Keith was not far off the mark. She barely remembered her mother, who died of leukemia when Lopez was only four. Her father had been her world. She would have given anything to have him back.

They said very little else after that. When the sun rose, Lopez went to her bedroom and came back with the jewelry box bearing the engagement ring she hadn't worn in weeks. He took the box back from her hand, hugged her briefly, and left without another word.

Most of the time, Lopez believed the demise of the engagement had nothing to do with the permanent void she felt following her father's death. She and Keith had different expectations from life. Ten years older, he was ready to settle. He wanted the house and kids. She still wanted to tackle the world. But at times like now, she had her doubts.

Arriving at the hospital, she shook off the memories. She parked in the same "Emergency Callback" spot as the previous visit and then headed up to the infectious-diseases ward. After checking with her manager, one of the nurses led Lopez straight to Marilyn Wales Carlyle's room. Lopez donned all the required body contact precautions, from cap and face mask down to booties, before entering the sterile windowless room.

Carlyle was sitting up over the side of the bed in her housecoat holding the newspaper on her lap. If not for the surgical mask covering her mouth, Carlyle could have passed for any person enjoying a lazy start to her day. She had medium-length gray hair, a full but not chunky face, and kind, brown eyes.

"Mrs. Carlyle, I'm Dr. Lopez."

"Ah, I get a sixth opinion," Carlyle said, though her tone was friendly.

"My clinical opinion isn't worth much." Lopez shrugged. "I'm an epidemiologist with the Centers for Disease Control."

"Oh." Carlyle said, sounding impressed. "How can I help, Dr. Lopez?"

Lopez took her response as an invitation, so she pulled up a chair close to her bed and sat down. "How are you feeling?"

"I have a sore throat," Carlyle said. "They tell me it's typical for strep throat, but otherwise I'm okay."

Lopez nodded. "I'm glad to hear it."

"But even if I don't deteriorate I will be in quarantine for at least a week." She paused to clear her throat. "I'll have to miss Dad's funeral."

"I'm sorry," Lopez said, feeling a sudden surge of empathy. "I was hoping to ask you about your father's infection."

Carlyle looked down at the newspaper. "Okay."

"How long was he in the hospital before it flared up so badly?"

"About three or four weeks. His bedsore had just begun to heal when, out of nowhere, it . . . ," she searched for the right description, "erupted."

"Which is typical for flesh-eating disease," Lopez said.

"So I've been told." Carlyle put the paper down on the bed beside her. "I hear that Dad picked up his infection from a girl named Tonya Jackson who was in the room next door. Something to do with the staff not properly washing their hands between patients."

Lopez began to halfheartedly defend the nurses. "Mrs. Carlyle, the staff couldn't have known that—"

"Oh, I'm not blaming them," Carlyle said. "They were wonderful to Dad. And you're right—How could they know? Even if they had . . ." She flushed and looked away. "Look at me. I was perfectly aware, and I still foolishly exposed myself to the organism."

"It happens," Lopez said. "You mentioned Tonya Jackson. Did you ever meet her?"

"Oh, yes." Carlyle nodded emphatically. "Poor Tonya. She was such a gaunt little thing. Couldn't have weighed ninety pounds. And she suffered so much in her short life." She shook her head and sighed. "You should have heard the stories. Sexually abused by her father. Living on the street when she was only thirteen. It went on and on."

Lopez cocked her head. "Sounds like you got to know her."

Carlyle laughed. "I'm a comptroller by profession, but Dad always said I should have gone into social work. He said that from the get-go I was always attracted to the runt of the litter." She shrugged. "Anyway, Tonya didn't get any other visitors. So, when Dad was sleeping, I used to drop in on her . . . before she became so sick." She sighed. "Tonya loved to talk. And she was so open, too. I never had the feeling she was making any of it up. She never portrayed herself as a victim."

Lopez shook her head. Too often she had heard variations on the same story when she worked at a vaccination clinic with street kids in downtown Atlanta. "Mrs. Carlyle, did Tonya ever mention why she ended up in the hospital?"

Carlyle nodded solemnly. "She had this awful sore on her left elbow. Apparently, because she was HIV-positive and used a lot of cocaine, she was prone to them. One of the nurses told me that this was where the infection began. She must have touched it before touching her mouth and. . . ."

Lopez wondered if Carlyle was reflecting on the similarities to her own predicament. She began to rise from her chair. "That's very helpful—"

Carlyle's eyes narrowed. "Tonya believed someone meant to make her sick."

"What?" Lopez said, dropping back into the chair.

"Tonya told me that she met this new drug dealer on the

street," Carlyle said. "He gave her free drugs. He told her it was just a sample, but she never saw him again. She thought this was very unusual. And she was convinced his drugs gave her the terrible infection. She thought he was 'cutting,' as she called it, the drugs with some chemical contaminants. Apparently, drug dealers will do that to save money."

Lopez felt more butterflies in her stomach. "Did she tell you anything else about him?"

"No, not really." Carlyle shrugged. "Except to say that he had the darkest eyes she had ever seen in her life."

"Dark as in color?"

Carlyle shook her head. "I think she meant it in the sense of opaque. She painted him as a scary person."

Lopez's chest thumped as she considered the implication of the accusation. She was so absorbed by the thoughts that she hadn't even heard Carlyle's next question.

"—don't you think, Dr. Lopez?" Carlyle asked expectantly.

Dazed, Lopez looked back up at Carlyle. "I'm sorry, could you repeat the question?"

"If I just end up with a bit of a strep throat, it would be good news for everyone. Right? It would mean this bug doesn't always cause terrible infections."

Lopez nodded distractedly. "There are two types of group-A strep, or G.A.S., infections," she said, beginning her rote explanation, her mind still dwelling on Tonya Jackson's accusation. "First, there's the more common, noninvasive form: strep throat, scarlet fever, mild skin infections, and so on. Second, is the much rarer invasive form. It causes infections like flesh-eating disease, toxic shock syndrome, and G.A.S. pneumonia."

Carlyle frowned skeptically.

"Only a few subtypes of G.A.S. cause such invasive infections," Lopez said, "but even with those strains, the bacterium still requires defects in the host's own immune system before infection can develop. Do you understand?"

Carlyle nodded slowly, her brow creased in concentration.

"You mean, even if you have the bad form of the bug, something has to be wrong with your immune system to get the bad disease?"

Lopez smiled vaguely. "Sort of. Though we can't predict whom, only certain people are susceptible. That is why we see only clusters of flesh-eating disease rather than epidemics."

Carlyle pointed at Lopez. "So this *is* good news."

Lopez nodded. "But there is a downside."

"How so?"

"It makes outbreak control much more difficult," Lopez said. "Take measles, for example. Everyone infected demonstrates classic symptoms. They all get a rash. Although it's highly contagious, we can quarantine those infected and protect the rest of the public."

"And with this G.A.S. infection?"

Lopez shook her head. "People can become carriers without ever showing symptoms."

"Carriers?" Carlyle grimaced in confusion.

"A carrier is a person who is infected with the disease—and capable of passing it on—but does not become particularly sick herself. You, for example."

Carlyle sat up straight. *"Me?"*

"Imagine that we didn't know about your exposure to your dad, and you were at home right now with a minor sore throat. You might inadvertently spread your infection to someone who then develops an overwhelming pneumonia or flesh-eating disease because he or she happens to be susceptible to invasive G.A.S."

"Dear God!" Carlyle's eyes went wide with recognition. "And, in the meantime, I could pass it on to ten others who also would become carriers of the bug."

Carlyle's logic hit Lopez like one of her cousin's childhood stomach punches.

What if this outbreak can't be contained?

20

Philadelphia, Pennsylvania

Horton sat at her desk with the door closed and her head buried in her hands. The pile of memos in her in-box threatened to topple over. She had 264 unread e-mails. Her voicemail was full, and would not accept new messages. Horton didn't want to hear from the outside world. Especially not another congratulatory message. Those had become unbearable.

Two days earlier she had heard that a third lab chimp on long-term Oraloxin therapy had died of bone marrow failure. And she had hardly slept an hour since.

Perhaps the bone marrow response was—as Martineau had assured her while she lay naked for the first time under his thick, fragrant down comforter—simply an idiosyncratic reaction specific to chimpanzees. Or possibly—as Martineau pointed out between the first and second time he clouded her thoughts with the most intense sex of her life—it would happen only to animals that took the drug for months rather than the maximum ten days it was intended.

Maybe Oraloxin posed no risk to humans in the appropriate doses for short courses, but if the FDA review panel saw the chimp data, they would immediately stop the human trials and reject the drug.

But Horton didn't report the findings. Instead, she shrank from her ethical duty like the coward and fraud she now saw herself to be. She couldn't sleep anymore. Nor eat. However, her vague fleeting fantasies had crystallized into a plan. She pictured herself drifting into oblivion in the garage with her favorite piece of music, Grieg's piano concerto, playing over the rumble of her car's engine. The thought of suffocation no longer evoked anxiety. Quite the opposite: The idea of her death, accompanied by the explanatory note she would leave behind, appealed to her scientific side as the only reasonable option.

She was pulled away from the fantasy when her door opened a crack. Her heavyset secretary, Sally, stuck her face through. "Dr. Horton, I know you said you weren't accepting calls . . . ," she said timidly.

"It's okay, Sally," Horton said gently.

"There's someone who insists on speaking to you," Sally said. "He won't take no for an answer. He made me tell you he was holding on the line."

"Oh," Horton said, trying to muster up a hint of interest. "Who?"

"Dr. Graham Kilburn from Vancouver, Canada. He says he's an old friend—"

Graham Kilburn. She hadn't spoken to him in almost ten years, since they graduated from McGill Medical School. "Sally, please transfer the call."

While Horton waited to be connected, she pictured Kilburn with his tawny blond hair worn short and uncombed long before it became the style. His T-shirt and sweatpants identified him as one of the class jocks. His rugged face with its square jaw, blue-gray eyes, and a crooked smile that generated so many crushes among classmates. She was one of the many. And once, after cramming all night together for a pathology exam, they came within an undergarment each of consummating the relationship. Only the arrival of Kilburn's roommate stopped them. But they never reached that point again. Theirs evolved into a comfortable friendship. After graduation, when she headed back to the States and he to Vancouver, they exchanged letters for a while, but the correspondence naturally tailed off as their lives grew hectic.

Horton's phone rang, startling her from the reminiscence. She picked it up. "Graham?"

"Ellen!" Kilburn said enthusiastically. "Ten years, Ellen! Can you believe it?"

"Ten years," she echoed in disbelief.

"Actually, thirteen since we dissected the King together," Kilburn said, referring to the obese cadaver in first-year anatomy lab that they had nicknamed 'the King' because of his passing resemblance to Elvis Presley in his last years.

"Good old Elvis." She smiled for the first time in days. "How are you, Graham?"

"Fine. Good. Hanging in there," he said with strange ambiguity. "And you? What's happened to you in the last decade?"

She flushed with sudden embarrassment. "Not much. The cloistered research life in Philadelphia. No husband. No kids. Pretty much as dysfunctional as I was in med school."

"Bull!" Kilburn said. "I heard about your research, El. My hospital is one of the centers involved in a study of your new wonder drug."

"I had a lot of help," she said distantly. Her smile faded. "And what have you been up to?"

"Me? I'm the poster child for mediocrity," Kilburn laughed. "Did my residency in infectious diseases out here at the University of British Columbia, went to New York for a fellowship in microbiology, then back home. I'm a consultant at St. Michael's Hospital with the predictable midlevel university appointment." He cleared his throat. "Lived with a great woman for about four years. Screwed that up. Now I'm single and childless."

"Mediocre, right! You're still as modest as you were at

med school, huh?" Horton said. "And your little sister." She searched for the name. "Chiara, was it?"

"Kyra," he said quietly.

"Last you told me, Kyra just had a new baby boy and had got her life in order," Horton said. "Is she still . . . you know . . . okay?"

There was a long pause. When he spoke, Horton detected a strained lightness to his tone. "New baby?" He chuckled. "Wow, we're aging. My *little* sister has a boy and a girl, ten and eight now. She's a single parent, though. I help out a little where I can."

"That's good of you." Horton said, not knowing what else to say.

"Listen, Ellen, have you heard at all about the new superbug in Vancouver?" Kilburn asked, his voice suddenly business-like.

"New superbug?" she said in genuine surprise. "I've been so tied up with Oraloxin and the FDA, I haven't even looked at the paper in over a month. I haven't heard a thing."

"To be fair, I'm not sure the news has gone national . . . yet." He sighed.

"What's going on?"

"El, we have an outbreak of group-A strep that is multiresistant."

"You mean to penicillin?" she asked.

"I mean to everything," he said slowly. "Nothing we've tried has even touched it."

"What? That's unheard of!" she gasped. Her bleak mood and morbid thoughts were pushed aside as her mind churned through the staggering consequences of an ultraresistant G.A.S.

"It's happened," he said bluntly. He told her about Tom Mallek's death and the mysterious connection to the young addict from the emergency room. Then he described Parminder Singh's grave condition. "Listen, Ellen, if we don't pull a rabbit out of our hats, she's going to die."

Horton's pulse sped. She suddenly realized where Kilburn was heading, but she refused to make the leap for him. "I'm sorry, Graham. That sounds tragic. I don't know what—"

"We're all out of conventional medicine," he interrupted. "I've got nothing left to offer, except . . . your new drug."

She took a slow, deep breath. "Graham, it's not approved for anything but clinical trials with MRSA."

"I hear you," he said. "But Oraloxin represents a whole new class of antibiotic, right?"

"In theory," she said circumspectly.

"So there's a chance it might offer something the others don't?"

She shook her head at the phone. "Have you even tested Oraloxin's response in the lab cultures to this resistant G.A.S.?"

"There's no time. Besides, I don't have any drug to test. All we have here are the study pills, which are blinded. So I don't know which are the real drug and which are placebo."

Horton swallowed. "I still don't see how I can help you," she said, though she did know.

"You can un-blind the samples, so I know which one is the real McCoy. And have SeptoMed release some more to me." His voice softened. "It would give me something to do for the patient. A glimmer of hope. Ellen, she deserves that much."

"Graham, legally . . . ethically . . ."—the word made her flinch—"I don't think I can."

"Damn it, she's only twenty!" Kilburn snapped, then his voice calmed. "She's got a new baby. And she will be dead within a day, for sure. What's the possible downside of trying it?"

She brushed the locks of hair away from the forehead. "I don't know," she said as much to herself as him.

"I don't expect Oraloxin to work. I honestly don't," he coaxed. "And no one would ever have to know we even tried. But, Ellen, imagine if it does help?" He paused to let the idea sink in. "Your drug—you—would have saved a young mom. And who knows how many are going to follow her?"

The conversation lapsed into a long silence. Horton weighed the options in her mind. She understood how sternly the scientific community would frown upon this kind of wild stab with an unproven drug. Yet she felt the first twinges of genuine excitement she'd had in weeks. It wouldn't make up for hiding the chimpanzee data. Nothing would. But if Oraloxin helped the woman? And as Kilburn had said—though she took a slightly different meaning from the reference—how much worse could it get?

"Ellen?"

"This is nuts, Graham," she sighed. "Totally irresponsible. But let me speak to my boss, the VP of R-and-D. Luc's the only one who can get you the information you need on un-blinding the study."

"Thank you, Ellen," he said earnestly. "You're doing the right thing."

If only you knew, Graham, she thought with another stab of guilt.

21

At ten minutes after midnight, Cohen and Leetch strolled down the same alley where Frigerator and Jimmy died. Unlike the relative quiet of that morning, the alley now hummed with nocturnal life like an Amazon jungle. Aside from the chalk marks and the partly torn crime scene tape, Cohen saw that the double murder had no effect on the illicit business carried on in the alley. He wasn't surprised. Death was commonplace for these downtown addicts. An accepted cost of doing business.

"Man, trolling skid row in the middle of the night beats the hell outta being at home with Gina and little Sophie," Leetch grumbled.

"Trust me, Rome, your family needs a break from you." Cohen shrugged with a slight grin. "Besides, we've come up empty-handed on the crime scene. Where else are we going to find any potential witnesses?"

"Yeah, I guess." Leetch pointed to his torn jeans and black

T-shirt that strained at the middle to contain his belly. "KC, you like my gear?"

Cohen nodded. "All you need are the words 'undercover cop' stenciled across your chest."

"And what about you?" He laughed as he thumbed at Cohen's suede jacket and khaki pants. "We're supposed to be casing the skids, and you look like you just stepped out of a Land's End catalog."

A few feet ahead, Cohen saw what looked like a woman in a miniskirt, tight sweater, and spike heels sitting against the back wall of an old warehouse. Her face was hidden by the shadows from the building's overhang, but she held her arms out in the weak light from the second-floor windows. Her pilled sleeve of her red sweater was pulled halfway up her left arm. In her right hand, she steadied a syringe against the skin of her left elbow.

Like Leetch, Cohen stopped and watched as she injected into her arm. The user pulled the needle out of her vein and then tucked the syringe away in her little cocktail-party purse. It wasn't until after she had put the rig away, that she noticed the two cops. "What the fuck do you want?" the addict asked in a voice that revealed "her" to be anything but feminine.

"We're detectives, darling." Leetch feigned a Southern drawl. "You mind having a tiny little chat with us?"

The transvestite struggled up to his standing height of over six feet. He was as thin as Carol was, and like her, he had open blisters on his lower lip. The pallid skin on his face had so little padding beneath it that his jaw and cheekbones stood out so that his face looked to Cohen like a skull decorated with mascara and rouge. He reeked of a cheap perfume that even from five feet away almost made Seth's eyes water. He swayed on his heels and pointed an unfocused finger at them. "You got nothing better to do than harass a lady?" he said in his deep baritone. Then, with both hands, he dramatically swept back the locks of his thick blond wig.

"Nah, I can't think of anything better," Leetch said.

"How about you, Seth? This pretty much as good as it gets for you, too?"

Cohen shook his head slightly and stared at Leetch, silently telling him to ease off.

"I'm Detective Leetch and this is Sergeant Cohen," Leetch said, the sarcasm gone. "We're Homicide detectives with Portland P.D."

"Homicide?" the man gasped in his deep tone. "I'm a lover . . . not a killer."

"Yeah, I thought as much," Leetch said. "What's your name?"

"Chavon will do, baby," he said with another sweep of his wig.

"It's a lovely name," Leetch said, and Cohen wasn't sure if he was mocking the man or not. "But it won't do for our report. What's your real name?"

"Douglas Evans," he said with a slight pout.

Leetch folded his arms over his thick belly. "So, Chavon, did you happen to know Jimmy and Frige?"

"Everyone down here did," Chavon said.

Leetch squinted at him. "Anyone you an think of who might have wanted to harm them?"

Chavon closed his eyes and chuckled. "Just about everyone."

Leetch held out his palms. "Can you be a tad more specific?"

"Honey, I don't know too many of us who pack heat." He held up his tiny handbag. "Mine's too small for a gun. Besides, it's not very ladylike."

"So who would be packing?"

"You should talk to Little Andrew." Chavon shuddered dramatically, and stumbled. For a moment he looked as though he was going to tip over in his spike heels, but he recovered his balance awkwardly and straightened his miniskirt. "Andrew had a hate on for Jimmy like you wouldn't believe."

Cohen recognized the name of the dealer, though he had never met him before.

"Where can we find Andrew?" Leetch asked.

Chavon floated a hand in front of him, making small circles with his bent wrist. "Oh, he's around, sugar. Just look for that white sports car of his. Porsche or whatever the fuck it is."

"Chavon, we hear there's a new supplier around," Cohen spoke up. "A guy in a track suit with frosted highlights. Does that ring any bells?"

"Oh, the cutie pie talks," Chavon squealed to Leetch. Then to Cohen, he said: "Sure I've seen him, baby. He was by here the other night."

"Did he sell you anything?" Leetch asked.

"Sugar, I don't buy drugs," Chavon said with a giggle. "That's illegal."

"Chavon, you remember Carol Wilson?" Cohen asked.

He moved his head quickly from side to side and frowned. "What do you mean, do I remember her?" he said indignantly. "Carol's my buddy."

"She died yesterday," Cohen said gently.

"Carol?" Chavon's face crumpled into a grimace. His eyes misted over. "Carol's dead?"

Cohen nodded. "We think it might have had something to do with the new guy."

"Carol's gone," Chavon repeated through a heroin-induced haze. "Poor, poor Carol." Then his eyes focused on Cohen as his words finally sunk in. "What did the guy to do her?"

"We're not sure," Cohen admitted. "But it would help if you can tell us whether he gave you any drugs."

Chavon nodded. "Yeah, I saw him two or three nights ago. He gave me some junk. Called it a freebie or something. Said he would be around with more of the same to buy."

"Have you seen him since?" Leetch asked.

"No," Chavon said, looking as if even he was surprised by his answer.

"The sample he gave you, Chavon," Cohen asked with a nod. "An eightball, right?"

Chavon nodded and readjusted his wig, setting it off kilter.

Cohen pointed at him with the knuckle of his finger. "How did you feel afterward?"

"Beautiful, sugar," he said with a laugh. "It was good stuff."

"Chavon, did you get sick at all?" Cohen asked. "Fevers or anything like that?"

Chavon shook his head.

"Do you remember where you injected it?" Cohen asked.

Chavon nodded. He reached down and rolled up the sleeve past the crease in the elbow of his cadaverous right arm. Then his eyes went wide in their bony sockets. At the crease, there was a matchbox-sized defect of missing skin. It was crusted at the edges with dried blood and pus, and a black scab had hardened over it, which looked as if it might slough off at any moment. "I thought it was just the coke. I've had the same kind of thing before when I missed the vein." He looked up from the suppurating wound. "But you know what, doll? I've been doing this a while." He stared right into Cohen's eyes. "I *know* I didn't miss that vein."

22

Philadelphia, Pennsylvania

Dennis Tyler was gone. The real Tyler had disappeared four years earlier while sailing off the coast of the Baja California. But the man who until recently had traveled the West Coast posing as a drug dealer, using Tyler's driver's license, had also shed Tyler's borrowed identity. According to his current identification, he was now Wayne Forbes, of Rockford, Illinois.

Like Dennis Tyler before him, the real Wayne Forbes had died at the hand of the man who now carried his ID. Conveniently, many of his previous targets had led shady and secretive lives. When they disappeared, they were not necessarily missed. Accordingly, it was sometimes convenient to borrow their names.

Forbes was delighted to have left Tyler and the assignment attached to his identity behind. A job is a job, he reminded himself. But he was enjoying the current assignment enormously, and staying in focus was easy. Anyone can pull a trigger, but this task was full of nuance and subtlety. It appealed to his creative side.

He sat, for the fourth morning in a row, parked a half block down from the Ukrainian Community Center, savoring a cup of tea. He had one eye on the newspaper and the other on the Center's entrance, but he could have taken a nap without missing his mark. The man spent exactly one hour working out in the Center's gym every morning before heading into work. After four days of following the man, Forbes had already learned that he was as predictable as the sunset.

Had the job been a simple termination, the mark's predictability would have been an advantage. But that was not what his employer had in mind. And for the fee attached to the assignment, Forbes intended to take his time and execute it perfectly.

Opportunity would come. The key was to be prepared when it did.

Forbes glanced at his watch, then neatly folded the paper and replaced the cap on his thermos of tea. Just as he started the engine, he saw his man emerge from the entrance of the Center. The squat bald man glanced to either side as if being followed—probably, Forbes thought, a habit left over from from his life as an Eastern bloc scientist—before turning down the sidewalk and heading for his car.

Forbes eased his own car out of the parking spot and slowly drove past his mark, knowing he would catch up with him again a few blocks later.

23

Impatiently, Kilburn checked his watch again. Nearly six P.M. He'd been waiting five hours to hear back from Ellen Horton's boss about releasing the Oraloxin study samples. Five hours that Parminder Singh didn't have to spare.

Kilburn had checked on her status every hour at St. Michael's ICU. At each visit, the relentless band of red had inched its way up her arm to the point where it now extended past her shoulder.

He headed back to the nurses' station and reached for the phone to call SeptoMed for the fourth time, when he heard his name being paged. "Dr. Kilburn, you have a call waiting on extension 26," the voice chimed.

He broke off his incompletely dialed call and pressed in the extension. "Dr. Kilburn," he said.

"Ah, Dr. Kilburn, I'm so sorry to have kept you waiting," the man said breezily. "I am Dr. Luc Martineau with R-and-D at SeptoMed. I work with Ellen Horton and the Oraloxin team. She told me that you and she were classmates at medical school."

"Yeah," Kilburn said, unwilling to draw out the pleasantries. "Dr. Martineau, I'm sure Ellen also told you about our case of necrotizing fasciitis."

"Absolutely," Martineau said gravely. "She tells me it is resistant to every antibiotic available." He exhaled heavily into Kilburn's earpiece. "It's been a long time since I have been anything but a paper-pusher, but I vaguely remember that group-A strep used to be universally susceptible to all antibiotics."

" 'Used to be' being the operative words," Kilburn sighed. "As I told Ellen, we've completely run out of options."

"So you would like to try Oraloxin now?" Martineau asked in a level tone.

"It's most certainly her last hope."

There was a long silence on the line. "Graham, Ellen clearly holds you in the highest regard," he said softly. "Forgive me for asking, but how does an experimental medication under evaluation—not yet approved, mind you—for an entirely different infection offer any hope to your patient?"

For a moment, Martineau's aptly articulated reasoning threw Kilburn off. He felt a fleeting moment of foolishness for even asking. But remembering the images of Parminder with her inflamed limb and her desperate husband, he quickly recovered. "From what I understand, Oraloxin has a novel mechanism of action at the cell wall level," he said. "I hear Oraloxin's results with MRSA, a similar bacterium to G.A.S., are staggeringly impressive."

"Yes, but—"

"It stands to reason that there is a chance Oraloxin might work against a sister organism," Kilburn said adamantly, "and it's unlikely our patient's G.A.S. would be resistant to an antibiotic that is a virgin to the bacterial community."

"You make a convincing argument, Graham, I'll give you that." He chuckled, before his voice took on a faraway sound, as if their divide had suddenly widened. "But what you're proposing is beyond the realm of compassionate release."

Kilburn clenched his fist. "Why?"

"Because apart from a well-crafted premise, you don't have a single shred of scientific evidence to back up your proposition," Martineau said flatly. "Frankly, from Ellen's description your patient sounds beyond hope for medical therapy even if we knew the bacteria would respond . . . might respond . . . to Oraloxin."

"You don't know it won't," Kilburn said, raising his voice.

"But you haven't convinced us it will," Martineau said in a more soothing voice. "Look, Graham, we have FDA approval for Oraloxin hovering over us any day."

"What's that got to do with anything?" Kilburn tapped his hand impatiently on the desk.

"Sadly, everything," Martineau said. "The FDA review panel looks for any opportunity to reject a new drug."

Kilburn fought the urge to crack the receiver on the desk. "And?"

"Imagine if your patient dies shortly after receiving our drug," Martineau said. "And let's be frank, Graham, you know that it is likely she will."

"Are you seriously worried that some idiot might blame your drug for her death?" Kilburn asked, flabbergasted.

"You have to admit, someone might at least *consider* the possibility."

"Fine," Kilburn said. "I promise you there will be zero paper trail. Unless this drug works, no one will ever know we tried it. Just give me access to the samples of the real drug, and you won't hear another word of it. Unless it works."

"Now, Graham," Martineau said, as if he'd been let down by a close friend. "You know I can't do that. I would be fired. And I might even go to jail."

Kilburn took three slow breaths, realizing that his fury wasn't going to help his case. "Luc, this is off-the-record stuff. I will take one-hundred-percent responsibility. I will tell them I threatened you with a hatchet and a grenade, if you want. Just give me the damn access and let me worry about the fallout."

Martineau didn't respond.

"A baby is about to lose his mother." Kilburn stressed.

"Graham, this is what I can do," Martineau said. "I will get you samples of Oraloxin to test on the culture plates against your resistant G.A.S.—"

"Fucking perfect!" Kilburn snapped. "I'll bring the plates to my patient's funeral to show her family!"

"I'm sorry, Graham," Martineau said calmly. "It's all we can offer."

Kilburn slammed the receiver into the cradle without saying another word.

He dropped his head to his arms on the table. He took a few more deep breaths, summoning the courage to go tell Gurdev Singh that the last hope for his wife had just vanished.

But as he rose from the desk, an idea struck him. "Screw you, Luc," he muttered under his breath. He grabbed for the phone and dialed the pager number from memory.

While he waited for his colleague and department head, Dr. Morgan Teal, to return the page, he considered the best approach. Though he would prefer to level with Teal, he doubted his by-the-book boss would agree to his request. And he only had one crack at this.

The phone rang, and Kilburn shot a hand out for it. "Morgan? It's Graham."

"Hello, Graham," Teal said in his ever formal tone.

"Morgan, are you still running that oral anti–MRSA drug study?" Kilburn asked.

"It's hardly mine, Graham. I'm merely the site investigator," Teal said with a hint of pride. "But yes, it is ongoing."

"Far as I'm concerned, it's your study," Kilburn fawned. "Listen, Morgan, I've got a good patient for the study downstairs in the ER. How do I go about enrolling him?"

"Graham, I'm confused," Teal said. "You're not on call this week for infectious diseases according to my schedule."

"Yeah, that's right," Kilburn said, his mind racing. He

could feel a drop of sweat running down his arm. "This is actually an office patient. I just got his C-and-S results today. He has an MRSA-positive wound on his foot. Not too sick. I think he would be perfect for the study."

"Sounds like a reasonable candidate," Teal agreed. "Why don't you give me his name?"

Shit, Kilburn thought, *Why didn't I think this through?* "Let me just get that info for you." He rattled some papers in front of him, buying time. "Okay, it's a Gurdev Singh," he said the first name that popped to mind. "He's twenty years old. Diabetic foot ulcer on the left heel." Then, in case Teal decided to check, he added: "He might not be registered in the computer yet, as I just sent him down to ER. You know how long that can take."

"I certainly do," Teal sighed.

"How do we enroll him in the study?"

"I'll page our research assistant, Lori," Teal said. "She will meet you in the ER and get you the application, consent form, and the drugs."

"Morgan, I'm in the hospital now, doing nothing but twiddling my thumbs," Kilburn said, as he cradled the phone against his shoulder and wiped his palms on his pant legs. "Why don't I get things started? Where do I find all the stuff?"

"I suppose it's relatively straightforward," Teal said reluctantly. "All the supplies for the study are kept in a lockbox in the ER's supply room. There should be a second key in the ER."

"Okay, Morgan, I'll go down and see if I can get the paperwork started."

"Graham, thank you for supporting our research initiative."

"Don't mention it," Kilburn said sheepishly. He hung up the phone, realizing he had just embarked on a game of Russian roulette with his own career. But he would worry about that later. Now he was anxious to get as much of a head start on the research assistant as possible.

He jogged out of the ICU to the stairwell, taking the stairs two at time. When he strode into the emergency room, the usual chaos prevailed. He darted through the patients, staff, and stretchers until he reached the back desk. He was pleased to see Maryanne manning the desk. In her early forties, Maryanne was tall and thin, with long red hair, freckles, full lips, and light gray eyes. He might have considered her pretty had she not always worn a little too much makeup to complement her slightly hungry expression. He understood why some of the residents referred to her as "the cougar of the ER."

"Well, hello stranger," Maryanne's eyes lit up. "How's my very favorite ID specialist doing?"

"Favorite of the moment, right?" He smiled widely, matching her flirtatious tone. "I'm not on call for ER, so I'm doing great."

"Nope. You're my *absolute* favorite." She shrugged. "So why are you here, if not on call? Just to visit me?" She bit her lip.

Kilburn laughed. "Mainly. Also, I just spoke to Morgan Teal. I need to get into those oral MRSA drug-trial supplies. He said they're in a lockbox in the office. And that you would have a key."

"I might be able to help." She reached under the desk and pulled out a chain with a single key attached. She dangled it above her like it was a hotel room key. "Can you find the supply room?"

"I'll manage." He took the key from her hand.

"Maryanne, the patient in bed seven is seizing again," a voice yelled from behind a curtain several feet from the desk.

"Got to go. See ya later." She shot out of her chair and dashed for the curtain.

Kilburn headed for the supply closet behind the nursing station. Feeling like a prowler, he slunk around the crowded room while looking for the lockbox. When he found the safelike box, marked RESEARCH: INFECTIOUS DISEASES, in the far corner of the room, he slipped the key in and turned the bolt. Once open, he reaching his hand inside and carefully moved some papers out of the way. He fished around and pulled out two small boxes marked *A* and *B* with the SeptoMed logo below each. He took two pill bottles from each, and then put the rest back in the lockbox.

Glancing around again to make sure he was still alone, he pocketed the bottles and strode out of the room. Keeping his head down, he hurried out of the ER and back to the ICU.

Outside Parminder Singh's room, he waved for the nurse, Nikki, to join him in the hallway. Nikki stepped out of the room. She slipped off her mask and gown and faced him in her scrubs. Thin and quiet, with wild locks of curly black hair, the thirtyish woman was known as one of the best in the ICU.

Standing in front of the room's sealed doors, Kilburn handed her one bottle of each of the *A* and *B* pills. "Nikki, this is an experimental antibiotic from a research study," he said.

"Which is?" she held up both bottles.

"I'm not sure," Kilburn admitted. "One is a placebo and the other is the trial medication. I just grabbed them from the ER."

She frowned. "I don't think I've seen this done before."

"You haven't," Kilburn said. He decided to gamble on the truth. "Nikki, I don't even have permission from the company to use this drug. But you and I both know that Parminder is dying. And this drug has shown good results with MRSA. So maybe. . . ."

Nikki regarded him for a long moment before she finally nodded. "You're the doctor. Write it on an order form and I'll give it. Down her nasogastric tube, I presume?"

"Bless you, Nikki." Kilburn grinned widely, resisting the urge to hug her. "You'll have to give the same dose of each bottle, because we don't know which is just a sugar pill."

Nikki nodded again, but she didn't return his smile.

Kilburn walked out of the ICU feeling vaguely elated. He understood how much trouble he might face for his actions, but he headed down to the microbiology lab, intending to get them to test both drugs A and B on the culture plates of Parminder's G.A.S. swabs, satisfied he had done all he could for his patient.

He made it only halfway down the hallway when his cell phone vibrated in his pocket. He glanced at the name display, which read "S & N Fischer." The name rattled around his consciousness, but he couldn't place it. He answered it anyway.

"Dr. Kilburn? It's Nancy Fischer. Angelica's mother."

Angie! He suddenly remembered the name of the teenage IV-drug user presumed to be responsible for the Vancouver outbreak. Days earlier he had left two messages on her parents' machine, but he'd given up hope of hearing from them. "Thanks for getting back to me, Mrs. Fischer."

"I'm not sure how much help I can be to you," Fischer said quietly. "I . . . we . . . haven't seen Angie in a long time."

"I understand," Kilburn said. "That must be tough." Fischer didn't respond, but Kilburn heard her swallow on the other end of the line. "Ah, Mrs. Fischer, it's very important that we find your daughter. She might have been exposed to an infectious disease."

"Oh, God," Fischer said and her voice quavered. "She has AIDS, doesn't she?"

"That's not why I was calling," Kilburn said, sidestepping the fact that the ER records established that Angie did indeed have HIV.

"What other infection could it be?" Fischer demanded.

"An unusual skin infection," he said. "We don't know too much about it yet, but it's important that we find her."

"Is it dangerous?" She began to sob quietly. "Of course it is. Why else would you call?" She sniffled. "In spite of it all, she's still my little girl."

"I know," Kilburn said. "But I can't really answer your questions until we find Angie."

"I don't know exactly where she is," Fischer said. "Before she was sixteen, I could get the child welfare authorities to track her down for me, but now that she's eighteen, I can't do anything legally. It's so stupid! She's just a confused little girl."

"Okay, Mrs. Fischer," he sighed. "Thanks for getting back to me—"

"But she still stays in contact with her brother," Fischer cut in. "Glen told me she called three days ago. She had gone down to meet her *boyfriend*." She hissed the word. "Dealer, more like it."

"Gone where?" Kilburn asked.

"The parasite is from the States. He moved back to Seattle last year."

"Seattle?" Kilburn blurted out. "Angie's been in Seattle recently?"

"You sound upset," she said.

"No, no," Kilburn said, recovering his composure. "It will just make it that much harder to track her infection."

But he didn't say what he was really thinking: *Has Angie already spread her deadly germs across the border?*

24

Philadelphia, Pennsylvania

Head down, Horton dodged the crowds on Walnut Street heading away from SeptoMed's headquarters. Lost in her thoughts, she barely noticed the warm sunny day on her way to the New York Deli. The diner was the closest thing the three key members of the Oraloxin development team had to a regular lunch spot, though they met there at most once a month.

Since Graham Kilburn's call the day before, the black veil shrouding Ellen's world had begun to lift. She'd even slept through most of the previous night. Inadvertently, Kilburn had offered Ellen the one thing her life had lacked during the past few weeks: hope.

Still, convincing Luc Martineau to release Oraloxin to Kilburn had taxed her powers of persuasion to the limit. Her boss initially balked at the suggestion, but he finally agreed to a compassionate release, "providing Dr. Kilburn abides by *all* the terms we set."

As she neared the deli, Horton felt a bubbling disquiet in

her gut. Today was not just a lunchtime get-together of friendly colleagues. Victor Leschuk had phoned her at home early in the morning and specifically asked to meet. Judging by his stiff, formal tone, she suspected he'd chosen the spot as an opportunity to get away from other eyes and ears at SeptoMed. Her suspicions were fueled when she arrived at the diner and discovered that even though the place was two-thirds empty Leschuk had chosen the most discreet spot in the far corner of the restaurant.

She had just sat down beside Leschuk, when Neil Ryland sauntered in. With exaggerated vigilance, he glanced around the room before sidling up to the table. "Spring has come early to Vienna. Maybe the birds will follow soon?" he said in the style of film-spy gibberish.

Leschuk closed his eyes and sighed.

"What's with all the secrecy, Viktor?" Ryland said as he threw his jacket over the back of the chair.

Leschuk scratched his neck, appearing uncomfortable. "Why don't we order lunch first?"

"You've made me a little too curious to eat." Ryland patted the thickness at his waist. "And that is saying plenty."

"Me too," Horton said. She tried to catch Leschuk's eyes, but he held them fixed on the table in front of him.

"Coffees then, at least," he said as their waitress stopped at their table. With short black hair and a wraparound blue tattoo on her forearm, her faraway eyes showed no recognition of them even though she had served them a number of times before.

After the server took their order and walked away, Leschuk shifted in his seat. "They say this weather will hold through the weekend," he said.

"Is that what you wanted to tell to us?" Ryland asked with a mischievous smile.

"No," Leschuk grunted, as if Ryland were serious. "It's just—." He shrugged self-consciously. "It will be good fishing weather."

"Are you taking the boat out?" Horton asked.

Leschuk nodded. "We're going to Struble Lake tomorrow. I've heard the trout have been biting all spring."

Horton nodded politely. She knew that aside from work, fishing was Leschuk's passion. But she had never fished in her life, and she never planned to. She had dodged all of Leschuk's previous invitations to join him and Oksana.

The waitress arrived with the coffees. As soon as she left, Leschuk leaned forward in his seat. "I wanted to talk to both of you about the drug trials," he said quietly.

Ryland stirred cream aggressively into his coffee. "What about them, Vik?"

"I saw the third chimp," Leschuk said. "I did the autopsy myself."

Ryland tapped his spoon against the side of his cup. "So?"

"His bone marrow simply turned off, you understand?" Leschuk said, barely above a whisper. "One day the monkey was fine. The next he had full-blown aplastic anemia. No white cells. No red cells. Nothing but wasted marrow." He held out his hands imploringly. "This is three chimps in a group of five hundred. In nature, you would expect to see this reaction less than once in fifty thousand chimps. The odds. . . ." He threw his hand up. "You cannot deny—"

"No one's denying anything," Ryland said. His voice lacked its previous edge. He sounded tired to Horton. Defeated, even. "Look, Vik, these monkeys have been on ten to fifty times the human dose for months and months. You can't necessarily extrapolate the results to people."

"I know, Neil," Leschuk said. "I know. But—"

"But what?" Horton spoke up.

Leschuk stared hard at the table. "I can't go on like this."

"Like what?" Horton asked.

"Like a cheat and a fraud," he said in a near whisper. "It is so unethical."

"What are you going to do?" Ryland asked.

Leschuk looked back at his colleagues with pleading brown eyes. "I was hoping to convince you that we should speak to the FDA review panel," he said. "Neil, we could explain, exactly as you have done just now, that this seems to be an idiosyncratic reaction specific to primates."

"They will shut us down," Ryland said evenly.

"Maybe, maybe not." Leschuk shook his open palms in front of him. "We might have to modify Ellen's formula. We've come this close. We can do it again."

"Who would fund us next time?" Ryland asked despondently.

"Hopefully SeptoMed."

"SeptoMed?" Ryland laughed bitterly. "Harvey Abram would see to it that we don't have a Bunsen burner left between us. You know how invested the CEO has become in this project. I don't think at this point he would accept an admission of failure—and let's face it, Vik, that's what you're proposing by going to the FDA—as an outcome."

"I'm sorry, but that is not my main concern. My conscience is," Leschuk said. He glanced at the others before returning his gaze to the table. "If you disagree, I will not stand in your way. I will not speak to the FDA." He shook his head emphatically. "But I will resign from the team. That much, I have to do."

There was a long silence. Finally, Ryland cleared his throat. "You know how premature I think this is," he sighed. "But far as I'm concerned, majority rules. If both of you want this, then count me in." He glanced from Leschuk to Horton and then shrugged. "Ellen?"

Horton scratched at nothing on the plastic tablecloth in front of her. She felt almost relieved that Leschuk had expressed the option of confessing to the FDA. And she felt another stab of guilt for not having had the courage to take the stand herself. Yet she couldn't shake the glimmer of optimism that Kilburn had instilled in her.

"Viktor, I admire your position here," Horton said. "I do. And two days ago I would have supported you wholeheartedly."

Leschuk looked up at her with a confused shrug. "What has changed?"

"There has been a development in Vancouver, Canada. A new bacteria."

Leschuk squinted at her. "What new bacteria?"

"An old school friend called me." She went on to tell them about the emergence of MRGAS. And she explained how Oraloxin was being tested on the new superbug.

Ryland leaned forward in his seat. Face flushed, he gripped the edge of the table. "*Well?* Did Oraloxin work?"

"I haven't heard," Horton said. "The patient would have just received her first doses."

Leschuk stared off in the distance. He shook his head slowly. "A group-A streptococcus resistant to every known antibiotic suddenly appears out of nowhere—"

"But it's happened, Vik," Ryland said with newfound urgency. "Ellen didn't make this up!"

Horton nodded. "And if Oraloxin is effective in treating this infection where no other drug has. . . ."

Leschuk sighed. "It would be unethical not to try it because of a theoretical risk seen only in monkeys. That is your point. Correct?"

"I guess," she said uncertainly.

Ryland stared wide-eyed at Horton. "Ellen, this is still your baby. What do you think?"

She looked down into her coffee cup. "I don't think it will make a difference if we wait a few more days. If Oraloxin doesn't work against MRGAS," she swallowed, "then I think Viktor's right. We have to go to the FDA."

"But if it does work?" Ryland asked.

She looked up at Ryland. His face was lit with boyish enthusiasm that she found appealing. Breaking into a spontaneous smile, she said, "Neil, let's just wait and see what happens in Vancouver."

25

Seattle, Washington

The convertible's soft-top thudded under the pounding of the relentless rain. Even at maximum speed, the window wipers had trouble keeping up with the torrential downpour. Lopez had a vivid memory of her CDC colleagues in Atlanta warning her before she accepted the job that it "always rained in Seattle." Not true. Long stretches of cloud-free sunshine highlighted Seattle's lush beauty, but when the rain did come, sometimes it seemed to last forever.

Lopez reached for the cell phone clipped to her belt. Keeping one eye on the road lines, which shifted in and out of visibility, she scrolled through the list of previously dialed calls and chose the long distance number. A husky voice answered on the second ring. "Dr. Kilburn's office. This is Louise."

"Hello, this is Dr. Lina Lopez calling from Seattle."

"Seattle! I love that town," Louise rasped. "Honest to God, that Northgate Mall has the best shopping in all of North America."

"Okay," Lopez said, simultaneously amused and bemused by Louise's digression. "I'm looking for Dr. Kilburn."

"You and half the doctors on this planet, honey," Louise said with a laugh. "But he's not in today."

Despite the secretary's unusual phone etiquette, Lopez warmed to her. "I'm with the CDC, Louise. It's extremely important I speak to him."

"Listen, Dr. Lopez, you've got me convinced," she sighed. "But I've got the who's who of the medical establishment *and* the media hounding my doctor day and night. Between you and me, I don't know how much more he can take."

Lopez changed tacks. "Sounds like he's lucky to have you there to protect him."

"Dr. Lopez, you're just too sweet," Louise grunted a cough. "I'll sit here and listen to your flattery all day long if you want, but I have to warn you, it isn't going to help your cause."

"I give up, Louise," Lopez said. "Truth is we—I—really need Dr. Kilburn's help. We have an outbreak here similar to the one in Vancouver. And I understand that he has more experience than anyone facing this new superbug."

"Hmmm," Louise said. "I'll give you this. You're more convincing than that jackass from the local news who keeps calling me. That boy reminds of me my high school prom date. Just won't take no for an answer." She chuckled a cough again. "That reporter is heading for the same well-placed kick my prom date got."

Lopez suddenly slammed on the brakes as a car swerved into her lane without signaling. "Asshole!" she muttered and hit her horn.

"You talking about me or the reporter?" Louise asked.

"Sorry, Louise, I was just cut off," Lopez said distractedly. "So this bug has hit the news in Vancouver?"

"Oh, yeah," Louise sighed. "Page three today. No doubt, front page tomorrow. The media can't get enough of this kind of stuff. Nothing terrifies the public like a new bug."

Lopez blew out her cheeks. "Great."

"I'll tell you what," Louise said. "I'll give you Dr. Kilburn's cell number. That's the best way to reach him. But I have to warn you, even that's hit and miss. He misplaces the thing all the time." She laughed heartily. "I'm thinking about having it surgically attached to him."

Lopez memorized the phone number. "Okay, Louise, thanks."

"Hey, Dr. Lopez, you sound young," Louise said. "You're not single by any chance?"

"Thirty-two. And as a matter of fact I am," she said, laughing at the latest surreal turn in their conversation. "Why, do you have a son?"

"Actually I do, but I don't think his battle-axe of a wife would appreciate me setting him up," Louise said. "No. I'd just love to see Dr. Kilburn settle down with a nice lady doctor."

"Even one who lives in Seattle?" she asked.

"Details, details," Louise said dismissively.

Lopez was still smiling when she tried Kilburn's cell number. After listening to the recorded greeting, she summarized her credentials and said: "I know you must be swamped, but it's vital I reach you. We have cases in Seattle similar to yours in Vancouver."

She put down her phone and drove the rest of the way with only the sound of the rain, which had slowed to a steady patter, in the background. In her head, she went over the interview with Marilyn Carlyle again. How did Tonya Jackson's dark-eyed dealer fit, if at all, into the spread of MRGAS?

She still hadn't come up with a plausible answer by the time she pulled into the underground parking lot of the State Health building.

Stepping into David Warmack's seventh-floor office, she sensed immediately that the news was not good. With his tie loosened and top button undone, he leaned back in the chair behind his desk. His forehead was creased with concern. The skin below his eyes drooped. For the first time ever, Warmack looked old to her.

"What is it, David?" she asked gently, sitting down across from him.

"There are four more confirmed cases, Cat," he said quietly. "And six possible others."

Lopez's stomach sank, but the news didn't surprise her. "Where?"

"Seven at Harborcenter," he said. "And three at the Kaster Hospital."

Lopez nodded. "Any link to Tonya Jackson?"

"Maybe with the Harborcenter cases." Warmack shrugged. "No obvious connection with the first confirmed case at Kaster. Then again, he's another IV-drug user."

"So we now have two super-infected hospitals in King County," she said flatly.

He lifted a copy of the *Seattle Times* on his desk. "And it's not a secret anymore, either."

Lopez leaned forward and read the headline: LETHAL SUPERBUG SPREADS THROUGH HOSPITAL. She took the paper from his hand and scanned the article that described Harry Wales's and Tonya Jackson's illnesses with only partial accuracy. She folded her arms across her chest. "It was bound to leak out, David."

"I know." His voice sounded as tired as he looked. "But we can't let innuendo run rampant. We need to make a statement."

"Agreed."

"I've called a press conference for noon. For both of us."

Lopez flipped the newspaper back on the desk. "This isn't the fifteen minutes of fame I was hoping for," she said glumly.

"Me neither, Cat." He shrugged. Then a smile crept into his expression, shedding years from his face. " 'No guts, no glory.' Isn't that what the marines say?"

"Whatever." Lopez leaned back in her seat. "David, we need to consolidate all King County patients infected with MRGAS in one hospital. The city's health care system will be paralyzed if this superbug gets into every Seattle hospital."

"We're working on it now," he said. "The tentative plan is to cordon off the entire fourth floor of Harborcenter—where the isolation rooms are—to contain all cases."

Lopez nodded. "I saw Marilyn Carlyle earlier," she said quietly.

Warmack frowned.

"Harry Wales's daughter. She's in isolation with MRGAS strep throat. She's hardly even symptomatic." She paused: "Imagine the repercussions of that! We may have carriers."

"That's all I've been thinking about, Cat." His face sagged again. "We have no idea how many are out there."

"So how do we control the spread if we don't even know who is infected?"

"That's tricky." He rubbed his eyes. "But we do the best we can. To begin with, we run throat and nasal screening swabs on everyone who has encountered a case. Including every single patient in Seattle-area hospitals."

Lopez rolled her eyes. "A logistical nightmare. And even if we succeed here in Seattle, there's still the Vancouver outbreak."

Warmack sat up straighter. He brought his fingers to his neck and buttoned up his shirt with one hand, before tightening his tie. "We can only take care of our own backyard," he said, "and hope that they do the same."

Lopez looked away from her colleague. "David, Marilyn Carlyle got to know Tonya Jackson before she died."

He dropped his hands from his collar. "And?"

"Tonya said that somebody deliberately gave her tainted drugs."

Warmack grimaced. "What?"

Lopez recounted Carlyle's description of the dark-eyed dealer. As she spoke, it dawned on her how tenuous the link was: a secondhand account from a less than credible original source.

"Cat, does that make any sense to you?" Warmack asked.

She shrugged. "At the CDC, we were taught always to consider intentional spread."

He viewed her skeptically. "But to an IV-drug user?"

She held up her hands. "Drug users are more susceptible to infections. Not only that but they're frequent hospital visitors, noncompliant, and difficult to track."

He shook his head. "I don't know, Cat."

Lopez felt a sudden resolve that almost made her shudder. "David, if someone wanted to deliberately introduce a new superbug in the community, what easier way can you think of than to give drug addicts contaminated drugs and turn them into unwitting vectors?"

26

Vancouver, Canada

Standing at his kitchen counter, Kilburn wrestled with the box of cornflakes, trying to find the seam to open the new bag. He grudgingly acknowledged to himself that his lack of sleep contributed to his impatience with the cereal box and every other aspect of the frantic pre-work and school preparations. He had called the ICU at two, four, and six A.M., checking on Parminder Singh's progress, and was relieved to hear each time that she was still alive.

Kilburn's ten-year-old nephew Matt sat at the counter watching his uncle with obvious amusement. "You're not a morning guy, are you Uncle Graham?" he asked matter-of-factly.

"Where do you hear these expressions?" Kilburn asked as he stabbed a hole in the side of the bag of cornflakes with a kitchen knife. "But to answer your question: No, mornings are not my strong suit."

"What's a strong suit?" Matt asked.

"Something you're best at," Kilburn grunted. He glanced

at his nephew with a half grin. "For example, Matt, one of your strong suits is irritating your uncle."

"I guess. But you make it so easy. I could irritate you in a weak suit." Matt giggled, which made his uncle laugh.

"Where's your sister?" Kilburn asked.

"You know, girl stuff." Matt rolled his eyes, and then pantomimed primping his own hair and dolling up his face.

"I hear you." Kilburn had watched his niece evolve from a six-year-old who refused to brush her hair or wear a dress to an eight-year-old who spent fifteen minutes in front of the mirror, doing and redoing her hair every morning. "Eat up, Matt, we have to get going very soon."

"Uncle Graham, why do you hang on to this house?"

Kilburn was caught off guard by his nephew's precocious question. "You want me to live on the street?" he said, dodging the issue. "That would make sleepovers way colder in the winter, wouldn't it?"

But Matt wasn't so easily dissuaded. "Mom says it's because you think Aunt Michelle's coming back."

"I forgot about your mom's ability to read minds," Kilburn grumbled. He had made the mistake of telling his sister that he had bought—but had not moved into—a new duplex in the ever-trendy Kitsilano neighborhood because it had offered the perfect fit for Michelle and him. Near to work, the beach, and the hip restaurants and shops of Fourth Avenue, the duplex had enough space for his niece and nephew. And the place could have easily housed the two kids of his own that he had once thought were in their near future. After Michelle moved out, he convinced himself that he didn't have time to go through the hassle of moving. He refused to admit that the hope of Michelle's return kept him in the four-bedroom house, but his nephew now had him wondering.

"C'mon, buddy, eat your cereal," Kilburn said. Then he yelled out: "Shayna. Downstairs—now!"

A minute later, his niece trudged into the room. Her chin hung on her chest. "Uncle Graham, I don't think I'm going to go to school today," she said with a huge sigh.

Kilburn folded his arms across his chest. "Would you like a second opinion on that?"

"Look at my hair," she said, pulling at her pigtails.

"Shay, they look cute."

"I wish I wasn't so ugly," she murmured.

"I do too." Matt giggled.

"Matt!" Kilburn snapped. Then he turned to his niece. "Shay, you don't believe that? Do you have any idea how many compliments I get when people see your photo in my office? They all say how beautiful you are."

"That's just grownups," Shayna pouted, but her lips broke into a partial smile. "Robby Markum called me the plainest girl in school."

"Oh, Shayna, don't you know anything?" Matt said with fraternal condescension. "That little twerp Robby only says that because he *likes* you."

Kilburn chuckled. "Your brother's right, Shay. Robby must be hot for you."

"Gross!" she squealed. And they all laughed.

Kilburn slapped another bowl of cereal on the countertop in front of her. "You have two minutes for breakfast." He glanced at his watch as if to time her.

The phone rang and he grabbed for the portable receiver without checking the caller ID. "Hello."

"Graham, it's Morgan Teal," his department head said tersely.

"Oh, um, Morgan, hi," Kilburn said.

"You had no right, Graham."

"Listen, Morgan, I had no other—"

"No, you listen," Teal cut him off. "You've put our hospital and me in a very awkward position. Not to mention potential legal actions. What were you thinking?"

Kilburn's discomfort dissipated, replaced by indignation. "I was thinking about a dying woman, Morgan. That's all." He looked up to see his niece and nephew staring at him intently. He pointed to their untouched cereal bowls and walked out of the kitchen into the privacy of the dining room, closing the sliding door behind him.

"So you went ahead and stole a completely untested drug because you think it *might* save your patient's life?" Teal's voice cracked with outrage. Kilburn had never heard him so angry.

"Morgan, I believed—in fact I still believe—that it's her only hope."

"And if she dies anyway?"

"Then she dies," Kilburn snapped. "But at least we—I—will know that she was given everything we could think of. She's only twenty, for God's sake!"

There was a long pause on the line. "That's just not good enough for me, Graham," Teal said grimly. "I'm going to have to take this to the hospital's medical director."

"Take it anywhere you want." Then a disturbing thought occurred to Kilburn. "Morgan, you're not going to stop the Oraloxin treatment now, are you?"

"By all rights, I should," Teal said. "But you've put me in an untenable position. If I write anything in her chart, including the order to discontinue the medication, then I expose myself legally."

"God forbid," Kilburn said sarcastically, regretting the remark as soon as he uttered it.

Teal grunted indignantly.

"Morgan, I'm sorry," Kilburn said. "I didn't do this to inconvenience you or disrupt your study. I did what I thought I had to do for my patient. For my own conscience."

Teal was silent for several moments. "It still doesn't excuse your actions, Graham."

"I guess not."

Drained, Kilburn hung up the phone. He stood motionless in his dining room, considering the implications of Teal's call. Only Matt's voice brought him back to the moment. "Uncle Graham, we're going to be late for school!"

Kilburn snapped into motion. He gathered Matt and

Shayna and shepherded them out to his Jeep. Barely able to focus on the kids' conversation, which mainly centered on Robby Markum and Shayna's dissatisfaction with her hairdo, he dropped the children off in front of the school. With a quick peck on Shayna's cheek and a high-five for Matt, he climbed back into his car and headed for the hospital.

Halfway there, his cell phone rang. He felt a sudden rush of foreboding, concerned it might be the hospital with bad news about Parminder Singh. He located the phone in his jacket pocket and brought it to his car. "Hello," he said.

"Dr. Graham Kilburn?" the woman asked.

"Yup."

"It's Dr. Lina Lopez calling from Seattle. I'm with the CDC—"

"Of course, Lina," Kilburn interrupted. "You're an EIS officer. I'm sorry. I was planning to get back to you this morning."

"No worries." Lopez said warmly. "I spoke to Louise. She told me how thin you're stretched these days."

"God knows what else she must have told you," Kilburn sighed.

"Plenty." Lopez laughed. "She's an interesting woman."

"One way of looking at it. But I would be lost without her." He cleared his throat. "What's going on in Seattle?"

Lopez told him what she knew of the confirmed and suspected cases in her region. "Our index case for the first outbreak, anyway, was an HIV-positive drug abuser."

"*Was?*"

"She died of MRGAS pneumonia," Lopez said. "I understand your known index case fits the same profile."

"Very much so," Kilburn said. "In fact, Dr. Lopez, I think I might know the connection between our outbreaks."

"You mean the pusher?" Lopez said excitedly.

"What pusher?"

Lopez gave him the quick lowdown on the enigmatic drug dealer Tonya Jackson had described to Marilyn Carlyle.

When she finished, Kilburn said, "I don't know anything about that drug dealer."

"Then what connection are you talking about?" She sounded disappointed.

"If I have my chronology straight, our first case predates yours by three or four days."

"And?" she said skeptically.

"Our index case, Angie Fischer, disappeared right after she left the ER," he said. "Her mom called yesterday. You'll never guess where she headed."

"Not to Seattle?" Lopez asked, her voice rising.

"Yup."

"Wait a minute, Graham. You think *your* index case is also *our* index case?"

"I would love to find out." Kilburn said as he turned into the St. Michael's parking lot. He pulled into a spot and switched off his ignition.

"How?" Lopez asked, her tone subdued.

"Angie's mom gave me the name of her boyfriend in Seattle," Kilburn said. "I think we should track him down."

"We?"

"If it's okay with you, I would like to come down to Seattle later today." Thinking of his conversation with Teal, he said, "If nothing else, I could use the change of scenery." As he said it, he realized he would have to ensure that Kyra or Corazón could take the kids overnight.

"Fine by me," she said. "You've got my cell number, right? Call me as soon as you get into town. Meantime why don't you give me the boyfriend's name? I'll see if I can track him down."

"Jacob or Jake Fasken. He's twenty-two. That's about all I know." He paused. "Though it sounded to me like he must have a criminal record."

"That might help. Means he should have a parole officer. I'll see what I can find out."

Having parked his car, Kilburn headed straight for the

hospital's elevator. Stepping out onto the fifth floor, he thought he heard a low-pitched noise. As he strode closer to the doors of the ICU, he realized it was the sound of a man crying.

Kilburn's heart pounded in his ears as he broke into a run.

Bursting through the opening of the translucent sliding glass doors, Kilburn saw Gurdev Singh. The young man stood beside the main ICU desk. His palms covered his eyes and his fingers reached to the edge of his turban. Shuddering, he rocked back and forth on his heels, while a few feet away the unit clerk clutched little Harjeet in her arms. But the baby's cries were drowned out by the plaintive sobs from his father.

Oh, shit! Kilburn knew without taking another step.

Then, more from reflex than reason, he sprinted for Parminder's room.

27

For the second night in a row, Cohen dreamt about his mother's death. In the dream, he sat on one side of the bed and his father on the other. Wearing a nightgown that looked two sizes too large for her gaunt frame, his mom lay motionless under a pale blue down quilt. Cohen couldn't tell if she was comatose or dead. In the dream, Cohen was his present age, but his dad was much younger—the robust woodworker of Seth's childhood, not the old man now crippled by rheumatoid arthritis and embittered by loss who lived in the basement of Seth's house. His dad never spoke a word throughout the dream, but a stream of tears ran down his cheeks and onto the quilt. Then, a moment before Seth awoke, his mom's eyes snapped open, and she turned to her husband, terror-stricken. "Please don't leave me!" Her voice quavered in the exact same way Carol's had before she slipped into her terminal coma in the ER.

Rising from his bed, Cohen wondered why an intravenous drug user he had barely known kept evoking memories of his elegant mother. Apart from their deaths, he could fathom no connection between the two women. Stepping into the shower, he realized he did not want to delve into the matter too deeply. He preferred not to know what Freudian turmoil raged in his subconscious.

After the shower, Cohen changed into a gray sports jacket and light blue shirt, deciding to forgo the tie. Firing up the espresso machine, he steamed some milk and then drank down the large latté that usually sufficed as breakfast. As he was contemplating a second cup, the steady tapping of a horn drew his attention from outside the kitchen window.

He locked his door, picked up the newspaper on the stoop, and headed down the front stairs. Stopping outside his father's suite, he dropped the paper in front of the basement door, knowing his dad would have finished both crosswords by the time he got home.

"Morning, KC," Leetch said warmly as Cohen slid into the passenger's seat of his partner's prized '97 Cadillac sedan. "Hey, how's the pappy doing?"

"About the same," Cohen said. "Still having trouble getting around with those arthritic knees of his. Still embarrassed that his son is a cop," he sighed. This ground was too familiar for both of them.

"Can't blame him on that one." Leetch chuckled. "Frankly, you're a disgrace to your whole family."

"Hmmm," Cohen agreed. "Since the day I enrolled in the academy, I've been hearing how Jews weren't meant to be in law enforcement."

"Very true." Leetch chuckled. "And I personally know a bunch of convicted murderers who strongly feel the same way."

Cohen nodded his thanks for the compliment.

"Speaking of murderers, I got a hunch today is the day we find us Jimmy and Frige's killer. Lovable son of a bitch that he must be!"

Cohen looked over to Leetch. "Rome, if he's half as good as I think he might be, then he's long gone."

"So?" Leetch shrugged. "Didn't stop us from nailing Marcus Hogan, did it?"

"True," Cohen said, remembering the ex-tech company CEO who murdered his financial VP and fled to Paris, before Cohen and Leetch lured him back to Portland with a phony inheritance scam.

"We'll find him," Leetch predicted confidently.

Cohen didn't share his partner's optimism, but he harbored as much, or more, determination as Leetch to track down the man he had come to think of as Carol's killer.

They drove in silence for several minutes. Eventually, Leetch turned onto Northwest Tenth Avenue, a few blocks up from the Willamette River. Cohen stared out the window at the posh downtown towers. "Little Andrew could live in worse neighborhoods," he said.

"Funny that," Leetch grumbled. "The guy's done hard time and never worked a day in his life, but he lives in a half-million-dollar loft and drives a Porsche. I ought to sign up with his financial planner."

Cohen sighed. "I think his *planner* works out of Bogotá."

"No doubt." Leetch pulled the car up to the curb in front of Riverside Suites.

They climbed out of the car and walked up to the building's intercom. Leetch read the number off the directory and typed in the code for Andrew Nagle. The bell rang unanswered ten times before it transformed into a steady busy tone. "Ah, drug dealers," Leetch sighed. "They do like their sleep in the morning."

Leetch slid a hand in his nylon jacket and pulled out his cell phone along with a slip of paper. Reading off the paper, he dialed the number and then brought the phone to his ear. After ten or fifteen seconds, he spoke into the receiver: "Little Andrew! How the hell are you?" He paused. "Now Andrew, what would your mother say about that kind of language?" The next time Leetch spoke, his tone was clipped and threatening. "Detective Leetch is exactly who the fuck I am," he snapped. "And my partner and I have wasted more than enough time outside your building. So let us in—*now!*"

No sooner had Leetch pocketed his cell than the front door was buzzed open. Leetch turned to Cohen with a cat-who-swallowed-the-canary grin and reached for the front door. He yanked it open, and Cohen followed him to the elevator. They stepped out onto the fifteenth and top floor. The door at the end of the hall was open, and Nagle stood in his doorway waiting for them in a navy bathrobe. Short and thin, with striking blue eyes and prominent cheekbones, his thick blond hair stuck out in tangled spears. "What's this about, detectives?" His open-mouthed smile showed off ivory-white teeth.

Leetch bowed his head slightly. "We've come to express our condolences at your loss."

"*My loss?*" The smile never vacated Nagle's lips.

Leetch's face broke into a smile as wide and insincere as Nagle's. "You know . . . at Jimmy and Frige's passing."

Nagle grunted a laugh. "That's funny, Detective."

Leetch walked past Nagle into the apartment. "I could sure use a cup of coffee."

Nagle chased Leetch inside. Cohen followed. They assembled in the spacious living room. Filled with overstuffed white couches, it had huge bay windows and a stunning view of the river. But the natural beauty was tainted by the lingering smell of cigarette smoke and stale wine. Leetch pointed around the spacious room. "Brutal being jobless these days."

A female voice called out from another room. "Who's here, Andy?"

Nagle hurried over toward the voice and pulled the door shut. "No one," he spoke through the closed door. "Just a couple of buddies."

"I'm touched, Little Andrew, I am. But technically we're not your buddies." Leetch plunked down on one of the couches and threw an arm over the pillow. "This is Sergeant Cohen." He nodded to Seth. "And I'm Detective Leetch with Portland Homicide."

Cohen sat down beside Leetch. Having been through this routine too many times to count, he was content to sit back and watch his partner lead the interview.

Nagle rejoined them in the living room, dropping into the chair across from them. "So you're here about Mitchum and Frigerator, huh?"

Leetch shrugged. "How about you confess now and give us the rest of the morning off?"

Nagle laughed again. "I wasn't even in the city the night they got whacked."

Leetch folded his arms across his chest. "Oh?"

"I've been in L.A. for the past three days," Nagle said, crossing his legs and adjusting his bathrobe to cover his exposed Hugo Boss boxers.

"Why?" Leetch asked. "You got a film script?"

"Visiting family," Nagle sighed.

"Of course. Your Colombian cousins!" Leetch brought a finger to each nostril and pantomimed snorting coke. "I assume you have witnesses to this family reunion?"

Nagle smiled coolly. "A few."

Picking up on Nagle's growing defensiveness, Cohen leaned forward in his seat. "There was no love lost between you and Jimmy, true?"

"If you mean, did I hate that little fucker," Nagle said, seemingly oblivious to his own short stature. "Then you'd be dead on."

"Why?" Cohen asked.

Nagle reached down and unhooked the belt of his bathrobe. He opened it up to reveal a long jagged scar that ran across the entire right side of his flat abdomen. "Took twenty pints of blood to save me after that bugger stabbed me in the liver."

"But you didn't kill him," Cohen said.

"No."

"Then who do you think did?" Cohen asked.

"Christ, how should I know?" Nagle rolled his eyes as he retied his bathrobe. "You think I'm the only guy he screwed over?"

"Have you heard anything about a new dealer in town?" Cohen asked.

"I don't do that shit anymore—"

Leetch waved his hands in front of him. "Save it, Andrew! Ten to one if we toss this place now, we'll find enough crack and rock to build an igloo." He glanced over at the room where the female voice had come from. "What say we start in there?"

Nagle stared at the coffee table. "There might be a guy," he grumbled.

"Description?" Leetch wiggled his fingers in front of him in his characteristic interview style.

"Tall, dark-haired guy with a bad highlight job. Thirties. Wears a track suit and a couple of gold chains. No class, you understand?"

"Good thing we're talking to Martha Stewart, here," Leetch sighed. "Was this guy handing out free samples?"

"Yeah! How did you know?" Nagle's head shot up. "But only to some of them. From what I heard, he only gave them to the most fucked-up of the junkies. Guess he was looking for easy marks." Then, as if talking to himself, he added, "Moron. Those are the ones who usually don't have any cash."

Cohen squinted at Nagle. "Is this new dealer still around?"

Nagle shrugged. "I only got back yesterday." He frowned and scratched roughly at his disheveled hair. "Wait a minute. You think this guy took down Jimmy and Frige?"

"We're still not convinced you weren't involved," Leetch said. "But it might help if you could tell us how to find this guy."

Nagle's eyes narrowed and his lips tightened, as if weighing his options. "And if I gave you a couple of ideas where to look, would you get off my back?"

Leetch shrugged. "Possibly."

Nagle looked up at the ceiling. "About four or five nights ago, I saw the guy in an alley. He was passing out a hit to this tranny, goes by Shania or Chevelle or something . . ." He snapped his fingers. "Chavon!"

"And?" Leetch rolled one index finger over the other.

"I was curious. Okay?" Nagle shrugged again.

"You were curious?" Leetch repeated skeptically.

"Look, I don't know where the fuck he came from or why he's suddenly doing business in my neighborhood," Nagle said defensively. "Besides, in any market it's important to keep tabs on the competition."

"'In any market.' You're priceless." Leetch rolled his eyes. "So how did you 'keep tabs' on your competition?"

"I followed him for a while."

"Followed him where?" Cohen asked.

"He loaded into this black SUV," Nagle said. "I tailed him back to his hotel."

Cohen felt a rush. "Which hotel?" he asked quietly.

"A little dump off Twenty-fifth and Graham," Nagle said. "The Lodger or something."

Cohen stared hard at Nagle. "Andrew, are you sure that's where he went?"

"I saw him pull up to a spot right in front. Then he walked through the front door."

Leetch cocked his head. "And you did what?"

"I hung around outside for a while," Nagle said. "I was thinking of having a talk with him, but then I saw a cop car pull up to the Denny's beside the hotel. So I fucked off."

Cohen glanced at Leetch, and they shared a slight nod. "Okay, Andrew, we're going check out this hotel, but if you're lying . . ." Leetch let the threat hang unfinished.

"I'm not," Nagle snapped.

Without another word to him, Cohen and Leetch got up and walked out of the condo. They headed out to Leetch's car and drove over to Twenty-fifth and Graham. On the northeast corner stood The Oregon Lodger, a dumpy-looking three-story brick building that Cohen assumed from the outside alone wouldn't have earned a single star from AAA. They pulled up in front of the main entrance on Graham Street.

Cohen followed Leetch into the lobby. The place smelled of cheap deodorizer. The linoleum floors were stained and curling up at the edges. Behind the desk, a fat bored-looking man in a polyester blazer and tie flipped through a newspaper. "You boys looking for a room?" he asked without looking up from his paper.

"Us boys are looking for someone," Leetch said, flashing his detective's badge to the unimpressed clerk. "We think he would have stayed a couple days, but he might've checked out two or three days ago." Leetch went on to describe the dark man with the frosted hair.

When he finished, the fat man shook his head. "Nope."

"You want to think about it," Leetch said, irritated.

"Don't need to," the man grunted. "I got thirty-two rooms in this place. I'm here six days a week. I know the guests. And I never saw the guy you just described. Believe me, he didn't stay here."

Deflated, Cohen glanced around the lobby. He saw a smaller door leading out to Twenty-fifth Avenue. Without a word, he walked out and stood on the street in the warm sunshine.

A moment later, Leetch joined him. "What's up, KC?" Leetch asked.

"Little Andrew drives a white Porsche, right?"

"I guess." Leetch frowned. "So?"

"Not the most discreet car for tailing someone."

Leetch's eyes brightened with a flicker of recognition. "No, it's not."

Cohen looked across the street. "And if our guy is the pro I think he is, he would've known Andrew was behind him."

"He might have," Leetch said, breaking into a grin.

Cohen pointed at the Econotravel Inn across the street. "If Andrew parked on Graham, he couldn't have seen our guy walk out the other door and cross Twenty-fifth."

"Not from Graham," Leetch agreed. "Let's go talk to the clerk."

The Econotravel Inn was a slight step up from the Oregon

Lodger. It had a similar, grimy lobby with an equally unidentifiable but unpleasant smell, but the skinny, nervous clerk behind the desk responded with far more deference to Leetch's badge. Even before Leetch had finished his description, the boy was nodding vehemently. "I remember a guy just like that," he said, his voice cracking. "Looked like a pimp, but he didn't talk like one."

"What does that mean?" Leetch asked.

"He was calm and quiet. Polite, even." The clerk nodded continuously. "But he was wearing a track suit and chains and stuff."

Cohen's heart sped up. He tapped his fingers on the desk. "And the name?"

"T-something . . ." The clerk typed at his computer keyboard. "Taylor . . . Tison . . ." He read the names aloud. "Here it is," he squeaked. "Dennis Tyler!"

"What did he leave for a room deposit?" Cohen asked.

"He paid in cash," the clerk said.

"But don't you take an imprint in case of incidentals?"

"That's right. Yeah." The clerk studied the screen. "He left a Visa card. Here it is. Name on the card is Dennis Lyndon Tyler. His address is in Fresno, California."

But Cohen had no interest in the address. He knew it would be bogus. Just like the name was. But it gave them a starting point for tracking the suspect. After all, how many Dennis Lyndon Tylers could there be?

Cohen looked at his partner and smiled, appreciating that they had just stumbled unexpectedly upon the fresh tracks of a man who in all likelihood rarely left a trail behind.

28

Honey Brook, Pennsylvania

The man who once went by Dennis Tyler, but now claimed to be Wayne Forbes, stood in the fish-and-tackle section of a small sporting goods store. Aside from the reels and flies, the store also sold a wide assortment of hunting rifles and handguns. Despite his line of work, Forbes found his country's obsession with firearms excessive. He saw no irony in his firm belief that guns were not a God-given right but should be limited to the domain of the professional.

After his father walked out on the family, when Forbes was only six, his grandfather began to take him along on regular fishing and hunting trips. Forbes couldn't stand the cantankerous old bastard, who always made it clear what a burden the boy was to him, but Forbes enjoyed the chance to escape the grime of the city. And from an early age, he got a rush out of tracking prey, especially deer, whose speed and perceptiveness made them a worthy challenge. They were a thrill to bring down.

Forbes had taken his last hunting trip soon after his fourteenth birthday. He never made it home from that trip, spending the rest of his adolescence in juvenile lockup. As an adult, Forbes had no interest in hunting or fishing. He considered it akin to a professional golfer going out for a round of minigolf. What was the sense in wasting time that way?

He browsed through the fishing rods, choosing one of the more expensive ones with just the right give in his hands. He carefully sorted through the flies and picked the ones he considered most eye-catching. He smiled to himself, realizing he was never going to use the gear. But meticulousness was what distinguished his work. He refused to compromise on detail.

He carried his selections up to the counter. Behind the counter sat a sullen young girl with a pale complexion. She appeared to be in her early twenties. She wore glasses and smelled of the bubblegum she loudly chomped. With barely a glance at Forbes, she began to ring in his purchases.

"Ma'am," Forbes asked. "How far is it to Struble Lake?"

The girl shrugged. "Five miles or so."

"And there's a boat launch there, huh?"

"Guess so," she said, still not meeting his eyes. "I see them come by with their boats and trailers all the time." She glanced out the window at the ten-foot trawler tied up to the back of his stolen minivan. "That one yours?"

He shrugged, then flashed her a coy smile. "Not much of a boat, but it's watertight and holds the fish. And I'm aiming to catch me a big one."

"Yeah," she sighed. "You and everyone else 'round here."

Very different fish, Forbes thought as he picked up his bag and new rod off the counter.

29

Seattle, Washington

With her hair pulled tightly back behind her head, Lopez wore a white blouse tucked into the midlength gray skirt of her most solemn suit. She sat at the podium beside Dr. Warmack, who looked authoritative and distinguished in navy. Sweating from the hot glow of spotlights and the adrenaline coursing through her system, the possible damage to her makeup from perspiration gave her one more worry she didn't need. Because of the subject matter, she had expected her first-ever news conference to pique the media's curiosity. But she never imagined such a zoo. The Department of Health's small conference room spilled over with reporters and cameramen to the point where the aisles were plugged with people.

Lopez rubbed her hands against the table, trying in vain to dry them. Her heart slammed against her breastbone. Glancing over at Warmack, she tried to absorb some of his calm.

"Time to face the wolves, Lina," he said quietly to her with a reassuring smile. Then he reached for the microphone in front of him and pulled it toward himself. "Good afternoon. I'm Dr. David Warmack with the Washington State Health Department." He casually lifted his reading glasses off the table, perched them on the bridge of his nose, and began to read his statement, indifferent to the camera flashes and the coughs, whispers, and other noises that filled the electrified room.

"Five days ago, Seattle's first case of multiresistant group-A streptococcus, now known as MRGAS, was admitted to Harborcenter Hospital. The patient succumbed two days later to pneumonia. The following day we received the lab confirmation of MRGAS in her respiratory secretions."

His tone was unruffled but commanding, and when he paused to look up at the reporters, the last few whisperers fell quiet. "In the past five days, there has been a second death, four more confirmed cases, and six suspected cases of this new superbug. All positive cultures so far have come from two Seattle-area hospitals. All live cases, whether proven or suspected, are now under strict quarantine in a specifically designated hospital unit."

Warmack stopped to sip from his water glass. "MRGAS is a mutated form of a common bacteria often responsible for mild infections such as tonsillitis, strep throat, and skin infections. On occasion, it can lead to more serious invasive infections such as we've seen in three patients." He looked up from his notes. "So far, all antibiotics that normally treat streptococcal infections have failed to work against MRGAS."

A collective agitated murmur broke out within the press corps.

Warmack dropped his notes on the table in front of him and pulled his glasses off his nose, using them to point at the reporters. "I want to emphasize that this organism is contagious only via direct contact spread. In other words, careful hand washing along with a simple mask and gown will suffice in preventing person-to-person spread. We are screening all contacts and hospital patients. We believe that we have successfully minimized the risk of any further spread within the hospitals and beyond."

Reporters shouted questions from every direction, but Warmack closed his eyes and shook his head until the noise died down. "I won't field any questions until Dr. Lopez from the CDC has had a chance to read her statement." He looked over to her with an encouraging nod and a concealed wink.

Lopez swallowed, trying to dislodge her heart from her throat. She leaned closer to her own microphone. "I'm Dr. Lina Lopez, the regional Epidemiological Intelligence Service officer with the Centers For Disease Control." She glanced down at her cue cards. "The new superbug Dr. Warmack described is similar to what we have seen with methicillin-resistant Staph Aureus, or MRSA, and Vancomycin Resistant Enterococcus, or, VRE." Realizing that her technical language might be over the heads of some members of the audience, Lopez decided it was too late to change her approach. "Bacteria commonly undergo spontaneous mutations and become resistant to certain antibiotics. The difference in the case of MRGAS is in the extent of resistance seen. As Dr. Warmack said, no antibiotic tested thus far has been successful in treating this infection."

The last statement led to another spontaneous eruption in the room.

"Please, please," Lopez waved for the crowd to quiet, feeling her confidence build with each turn of the cue cards. "This is not the first bacterium to be resistant to all antibiotics. For example, since the late 1990s we have seen multiresistant tuberculosis develop in the inner-city areas of New York and San Francisco. In fact, up until the early 1930s—the so-called preantibiotic era—there was no specific therapy for *any* bacterial infection. Yet most people survived such infections.

"However, the CDC and the World Health Organization have identified this pathogen as a level-one public-health priority. We are working together to respond to the outbreak in Seattle and the simultaneous emergence in Vancouver, Canada. A joint task force of local experts—in public health, epidemiology, and infectious diseases—has been assembled to coordinate the Seattle response with the CDC and WHO."

She glanced over to Warmack, who nodded to her once. Then she turned back to the reporters and cameramen. "We will try to answer some of your questions now, but please bear in mind that we have only known about the pathogen for less than forty-eight hours."

Warmack waved down another noisy collective outburst. He pointed to a woman waving her arm above her like a flag. She jumped to her feet. "Is this the same organism that causes flesh-eating disease?" she called out.

Warmack pulled the microphone closer. "Several bugs can cause necrotizing fasciitis, as we call it. And regardless of the bug, only a minority of people are susceptible to developing fasciitis. But, yes, this pathogen is *capable* of causing the disease in the right—or maybe wrong would be a better choice of words—person."

Warmack pointed at another man casting his arm about as if trying to hail a passing plane. The man popped out of his chair. "Jack Mavis, KIRO news," he said. "Is it true this bacteria came from the drug addict and AIDS patients?"

Warmack turned to Lopez with a frown. "Yours?" he whispered.

Lopez nodded and leaned toward her microphone. "At this point, while the investigation is in its infancy, we simply don't know the source." The anger welled inside her. "But if you're looking to point fingers, you'd be far better to blame society's flagrant overuse of antibiotics than any particular segment of the population."

"I don't follow you, Dr. Lopez," Mavis shouted, still flailing his arm. "What's overuse got to do with this superbug?"

Lopez paused. She realized she had successfully dodged the reporter's loaded scapegoat question but only by stepping into an equally sensitive area. Warmack reached for his mike—and Lopez knew he intended to bail her out—but she stopped him with a hand placed gently on his. She had no intention of backing down from her remark. "What I mean *is*," she said pointedly, "bacteria develop antibiotic resistance only after repeated exposure to an antibiotic." She tapped the tabletop with an index finger. "There are still lots of doctors out there treating colds and flus with powerful antibiotics that are of no use against viruses, and they do so mainly because patients demand it. And many of those same people don't even finish the courses of antibiotics they begin, making it easier for bacteria to survive and develop resistance." She shook her head angrily. "Then there are the corporations. Drug companies actively promote the use of the newest and most expensive antibiotics for infections when older, less precious treatments would easily suffice. Leaving us little in reserve for the worst infections. And the livestock industry puts antibiotics in their feed to produce better growth among the chickens and cattle." She held up her palms, too incensed to care that she might have just offended everyone from doctors to farmers. "The cumulative effect? Bacteria are repeatedly and *unnecessarily* exposed to antibiotics. It's only inevitable that they go on to develop resistance."

She inhaled a slow deep breath. "Not only can the microbes pass their resistance on from colony to colony, it can jump to different species of bacteria. So it's not a huge surprise that with global abuse of antibiotics, we've created a bacterium that has managed to collect a perfect set of antibiotic resistances." She stared hard at the still-standing reporter. "So if you're looking to blame someone, you might as well start with the people in this room."

As Lopez leaned back away from the microphone, hands shot up around the room while others called out to her. Her anger spent, she suddenly felt acutely self-conscious.

Warmack pointed to a petite woman in the front row. "Yes?"

The woman rose to her feet but didn't stand much taller than the man seated beside her. "You said earlier that all cases have come from two hospitals." She tapped a pen against her lips. "Does that mean that you can only acquire the infection *inside* a hospital?"

Warmack grabbed for his microphone. "We don't think this superbug originated inside the hospital. However, the only spread we know of so far has happened in hospital."

"So you're saying people in the community aren't at risk?" the woman demanded with the pen still glued to her lips.

Warmack shook his head, resignedly. "I'm not saying that at all."

A man from several rows back shouted out, "Aren't you worried that people who need hospital care will stop going out of fear?"

"That's a real concern," Warmack said grimly. "It's why we've made every effort to quarantine known infections from other patients. But we've seen only a handful of cases. And while it might make sense to avoid hospitals for minor ailments, the risks of not seeking attention for serious medical problems far outweighs that of becoming infected with MRGAS."

Warmack pointed to a hulking man standing in the near aisle.

"Adam Pearson, KOMO news," the man said with an easygoing smile. "Docs, isn't it possible there are people out there who have this bug without knowing it?"

Lopez's chest thumped a little harder. She was about to answer, but again Warmack spoke up. "We call such people 'carriers.' And, yes, it's possible there are carriers we haven't yet recognized."

"And these carriers could potentially spread the infection?" Pearson continued.

"Potentially," Warmack said.

"So let me get this straight, docs." Pearson's eyes narrowed, and his laidback manner disappeared. "You don't know where this bug came from. You have no treatment for it. You don't know who is infected. And you don't even know if it is containable. Have I got it right?"

Lopez glanced over to Warmack who, for a fleeting moment, looked uncertain. He reached for his water glass and took a long sip. Then he put it back down on the table, his poise regained. "This outbreak is less than two days old to us. Like every other emerging pathogen I've seen in my nearly forty years as an epidemiologist—and trust me, I've seen my share—the questions always dwarf the answers in the early days. But answers do come with time." He paused and stared directly at Pearson. "Until then, it's our job—*and yours*—to keep the public informed without panicking them."

More arms waved and people yelled out, but Warmack said, "That's all the time we have for questions today. We'll convene another news conference as soon as we have more information to share." He pushed his mike away and rose from his seat.

Lopez stood up from her chair and followed Warmack out the door behind the podium. He hurried down the hallway and into the stairwell. She didn't catch up with him until the fourth-floor landing where he stood smiling. "Little trick for you, Cat. Never hang around after a press conference. Those wolves will hunt you down like you're a wounded elk."

She nodded. "Sorry, David," she said, biting her lip.

His eyes narrowed. "For?"

She pointed down the stairs. "Losing my cool back there."

"That reporter deserved it. He was looking to make scapegoats out of AIDS patients and drug users with that ignorant, inflammatory question." Then he smiled. "Besides, that's what makes you so much fun to work with."

She looked down at her feet. "My unpredictability?"

"That. . . . your fiery temperament . . . your stubborn streak . . . but most of all, your fierce devotion to principle. It's time they heard the message about antibiotic abuse." His face broke into a paternal smile and, for a moment, she saw Papa staring back at her. "I was proud of you in there, Cat."

She felt her spirits lift. She chuckled and punched him softly on the shoulder. "But you weren't going to let me squeeze another word in edgewise, were you?"

"Not on your life." He laughed. "I didn't want to see any of those reporters carried out of there on a stretcher!"

"I wouldn't have minded seeing that last guy go out that way. But I guess everything he said was true," she sighed. "You handled it beautifully, though. Maybe there are still a few tricks I can pick up from you."

"One or two." He chuckled. "I'm not in the ground yet, you know."

Lopez's cell phone rang, and she grabbed for it. "Hello."

"Lina, it's Nelson Amar," her boss said in his usual curt tone.

"Oh, hi," she said. "You caught me just after our press conference."

"I watched it," Amar said impassively.

"In Atlanta?" She grimaced at Warmack.

"We picked it up on satellite," Amar said.

"And?" Lopez asked.

"You made your point, Lina, I'll give you that, but you can't afford to lose your cool with the press. Ever." Amar paused. "Otherwise, I thought it went fine."

"Thanks," she said distantly.

"Lina, have you managed to contact Dr. Kilburn from Vancouver?"

"Yeah. He's coming down today." Then she stopped to take a breath. "Nelson, it seams there may be a plausible connection after all between the Canadian outbreak and ours."

"Oh?" Amar said.

She told Amar about the teenage drug addict, Angie Fischer, and her connection to the first Vancouver case. "According to her mom, she came to Seattle to visit her boyfriend. It would've been within a couple of days after having her MRGAS abscess was drained. This was before we saw our first case in Tonya Jackson, a fellow user."

Lopez took a breath and braced herself for the expected I-told-you-so reproach, but instead, Amar said: "Good work, Lina. This could be crucial. Have you found the girl yet?"

"I have an address for the boyfriend from his parole officer," Lopez said. "I'll start there. Finding her is our number-one priority."

"Should be. She needs to be interrogated and quarantined." Amar's voice dropped lower. "And under the Communicable Diseases Act, we don't need her consent to do either."

"I know," she said.

"Good. I would like to interview her myself when I get to Seattle tomorrow," Amar said. "The day after at the latest."

"I can handle it here, Nelson," Lopez said, more defensively than she had intended.

"No one says you can't," Amar said. "But after I report to the secretary of health and the surgeon general in DC, I want to review the situation in person. Besides, I'm planning to visit Vancouver and San Francisco on the same trip."

"San Francisco?" Lopez said.

"You haven't heard?"

"Heard what?"

"There are two confirmed MRGAS-related deaths in the Bay Area," Amar said flatly. Lopez's heart sank. *San Francisco!* How far can the reach of one teenage junkie extend? Then a bleak thought hit her: not as far as the reach of Tonya Jackson's dark-eyed dealer.

30

Vancouver, Canada

Five minutes past noon, Kilburn walked into his empty waiting room. The moment Louise looked up and saw him, she dropped her pen. "Oh, Dr. Kilburn," she groaned. "Not Parminder!"

"Yeah," Kilburn said.

Louise rose from her desk and hobbled over to Kilburn. She swept him into another enveloping hug, which felt as unexpectedly comforting as the last one. When they broke off the embrace, he forced a smile. "We keep doing this, people will talk."

"Damn that little parasite!" Louise huffed.

Technically, bacteria weren't parasites, but he nodded in agreement.

Louise stood so close that Kilburn could smell the remnants of cigarette smoke along with the toothpaste and perfume that she used to conceal her habit. "How's that Gurdev going to manage alone with his son?" she asked. "He doesn't sound like much more than a boy himself."

"I don't know, Louise. I truly don't."

She frowned. "And you?"

"What about me?" he asked, stepping back.

"Not your best week."

"No," Kilburn agreed. "I've lost two in a row."

"C'mon, Dr. Kilburn, don't give me that," she growled. "You didn't lose anyone. They had the best. The damn shame is that no one or nothing could help them."

Kilburn nodded. He had no illusions about being 'the best,' but he doubted anyone could have done more for Tom Mallek or Parminder Singh. Who's next? he wondered again miserably.

As if reading his mind, Louise asked, "How many others are going to go the way of Thomas and Parminder? Or Annie and Gurdev, for that matter."

Kilburn shrugged. "If this bug spreads into the community . . ." He left the remark unfinished.

Louise stared at him in rare silence. From her furrowed brow, Kilburn knew she had more to tell him. "What, Louise?"

She limped over to her desk and grabbed two pieces of paper. "I considered hiding this for a while, but you're going to see it sooner or later."

He walked over and took the pages from her. He flipped past the fax cover page with CONFIDENTIAL emblazoned across it and scanned the brief letter from the hospital's medical director. Even before he read the opening "we regret to inform you" clause, he knew that his hospital privileges had been suspended.

"Thanks," he said, handing the papers back to her.

"That's it?" Louise said, looking incensed. "Why, Dr. Kilburn? Why would they do that?"

"I broke the rules," he said with a shrug. "I deserve this."

Her eyes narrowed. She shook her head vehemently. "Not buying it."

"You really want to know?"

She sat back in her chair and eyed him expectantly.

Kilburn briefed Louise on his unauthorized access to the trial drug Oraloxin. Then he said: "I can't blame them, too much. I left them in a delicate position, legally."

"Screw their legal position! And screw them," Louise croaked. "You were trying to save a woman's life. What's that count for?"

"Not much apparently, if you don't actually save her," he said softly.

Without another word, Louise's head disappeared under her desk. When she emerged, she held a bottle of scotch bourbon in one hand and two plastic cups in the other. She flashed an impish smile. "Good news, Dr. Kilburn. I'm better prepared than last time." She shook the bottle gently in her hand.

Kilburn laughed affectionately. "Tempting, but I better not," he said. "I've got a long drive ahead of me. You go ahead."

"One thing I hate to do is drink alone," she said, putting the bottle and glasses back under her desk. "No wonder I hang around bars so much."

Kilburn smiled. "Which reminds me, has Kyra called this morning?"

She shook her head.

"I have to get the kids back to her today," he said, speaking more to himself.

Louise sighed. "Frankly, Dr. Kilburn, sometimes I don't know how you put up with her and her drinking."

He shrugged self-consciously. "Maybe it's because I'm partly to blame."

She frowned. "What does it have to do with you?"

He hesitated, then said, "I never told you about Toronto, huh?"

Louise shook her head.

He hesitated. Michelle was the only person he had ever told. But looking into Louise's understanding eyes, he began talking without consciously deciding to. "I spent the summer after second year university working as a lab assistant."

His voice lowered out of reflex. "Kyra had just finished eleventh grade. She begged our parents to let her fly East to visit me there." He shrugged. "I thought it would be fun to have my little sister around. She was a good kid." He cleared his throat. "I worked with a pretty wild crowd of students in the lab. Especially this one kid, Dale McLean. Rich. Good looking. Edgy. He had his parents' swank house in Rosedale all to himself for the summer. Dale's parties were legendary. I never got invited, until—" Kilburn broke off the story and eye contact, flooded with the familiar sense of shame.

"Until Kyra showed up?" Louise prompted, leaning forward in her seat.

Kilburn nodded. "One day Kyra came to meet me at work. Dale took a shine to her. Suddenly, I—we—were invited to the best party in town. I knew what he was up to, but I was nineteen and desperate to get into the *Playboy* Mansion, as we used to call the place."

"And what happened to Kyra there?" Louise asked.

"I know she had a few drinks by the time she was seventeen. Maybe even smoked a joint or two before." His face flushed. "But that night I was preoccupied with the girls, the beer, and the pool. By the time I found Kyra in one of the upstairs bedrooms she was so drunk and stoned she couldn't even talk. She was lying in her underwear on top of the bed with Dale. He was nearly as far-gone as she was. Maybe that's why I didn't kill him."

"I doubt they were the first two teenagers to get too drunk and fool around," Louise said with a half-hearted smile. "What's the big deal?"

Face burning, Kilburn looked her in the eyes. "*The big deal* is that Kyra and I went back to Dale's place the next day, and the day after, and so on. By the end of that month, my naïve little sister had turned into a lush who dabbled in coke and was heading for an abortion thanks to Dale." He shook his head. "Kyra was never the same after visiting her big brother."

Louise's mouth fell half open. "Oh, the poor kid," she said hoarsely.

"I could argue—and I used to—that Kyra insisted on going back to Dale's place. That she would have gone with or without me." He stopped to swallow away the lump in his throat. "But that's a pile of crap. Truth is, despite what was happening to my little sister, I wanted to go back to party at the mansion. And by the time I opened my eyes to it all, I think it was too late for Kyra. When she got back home, the eleventh-grade honors student barely scraped through the twelfth grade. The partying, the boozing, the drugs—sometimes I wonder if her whole future wasn't spent that summer in Toronto."

Louise stared at Kilburn wordlessly for several moments. Then she ran a hand through her thick puff of gray hair. "You honestly believe things would've all worked out for Kyra if only she never visited you?"

"I don't know," Kilburn sighed. "But I've never been able to shake the doubt."

"Addiction is a disease." Louise sighed. "You don't end up an alcoholic by going to the wrong party."

"But just maybe you get started down the wrong path at the wrong time in your life," Kilburn said.

"I don't buy it." Louise frowned. "But whatever happened back then, I'm pretty sure you've made it up to her—and then some—since."

Too little, too late, he thought without verbalizing it. He was anxious to change the subject. "Louise, I need you to clear today's and tomorrow's schedule. Maybe the whole week."

She looked at him skeptically. "This isn't because of your hospital suspension, is it?"

"No," he said. "I have to go to Seattle."

Louise's round face broke into a Cheshire cat–like grin. "Ah, to meet up with Dr. Lopez?"

"That's right," he said slowly.

"Dr. K, this might be inappropriate of me to say—"

He cut her off with a laugh. "When has that *ever* stopped you?"

"Never," she said matter-of-factly. "I like how Dr. Lopez sounded. Real spunky. I think she's a sparkplug." She raised an eyebrow suggestively. "And she sounded awful cute too."

"You can tell that from a phone call?"

"Yup." She flashed another mischievous smile. "And I happen to know that she's single."

"Louise, you're unbelievable." He laughed again and turned to go to his inner office.

Kilburn spent the next hour clearing paperwork off his desk. As he was getting ready to leave, his phone rang. He grabbed for the receiver. "Gray, it's Kyra."

Kilburn felt a rush of warmth at the sound of his sister's voice. "You okay?"

"I'm good. Honest." And he realized, with relief, that she sounded sober. "Gray, thanks for yesterday. I really appreciate your help."

"No problem," he said. "Are you planning to take Matt and Shayna home tonight?"

"I was hoping to, if that's okay with you," she said deferentially. "I'm going to attend a meeting this afternoon before I pick them up from Corazón."

He knew she meant an AA meeting. "Sounds like a good plan."

"They always say 'one day at a time'," she said with a self-conscious laugh. "And I'm almost at a full day without touching a drop." She paused. "I made it three months last time."

"You're getting there," he said encouragingly. "Kyra, I have to head out of town for a few days."

"Everything okay?"

"I've got to go to Seattle on business," he said evasively.

"I hope you get a couple days off down," she said, "You work too hard, Gray. How are you ever going to meet Ms. Right with your crazy schedule?" She swallowed. "Of course, having an albatross like me around your neck doesn't help much."

"Don't go taking credit for that!" he said. "I'm more than capable of fucking up a relationship without your help."

They shared a laugh. "I'm sorry you two broke up," Kyra said. "I liked Michelle. She's a good person."

"Yeah," Kilburn said distantly. "Kyra, I have to go."

After leaving his office, he stopped by his house to pack an overnight bag before heading out on the highway. At the Canada–U.S. border, thirty miles south of Vancouver, he was relieved to have to wait only twenty minutes to cross—a rarity in these post–9/11 days heightened security. The beefy and balding U.S. Customs agent viewed him suspiciously at the booth. Realizing the mention of his work-related motive might lead to a prolonged interrogation and even refusal of entry, Kilburn stretched the truth and told the officer he was going to Seattle "to escape work."

Once he drove onto Interstate 5, he was reminded of the last time he had driven the same stretch of freeway, heading to the Olympic Peninsula on the last vacation he ever took with Michelle. He couldn't stave off the memories of her any longer.

On the day Michelle left, two and a half months earlier, she had termed her departure a trial separation. "A chance for both of us to get our acts together," she had said tearfully. They had spoken only a handful of times since. Neither had mentioned working toward reconciliation though Kilburn thought of it often. He missed her, especially their lazy mornings together. He loved to wake up before her and watch her sleep. Michelle never looked more beautiful than with the strands of blond hair draped across her oval face. At thirty-two she had a wrinkle-free complexion dotted with numerous freckles and flat moles, which only intensified her fragile beauty. She was so peaceful in sleep, never moving an inch. She always slept in an oversized T-shirt, facing him on her side with arms tucked close to her body. He loved to wake her up with kisses or a gentle neck massage. Sometimes they would make sleepy love. Other times they would curl up in bed together and share sections of the paper over coffee and croissants.

Resisting the temptation to pick up his cell and call her, he popped his niece's John Mayer CD in the stereo. It wasn't much of a distraction. The melancholic lyrics reminded him even more of Michelle.

Frustrated, Kilburn tried to suppress his memories of Michelle, but only bleak thoughts took their place. He envisioned the funerals of Thomas Mallek and Parminder Singh. The oppressive grief felt for the young victims must have been palpable on both occasions.

Had Angie Fischer unknowingly spread that same anguish to Seattle?

31

Struble Lake, Pennsylvania

By 6:45 A.M., the sun had risen above the low clouds on the horizon and the cool dawn had given way to morning. The man carrying Wayne Forbes's ID slipped out of his fleece jacket, enjoying the growing warmth.

The moment he shut off the engine on the stolen ten-foot boat, the lake grew remarkably still. Without another vessel in sight, it looked as if he could have stepped off the boat on a pair of ice skates and skated the half mile to shore.

Forbes carefully disassembled his fishing rod. He loaded the rod, reel, and other accessories into the triple-layered plastic garbage bag with a cinder block at the bottom. He triple-tied the knot on the bag. Lifting the bag over the side of his boat, Forbes gently lowered it into the water. Then he watched the spot where it had sunk for at least five minutes until he was convinced it had gone to the bottom.

Forbes cracked his neck from side to side and stretched. It felt good to have finished his work so early in the day. He sat down and poured himself a cup of tea from his thermos.

Relishing the warm brew, he looked back over to the spot from where he had come. In the distance, he could still make out the overturned white hull of the small boat. The area beside it, where minutes earlier the water had thrashed and churned from the man's desperate struggle, was now still.

The man's fishing jacket and gray hat were nowhere to be seen.

Forbes lifted the cup to his mouth for another sip of tea.

32

Seattle, Washington

Kilburn pulled up to a parking meter in front of Lopez's office building. Realizing he had only Canadian currency on him, he was pleasantly surprised to discover that the meter graciously accepted his foreign quarters. He ran up the stairs two at a time to the eleventh floor. Panting more heavily than expected as he reached the last step, he vowed to return to the gym. He stepped out through the fire door and into the CDC regional office that occupied the entire floor.

An eager young receptionist with her hair pulled back and dressed in a power suit (that had the likely unintentional effect of making her look even younger), led Kilburn down the corridor. The door at which they stopped opened before the receptionist had a chance to knock. On first sight, Kilburn realized Louise's prediction had proven accurate. With thick wavy black hair, huge brown eyes, upturned nose, and a flawless dark complexion, Lopez was extremely attractive. Despite black leather pumps, she still stood more than half a head shorter than him.

Lopez's dark red lips parted in a welcoming smile, and she extended a hand to him. He caught a whiff of her pleasant jasmine scent.

"Good to meet you, Graham," she said.

"Likewise." He met her handshake and reciprocated her smile. He was about to step into her office when she walked past him in the opposite direction.

She turned back to look over her shoulder at him. "Hope you don't mind, but I thought we'd go try to find Angie Fischer straight off. We can catch up in my car."

Watching her disappear into the stairwell, Kilburn realized that it didn't matter whether he minded or not. He hurried to follow her down the twelve flights of stairs to the parking lot below her building. She walked with a brisk gait that he suspected was born of habit rather than the urgency of finding Angie.

When they reached her black Audi convertible, he ran a hand over the vinyl roof above the passenger's side door. "Nice car," he said.

"My pride and joy," she said unapologetically as she slipped into the driver's seat, quickly pulled out of her space, and left the lot.

Kilburn stared out the window at the shops and buildings of Fifth Avenue. "I love this city," he said.

"Guess you like rain, huh?"

Kilburn glanced over to Lopez and laughed. "You kidding me? I'm from Vancouver. Up there, we don't tan, we rust."

She groaned at the old, old joke. "I grew up in Phoenix. Did my med school at UCLA, and fellowship in Atlanta. Rain was kind of a novelty for me until I moved here to become the EIS regional officer."

"So why did you move?"

Sweeping a hand toward stunning Puget Sound at the bottom of the hill, she said. "Who could turn down this kind of natural beauty?" Her lips broke into a smile and her features softened. "And I never said *I* didn't like the rain, just that you have to like it to love this town."

Kilburn chuckled. He had a sense that Lopez was not the type to back down from any argument, even one as trivial as regarding Seattle's rainfall. Louise was right again; Lopez wasn't lacking in spunk. "How long have you been doing this job, Lina?" he asked.

"For a year and a bit."

"Is this your first public-health crisis?"

She glanced at him with an expression that straddled amusement and gravity. "Before this, I spent most of my time combating West Nile Virus, which has never even been reported in the Pacific Northwest."

"Same for us." He nodded empathetically. "So far, in Vancouver, West Nile is the microbiological equivalent of the bogeyman."

"Exactly!" Her smile abruptly faded. "But there's nothing imaginary about MRGAS."

"No," he said quietly. "Lina, can you tell me a little more about the Seattle cases?"

"Sure." She gave him a concise chronological recap of the spread through the Seattle area. "After you and I spoke this morning, I heard from my boss in Atlanta. Cases have been reported in San Francisco. Similar pattern of spread through an infected drug user. There already have been four deaths."

Kilburn felt as if he had been punched. "MRGAS has made its way to the Bay Area?"

She nodded at the windshield.

He rubbed his eyes and temples with a hand. His stomach sank. Suddenly he felt weary. "Lina, this thing is spiraling out of control."

"Hmmm," she murmured. She glanced over at him and her expressive eyes burned with curiosity. "Graham, I'm not a clinician, but you've managed a couple of cases of MR-GAS, right?"

" 'Managed' might be a stretch."

Lopez looked back at the road. "And?"

"Both were parents of young kids. And both died miserable deaths." He looked down at his hands. "I don't think I've ever felt more useless as a clinician."

She offered him a sympathetic smile. "This is one miserable son of a bitch, huh?"

"That's putting it mildly," he sighed. "We've got to stop it in its tracks," he said, but his words rang hollow even to him.

Her eyes pierced into his. "And if we can't?"

Kilburn shook his head. "Then we're in deep, deep shit." He'd avoided the thought as much as possible, but he knew she was right to consider the possibility. "In the past twenty years, the world has learned to live with MRSA, Ebola, VRE, and HIV, to name a just few pathogens. Somehow we'll cope. We always do." He shrugged. "With six billion of us on the planet . . ."

"There are a few of us to spare, huh?" She chuckled grimly. "That's not exactly the party line the CDC likes us to toe."

"I guess not," he said, deflated.

In silence, Lopez drove onto the cobbled streets of Pioneer Square and followed them until they gave way to a seedier-looking neighborhood. As they slowed to pull up in front of a decrepit brownstone on Jackson Street, Kilburn noticed the smell of garbage that wafted into the car.

"Jake Fasken's abode," Lina said as she opened her car door.

Stepping out of the car, Kilburn spotted two police cruisers and an ambulance parked across the street. Confused, he glanced at Lopez.

"We can't afford to let Angie go anywhere else," she explained, waving to the uniformed cops and paramedics who sat in their vehicles. She held her phone up to Kilburn. "They've promised to keep out of the way unless we call for help."

The idea of bringing police backup to a patient interview struck Kilburn as surreal, but he understood the rationale behind it. If Angela Fischer was the Typhoid Mary for MR-GAS, then they couldn't afford any further flight risk. "Do you even know if she's here?" he asked.

"Let's find out." Lopez turned and marched for the door.

The rancid smell was stronger inside the building. Flyers and junk mail littered the floor while a neglected garbage can overflowed in the corner. Lopez headed straight through the foyer for the stairwell. Kilburn followed her up the stained carpeted stairs and down the second-floor hallway. A skinny gray cat missing part of its right ear wandered indifferently past them. Somewhere, a door slammed. The sound of tinny hip-hop music echoed in the hallway. The noise grew with each step.

They stopped outside the door from where the music originated. Lopez knocked. No response. She pounded on the flimsy door so hard that it shook.

A male voice shouted gruffly from the other side. "What?"

"Jake Fasken?" Lopez yelled.

The music cut off in midnote. "Who wants to know?"

"Dr. Lopez, a medical health officer."

Nothing.

"Your parole officer gave me your address," she said to the door. "He told me to tell you that you'd be real wise to cooperate with us."

The door jiggled before it opened a crack. A bloodshot eye stared back at them. "Who's the guy with you?"

"Dr. Kilburn. He works with me. Now let us in, Jake," she demanded.

Fasken hesitated a moment before pulling the door further open. Barefoot, in ripped jeans and a T-shirt that reached his navel, Jake Fasken was of average height. He had greasy blondish hair and a thin face scattered with pimples. The pupils of his pale blue eyes were dilated. He yawned and stretched, exposing more of his indrawn abdomen. "What do a pair of doctors want with me, anyway?" he asked blankly.

"Not you," Lopez said. "We're looking for Angie Fischer."

Fasken yawned again. "She's not here."

Lopez looked over his shoulder into the room. "Mind if we see for ourselves?"

Fasken folded his arms across his chest defiantly. "Matter of fact, I do."

"Okay." She reached for her phone and started to dial.

"Who are you calling?" Fasken asked.

"I promised I'd let your parole officer know if there were problems," she said without breaking the rhythm of her finger.

"Okay, okay. Shit!" he huffed. "You can come in." He stepped out of the way.

They walked into the filthy apartment, which reeked of cigarettes, beer, and stale mustiness. A mattress lay askew on the floor with blue sheets and a gray blanket wadded into a ball on top. The only sofa in the bachelor unit was covered with empty beer cans and old pizza boxes. Plates, cans, and plastic wrappers were piled on every square inch of countertop in the galley kitchen. "See?" Fasken sneered. "You want to leave now?"

"Sure," Lopez said. "Soon as I borrow your bathroom."

Fasken hesitated a moment then shook his head. "Ah, fuck!" His eyes rolled back until only the whites appeared. He ambled over to the only door in the room and banged on it. "Come out, Ange. They're not going anywhere."

The door opened. A girl with dyed blue hair, wearing a red halter top and tartan skirt, stumbled out. Her arms and legs were skinny to the point of bony. Sallow in coloring, she had hollow cheeks and thin lips; her strikingly high cheekbones, however, complemented her sculpted facial features. Her eye color was hard to determine, because her widely dilated pupils made them look entirely black.

Kilburn had seen enough drug addicts at St. Michael's to recognize the signs of crystal meth intoxication from eight feet away. He wondered if that was why she was hiding. Or maybe her brother had given her the heads-up that the authorities were searching for her. He realized he probably would have done the same for Kyra.

He glanced down to Angie's left thigh where, at the skirt's hem, he noticed a sore with a half-inch-long crusted opening surrounded by salmon-pink skin. He judged that the wound was healing despite the lack of proper attention to it. It looked so innocuous—like ones he had seen countless times at St. Mike's. But he knew the pus inside had proven lethal to Tom Mallek and Parminder Singh and possibly, indirectly, to countless others.

Unsteady on her feet, Angie twitched and writhed constantly, looking like someone with a desperate need to pee. "What do you want from me?" she asked in a weak voice as her eyes darted around the room.

Kilburn pointed to the sore on her leg. "Did you have that abscess drained at St. Michael's in Vancouver?"

"Maybe." Angie's head and arms twitched. "So what?"

"Angie," Kilburn said evenly. "We're concerned you might have contracted a rare and dangerous infection in that leg."

"It's getting better." Angie yanked up the skirt's hem, momentarily exposing her leg to the upper thigh where the pinkness ended. "Doesn't even hurt anymore."

"That's good, Angie." Kilburn nodded. "But we think your infection might have spread to other people."

"I didn't spread nothing to nobody," she snapped, practically dancing on the spot.

"Chill, Ange!" Fasken spat, more out of annoyance than reassurance. "Fuck."

"Of course, not on purpose, Angie," Kilburn soothed, patting the air in front of him with both palms. "You wouldn't have even known, but when the doctor drained your abscess we think the infection could've accidentally spread to other patients at the same hospital."

Ignoring Kilburn, she turned to Fasken. "Jakey," she pleaded, "I didn't do anything."

Lopez took three steps closer to her. "We're not accusing you. But we need to know more about your infection." She pointed at Angela's thigh. "Tell us how it happened."

Angie mussed her blue hair aggressively with a jittery hand. "I don't know. I muscled some coke. It got infected. It happens, 'kay?"

Lopez nodded. "And where did you get the coke from?"

Angie looked at Fasken and chewed on her lower lip. "I don't know. A friend."

"Which friend?" Lopez said.

"Randee or Jenny." Angie wrung her hands rapidly as she spoke. "Shit, I don't remember."

"What about the tall guy with dark eyes and frosted hair?" Lopez said. "Didn't he give you a sample?"

Angie's face twitched wildly. Her head snapped forward. She stared at her own shuffling feet. "I don't know any guy like that."

"Angie, listen to me," Lopez said, her tone stone firm. "This is vital. Tell us about the man who gave you the drugs."

"I told you already." Her twitching became a series of shoulder jerks. "Randee or Jenny. One of them gave it to me."

Fasken turned to Angie. His eyes narrowed to slits. "What's she talking about, Ange?"

"Nothing, Jakey." She kept shaking her head. "I don't know any dark-eyed guy!"

Lopez raised a finger and looked as if she were going to pursue the point, but instead she shook her head and sighed. "Okay, Angie. We need to take you to the hospital now."

"No!" Angie cried. "I told you I'm okay. I don't need the hospital."

"We need to run some tests," Lopez said. "I'm afraid you don't have a choice."

Angie ran over and hurled herself on Fasken. He let her hug him for a few seconds before pushing her away. "Ange, whatever they're talking about, you better not have given it to me!" he warned. Then he turned to Lopez and Kilburn. "You got nothing to hold me on, right?"

"No," Lopez said, sounding disappointed.

"Jakey!" Angie cried but didn't move toward him.

Without any assistance from Fasken, it took ten minutes of cajoling and reassuring to calm Angie to the point where she agreed to go with them voluntarily. Fasken walked with them only as far as the room's door. When Angie tried to hug him again, he turned and walked away. "Later, Ange," he called out over his shoulder.

After they loaded Angie into the waiting ambulance, Lopez and Kilburn walked across the street to her car. Once inside, Lopez pulled a disposable alcohol wipe out of her glove compartment and offered one to Kilburn. They cleaned their hands in silence.

After tossing the wipe in the plastic garbage container by the ashtray, Lopez looked up at Kilburn with a frown. "She's lying, Graham."

"Maybe," Kilburn said. "But she's so strung out on crystal meth, it's hard to know what's going on inside her head. She might just be paranoid."

Lopez shook her head slowly; her face was etched with determination. "Did you see how spooked she got when I mentioned the dealer? She knew exactly who I was talking about."

Before Kilburn could respond, his phone vibrated in his pocket. He dug a hand inside and pulled it out. "Graham?" the voice asked gruffly. "It's Lonny."

"Hey, Lonny," Kilburn said, surprised to hear from his favorite microbiologist, Lonny McKee. "It's already after lunch, aren't you done for the day?"

"Funny," McKee grunted, "I thought you might be interested in my news."

"What news?"

"Those pills you dropped off at the lab and made such a big fuss about us testing," McKee said.

"What about them?" Kilburn felt the anticipation rising.

"Well bottle *A* wasn't worth a damn. I might as well have pissed on the culture plates for all the use they showed." McKee paused, deliberately drawing out his disclosure. "But bottle *B* was a different story."

"How different?" Kilburn snapped, breaking into a big smile that drew Lopez's wide-eyed attention.

"Very. Those pills worked like a hot damn on three separate MRGAS culture samples," McKee said merrily. "They cleared out the colonies around them like Napalm on a dry forest."

"Get out!" Kilburn chirped. "MRGAS is sensitive to Oraloxin?"

"Extremely sensitive."

Relief swept over Kilburn like a wave. He felt as elated as if the failed brakes on a runaway car had just kicked back in.

But one thought nagged at the back of his mind: If Oraloxin works so damn well, why is Parminder Singh dead?

33

Portland, Oregon

Cohen sat hunched over a copy of the *Portland Tribune* spread open on his desk. He rarely read the paper at work but while walking through the reception area, a headline from the front page had jumped out at him.

Just as Cohen finished reading the article a second time, Leetch breezed into his office. His ruddy round face beamed. "I should get a photo of this." He pointed to the paper on Cohen's desk. "The Portland taxpayers would be tickled pink to see they're paying for you to catch up on obits and game scores."

Cohen ignored the barb and held up the paper. "Rome, did you see this?"

Leetch plopped down in the chair across from Cohen. "I didn't see nothing!" He pressed the joke. "If anybody asks, I'll swear you were out on surveillance."

"This." Cohen shook the paper and tapped the headline on the bottom of the page: FLESH-EATING BUGS BREED INSIDE SEATTLE HOSPITALS.

Leetch reached forward, pulled the paper from Cohen's hands, and read the article. He tossed the paper back onto Cohen's desk and whistled. "Great! Like we didn't have enough to worry about out there—" he pointed vaguely out the window—"without a plague that you can pick up by going to see the doctor."

"I think there's a connection, here," Cohen said slowly.

"Oh. Of course you do, Seth." Leetch tapped the headline on the desk. "You think this flesh-eating bug is what did in Carol, don't you?"

Cohen nodded.

Leetch sighed. "And you still think our hitter deliberately infected her with it?"

"You keep calling him our hitter. What if he came to Portland to spread this," he nodded to the paper, "and Jimmy and Frige just happened to get in his way?"

Leetch shrugged. "Whatever Dennis Tyler was in town for, it was his first appearance in some time."

"Oh?"

"I just tracked down a cousin of his in Fresno. According to this cousin, Tyler disappeared about four years ago during a solo sailing trip off the coast of Mexico. They never found the body. Or the boat. The cousin figures Tyler is probably dead."

"Why probably?"

"Apparently, old Dennis had a big-time gambling problem. Owed a number of people some serious coin." Leetch rubbed his thumb and index finger together rapidly. "The cousin thinks there's a chance Tyler faked his death and just sailed away from all that debt."

"Did his cousin say who Tyler owed?"

"Not by name." Leetch grinned. "But if he owed the kind of people it sounds like he did, then there's a good chance his boat sailed head-on into a gale-force Sicilian storm, if you know what I mean."

Cohen rolled his eyes.

"Anyway, after treading water off the coast of Mexico for

about four years, Tyler suddenly surfaced last month. He opened up a bank account in Philadelphia and then applied for a new Visa card." Leetch dug a hand in his back pocket, pulled out a single sheet of folded paper, and handed it to Cohen.

Cohen unfolded the page. He scanned the short list of items on the credit card statement. "Not many charges." He studied the list of locations. "What was Tyler doing in Philadelphia?"

"Not what you'd expect a sailor to do," Leetch said. "He dropped a couple grand on clothes and jewelry. I recognize a couple of these places too. High-end gangsta rapper wear. Pricey stuff, but it fits with his nouveau pimp outfits. He stayed two nights at the Intercontinental. But whatever other trouble Tyler—or whoever now has his ID—got up to, he did it in cash."

"If he paid at all," Cohen murmured. His eyes rested on the last item on the list, bearing the name of a major national airline. The purchase was dated more than three weeks earlier. "Where did Tyler fly to that cost over two grand?" he asked.

"I just got the statement," Leetch said, "and you wouldn't believe the fast-talking and charm I had to use to get it. I haven't had a chance to follow up line-by-line yet."

"Good work, Rome," Cohen said with a nod. "Okay with you if I track this one down?" He picked up a pencil and underlined the airline charge at the bottom of the statement.

"What can I say? You outrank me." Despite the longstanding joke, Cohen knew it wasn't a source of friction between them.

After Leetch left, Cohen picked up the phone and dialed the toll-free number for the airline listed on the statement. Finally, after speaking to three operators, he was transferred to a manager who had the authority to release the information he required. "We are very protective about this sort of thing, Sergeant," the man said in a nasal, officious tone. "These days, you can imagine how sensitive an issue it is."

"Absolutely," Cohen said, though he had the distinct feeling the man was lording his limited power over him. "But this could be the key evidence in a double-homicide investigation. If we have to subpoena the records, we might seek out even more privileged information like the passenger lists and so on."

"I see." There was a long deliberate pause. "Okay," the man sighed. "Let me call up that information. Can you give me a confirmable number to call you back at?"

Cohen gave him the Portland Police Department's main number as well as his direct line.

Five minutes later, his phone rang. "On the nineteenth, Mr. Tyler booked a roundtrip ticket to Vancouver, Canada," the airline manager said.

Vancouver! Alarms went off in Cohen's head. He pulled the newspaper off his desk and scanned through the article until he found the sentence: "Public-health officials in Vancouver, B.C., are wrestling with an identical outbreak."

"Sergeant?" the manager prompted. "Are you still there?"

"You said 'roundtrip'?" Cohen's voice was calm but his mind raced.

"Yes, he booked an open-ended return for the twenty-third. . . ." The man's voice trailed off as he tapped away at the keyboard. "It seems that Mr. Tyler has yet to take the return flight back. At least not with us."

Maybe the man who called himself Dennis Tyler drove down to Seattle instead of flying home, Cohen thought after he hung up. He turned back to the article and scanned it for timelines. It didn't say when the first case was reported in Vancouver—and Cohen didn't have a clue how long it would take between exposure and development of infection—but by doing the math he realized that Tyler flew to Vancouver ten days before the first case was seen in Seattle and almost two and a half weeks before Carol met Tyler in Portland. *Was Tyler the connection between all three cities?*

34

Horton sat at her desk, chewing on a fingernail and staring at her phone. Two days had passed without word from Dr. Kilburn as to how his patient with flesh-eating disease had responded to Oraloxin. Hope had begun to fade. Her self-destructive musings, which briefly disappeared, had crept back. And after two decent nights, sleep was again as elusive as ever.

A new worry had wormed its way into her thoughts concerning the emergence of the latest superbug. The more she had read in the past days about the MRGAS outbreak, the more her unease grew. Something was disturbingly familiar about this new strain of multiresistant strep. Something from her own labs.

Horton desperately wanted to talk her concerns through with a friend. She picked up her phone and called Neil Ryland's office again but was met only by his upbeat voicemail greeting. She dialed Viktor Leschuk's phone number. No answer. Horton considered calling Luc Martineau, knowing she could count on him to bolster her spirits, but she decided against this. His reassurances were at best fleeting; they seemed to evaporate as soon as she was away from his dizzying physical presence.

The ringing phone startled her into action. She grabbed for the receiver. "Ellen! It's Graham Kilburn."

"Oh, Graham." Her chest tightened with an equal mix of apprehension and anticipation. "What's happening with your patient?"

"She died, but I don't—"

"Oh, Graham, no!"

"Ellen, listen to me," Kilburn said evenly. "Oraloxin. never stood a chance with her."

"What does that mean?" she asked despondently.

"The patient was in flagrant septic shock when we started her on treatment. She died within fourteen hours of her first dose. You know antibiotics take a minimum of twenty-four hours to make a dent in any infection." He sighed. "Her body had already shut down by the time we started the Oraloxin. She didn't survive long enough for us to know whether it might have helped."

"What makes you think it would have?" Horton muttered, gnawing at a fingernail.

"The culture results."

Horton felt a flicker of excitement. "What about them?"

"We plated the Oraloxin samples against MRGAS," Kilburn said. "And Ellen, it worked!"

She rose from her chair. "It did?" she said, stunned.

"Congratulations, Ellen!" He laughed. "You have created the only antibiotic shown to work against MRGAS."

"I did?" she mumbled. "Have you tried it on other patients?"

"Not yet," he said. "We only got the word on these results last night. But Ellen, I suspect we'll need a lot more Oraloxin in a big hurry. Will that be a problem?"

"Shouldn't be," she said, feeling the excitement build. "We're expecting FDA approval any day. The plant is all set up. We've already begun to manufacture pills in large quantity." She paused. "But of course, I'll have to run it by Luc."

"Oh," Kilburn's tone chilled. "Dr. Martineau."

"What's wrong, Graham?" she asked.

"Let's not forget how Martineau refused to authorize my use of Oraloxin for my dying patient," Kilburn grumbled.

Horton dropped back down in her chair. "He *what?*"

"You didn't know?"

"No," she said, stinging from the betrayal. "But I'll definitely have a talk with him."

"Do you foresee a problem with access to more of the drug?"

"No," she said distractedly. "I don't."

"Good." On an upbeat note, he added, "And if I can speak on behalf of the entire planet: thank you."

"Let's hope that a planetary thank-you isn't a bit premature," she said. "I'll give you a call as soon as I've had a chance to discuss this with Luc and my other colleagues here."

After hanging up, she headed for the elevator, filled with a tumultuous mix of elation and anger. When she stepped into the forty-fourth-floor reception area, she stormed past Luc Martineau's receptionist, yanked open the brass handle on the large mahogany door, and marched inside.

Martineau leaned comfortably back in the leather chair with an arm folded behind his head. Looking equally relaxed, Andrea Byington sat on the other side of the large oak desk with her legs crossed. Though separated by the desk, there was something painfully intimate to Horton in their body language; like two people taking a breather between episodes of lovemaking.

"Good morning, Ellen," Byington said cheerily.

Martineau smiled broadly and stood to his feet. "Ellen, we were just talking about you."

"And I you," Horton said coolly, stopping beside his desk.

Martineau stepped forward, grabbed her shoulders with his strong hands, and then kissed her on either cheek.

Breathing in the scent of his familiar cologne, Horton began to feel her resolve buckle. "Should my ears be burning?" Martineau smiled, freeing her from his grip.

"Maybe," she said humorlessly. "I was just talking to Graham Kilburn."

"Ah, Dr. Kilburn." The smile left Martineau's lip. "He is no fan of mine."

Horton folded her arms across her chest. "Luc, why didn't you tell me you turned down his request for a compassionate release of Oraloxin?"

"I thought you understood," he said unapologetically. "It was an impossible request! I had neither the authority nor the right to jeopardize the project by entertaining such a rash long shot."

"I have to agree with Luc," Byington said calmly. "You can't cut corners like that. I'm sure in the cold light of day, Dr. Kilburn understands too."

"I wouldn't be so sure," Horton huffed. She didn't know which she resented more, Byington's patronizing tone or her obvious closeness to Martineau. Regardless, she decided that she didn't like Andrea Byington.

Martineau cocked his head. "What makes you say that, Ellen?"

"Because Graham went ahead and used Oraloxin without your permission."

Byington sat bolt upright in her seat. *"He what?"*

Martineau's blue eyes darkened to the point of opacity. He squinted at Horton and said, in just above a whisper, "He used our drug after I forbade him to?"

Taken aback, Horton dropped her arms to her side. She was unnerved by Martineau's cold ferocity, something she'd never seen before in him. "But Luc, Oraloxin *worked*," she sputtered.

Martineau did a double take. "What?"

"On the culture plates anyway." Horton told them about MRGAS's exquisite sensitivity to Oraloxin on the culture plates.

By the time she finished, Martineau's scowl had been replaced by a gaping, matinee idol smile. "Ellen, this is wonderful news! Can you imagine the implications of producing the only drug that treats MRGAS?" He threw his arms around Horton and squeezed her tightly. Despite her ambivalence toward him, the contact stirred up primal warmth inside her.

Byington rose and joined them by his desk. She laid a hand on Ellen's wrist and another on Martineau's shoulder. "Luc's right, Ellen. This is one hell of a feather in your cap!"

Conflicting emotions swirled in Horton. Validated by their praise and aroused by Martineau's proximity, she hadn't shaken off the bitterness of his deception.

Suddenly, the office doors flew open, and Neil Ryland burst in. Even before she saw his face, she knew from his slumped shoulders that something was very wrong.

"Neil! Have you heard the news?" Martineau held out a hand triumphantly to him. "MRGAS is sensitive to Oraloxin! And we have the only—" He stopped in midsentence.

Ashen, Ryland's eyes were bloodshot and his expression blank. He looked directly at Horton and spoke to her as if the others weren't even in the room. "Ellen." He stepped closer to her and took her hand in his. "El, it's Vik. . . ."

35

Lopez slept fewer than three hours, but when she woke at 5:05 A.M. she felt as energized as if she had slept twelve. After dropping Kilburn off at his hotel, she'd exchanged phone calls and e-mails into the early hours of the morning with her colleagues back in Atlanta, eager to share the news of Oraloxin's success, the first break in the MRGAS crisis.

When she stepped out of the shower, her dog waited outside the bathroom door frantically wagging her tail. "I know, Rosa, Mommy will take you out for a quick walk." Before she had Rosa, she used to shake her head at people who tried to engage their dogs in conversation, especially the ones who referred to themselves as "mommy" or "daddy". She realized she had become as nutty as those other childless dog owners.

"Maybe I'm more ready for kids than I thought," she told Rosa. She reached down and swept the dog up in her arms, enjoying the lingering shampoo scent from Rosa's recent grooming. "Ready or not, girl, without a decent man in sight, you're my only baby now."

Although, Lopez had begun to notice the many babies and toddlers around her in parks, supermarkets, offices, even in her own building, she refused to attribute her increased awareness to a ticking biological clock. Instead, she blamed the neighbors next door and their adorable eighteen-month-old daughter, Alicia. In one of an array of heart-stoppingly cute dresses or overalls, Alicia wobbled up and down the hallway daily. If she caught sight of Lina, she would go right up to her. With saucer-brown eyes and an ear-to-ear smile fixed on her elfin face, the toddler would open her arms wide. Lopez would swoop down, lift Alicia under her arms, and zoom her up and down while Alicia giggled gleefully.

As a child, Lina had loved to fly the same way in Papa's strong hands. The memory brought a pang of melancholy. She knew Papa would have loved grandchildren, and they him. He had clicked with kids of all ages.

Laying aside such thoughts, she leashed up Rosa and headed for the door. Silently promising not to converse with her dog in public, Lopez led Rosa to the elevator and out to the street. Dawn was just breaking, but the streets were already busy. Joggers, businesspeople, and fellow dog-walkers all hurried through the crisp, clear Seattle morning.

Walking the block to the small park on her street corner, Lopez slipped an earpiece in and tuned into the six A.M. newscasts on her smartphone. Coverage of MRGAS dominated the news. No matter where she turned the dial, she couldn't escape her own voice, recorded at the previous day's news conference. She felt slightly uncomfortable listening to herself speak. And when her tone rose in response to the loaded question regarding who was to blame for MRGAS, she noted the distinctly Latina inflection in her pronunciation. Nevertheless, she didn't regret one word of her answer.

The newscast was interrupted by a long steady beep. She pressed a button on the device, switching it from radio to phone. "Lina, it's Nelson. Have I caught you at a bad time?" Amar asked, even though his gruff tone suggested he didn't care how or where he had caught her.

"No, it's fine."

"What do you know about this drug?"

"Oraloxin?"

"Yes."

"It's a new class of antibiotic that specifically targets the cell wall. It was developed for MRSA," Lopez said. "But Graham Kilburn tried it without permission on a MRGAS patient." She had trouble keeping the admiration from her voice. "The patient was already too far gone to respond, but the culture results were dramatic. So far, all MRGAS samples tested in the lab are sensitive to Oraloxin."

"Hmmm," Amar grunted. "Have we tried it on other patients?"

"We're starting today," Lopez said.

"Is it safe?" he asked.

"Far as I know," she said, but she realized she hadn't asked. "Human trials have been going on for six months and FDA approval is expected, so I assume it has to be."

"Then there's no excuse for delay," Amar grunted. "Who is liaising with SeptoMed?"

"Graham went to med school with the scientist who developed it," she said. "He's talking to her this morning. SeptoMed has been running a MRSA trial in the Seattle area, so we don't anticipate any delay in getting the drug."

"Fine," he said. "I'll need to find out if the same trial is running in the Bay Area."

She suddenly remembered that her boss was in San Francisco. "What's the latest there, anyway?"

"Not good, Lina. Twenty-eight more cases were reported yesterday, sixteen of them in Oakland, where there have already been seven deaths. MRGAS has decimated the Oakland County Hospital. They've had to shut it down."

"Closed the whole hospital?" Lopez felt a sudden chill. "Hard to imagine the impact."

"That's the irony of it," Amar grunted. "There is *no* impact. Other hospitals are setting records for low volume. Everyone is avoiding them."

"We predicted this, Nelson," she sighed. "People are panicking."

"Or maybe they're being sensible."

Not true! she thought. "But hospital spread of MRGAS can be stopped with common-sense measures," she said. It's the inevitable community spread I worry about."

"And spreading it is," Amar grumbled. "I just received word of a positive culture in Portland, Oregon."

"Portland?" she said. "Damn it! This thing is chewing up the entire Pacific Northwest."

"Same old story," Amar said. "Portland's first known case was an HIV-positive junkie who died of overwhelming sepsis."

Lopez's suspicions rose; yet another infected drug addict hundreds of miles removed from the other cases. "Nelson, we found Angie Fischer," she said. "The Vancouver index case."

"And have you connected her to the Seattle outbreak?"

"We've got her in quarantine at the Harborcenter Hospital," Lopez said. "We've taken swabs and cultures from her wounds. The microbiologists should be able to tell us how closely her MRGAS strain is genetically related to the Seattle cases."

"Let's get back to basics," Amar said. "Keeping in mind the two- to four-day incubation period, has that girl been in Seattle long enough for the timing to make sense?"

"Yes," Lopez said. "But—"

"But what, Lina?"

"I think Angie might have met the same dealer who gave Tonya Jackson, the first Seattle case, her suspect drugs."

"You *think?*" Amar snapped. "Did Angie tell you she met this dealer?"

"She was wired on drugs when we talked to her. She wasn't very cooperative."

"What exactly did she say?" Amar asked.

"She denied meeting him," Lopez admitted, "but it was the *way* she denied it! You should have seen how she reacted. I know that—"

"No, Lina!" he said sharply. "Stop trying to fit a square peg into a round hole. We have a perfectly good explanation for the bug's spread. This jumping distribution from one inner city to another is classic for infections spreading among IV-drug users. You know that."

"I guess," she said.

"Okay. We're agreed, then. You make sure that Oraloxin gets rolled out ASAP," he said, his tone businesslike. "I'm going to stay in the Bay Area until things get better sorted out."

After hanging up, she glanced at her watch. She knew she had to hurry to be on time for her breakfast meeting with Kilburn. Jogging home, she considered what to wear. She felt embarrassed to realize she was weighing clothing options as if this were a date rather than a business meeting. Besides, despite Kilburn's charm and intense blue-gray eyes, she sensed an air of unavailability about him.

Lopez and Rosa headed home. Once there, she refreshed the dog's water and put out a breakfast bowl for her. Then Lopez clipped her hair back, changed into a black skirt and a pale green top, and headed down to her car. She wavered on whether to lower the vinyl top, concerned how it might affect her hair. "You're acting like a schoolgirl," she chided herself in the rearview mirror. Then she reached for the button and lowered the top all the way.

When she arrived at the hotel restaurant, Lopez spotted Kilburn sitting at a table with the newspaper open in front of him. As she neared, he put down his coffee cup and held up the paper to show Lina a photo of herself from the press conference. He broke into a warm, crooked grin. "I had no idea what a celebrity I was dealing with. No doubt we'll have to duck the paparazzi at any moment."

She gently pushed the paper down to the table. "I don't think my Chicken Little act will hold their attention too long."

"I liked what you had to say, Lina. Time the world woke up. Maybe now people will finally get the message that we can't toss around antibiotics like confetti without facing the consequences."

"I wouldn't count on that, Graham."

"You're probably right." He passed her a menu. "Hungry?"

"Famished," she said. "And I can put away a good-sized breakfast."

He grinned. "Which of course means you'll have the small bowl of the carb-free Muslix with fat-free yogurt."

"That's incredibly sexist!" She feigned indignation, but couldn't hold back the laughter. "No. My dad used to make us a mean breakfast every morning. Sausages, huevos rancheros, the works. He used to say that a hearty breakfast was the key to a hearty life." She looked down at her menu. "Then again, no doubt those big breakfasts contributed to the heart attack that did him in at fifty-six."

Kilburn nodded sympathetically. "That's far too young."

She dismissed the memory with a forced smile and studied her menu. "It hasn't slowed me down. I can just hear the three-egg, ham, and cheese omelet calling my name."

"I predict an extremely hearty life for you." Kilburn laughed after she placed the order. "I spoke to Ellen Horton this morning."

"Oh?"

"She doesn't foresee a problem in SeptoMed releasing Oraloxin to us." His brow furrowed. "Strange, though."

"What was?"

"Ellen had no idea that her boss blocked my access to the drug," he said. "She seemed taken aback when I told her."

"I'm not surprised," Lopez sighed. "Don't forget, your friend is a scientist. She wouldn't see things the same way as do the lawyers and bean counters who run those companies. To them 'compassionate release' equals lost money and potential lawsuits."

Kilburn nodded. "I suppose."

"Graham, my boss called this morning," Lopez said.

"There's trouble in San Francisco." She updated him on the rapid spread, the closed hospital, and the newly reported case in Portland.

Kilburn took a long sip of his coffee. "Lina, if Oraloxin doesn't pan out in the real world as well as it has in the lab, we could be talking about millions of . . ."

She shook her head. Eager to redirect the conversation, she asked, "When are you heading home?"

"Wow, people usually wait until the food arrives before they start trying to get rid of me."

"I'm not trying to get rid of you." Then she added with a smile: "Not yet, anyway."

"If it's alright with you, I was kind of hoping to see how things turn out in Seattle for the next few days." He shrugged. "After my little stunt in Vancouver, I'm persona non grata around my hospital."

"But you and your so-called little stunt might end up saving a lot of lives."

He looked down at his coffee cup. "That's a bit of a stretch, Lina. Even if Oraloxin does work, someone else at one of the other study centers was bound to have given it a try."

"Maybe. Maybe not." Lopez frowned. "Where are the other study centers?"

"There are separate Oraloxin trials in Chicago and Europe." He tapped his chin. "But the centers I know of on the West Coast trial include Vancouver and Victoria in, Canada, and Seattle, Portland, San Francisco, and San Jose in the States."

"That's kind of a coincidence, huh?" she said.

"What is?"

"All four MRGAS outbreaks have occurred in cities with ongoing Oraloxin trials."

He frowned. "When you put it that way . . ."

The waiter arrived with their omelets. As he turned from the table, Lopez's phone rang. "Excuse me, Graham, it could be important," she said reaching for her phone. "Hello."

"Dr. Lopez, my name is Sergeant Seth Cohen," he said in

a soft deep voice. "I'm a homicide detective with the Portland Police Department. I'm sorry to call so early."

"Portland Homicide?" she said, thinking of Amar's news about the first positive MRGAS case in Portland. "What's going on, Sergeant?"

"Hope I'm not wasting your time," Cohen said, "but I was reading about your involvement with the MRGAS—" he pronounced it correctly but tentatively—"outbreak in Seattle."

"Okay," she said. "How might that be connected to Portland Homicide?"

"Probably isn't," Cohen said. "Let me take a step back. We've been investigating a double-homicide of two local drug dealers. One of the few witnesses in the case was a female drug user who was in the same alley the night the two victims were gunned down."

Lopez's heart sped up, but she didn't interrupt.

"The witness in question met a man who we believe was involved in the murders," Cohen continued. "But shortly after we interviewed her, our witness died from a blood infection that started with an abscess at her elbow. I wonder if she might have suffered from the same MRGAS infection as seen in Seattle and Vancouver."

"It's possible," Lopez murmured.

"I was hoping you could give me a sense of the timeline," Cohen continued in his even tone. "What's the incubation period—I hope that's the word—for this infection?"

"Two to four days," she said.

"And do you happen to know if the Vancouver outbreak predated the one in Seattle?"

"Yes," she said numbly. "By at least four days."

"Okay, that's mainly what I needed to know—"

"Sergeant Cohen," she cut in. "Where do you think your witness acquired her infection?"

"This is pure conjecture," Cohen said. "But the suspect— a drug dealer, or at least someone posing as one—gave our witness heroin and cocaine three days before she died. And I think it might be related."

"Gave her?!" Lopez raised her voice.

"Yes," Cohen said. "According to our witness, he called it a 'sample'."

Lopez felt the blood draining from her face. "This man," she said hoarsely, "was he tall with very dark eyes?"

Cohen was silent for a moment. When he spoke, his voice had dropped to a near whisper. "How did you know?"

36

Philadelphia, Pennsylvania

Her bare skin wrapped tightly in the silkiness of the goose feather comforter, Horton stared up at the faux finish of the ceiling trying to figure out how she had wound up in Luc Martineau's bed again. She had agreed to meet for dinner only to let him know that their personal relationship—whatever that amounted to—was over. But after polishing off a bottle of wine while listening to his charmingly persuasive arguments, she'd found herself in the back of a limo, half-dressed and emotionally disoriented.

When her post-orgasmic euphoria faded, all the disasters of her world came flooding back. She felt ashamed of herself for allowing Martineau to seduce her the day after Viktor's corpse was found tangled in the reeds of Struble Lake. And she knew that Neil, who had taken Leschuk's death particularly hard, would have been horrified. "Sleeping with the enemy," he would have labeled it.

Oraloxin. The mere name had once brought butterflies of anticipation to her stomach. Not any more. Now she associated it with misadventure and tragedy. Even its apparent ability to fight MRGAS engendered no pride. On the contrary, it brought her unease.

She was pulled from her dark thoughts when Martineau, bearing two fresh glasses of red wine, strode into the room in only his silk boxers. Horton suspected he relished any opportunity to show off his hairless chest and lean muscular body, the product of his obsessive workout regime.

He stopped and eyed her from the edge of the bed. "What is it, Ellen?"

"Nothing." She shook her head. "Just thinking about Vik."

"Ah." Martineau closed his eyes and shook his head. "*C'est vraiment tragique.*"

"Luc, did you know that Vik was an experienced fisherman?"

"Even experienced fishermen have accidents, Ellen. Especially when they go out on the water alone before dawn."

She took no solace in his remark. "Of the three of us in the lab, Vik took the bone marrow complications the hardest."

Martineau put the glasses of wine on the bedside nightstand and sat down on the side of the bed. He stared at her. "What are you suggesting, Ellen? From what I've heard, there was no evidence of foul play."

"I'm just thinking aloud," she said, troubled by her own line of reason. "I'm sure Vik had life insurance. And if he wanted to provide for Oksana and his two kids at college . . ."

Martineau brought a finger to his lip and gazed up at the ceiling. "You think he might have *deliberately* drowned himself?"

"I don't know what to think anymore, Luc." Horton had not cried since hearing of Leschuk's death, so she was surprised by the sudden torrent of tears that streamed down her cheeks.

Martineau dabbed at the tears with a thumb and forefinger. "Everything will be okay, Ellen. You'll see."

She buried her face into his chest. "I can't imagine how," she sobbed.

He stroked her hair with his hand. "Well, to begin with I don't think we have to worry about the FDA any more."

She pulled back and looked up at him. "What do you mean, Luc?"

"If Oraloxin is the only treatment option for MRGAS." He shrugged. "Then I don't think it matters how many monkeys die. They will have no choice but to approve the drug."

She sniffed and wiped her eyes roughly. "No doubt Viktor would have taken great comfort in that," she said bitterly.

Martineau cocked an eyebrow in confusion. "But isn't that what we've been struggling for all this time, Ellen?" He shook his head. "I'm sorry about Viktor. I truly am. But life marches on. And we have—" He smiled. "*You* have done something great. Once we have the FDA approval, the world will see it too." He stroked her cheek gently.

Horton picked up on the sexual innuendo in his touch, but she moved away from his hand. "Is that what this is about?" she asked quietly.

"What do you mean by 'this'?" Martineau asked with a soft laugh, as he reached out and fluttered a hand over the skin of her abdomen.

"This!" Horton snapped, pointing a finger from him to her. "You lowering yourself to sleep with the likes of me."

"Ellen," he said, his tone even but his expression wary. "What does this have to do with anything?"

She looked away, suddenly self-conscious of her nakedness. "Was it part of the strategy for stopping me from going to the FDA about the dead chimps?"

His eyes narrowed. "What 'strategy'?"

"I don't know." She looked away from him. "The one you and Andrea Byington dreamed up."

"You can't be serious," he said with cold indignation. "You honestly think Andrea and I planned what happened between you and me?"

"I don't know what I think," she said in a whisper.

"I'll tell you this, Ellen. I never had a strategy for keeping you away from the FDA." He paused. "Look at me, please, Ellen."

Seeing the hurt burning in his eyes, she felt guilty for having leveled the accusation.

"And I'll let tell you something else, *ma chérie*," Martineau said in the same quietly incensed tone. He gestured around his bedroom. "What goes on here has nothing to do with work. In fact, until you came along, my practice was to never mix work and romance. After all, Ellen, I'm your boss. I could lose my job for *this*, as you call it. But your genius, your dedication, your passion—they were like aphrodisiacs for me. And maybe you aren't aware of it, but long before you came into my bed, I recognized your sexuality."

Horton felt herself reddening.

Martineau sighed. "And yes, I admit it. I wanted—I want—to see us succeed. Not only for the world's benefit, but for yours and mine too." He stopped and stared at her for several moments. "But don't flatter yourself, Ellen. I wouldn't whore myself for the job, regardless of how important you think your cooperation is."

He stood up and walked for the door.

Horton jumped up from the bed and followed after him. Catching him at the door, she wrapped her arms around him and hugged him from behind. "I'm sorry, Luc. I had no right to say any of that. I'm so confused right now. Viktor . . . those chimps . . . the FDA . . . I've never felt so lost before."

Martineau turned slowly. He nodded but his distant expression suggested he had not forgiven her. She leaned forward and pressed her bare breasts against his chest. She kissed him on the lips. When his growing hardness pressed against her pelvis, she felt the heat rising between her own legs.

He pulled her back to the bed. His slow, gently teasing approach of previous encounters was gone. Now his aggressive animalism only heightened her arousal. She wanted him to find relief from the hurt of her earlier accusations.

Some time later, spent, they lay on their backs, side by side. For a while both stared at the ceiling lost in their own thoughts. Finally Horton spoke up. "Luc, there's something else I haven't told you about Oraloxin."

He turned to her. "Oh? What's that?"

Horton didn't know how to broach the subject. She suddenly regretted raising it at all.

Martineau sat up in the bed and looked down at her suspiciously. "What is it, Ellen?"

Horton pulled the comforter tighter around her neck. "This new superbug, MRGAS. It reminds me of another bacterium."

His eyes narrowed. "Which one?"

"Well, it's not really . . . ," she began awkwardly, "it's nothing seen in nature."

His face reddened. "Ellen, what are you talking about?"

"In the lab, we engineered a bacterium to test against Oraloxin," she said. "We wanted to see how it performed on staph aureus that was more than just methicillin-resistant. In other words, something worse than MRSA."

His shoulders stiffened. "And?"

"We came up with a form of staph aureus resistant to every known antibiotic."

Martineau's eyes narrowed. "But what you engineered was a form of staph aureus, not group-A strep, correct?"

"Yes." She nodded. "But it would be so easy to pass that same resistance from the staph to strep species."

"*Merde*, Ellen!" he said through gritted teeth. "Are you suggesting that someone at SeptoMed created MRGAS?" His voice dropped to a menacing whisper. "Is that what you're accusing us of?"

"No, no, no!" She waved her hands frantically, suddenly afraid of the enraged face and icy eyes hovering over her. "Not on purpose," she said contritely. "Anyway, it's probably just a big coincidence, Luc, nothing more. But—"

"But what?" he snapped.

She shook her head and tried to swallow but her mouth was too dry.

"Say it, Ellen," he hissed.

She held up her hands helplessly. "Maybe somehow our engineered staph areus escaped our lab and transferred its resistance genes to a group-A strep species it came in contact with in the community. That's all."

Martineau shook his head ferociously and sneered at her. "What the hell is wrong with you? You think ours is the only lab experimenting with bacterial resistance?" He shook a finger at her. "You can't accept this as a simple chance happening. No. You have to see a conspiracy everywhere, don't you?"

"Luc, listen—" she started.

"No." He leapt off the bed. "I'm through listening to this." He snatched his wine glass off the nightstand and strode out of the room, muttering angrily to himself in French that she didn't understand.

37

Seattle, Washington

Haley Vallance blinked several times wishing the nightmare away. But every time the ten-year-old opened her eyes, she saw the same tubes and wires running from her body and hanging around her like a giant spider's web.

Then, piece by piece through the fog, she remembered. The sore throat and cough had come while she sat in Ms. Jergen's music class. By the time her mom picked her up at recess and brought her home, she was having trouble breathing. She felt awful that her dad—who had only been home two days from his appendix operation and was still hoarse from his cold—had to drive her back to the same hospital.

As soon as they had reached the emergency room, the doctors and nurses rushed Haley into a special room with bright lights and huge poles. Despite reassuring words, everyone around her looked so worried. There were too many awful needle pokes to count. They took an x-ray of her chest. Everyone, even her parents, put on masks like she had seen in hospital movies. They all kept saying how it was "going to be fine," but her mom kept crying.

Then everything went so fuzzy. All Haley remembered was hearing her doctors telling her parents that she had a case of something that sounded like mermaid. That made no sense to her, but nothing was clear. The next moment she opened her eyes in a new room. It smelled funny, like her doctor's office. And she suddenly realized there was something filling her mouth. It was like a snorkel except she felt it running back behind her tongue. And every time the television-sized machine beside her head whirred, air rushed into her as if the machine was breathing for her. She wondered if that was why she felt so breathless and dizzy.

She lifted her head off the bed and frantically searched the room for Mom and Dad. She heard their voices before she saw them. "Haley, sweetie," her mom cooed. "Mommy's right here. Everything is okay."

Her dad said, "We're here, Haley-Bear. You just keep hanging in there."

Her eyes swam as she turned her head and saw them hovering over the side of the bed. Except now they both wore green pajamalike tops and bottoms with white masks and blue caps. "Mommy, Daddy, why are you dressed like doctors?" she tried to say, but the tube in her throat choked off the words.

Haley felt so winded. And tired. She had trouble focusing on her mom's swirling face, but she could hear the sounds of her sobs. "Stop crying, Mom. It will be okay," she wanted to say to her but nothing escaped past the snorkel.

It was the strangest nightmare Haley had ever had. She so badly wanted to wake up, but she couldn't keep her eyes open any longer.

38

Portland, Oregon

Cohen stood at his kitchen counter, steaming a mug of milk for the lattés. Leetch sat on a barstool on the other side, shaking his head as he watched. "You sure you don't have any instant coffee?" Leetch asked. "What would people say if they knew I was drinking these frou-frou drinks?"

Cohen smiled. "Maybe that you were slightly less of a redneck than they originally thought."

Leetch put a hand to his chest. "Hey Kosher Cop, don't go belittling my ethnicity!"

Cohen poured the milk over the shots of espresso. To further annoy his partner, he used drops of extra coffee to inscribe the initials 'RL' into the steamed milk on top.

Leetch took the cup from Cohen's hand. "What, no umbrella?" he asked in mock outrage. But he wasted no time in taking a big gulp from the cup.

"When do I get to see Sophie again?" Cohen asked.

"Yeah, Soph was asking me about Uncle Seth just this morning," Leetch said. "How about Friday for dinner? It's

Sophie's fifth birthday on Saturday and we're having a little family get-together." He chuckled. "Plus now that Gina's given up on trying to set you up, she'd kill for another chance to shamelessly flirt with you."

"Five, huh? I can't believe how quick Sophie is growing up." Cohen shook his head. "I would love to come, but I don't think I'll be in town on Friday."

Leetch squinted at him. "You got vacation time I didn't know about?"

Cohen shook his head again. "I heard from the hospital earlier, Rome. Carol's blood was growing that MRGAS bug. She's Portland's first confirmed case."

"Oh, crap," Leetch muttered, slowly putting down his cup. "Are there others?"

"The doctors here seem to think so." Cohen sipped his coffee. "I spoke to a Dr. Lopez from Seattle earlier this morning."

"And?"

Cohen stared at him. "There was a case in Seattle almost identical to Carol's."

Leetch frowned and deep lines cut into the normally smooth skin at the corner of his eyes and mouth. "You mean, another drug addict who got this bug from a mysterious dealer?"

Cohen nodded. "Right down to the sample he gave her."

"Son of a bitch," Leetch grumbled. "I got to admit, KC, you might be right for a change. I'm beginning to think Dennis Tyler didn't come to town to clean up our garbage after all. Maybe he *was* here to spread that shit."

"That's why I can't make dinner. And neither can you. I think we need to go to Seattle and meet Dr. Lopez and her people. And after that, to Philadelphia."

Leetch put his cup down. "Since when did we become worldwide bounty hunters?"

"We have the best lead—the *only* lead—on Tyler, so far." Ever since his conversation with Lopez, Cohen had mulled over the next steps to take and decided they had to follow the trail themselves. "We have nothing concrete to connect Tyler to MRGAS. And except for one unreliable transvestite, our potential witnesses are all dead. According to Dr. Lopez, her higher-ups at the CDC don't buy the fake drug dealer theory. And you can imagine what will happen if we go to the FBI now with what little we have."

"Oh, yeah." Leetch blew out his lips contemptuously. "Special Agent The-Sun-Shines-Out-Of-My-Ass will thank us politely and then file it *below* the UFO sightings for the week on his to-do list."

Cohen finished the last of his coffee. "So are you coming to Seattle?"

"With Gina's parents in town and Sophie's birthday, this is a crazy week. I promised Gina I would help out with Sophie's party," Leetch said, almost sheepishly. "Okay with you if I stay here and do the legwork from this end? I can meet up with you later in Seattle or Philadelphia—or for that matter, Outer Mongolia—once we've got a better line on Tyler."

Cohen nodded. "I think that would work. Rome, this guy hasn't used Tyler's credit card in over three weeks."

Leetch shrugged. "But he used the name at that fleabag motel here within the last week."

"But he might have moved on to a whole new identity by now."

"Not much we can do about that."

"Yeah," Cohen said distractedly. He knew picking up the trail a second time could prove very difficult with someone as slick as Tyler.

Leetch passed his empty cup across the counter. "You got any more of that girly drink?"

Cohen grabbed the cup and turned the espresso machine back on. "Rome, while I'm gone, do you mind checking in on Dad for me?"

"*Do I mind?*" Leetch bellowed. "I love dropping in on your pappy! We can bond over what a big disappointment you turned out to be." He listed the points on his fingers. "A cop . . . no grandkids . . . divorced . . ."

Cohen rolled his eyes. "That was twelve years ago. I was barely twenty-five."

"I know." Leetch nodded happily. "And the shrew walked out on you. Good riddance from the sound of it too. But Pappy and I don't quibble." He laughed, clearly enjoying himself. "The point is, between discussing your shortcomings and how bad the Trailblazers suck these days, Pappy and I can talk for hours."

"Thanks," Cohen sighed. He poured Leetch another latté. This time he used the extra coffee to drizzle the letters "SOB" into the steamed milk. "I think I'm going to take advantage of the late-morning break in traffic and head up to Seattle soon."

"Makes sense." Then looking down at the letters on top of his coffee, he grinned and said: "Now that's totally uncalled for." His smile waned. "Seth, if we're right about what Tyler is up to—"

Cohen nodded. "Then there are others behind him."

Leetch's face scrunched into a grimace. "Listen, KC, you be careful up there."

39

Wayne Forbes—on the verge of permanently dumping that
particular identity—was on his way to a long-anticipated
month on the quiet island of Antigua. With an hour to kill, he
checked his temporary e-mail address while waiting to
board his flight and found a message requesting contact. He
thought long and hard before responding to the query.

Forbes found a pay phone and dialed the number. The
phone rang once before he heard the now familiar voice on
the other end of the line. "Yes?"

"Wayne Forbes, returning your page," he said impassively.

He listened for two minutes without interjecting a word as
the person outlined the latest request. Instead of refusing
outright, as he had planned to, Forbes found himself saying:
"I will let you know in thirty minutes."

Forbes hung up the phone, but his curiosity was piqued.
The offer was the best one yet. The money would allow him
to accelerate retirement plans; not that he felt any urgency to
retire at age forty-two, but he liked having the option. Cash

payment aside, the job would demand his utmost creativity. Even artistry. The challenge tempted him more than the money.

Still, Forbes recognized the inherent danger of associating for too long with one client. Such long-term relationships always heightened the risk of exposure. Or betrayal.

Weighing these factors over a cup of tea at the downtown Internet café, in the end he found the offer too appealing. With some misgivings, Forbes sat down at a terminal and e-mailed back his acceptance.

As soon as he hit the SEND button, his thoughts turned to logistics. He planned to return to Philadelphia on the first available flight. But he realized that another "accident" wouldn't work. And time constraints were far tighter. Rather than having the luxury of waiting for opportunity to arise, he would have to create his own opportunity.

I will do this, he thought. *Focus.*

Then he took another sip of his barely drinkable tea.

40

Seattle, Washington

Kilburn was thankful for the change of scenery Seattle brought. The suspension of his hospital privileges had yet to sink in, and he didn't miss his on-call pager. Even the break from Kyra was welcome. And from her phone silence, he inferred that she'd stayed sober.

He stuck a hand out into the warm wind blowing by the convertible's windshield. He looked over at Lina Lopez who was staring at the road ahead with chic sunglasses resting on her nose. He grinned at her attractive profile.

Lopez glanced over at him. "What's so funny, Graham?" she asked.

"Nothing," he said. "I'm feeling a bit more upbeat. That's all."

"Doctor, are you holding out on some good news?" she demanded with a playful frown.

He laughed. "Hardly. It's just that I think there's a good chance Oraloxin will help stem the spread of this little monster."

"I wish I were as convinced as you are," she sighed.

"Lina, I'm not at all convinced, either. But if you have a better strategy than groundless wishful thinking, I'd love to hear it."

Pulling up to a red light, she turned to him with a smile. "That's better than anything I've come up with. That is, unless you're partial to my plan to join a survivalist colony in Idaho." The light went green, and as Lopez turned back to look at the road, her smile faded. "Graham, there won't be any delay in getting Oraloxin to those who need it, right?"

"No," Kilburn said. "SeptoMed has un-blinded the study drugs. They should have already given the first doses this morning at Harborcenter."

"And we'll know within forty-eight hours if Oraloxin is going to work?"

"We might have an idea within twenty-four," he said. "How many cases are in quarantine at the hospital?"

"As of last night, there were eight critically ill patients with invasive MRGAS," she said. "Three with necrotizing fasciitis, three with pneumonia, and two with sepsis. Fifteen others have milder forms of MRGAS—strep throat or skin infections similar to Angie Fischer's. Twelve people have no symptoms at all, but their swabs grew positive cultures on routine hospital screening."

"Sure, the carriers." Kilburn exhaled heavily. "I'll be curious to see how all three groups respond to treatment."

"*Curious.* And you accused *me* of understatement!"

Kilburn's attention was suddenly drawn by the noise outside the car.

"Oh, shit!" Lopez said as she turned the corner.

The entire block was lined with news trucks and vans. The street was so congested that she had to circle twice before finding a space. As soon as she put the safety brake on, she hit the power button to raise the vinyl roof. But it was too late. The reporters recognized her. Cameras and microphones swarmed them as soon as they stepped out of the car.

"How much worse is it today, Dr. Lomas?" a chunky woman called out, muddling Lina's surname.

A man pushed a mike in front of Lopez. "Has there been further spread?"

"Is San Francisco hit harder than us?" another female voice yelled.

Lopez lowered her head and pushed her way through the throng of reporters. Kilburn had trouble keeping up with her because the gaps closed as soon as she squeezed through. But he followed her lead and shouldered his way through the scrum.

At the doors to the Washington Health Department building, which housed Warmack's office, two burly security guards waved the media types back from the door. Lopez flashed her ID badge. After scrutinizing it carefully, the guards allowed them to pass.

"This is fun," Lopez grumbled as she trooped toward the elevator.

"Lina, I can't see it getting anything but worse in the short term. This story is huge."

On the seventh floor, Kilburn followed Lopez down the hallway to the office in the far corner. The door was open a crack. She knocked but didn't wait for an answer before pushing it further open and walking inside.

The handsome older man behind the desk pulled the reading glasses off his nose and stepped around the desk to greet them. He pecked Lopez on the cheek. "Hello, Cat."

Kilburn raised an eyebrow at the nickname but said nothing when he caught Lopez's cautionary glance.

Warmack turned to Kilburn with a smile that didn't diminish the concern in his gray eyes. "Graham, I'm David Warmack. Good to meet you." He shot out his hand and pumped Kilburn's firmly. Then he pointed to the chairs. "Please." They sat down across from him. "Shall I start?" he asked, laying his hands palm-down on the desk.

Lopez nodded.

"A tough night for the city," Warmack said. "Four patients in quarantine have died. And in the last twenty-four hours, we've had twenty-two more cases admitted to the MRGAS unit."

The last remnant of Kilburn's upbeat mood slipped away. "Sounds like MRGAS is nearing critical mass in Seattle and San Francisco. No doubt in Vancouver, too," he said, "and once it does . . ." He didn't need to finish. It was basic epidemiology. Once a sufficient pool of cases was established, the infection would spread at an exponential rate.

"Twenty-two more." Lopez whistled. "How sick are they?"

"Four are already on life support," Warmack said. He rubbed his eyes with one hand. "One case is particularly alarming, not to mention sad."

Kilburn sat forward in his chair. "Why?"

"She's only ten years old. Even more distressing, she hadn't gone near a hospital before she became ill."

Kilburn imagined his niece Shayna struggling for life on a ventilator; the image turned his stomach. "Who or what was the girl's contact?" he asked, wondering for a fleeting, paranoid moment if a ten-year-old might be dabbling in street drugs.

"Her father underwent an appendectomy five days ago," Warmack said.

Lopez frowned. "But his daughter never saw him in hospital?" she asked skeptically.

"That's the irony," Warmack sighed. "The parents didn't want their daughter to be exposed to potential germs at the hospital. They never counted on the fact her father might bring home more than just stitches."

Lopez ran both hands through her thick hair. "So now we officially have community spread," she groaned.

"Yes," Warmack said. They lapsed into a gloomy silence. After a moment Warmack spoke up. "At least now we're going to find out if Oraloxin works outside the lab. All quarantined cases have received their first dose."

"Including the little girl?" Kilburn asked.

Warmack nodded. "The pediatricians had to guess at what dose to give her. Oraloxin has never been tested in children. But they don't expect her to survive without—"

"A miracle," Kilburn said.

"Damn it!" Lopez muttered.

Warmack forced a smile. "And what good cheer have you brought me?"

Lopez glanced at Kilburn before turning back to Warmack. "David, we're fairly certain someone spread this bug on purpose."

Warmack's mouth fell open slightly. "Because?" he asked quietly.

Lopez began to explain when Warmack's phone rang. He listened a moment and then said, "Okay. Send him down."

"Who is it?" Lopez asked.

"There's a Sergeant Cohen with the Portland Police. He says he's here to see you."

Lopez nodded. "If nothing else, his timing is impeccable."

Warmack rose from his chair, but Lopez waved him back down. She stood up and opened the door. Seth Cohen stood on the other side. As tall as Kilburn but with a sinewy runner's build, Cohen had short black hair and an olive complexion that complimented his chiseled facial features and brown eyes. He smiled shyly as he stepped into the room.

Warmack came around the desk to shake hands and introduce him to the others. "I'm sorry to interrupt your meeting," Cohen said.

"It's Lina, please," she said with a smile. "I'm glad you did. We were just about to discuss your involvement with MRGAS." She held out her small hand to him. "Seth, maybe you could tell David and Graham what you told me earlier?"

Cohen nodded and pulled an extra chair up to the desk. "My partner and I are investigating a double-murder in Portland." He recapped his connection to Carol, Portland's first MRGAS victim, and the murder suspect who posed as a drug dealer. "The man was still using Dennis Tyler's name as recently as last week in Portland, but it's possible—probable, even—that he's assumed a new identity by now."

Lopez tapped the table in front of her. "You see, David! This Dennis Tyler guy is the link for all the outbreaks. He was Tonya Jackson's 'dark-eyed dealer,' I am sure of it."

Face creased and eyes troubled, Warmack viewed her for several seconds. Then he turned to Kilburn. "A bug like MR-GAS could survive in powdered-form cocaine or heroin?"

"Wouldn't require much moisture at all." Kilburn nodded. "A form like rock or crystal cocaine would be especially suitable. We've seen it before with MRSA."

"All right," Warmack said, turning to Cohen. "Supposing his drugs were contaminated. Is it possible this drug dealer didn't know?"

Cohen shook his head. "We don't think Tyler is a dealer at all. The murder scene suggests he's a proficient killer." He looked down at his hands. "What's more, it looks as if he never sold any drugs, but only gave away free samples. Best we can tell, he targeted the users who looked sickest."

Lopez nodded vigorously. "Which makes perfect sense if you're trying to deliberately disseminate an infection. Establish a foothold in immune-compromised patients and let them spread it to the hospitals and other users."

"Pardon my ignorance, doctors." Cohen cocked an eyebrow. "But this MRGAS has never been seen *anywhere* in the world before, right?"

"True," Lopez said.

Cohen frowned. "So where would Dennis Tyler get it from?"

"My guess is someone made it for him," Kilburn said flatly.

"Made it?" Cohen said.

"It wouldn't be that hard," Kilburn said. "Bacteria store resistance in their genes or DNA. There are three common mechanisms for transferring resistance between cells." He lapsed into the lecture he had given many times before to med students but tried to keep his tone conversational, rather than didactic. "Transformation: where bacteria soak up free-floating DNA in the vicinity. Conjugation: essentially a form of sex between cells where strands of DNA called plasmids are transferred. And transduction: in which a virus acts as the 'middleman' passing DNA back and forth between cells. All those mechanisms can be reproduced in a lab. You would have to collect bacteria resistant to each antibiotic, slice up the DNA, and transfer the resistance genes into a waiting group-A strep colony." He snapped his fingers. "Presto—you have MRGAS."

Cohen shook his head in disbelief. "It's that easy?"

"Not quite," Kilburn said. "But certainly doable for a microbiologist with the right equipment."

Warmack leaned forward until his elbows touched the desk. "Now you have the how and maybe part of the who. But the one question you haven't answered is *why*. Why would anyone go to the trouble of creating a brand-new superbug?"

41

Haley Vallance awoke in the same strange room as before. The tubes and wires still criss-crossed the bed. The machine still whirred by her head. And the same tube was stuck down the back of her throat. She gagged again, which sent her into a spasm of coughs. Her body shook with each cough, but no sound emerged from her lips.

Panicking, she lifted her head off the bed and looked around for Mom or Dad.

Still wearing the funny green pajamas and masks, her parents stood in the same spot by the bed. Mom held her hand; Dad squeezed her arm. The sight of them calmed her. The coughing fit passed. Nothing had changed.

Then Haley realized something was different. Staring up at Mom, she noticed her eyes were dry. Mom was smiling through her mask. She turned to Dad. He was smiling too.

Am I in heaven? she wondered. She tried to ask, but the tube blocked her words.

"Oh, Haley . . ." her mom began to say, but she dissolved into sobs.

"Haley-Bear, the doctors say you're getting better." Dad squeezed her arm gently. "They say you're going to be okay." His voice cracked in a way she had never heard from him before.

As soon as he said it, Haley realized she didn't feel so winded any more. Every time she tried to breathe, the big machine still forced air into her chest, but the choking sensation was gone. And she didn't feel dizzy either. She squeezed her mom's hand. She tried to smile at her dad but the tube felt strange between her lips.

Dad was the first to laugh. And then Mom, still crying, joined in. Soon Haley was laughing around the snorkel too. That sent her into another coughing spasm. But she didn't care.

She knew she was going home.

42

Philadelphia, Pennsylvania

Still in a fog, Horton walked into her office just after seven
A.M. She hadn't slept after her early-morning altercation
with Martineau. In her urgency to flee his penthouse suite,
she'd spilled the contents of her purse on his living room
floor. He never even glanced her way when she knelt down a
few feet from him to collect the items. Heading home in a
cab, she tried to resist the combined assault of nerves and alcohol on her stomach. But it was no use. Mortified, she
asked the driver to pull over to the curb where she threw up
repeatedly. Once inside her house, she downed three sleeping pills with another glass of wine. They didn't help her
sleep; they didn't even quell the tremor in her hands.

Now she sat at her desk, holding her throbbing head in her
tremulous hands and wondering why she had even bothered
to come in to work. What could she hope to accomplish?
Thanks to her rift with Luc, she might even have to clear out
her desk by day's end.

The phone rang, making her jump. Vaguely intrigued by the call display that read SPAIN, she reached for the receiver.

"Ah, Dr. Horton. I am honored," the man said in a rich Spanish accent. "I am Dr. Emanuel Zapatero telephoning from the Hospital General de la Valle d'Hebron. I am the—"

"Of course, Dr. Zapatero," Horton cut in. "You're the principal investigator with the Spanish Oraloxin MRSA trial."

"Exactly so!" he said, sounding pleased.

"How can I help you, Dr. Zapatero?"

"Dr. Horton, let me congratulate you on this marvelous drug," Zapatero said, his musical accent echoing slightly on the line. "While our data has not been collated, it is clear to me already that Oraloxin will prove as good or better than the intravenous medications."

Weeks ago, his praise would have lifted her spirits. Now it served only to heighten her guard. She doubted Zapatero would call to congratulate her before their data had even been compiled. "There's something else, isn't there, Dr. Zapatero?"

He cleared his throat. "A matter of a question, really," he said, sounding suddenly less certain of his English. "I am hoping you have seen enough to know if it is even of significance."

"If *what* is of significance?" she asked.

"A patient from the Oraloxin group. A middle-aged man with MRSA infection of the leg. You understand," Zapatero said. "His infection was treated beautifully. But yesterday, on the fourth day of treatment, his white blood cell count . . ."

Horton's stomach tightened. "What happened to the white count?"

"It fell." His voice lowered to a hush. "Significantly."

Her throat began to squeeze shut. "How significantly?" she choked out.

"It went from 11,200 down to 1,100 in two days." He hurried to add: "The patient has no symptoms. But we have not seen this before in the treatment groups. I do not know whether we should continue with—"

"Stop the damn drug!" Horton barked into the receiver. "For God's sake, don't let him have another dose!"

"Please, Dr. Horton." Zapatero said defensively. "I am merely turning to you for advice."

"I'm sorry, Dr. Zapatero," Horton said, unable to keep the quaver from her voice. "We've seen this in a few lab animals. Oraloxin can occasionally cause bone marrow suppression, even—" She stopped herself before saying bone marrow failure.

"Is this *suppression* reversible?" Zapatero asked, his earlier Mediterranean warmth replaced by suspicion.

"I think so," she said uncertainly. "But it is vital to avoid further exposure to the drug."

"I see," he said coolly. "Is this reason to stop the study?"

"Yours is the first human case I have heard of." Horton was going to caution against overreacting, when she realized that she no longer cared whether he stopped the trial. "But I would leave the decision to you, Dr. Zapatero."

"I see," Zapatero said curtly. "I will bring this forward to our research committee for further consideration. I will apprise you of the committee's decision."

Hanging up, a cold emptiness filled her. She had a vivid and comforting image of drifting off in the front seat of her car, the motor running and Grieg playing in the background. She dropped her head into her arms on the desk.

"El?"

She lifted her head up to see Neil Ryland standing across from her. Her friend's deep green eyes peered down at her with worry. "El, what's going on?"

Horton shrugged. "Just daydreaming about warming up my car for an hour or two extra in my garage."

"That's not even funny, Ellen!" Then his expression softened. "You're kidding, right?"

She waved her hand in apology, dismissing the idea. "Of

course. I'm sorry, Neil. Awful joke." She smiled weakly. "I was just thinking about Viktor."

"I know." Ryland broke into a downcast grin. "We were like the three misfit musketeers." His smile withered. "I miss the guy more than I ever would have guessed."

She sat up straighter in her chair. "Neil, what I meant was that Viktor was right all along."

Ryland cocked his head skeptically. "About?"

"The risks of Oraloxin." Then she told him about the patient in the Spanish study.

Ryland's eyes widened and the color drained from his cheeks. He fell into the seat across from her. "Oh, crap," he murmured.

"Another day, another disaster," she said.

A troubled frown glued to his lips, Ryland stared at her desk.

"Neil, I think it's over."

He kept his eyes fixed on the desk. "What about MR-GAS?" he asked in a monotone.

She shook her head and shrugged.

"According to the paper, it's raging out of control in San Francisco, Seattle, and Vancouver," Ryland said. "Far as I've heard, Oraloxin is still the only hope for a cure."

"We don't even know if the drug works in real patients," she snorted. "Maybe it's only useful in petri dishes."

Grimly, Ryland looked up at her. "Its effectiveness is the only thing that matters from here on."

She shook her head, confused. "How so, Neil?"

"Don't you get it, El?" He sighed. "Viktor would have loved the irony of this. We were so worried about how quickly they would shut us down if they learned about the chimps. But if Oraloxin works against MRGAS, we could show the world a mountain of dead monkeys and they wouldn't let us stop the Oraloxin project."

"I never thought of it like that," she said slowly. "Oraloxin's future depends solely on how well it works against MRGAS." As the words came out of her mouth, she was struck by a sinister thought that set her heart pounding.

No! It couldn't be!

Ryland leaned forward and grabbed her gently by the wrist. "El?"

She hesitated, afraid to even put her wild hypothesis into words, and swallowed. "I've been thinking about the various bacteria we tested Oraloxin on, Neil. You know that multiresistant staph aureus we engineered for sensitivity testing with Oraloxin?"

He let go of her wrist. "What about it?"

"MRGAS came around pretty soon after we developed it."

"Coincidences like that happen all the time in microbiology, El. Remember how vancomycin-resistant enterococcus emerged almost simultaneously in Japan and Europe?"

"I know. But what if the multiresistant bacterium we engineered is related to MRGAS?"

His brow furrowed and his eyes darkened with concern. "You mean, what if that bug somehow escaped into the community and cross-pollinated with group-A strep?"

"No." She shook her head slowly. *"I mean, what if someone deliberately released it?"*

43

Lopez awoke at 5:20 A.M., burning with determination. Since Detective Cohen had put a name to the man behind the spread of MRGAS, her last shred of doubt had vanished. Though her colleagues at the CDC refused to accept it, she knew that the world's latest superbug was not another example of nature venting its fury. MRGAS was man-made. And spread by humans, not by chance.

She grabbed the leash to lead a wired Rosa downstairs and out to the park. Walking briskly along the trail in the cool dawn, Lopez's thoughts turned to Seth Cohen. She sensed a profound character beneath his quiet exterior. And she found his sharp features, dusky complexion, and deep brown eyes easy on her own eyes. As was Graham Kilburn. Fair-skinned with a square jaw and a crooked smile, he looked nothing like Cohen. But Lopez found his outdoorsy looks and laid-back charm appealing. None of the men she had dated in the past two years seemed as interesting in comparison as either of these two.

"Snap out of it, Lina!" she scolded herself. She felt silly for having entertained the thoughts about the men whom she barely knew professionally, let alone personally, and who lived more than a hundred miles on either side of her.

Returning from her walk, she refilled Rosa's water bowl, showered, and then sat down at her computer. The sixth of twenty-nine new overnight e-mails caught her eye. One of them, from the CDC's surveillance center, read: "Two cases of MRGAS were confirmed at Orange County Hospital. One patient, a known intravenous drug user, has died from necrotizing fasciitis."

"Not L.A.!" she groaned to the dog who lay at her feet. With a population of ten million people to hide among, Lopez wondered how they could ever to hope to root MR-GAS out of Greater Los Angeles.

Her phone vibrated and she brought it to her ear. "Lina, it's Graham. Sorry to call so early."

"No problem." She checked her watch, which read 6:55 A.M. "I've been up for a while."

"Have you heard?" Kilburn asked excitedly.

"About L.A.?"

"Has MRGAS reached Los Angeles?" he asked calmly.

"Yes." She read the e-mail aloud to him.

"Hmmm," he said with surprising indifference. "Good thing Oraloxin seems to work."

"It's *working?!?*" Lopez sprang up so quickly that Rosa jumped in surprise.

"Some very promising developments at Harborcenter," he said. "I'll give you the full lowdown over breakfast."

Too impatient to wait even a few minutes to hear the details, Lopez tried David Warmack's number but reached his voicemail. Keyed up on adrenaline and bursting with curiosity, she grabbed her purse and raced out the door. Hair still damp, she hopped into her car, not bothering to lower the top, and sped over to the restaurant.

She ran into Kilburn standing at the PLEASE WAIT TO BE

SEATED' sign at the front of the restaurant. As soon as he saw her, his face broke into a huge smile. "Lina!" He startled her by wrapping her in a tight hug.

Releasing her, he cleared his throat and glanced down "Sorry . . . er . . . guess I got a bit carried away by the moment," he said. "It's nice to have something to celebrate for a change when it comes to MRGAS."

She laid a hand on his shoulder. "Definitely a huggable turn of events, Graham."

A tall young hostess with long dyed-blond hair approached them. "Your table's ready," she said perkily and led them to a table in the corner.

Once seated, Lopez pointed to the third place setting at the square table. "Seth?"

Kilburn nodded. "Yeah. I caught him as he was heading out for a run. He said he would try to catch up but to go ahead and order without him."

"Okay." Lopez brushed off as juvenile the slight sense of letdown. "Okay, Graham, what's going on at Harborcenter?"

"You remember the little girl David told us about?"

Lopez nodded. "The ten-year-old with MRGAS pneumonia?"

He smiled. "She's going to be off the ventilator by day's end."

Lopez shook her head in surprise. "But she's only had twenty-four hours of treatment!"

Kilburn beamed. "Her doctors are pleasantly astounded by her response."

"No chance this is just a coincidence and not related to Oraloxin?"

"Lina, yesterday morning they were planning her funeral. Today they're planning her discharge. It's no coincidence." He shook his head emphatically. "And she's not alone. She's the most dramatic responder, but all of the patients on Oraloxin are showing signs of improvement, or at least stabilization, this morning."

"A toast." Lopez raised her water glass to Kilburn. "To the genius who thought of trying this obscure experimental drug in the first place."

"A stab in the dark." Kilburn shrugged. "No. The real genius we have to thank is the one behind Oraloxin, Ellen Horton." He raised his glass and touched hers. "To Ellen."

"To Ellen." Lopez put her glass down. "You two are friends from med school, huh?"

"We've lost touch in recent years," he said with a sigh, "but we were close in school. We met as anatomy lab partners, Ellen and I became study partners afterward."

"What's she like?"

"Ellen?" Kilburn looked down at his glass, considering the question. "Aside from brilliant, she's very driven. But she's also sweet, soft-spoken, and . . ."

She picked up on his hesitation. "And?"

"Like most overachievers I've ever met, Ellen has always been her own worst enemy," he said. "Nothing was ever good enough. She had low self-esteem. And she suffers—or at least used to—from bouts of deep depression."

Lopez recognized the genuine affection in Kilburn's words. "It's true about overachievers. Some of the most renowned people I worked with in Atlanta were also the most miserable."

"See?" He grinned playfully. "That's why I revel in my mediocrity."

"As if." Lopez rolled her eyes and chuckled. "I think my dad had the best perspective on overachievement."

"Which was?"

"Papa recognized my ambitiousness long before I did."

"You?" Kilburn uttered in mock surprise. "*Ambitious?*"

"You won't find an EIS officer who isn't," she said unapologetically. "One time I was bragging to him about a class prize I had won in the fourth grade. He gave me a hug and a kiss on the cheek. Then he sat me down and looked me square in the eye." She affected a huskier voice and a thick Hispanic accent. " 'Cat, no one is prouder of you than me.

But promise me you won't ever look for happiness in a diploma on the wall or your name in bright lights. You will never find it there, *ángel. Comprende?* ' "

Kilburn chuckled. "Sounds pretty sharp, your dad."

She nodded and reached for her menu, suddenly feeling shy about her disclosure.

Kilburn's cell phone rang. He listened for a few moments. "We'll pick you up on the way." He disconnected and said to Lopez: "Seth is running late. Literally. Said he got lost out on his run and went further than expected."

As soon as the waitress came by, they ordered breakfast. Cohen's jogging misadventure reminded Lopez that she had missed the gym four days in a row, so she reluctantly opted for the cereal and yogurt breakfast. Kilburn ordered the same.

Over their meals they discussed their career choices and directions. Then the conversation veered toward more personal territory. "Lina, do you have kids?" Kilburn asked.

She shook her head, willing herself not to flush. "Closest I've come is in the form of a wheaten terrier named Rosa." She looked away. "I was engaged once, but things didn't work out." She looked back to him and cocked her head. "And you?"

"I've got a niece and nephew—eight and ten—who I'm close to." Kilburn cleared his throat. "My sister is a single mom. I help her out with the kids where I can. Truth is, they're great kids. I love having them." He shrugged. "But on the home front, my girlfriend—ex-girlfriend, I guess— moved out a few months ago."

"Oh," Lina said. Graham's tone suggested, as she had suspected, that he was still emotionally invested. "Were you together long?"

"Almost four years," Kilburn said. "We lived together for three."

Lopez nodded understandingly.

"Michelle's an architect, a junior partner in her firm. My practice is pretty well established." His gaze fell to the table. "I thought we'd both reached that settling-down stage. We talked about marriage. And I'd just assumed . . . hoped, I guess . . . that we'd have kids of our own." His voice trailed off, and he suddenly reddened.

Lopez smiled, sympathetic to his hurt and vulnerability. "Well, aren't we just a perfect pair of losers?" she said.

He glanced at his watch. "Wow! Losers who are late too."

Kilburn insisted on paying. After leaving cash on the table, they rushed out to Lopez's car. She drove them to the waterfront Marriott where Cohen was staying. He stood by the front door of the hotel, waiting for them to pick him up. After exchanging greetings, Lopez asked him whether he had heard the good news about Oraloxin.

"A little," Seth said as he clipped his seat belt in place. His eyes scanned the interior of Lopez's car. She wondered whether he was pricing it in his mind, but he made no comment.

During the ride to Harborcenter, Lopez and Kilburn took turns updating Cohen on the specifics of the patient responses to Oraloxin. When they arrived at the hospital, Lopez hurried them inside and up to the eighth floor MR-GAS quarantine unit, or "The Unit," as the entire floor had become known. At the provisional security screening post, a guard carefully inspected Lopez's ID. After ten minutes of walkie-talkie conversations, Kilburn and Cohen were also granted permission to enter.

Inside the makeshift women's changing room, Lopez changed into scrubs, mask, cap, gown, and booties. When she stepped onto the floor, Kilburn and Cohen waited, looking like a couple of lost surgeons.

The Unit was divided into two sections. The larger section held several rooms where less-sick patients and carriers were cared for. The other section enclosed a functional ICU with isolation rooms that held four critically ill patients. The place smelled to Lopez of iodine and ammonia-soaked sterility.

The charge nurse, Janice, a gregarious, chunky woman with a throaty Southern drawl, guided them around The

Unit. She pointed out the fourteen empty rooms in the ICU section. "We're still worried we might run out of capacity. Then again—" she laughed heartily—"we're praying that with this wonder drug Oraloxin, we might not need 'em after all."

Janice led them to the door of one of the rooms. She pointed to the large, double-paned, scored window. "This is Haley Vallance's room." She smiled. "That little girl is our number-one success story. The staff are already calling her the Oraloxin poster child."

Peering through the glass, Lopez saw a cute girl with auburn bangs sitting up awake in the bed. An endotracheal tube led from her mouth but her eyes were open and she moved her arms animatedly. A man and a woman, presumably Haley's parents, hovered over the sides of the bed. Lopez's spirits rose just watching the scene. Medical gadgetry aside, Haley looked too well to be in an ICU.

Lopez assumed Kilburn was thinking the same, because he glanced at her; his eyes smiling over his surgical mask. "I'll bet Haley gets kicked out of the ICU soon," he said.

"Maybe tomorrow," Janice said as she led them past the other ICU MRGAS patients, each of whom appeared sicker than Haley, but Janice assured them that all were looking better than the previous day. And she added, as if it were a massive accomplishment, "No deaths in fourteen hours."

Janice steered them out of the ICU section and into the other side of The Unit, which looked like the hospital ward it was. Some of the doors were wide open. A few masked patients even milled about in the hallways. They stopped in front of a room. "Angie's in here. Legally, we have to keep the door locked, but she's been pretty cooperative so far." Janice called over to a security guard who unlocked the door. "Angie hates wearing the mask. And since she's not growing any MRGAS in her sputum, we don't force her."

Janice led them into the room. In a hospital gown that draped over her skinny body, Angie Fischer sat upright over the side of the bed reading a teen magazine. Her hair was still blue, but now it was neatly combed back and pinned with barrettes. With her face tidied and her formerly crystal meth–dilated pupils no longer hiding her bright green eyes, Lopez realized that Angie was a nice-looking kid despite the scrawniness and pallor.

"Angie, I believe you've met Dr. Kilburn and Dr. Lopez before," Janice said.

Angie nodded shyly.

"And this is Sergeant Cohen," Janice pointed to Seth. "I'm going to leave you in their good hands for a while." She sauntered to the door and turned back to the visitors. "Give us a holler when you're ready to come out." She closed the door, and Lopez heard a lock click.

Kilburn pulled up three chairs to the bedside. Lopez sat between the men, facing Angie directly. "Angie, how are you?" she asked.

"I was already better." Angie pouted slightly. "I told you that at Jake's."

"And we explained why you had to be quarantined," Lopez said evenly.

Angie didn't protest. She looked down at her bed for a moment. When she looked up, her eyes were red. She pointed beyond the door. "Did I really make all these people sick?"

Lopez shook her head. "We don't think you did."

She swallowed. "But some of the others around here said that I spread this thing from Vancouver to Seattle."

"That's not true." Lopez leaned forward in her chair. "But Angie, we do need your help."

"Jake hasn't come to see me since I got here," Angie digressed. "I bet those rent-a-cops have stopped him from getting in."

"Or maybe he's too scared," Lopez said.

"Yeah, maybe." Angie sniffed and nodded. "You think he'll come later?" She looked at Lopez desperately. "He will, don't you think, Doctor?"

Lopez wanted to tell the poor kid that Jake Fasken and

snakes like him were the reason she had ended up here. Instead she just smiled and said, "How's your leg?"

Angie pulled her gown up on the left side. In the two days since they had last seen her, the wound had healed dramatically. Now it was just a superficial scab without any surrounding redness. Lopez wondered whether Oraloxin or simple decent wound care deserved the credit. She pointed to Angie's thigh. "We need to know who gave you those drugs."

Angie's shoulders stiffened. "I told you already." She licked her lips. "One of my friends, Randee or Jenny, maybe."

Lopez shook her head. "We don't believe you."

Angie folded her skinny arms across her chest. "Why would I lie?"

"We know about the dealer who gave you the samples," Lopez pressed. "He *meant* to make you sick, did you know that?"

She didn't reply.

"Listen, Angie, if you can't help us, he'll do the same to others," Kilburn said.

Angie shook her head. "I never met that guy," she said in just above a whisper.

Kilburn looked at Lopez with frustrated concern. Before either had a chance to say more, Cohen spoke up. "Angie, I'm a cop from Portland. You want to know why I'm here?"

Angie stuck out her lower lip. She shrugged without looking at him.

"I met a woman in Portland," Cohen said. "A few years older than you, but you remind me of her. Same defiant streak. Her name was Carol Wilson. She was a witness in a murder there."

"So?" Angie said softly.

"I wound up spending some time with Carol. She told me her life story. I'm sure you've heard it before." Cohen sighed. "A good kid from a loving family who stumbled into the wrong crowd. The wrong guy. Drugs. She was hooked right off the bat. Try as she might, she just couldn't shake the habit."

Angie kept her head down, but from the occasional sniffle and the way she tilted her head Lopez knew she was listening to Cohen's narrative.

"Carol was a wreck when I met her. Couldn't have weighed more than eighty pounds. And she was already very sick from the infection." Cohen paused a moment. "But Carol wasn't just a drug addict or a street girl. She was someone's daughter. Someone's big sister. And there was something special about Carol. She had a real spark."

"Had?" Angie croaked softly.

"Carol is dead," Cohen said matter-of-factly. "Like you, she developed an infection at the site where she shot up. But hers just kept getting worse until she collapsed at my feet. And she knew who killed her. She described him to me. Said he was tall and handsome, but he had these eyes that look dead." Cohen shook his head. "But you want to hear the worst part? Not only did he kill Carol, he used her to spread this awful infection. And he let her die thinking she was responsible. This guy used you for the same purpose, Angie."

Angie sniffled a few more times, but she didn't reply for a long time. Unlike the last time Lopez saw her, wired on drugs and writhing like a patient with a neurological disorder, Angie kept very still. Finally, she looked up at Cohen. "His eyes *were* dead," she whispered.

"You did meet him," Cohen said encouragingly.

She waved her palms in front of her. "But you can't tell, Jake. He's so jealous."

"Not a word," Lopez promised.

Angie's eyes pleaded. "Jake would kill me if he knew that I got stuff off this guy. I got no money. Jake would think for sure that I screwed him for drugs, but I didn't! The guy gave them to me free." She shook her head bitterly. "Now I know why."

Lopez and Kilburn shared a glance, but Cohen kept his eyes on Angie. "Angie, we need your help to find this guy," he coaxed. "What do you remember about him? His voice. His smell. His clothes. Anything?"

"His face," Angie said emphatically.

"What about it?"

"I'm good with faces. Mom—" she swallowed—"my mom used to tell me I had a photographic memory. I can still picture the guy's face."

"If we brought a police artist in here to talk to you . . ." Cohen suggested.

"I'm a good portrait painter. My tenth-grade art teacher said I was going to grow up to be an artist." She made fleeting eye contact with Cohen. "Guess not, huh?"

"You can draw him?" Cohen asked.

Angie shifted her butt up the bed. She reached for the nightstand, opened the drawer, and pulled out a notepad. She flipped it open and leafed through some doodles and drawings. Even though Lopez glimpsed it only briefly, one portrait bore a striking likeness to Angie's boyfriend Jake. Angie reached a page and stopped. She turned the notepad outward to show them the sketch.

Lopez's heart skipped a beat. The man was handsome in a cold, detached way. His hair shot off his head in short spears. His expression was unreadable, his eyes deadly. An unfamiliar feeling overcame her. It was fear.

44

Mt. Airy, Philadelphia, Pennsylvania

Forbes yanked hard on the choke collar around the neck of the two-year-old Lab-shepherd mix, snapping the dog's head back. Whether from the rough corrections or the exertion of the two-hour morning walk, the mutt seemed to finally be learning. He made far fewer of his senseless lunges—at any person or dog coming in the opposite direction—than he had when Forbes first borrowed him from an animal shelter the previous evening.

Forbes had previously taken advantage of the various programs that allow people to bring animals home from shelters for a twenty-four-hour trial period. He could have just as easily bought the dogs, but in principle that offended his frugal nature. He had no intention of keeping the dogs—he wondered why anyone would—but he found the animals useful for providing cover, especially when staking out suburban neighborhoods in broad daylight.

At 8:25 A.M., after quickly circling the trail in Fairmount Park, Forbes jerked the dog back toward the street. He trotted the block and a half toward his target's house, slowing only when he could see it. He was approaching the house in the middle of the street for the third time that overcast morning when he saw the dated brown Ford Taurus sedan pull out of the driveway. He squatted down and pretended to fawn over the dog, hiding most of his face in the mutt's coat. But as the car passed, he saw that the driver didn't even glance his way.

Forbes waited until the car turned the corner at the end of the street before straightening up. Then he pulled a packet from his jacket, tore it open, and removed the cleaning wipe. The sterile alcohol scent was a welcome change from the nauseating wet-dog odor. After wiping the dog's smell off his face and hands, he turned and headed leisurely for the now empty house. After scoping out the house, he intended to drop off the dog. And then he would have the rest of the day to set up.

45

Seattle, Washington

Kilburn had just walked out of Harborcenter Hospital when his cell rang. Stepping away from Lina and Seth, he dug into his pocket and pulled out the phone. To dampen the traffic noise from the street in front of the hospital, he cupped a hand over one ear.

"Hey, Dr. Kilburn, remember me?" Louise asked gruffly.

"Vaguely." Kilburn smiled. "Aren't you the woman who tends bar at my office?"

She laughed. "I wish. How's Seattle?"

"So-so," he said. "How are things in Vancouver?"

"Not so hot," Louise sighed. "There are a bunch more cases. Several people caught it outside of the hospital. Talk of the bug is everywhere," she sighed. "People are scared, Dr. Kilburn."

Though not surprised, Kilburn felt deflated. Louise was anything but alarmist. "Help might be on the way," he said.

"You figure?"

"Hang on a sec." He covered the phone, and yelled to his

colleagues: "Lina, Seth, go on ahead. I'll catch up." Then he put the receiver back to his ear and updated Louise on Oraloxin's promising early clinical trials in Seattle.

"Ha—you were right all along!" Louise trumpeted. "That explains it."

"Explains what?"

"Why the powers-that-be keep calling from St. Michael's," she said.

"My privileges have been reinstated?"

"You got that right. Dr. Teal has called at least three times and faxed as many letters," she snorted. "If that stuffed shirt could figure out a way to fax over the key to the hospital, our machine would be spitting out metal by now."

Kilburn laughed. "C'mon Louise, he did what he had to. Anyone else looking for me?"

"Everyone," she groaned. "I expect to see your face on the back of milk cartons soon."

"Has Kyra called?"

"Once." Before Kilburn could ask, Louise added: "Don't worry. She sounds fine, Dr. Kilburn. She saw all the news coverage, and she was concerned about you."

The relief was immediate. If Kyra weren't sober, he knew Louise would have picked up on it. "Who else?"

"Let's see." Kilburn heard Louise shuffle through papers. "A bunch of S.O.S. calls from local docs. A couple of calls from Atlanta and Geneva. None of them sounded urgent enough to bug you about. And one call from an old classmate of your . . ."—he heard more pages rustled—"a Dr. Ellen Horton in Philadelphia. She called this morning."

Kilburn cursed himself for not getting back to Horton sooner about the Seattle results.

"Oh, I almost forgot one other message," Louise said, but he knew she never forgot anything. She must have been saving the message for last. "Michelle called yesterday."

Kilburn had a painfully clear vision of Michelle in jeans and a T-shirt kneeling on the sofa. He pictured her holding a mug of coffee in both hands and pinning the phone to her ear with a shoulder. "What was she calling about?" he asked.

"She said it could wait," Louise said offhandedly. "Said she'll try you later in the week."

Kilburn knew his receptionist would have gotten far more out of Michelle, but he didn't dare ask, apprehensive of what he might learn about Michelle's new life. "Thanks, Louise. I better catch up with the others."

"Hey, Dr. K.," she said. "Was I right about Dr. Lopez?"

"Not far off," he said evasively.

"And?" Louise prompted.

"And what, Louise?" He realized how his words might have come across as defensive. "Things have been going to hell in a handbasket around here." He forced a laugh. "Doesn't leave much time for chatting up the ladies."

"You know, Dr. Kilburn," Louise said, undeterred, "if you catch the traffic right, it's only two and a half hours from Vancouver to Seattle."

"Bye." He hung up the phone and hailed one of the cabs idling a few feet away in front of the hospital's main entrance. As he climbed into the backseat, Kilburn heard a voice on the radio in a language that he guessed was Turkish. The young driver with the crew cut glanced at him in the mirror. "Where to, sir?" he asked in a thick Middle Eastern accent.

Kilburn gave him Lopez's office address. As soon as he'd buckled his seat belt, he dialed Horton's direct line at SeptoMed. By the fifth ring, he was expecting voicemail, so he was surprised to hear her answer. "Ellen, it's Graham," he said.

"Hello, Graham," she said distantly.

Kilburn couldn't keep the smile from his face. "Are you sitting down?"

"Hmmm," Horton murmured.

"Oraloxin works, Ellen. It really works!" Kilburn said. "All ten patients in Seattle are showing some degree of response after twenty-four hours!"

"That's great," she said, but her tone conveyed neither surprise nor enthusiasm.

"Oraloxin saved the life of a little girl. Ten years old and on the verge of death! But, Ellen, your drug saved her."

"That's terrific," Horton said remotely. "But it's not my drug alone. I worked with a team."

"I don't understand," Kilburn said. "Oraloxin is making an impact that you can't have imagined in your dreams. Why don't you sound more pleased?"

There was a deathly long pause on the line. Finally, she said in a subdued tone, "A colleague and friend, Viktor Leschuk, died a couple days ago. We worked together for nearly five years. He was a key part of Oraloxin's development."

"Oh, I'm sorry," Kilburn said in genuine sympathy. "What happened?"

"Fishing accident," she said. "The coroner ruled it an accidental drowning."

Kilburn was perplexed by her choice of terms. Before he could ask about it, he heard a soft whimpering. He realized she was crying. "Ellen? Are you okay?"

"No, I'm not sure that I am."

"Ellen, I'm so sorry about your friend—"

"It's not just Vik," she sobbed. "Nothing is right around here, Graham. I don't know what to think anymore."

"Slow down, Ellen," he said. "I'm not following you. Tell me what's going on."

Her voice steadied. "Look, there have been problems with Oraloxin for months. We've known about them in the lab. I should've said something sooner." Her voice took on an anxious edge. "The testing wasn't complete when we started our clinical trials, but there was a lot of pressure to move forward. So much riding on the line . . ."

Kilburn waited for her to explain, but she lapsed into silence. "What problems?" he asked. "Why wasn't it ready?"

"It's, um, hard to explain," she stammered. She sniffled. "Maybe, if I could tell you in person, if you came to Philadelphia . . ."

"Ellen, I'm stuck here in Seattle," he said. "And I have a mountain of commitments waiting for me in Vancouver."

"Of course, Graham. Sorry. It was a dumb idea." She cleared her throat. "I don't know what got into me. I'm not sleeping well, with FDA approval looming and all. Excuse me, I say wild things."

Kilburn's unease grew. In the course of their short conversation, Horton had gone from despondent to anxious and now sounded evasive. "Listen, Ellen, maybe there's a more private time to speak. I have my cell on me. You can call me any—"

"No, no. Don't worry. I'm sorry I unloaded on you." She laughed nervously. "Apart from the lack of sleep, I'm still in a bit of shock over Vik's death. But now that I've had my little-girl cry, I feel better already."

"Ellen?" he said dubiously.

"Graham, it's great news about Oraloxin," she said, suddenly perkier. "The people here will be over the moon. Thanks for letting me know. I'll talk to you soon."

Before he could say another word, the line went dead.

46

Horton's heart slammed against her ribcage as she hung up the phone. During her conversation with Kilburn, she had stared aimlessly out the window. Not until three-quarters of the way through, when she reached for the tissue box on her desk, did she notice the two pairs of eyes watching her through the partly open door.

How long had they been there? Her throat tightened. What had these people heard?

But Andrea Byington was all smiles as she stepped into the room. And Martineau—who was so enraged the previous evening that he wouldn't make eye contact when she left his apartment—approached amiably as if nothing unpleasant had ever occurred between them.

"Oh, Ellen, what's wrong?" Byington's brow furrowed. "You've been crying."

Horton sniffled a few times, deliberately buying time. Her mind raced, trying to calculate how much to tell the two people she no longer trusted. "I'm okay," she said. "I'm just a little overwhelmed by the good news."

Byington's eyes widened and her face lit up with delight. "You've heard about the success in Seattle, then?"

Horton nodded. "I just spoke to Graham Kilburn."

"Isn't it marvelous? Think of all those lives you've saved." Byington beamed. "What you've created here is nothing short of miraculous!"

"Doesn't surprise me," Martineau said proudly. He spoke to Byington but his eyes focused on Horton. "I knew when Ellen joined us at SeptoMed that great things were possible."

Horton's vigilance relaxed slightly. Perhaps they hadn't overheard anything of significance.

Still smiling, Byington eyed her silently for a few seconds. "Ellen, when word of Oraloxin reaches the media, you'll become an overnight sensation. At least in the short term, your life is going to change dramatically." Her grin gave way to an expression of concern. "You do know that, don't you?"

Horton nodded, fighting off a shudder. In the past, she had felt ambivalent about the attention Oraloxin might bring her. Never one for the spotlight, she still welcomed the validation and praise she might have expected from her peers and colleagues. However, she never dreamt of the kind of international celebrity that news of Oraloxin's effectiveness against MRGAS might bring. She wanted no part of that circus.

"Andrea's right, Ellen." Martineau said with a nod. "It may take a few days for the media to learn of Oraloxin and you, *n'est-ce pas*? But Ellen, once they do . . . ," he said, holding out a hand to her, as if helpless to intervene, "you can expect their full attention."

"They'll call you at all hours," Byington added, "and they'll wait for you outside the office and home, hoping for an interview, or at least a sound bite."

"I can imagine," Horton said distantly. She had a sudden flash of insight as to where the conversation was heading.

"Trust me, Ellen." Byington leaned forward and patted

Horton's arm. "They're experts at twisting words and taking things out of context. Luckily, we have a perfectly able communications department here. Their job is to keep you at arm's length from the media."

Horton was tempted to pull her arm away, but instead she just nodded.

"Communications has already drafted a press release. You should be getting the e-mail any time." Byington glanced to Martineau, before turning back to Horton straight-faced. "We think it might be best for you not to comment publicly to anyone until you've cleared it through Communications and us."

"That makes sense," Horton said, silently adding, *For you*. From the bone-marrow side effect to MRGAS's similarity to the bug engineered in SeptoMed's own lab, Oraloxin's closet was rapidly filling with skeletons. She now understood that Byington and Martineau were desperate to keep the press from opening that closet door.

Martineau's expression was as placid as ever, but his eyes had crystallized with the same icy dangerousness she glimpsed the previous evening. "Ellen, it would be in everyone's best interest—especially yours—if you didn't speak to anyone about Oraloxin." He took a step closer to her. She smelled his rich cologne and felt his hot breath against her cheek. But this time, it didn't stir arousal. Instead, she experienced a chill, aware of the menacing undertone to his silence. "Do you not agree, Ellen?"

47

Seattle, Washington

Cohen sat in the passenger seat of Lopez's Audi and stared out at the buildings passing by in the bright morning sunshine. He'd yet to shake his fish-out-of-water discomfort at having stepped from a criminal investigation into a public-health probe. But he appreciated that both had the same ultimate endpoint: finding Dennis Tyler and the people behind him. He had never lost sight of his quest to find Carol Wilson's killer.

Cohen appreciated the way Lopez and Kilburn took the time to explain the technical jargon without patronizing. He enjoyed their company, too, but he couldn't ignore the chemistry he sensed between Kilburn and Lopez. That, not his jog, was what had actually kept him from joining them at breakfast. Cohen had no desire to be a third wheel. And the more time he spent around Lina, the more difficulty he had focusing on the job. Latina good looks aside, her rocket ship personality wowed him more than anyone had in a long time.

"What are you thinking about?" Lopez asked, adjusting her sunglasses.

"Medicine," Cohen said obliquely.

"You looking for a career change?"

"Not when the job is even more depressing than Homicide," he said with a slight grin. "I was thinking, though, that there are more similarities between our jobs than I'd have ever guessed."

"Absolutely." She nodded. "Particularly what I do. Epidemiology is all about following the broken trail of evidence back to a source. In fact, during my fellowship I had to take a few criminology courses on the principles of police investigation. I loved them."

"So maybe you'll be the one switching jobs?" Cohen suggested with a smile.

"Never." She brushed back a few strands of hair that had drifted over her forehead. "I love what you do *except* for the criminals themselves. I'd rather deal with homicidal bugs than homicidal people any day."

"Lina, I think right now you're dealing with both."

"Yeah, I guess," she murmured. "So how did you wind up as a cop?"

Cohen chuckled. "That's what my dad always asks."

Lopez flashed a toothy smile. "He's not proud of his detective son?"

"Not outwardly." Cohen said, thinking of his father's tendency to substitute wit for affection. "He calls me the Jewish Charlie Chan. Claims he doesn't have a clue why I do it."

"Why do you?"

He cleared his throat, uncomfortable at being the subject of conversation. "My partner jokes that I have an overdeveloped sense of revenge."

Lopez frowned without taking her eyes off the road. "Any truth to that?"

"I guess I like the balance," he said with an awkward

laugh. "Someone breaks the law. I help bring him or her to justice. And it's all a wash . . . theoretically."

"Okay." She sounded unconvinced.

"I couldn't have gone into medicine," Cohen said quietly. "My mother died of breast cancer when I was a kid. As far as I know, she had good medical care. Everyone did everything they could. No one was to blame for what happened to her." He swallowed. "And in a bizarre way, that was part of the problem for me. She was taken from us so young, yet there was nowhere to lay my anger or hurt. It was as if I had no retribution for her loss." He looked away, embarrassed. "I'm not making any sense."

"I know exactly what you mean, Seth," Lopez said softly. She reached over and touched him gently on the elbow. "I went through the same when Papa died." She paused. "It was so unfair. Like I was cheated, you know?"

"Exactly," Cohen said, pleasingly aware of her fingers resting on his arm. "I think that's what got to me about the death of our witness, Carol Wilson. She kind of resembled my mom at the end. Young, but so gaunt and pallid. I was with both of them when they died. But in Carol's case, I knew someone was responsible. Someone who could be made to answer, you know?"

She nodded and squeezed his arm gently, before pulling her hand back.

Though he inferred a pleasant intimacy in her gesture, Cohen felt self-conscious for having opened up to a woman he barely knew. "How about you?" he asked. "Why medicine? Why epidemiology?"

"The medicine part is easy," she said with a chuckle. "It's in my blood. Both my parents were doctors in Guatemala, but neither of them could get licensed in America. Papa was a surgeon in the old country, but he ended up as a radiology technician in Phoenix. He made it pretty clear from as long as I remember that his only child was going to be a doctor—come hell or high water!"

"And why epidemiology?"

"It seemed so cool to me when I was a med student. The outbreaks. The exotic bugs. The travel. The drama. And best of all, no night call!" Her tone took on a serious edge. "And the scale of it appealed to me. I had this kind of naïve idea that if I did my job right, instead of having an impact on just one patient I could make a difference for many." Her face flushed. "I think I must have a hero complex or something."

Cohen smiled, admiringly. "Seems to me you *are* making a difference now."

"Don't know if the stats would bear you out, now that MRGAS has hit L.A."

"That's hardly your fault." He wanted to provide better reassurance but was at a loss for words. Instead, he said, "Lina, do you think Dennis Tyler is still spreading this infection?"

"Not sure he needs to anymore. It might be overkill."

"I don't follow."

She bit her lip and frowned. "Arson might be the best analogy for what Tyler and the others are up to. No question, someone can start a fire in a building with a single match. But each extra spark, each new flame, increases the likelihood of reaching flashpoint. Once you reach that point—'critical mass' in epidemiological terms—the fire is self-propagating. In other words, you don't need to walk into the middle of a burning building with a can of gasoline to keep it going."

Cohen nodded.

"And as with arson, the more extensive and damaging the fire, the harder it sometimes is to uncover the cause. The evidence gets consumed in the flames." Lopez shot a steely glance at Cohen. "And you know what, Seth? Since no one has come forward to claim responsibility, my guess is that this what these bastards counted on: The outbreak would rage so out of control, no one would be able to track the source back to them."

"They never counted on you."

"Hardly." She broke into a glowing smile. "You're the one who dug up Tyler's name."

Cohen shrugged. "He probably goes by a hundred different names."

A musical tone rang from Lopez's waist. She reached down and brought the cell phone to her ear. "Sure, Karen, patch him through." Another pause. "No problem. Just hold on a sec, please."

Lopez surprised Cohen by passing him the phone. "For you," she said.

He brought the phone to his ear. "Seth Cohen."

"KC," Leetch boomed. "Is that lady with the sexy voice Dr. Lopez?"

Cohen ignored the question. "What's up, Rome? Is Dad okay?"

"Pappy's doing good. Saw him this morning. He wanted to know, since when did our jurisdiction extended to Seattle." Leetch chortled. "So do I for that matter!"

"Rome, I'm on a borrowed cell phone here," Cohen pointed out.

"Hey, how come I hear so much background noise?"

"I'm in a convertible."

"Ah, very nice!"

"Rome . . ."

"Okay, okay," Leetch said. "While you're out cruising with some babe with the top down, I've been slogging away at my desk. I came across something interesting."

"Oh?" Cohen leaned forward in his seat.

"I was working my way through Dennis Tyler's credit card bill," Leetch said, and Cohen knew he was going to draw out his revelation. "I finally tracked down the clerk at the Intercon in downtown Philly who checked Tyler in. Her name's Tara Newbridge. Giggly girl but sweet."

"She remembered Tyler?" Cohen asked impatiently.

"She said she thought he was hot."

"Just the break we've been looking for," Cohen sighed.

"Tara works only part-time for the downtown Intercon," Leetch continued as if never interrupted. "She also works out at the Airport Intercon, picking up shifts here and there.

Four days ago, Tara was working the late shift at the bell desk out at the Airport—"

"And she saw Tyler?" Cohen shot.

"Patience, Seth," Leetch said gleefully. "In walks this guy. Except, unlike Tyler, this guy is dressed in a suit and tie and his hair is all one color. But our Tara doesn't forget a face or a name when the guy's a real cutie. So after he checks in, Tara hustles over to see her friend at the check-in desk, wanting to know how long old Dennis is planning to stay. But guess what?"

"His name is not Dennis Tyler," Cohen said, drawing Lopez's wide-eyed attention.

"His name is not Dennis Tyler!" Leetch echoed enthusiastically. "The guy checking in claims to be Wayne Forbes from Illinois. But Tara knows Wayne and Dennis are the same person. Still, she doesn't pry. People check in under aliases all the time. Tara even starts wondering if he might be a movie star or something. He was cute enough—"

"*Is he still there?*" Cohen interrupted.

"No. Wayne checked out early the next morning."

"What do you know about Wayne Forbes?" Cohen asked.

"Well, if he's the same Wayne Forbes the Illinois DMV thinks he is, then like Dennis Tyler, Wayne just awoke from about a two-year nap. And like Tyler, he's run into trouble with some bad folks in his shady past."

"And as of three days ago, he was in Philadelphia," Cohen said slowly.

"According to Tara," Leetch said.

Lopez drew Cohen's attention by laying her hand on his. "Tyler is in Philadelphia?" she asked, her eyes afire.

Feeling the rush of another fresh trail and the warmth of her touch again, Cohen nodded. "Except he's going by the name of Wayne Forbes." He paused. "These days, all roads seem to lead to Philadelphia."

48

Mt. Airy, Philadelphia, Pennsylvania

Halfway through the day, Forbes realized that he'd budgeted too much of his limited time for preparation. Assuming the bungalow would have some kind of alarm system to overcome, he was surprised to discover that a flimsy deadbolt represented the extent of its security. The ease of access created a dilemma. Forbes had no idea when his target might return home and, intent on completing the contract within the narrow time frame he was allotted, he was not willing to chance missing the arrival. So, once the house and garage were prepared to his satisfaction, he settled into a chair in the kitchen and pulled out his book, Dan Brown's *Angels and Demons*. Fascinated by the rituals of religion, he was drawn to books about Church intrigue long before the popularity of *The Da Vinci Code*. Settled in with a book and a full thermos of tea, he realized the afternoon was shaping up all right.

At 6:34 P.M., Forbes heard the car approach followed by the sound of tires crunching on the house's driveway. He tucked his book into his jacket pocket, slipped on a pair of gloves, and pulled the knife from the sheath clipped to his belt.

He calmly rose from the chair and strolled into the kitchen to the spot he had chosen behind the back door. Through the translucent window shade, he saw the solitary figure approach. He heard a key rattle inside the lock. The bolt turned. The door opened. He pressed flatter against the wall, as the door's edge swung within an inch of the toes of his shoes.

Before she had even walked through the doorway, she called out: "Malcolm." And then she clicked her tongue encouragingly. "Come on, Malcolm."

For a split second, Forbes felt apprehensive. Then he remembered the smell of cat litter from the bathroom and realized she was calling the cat that he'd yet to encounter in her house.

"Even you've given up on me, huh, Malcolm?" she sighed, as she walked in and closed the door behind her.

With the knife dangling at his side Forbes stepped forward and said, "Dr. Horton?"

Horton gasped in surprise. Spinning to face him, she lost her balance. She had to grab the countertop beside her to steady herself. Her hands trembled and her eyes went wide.

"What do you want?"

"To talk," Forbes said quietly.

Horton backed up until she banged into the cupboard behind her, which sent the plates inside rattling. "Why the knife?" she asked, her voice cracking.

Forbes glanced down at his hand. "I don't want you to leave unexpectedly."

Horton took several slow breaths. "I've got money in my bedroom. And some jewelry. It's not worth much, but—"

He waved his palm slightly in front of him and smiled. "Don't worry, Dr. Horton. I'm not going to take your money or your jewelry."

"What, then?" she asked weakly, still leaning against the cupboard.

"How about a drink?" He pointed to the small round kitchen table where, apart from a notepad and pen, the bottle of red wine he'd uncorked earlier stood beside a solitary wineglass.

Horton shook her head wildly. "I don't want a drink."

Forbes smiled and nodded understandingly. "I think it might be a good idea, Dr. Horton."

Her eyes darted around the room. "How do you know my name?"

He smiled again. "It's what I do."

Suddenly her eyes locked onto his. "*What* do you do?" Her tone verged on pleading.

"I clean up other people's messes," he said evenly.

Her face creased. "Whose mess am I?" she whispered.

He shrugged. "I really don't know," he answered. "I'm hired strictly on a need-to-know basis."

Expecting to see tears, Forbes braced himself. He never got accustomed to seeing them cry. Other than fear and anger, he was acutely uncomfortable with people's emotions. *Focus*. He repeated the mantra in his head. *A job is a job*.

But Forbes was relieved to see that she didn't burst into tears. Instead, her eyes narrowed and she nodded to herself. "I know who hired you."

"It's really none of my business." Forbes pointed to the glass again. "Dr. Horton, will you reconsider that drink now? It might help."

She nodded. Still shaky, she stepped away from the kitchen cabinets and moved cautiously toward the table. She reached the far side of the table and pulled out the chair behind it. She reached forward and picked up the wine glass in her right hand.

In one rapid motion, the speed of which surprised even Forbes, she hurled the glass at him. He dodged to his left just as it flew by his ear and exploded against the wall behind. He saw her disappear through the kitchen doorway into the hall.

Standing on the spot, Forbes smoothed his hair and sighed. *They always run.*

49

Mt. Airy, Philadelphia, Pennsylvania

The blood pounding in her ears, Horton sprinted the ten paces down the hallway to the front door. She grabbed for the door handle and pulled. It didn't budge. With both hands, she yanked harder. Nothing. Desperately, she dug in her heels and heaved with all her might but she realized with welling panic that the door didn't move an inch.

"Dr. Horton," the man said in his chillingly calm voice. "It's not going to open."

She glanced over her shoulder and saw him sauntering nearer. He pointed with the knife to the door's hinges. She looked over and saw the metal clamps locked around them.

Releasing her hold on the doorknob, she turned and faced him.

"I'm sorry, Dr. Horton, but I had to ensure the house was secure." Like every other one of his comments, the remark was devoid of emotion. His lifeless eyes were the perfect match for his tone. She knew then, with abrupt finality, that she wouldn't escape. Her panic subsided, replaced by the cold numbness of resignation.

"Would you reconsider that drink now, Dr. Horton?" he asked.

She nodded. She trudged toward him. Out of reflex, her heart still skipped a beat and her throat tightened as she walked past him and into the kitchen. She noticed that he had already replaced the broken wineglass with a new one placed beside the bottle.

She pulled out the chair and sat down. Walking around the table, his feet crunched on the broken glass. He stood directly across from her. His expression remained as relaxed as ever, but he kept an attentive eye on her hand near the new wineglass.

As if dreaming, Horton viewed her captor dispassionately. With short groomed hair and a square jaw, he was undeniably handsome. But his dark eyes held the same frigidity she'd seen in Martineau's the night before. A surge of disgusted indignation tore through her. A day earlier she had slept with Martineau. *And now he's sent this quiet monster for me,* she thought. Clearly, Byington and Martineau hadn't trusted her to protect Oraloxin's dirty secrets.

She wished she'd had the guts to speak out sooner, as Viktor had begged her. Maybe none of this would have happened, she thought bitterly.

Viktor! It suddenly clicked. She turned to the man angrily. "There was no fishing accident, was there? You killed Viktor Leschuk, didn't you?"

He stared blankly. "I don't discuss my work with anyone."

She took his answer for an admission. "You bastard," she murmured.

He didn't respond.

Horton's eyes focused on the pen and notepad in front of her. "You expect me to write a note, don't you?"

"Yes."

"Do you really believe I would fake my own suicide note?" she asked, shaking her head.

"Why don't you have a glass of wine? Then we can discuss it."

She shook her head vehemently. "The whole bottle won't change my mind."

He lifted his hand with the knife and tapped it against his other palm. "Dr. Horton, you may reconsider still."

Horton swallowed hard, but her resolve held firm. "I'm dead anyway. What more can you do to me?"

He frowned almost imperceptibly. "What makes you think I'm talking about *you?*"

At first, his words struck her as an empty threat. Both her parents were dead. She had no other family. The closest she came to a significant other was Martineau. And the thought of harm befalling Martineau appealed to Horton. Then it dawned on her. Neil Ryland! Neil was the final member of Oraloxin's inner circle. She realized her death could serve a purpose. If only she could use the note to warn Ryland.

Reaching for the wine bottle, the violent tremor in her hand surprised her. She pulled the cork out of the bottle and filled her glass, spilling a few drops as she did so in the process. She took a sip of the dry wine. It tasted better than any wine she remembered. Composing her thoughts, she finished the glass in absolute silence and then refilled it. She drank the next glass even more slowly, buying time while she considered precisely how to phrase her note, knowing the wrong word would nullify her effort.

She pushed the glass away and reached for the pen and paper. She looked to her captor with undisguised contempt. "What would you want me to say?" she said.

He flashed a brief smile, which only emphasized his iciness. "How about good-bye?"

She felt a visceral sense of loss. She shook off the emotion and forced herself to concentrate. She brought the pen to the page and began to write:

Dear Neil,

I am very sorry to have to leave you like this. But please try to understand. I am so very tired. And I've run out of options.

That day at the New York Deli when you asked me to marry you was the most important day of my life. You were so sweet when you told me how you wanted to let the rest of the world know how you felt. But I told you not to. You know why, Neil? I was scared what might happen if people found out about us. But I didn't need to be scared of the world. The risk was all inside. And I can't live with myself any longer.

Realizing our dream has proven such an empty experience for me. There is a huge price to pay for the fame we craved. And I can't pay any more.

All my love,
El

Without reading it over, she put down her pen and pushed the notepad away.

He reached over and picked up the pad with a gloved hand.

Heart pounding, Horton watched as he read the letter impassively. Without saying a word, he slid the notepad, page open, back onto the table beside the wine bottle.

Overcome by a surreal sense of relief, Horton put the pen down beside the notebook. She prayed that Neil might recognize the absurd note for the warning it was meant to be. She had done all she could. She felt strangely contented.

"Another glass of wine?" he asked.

She shook her head.

He gestured with his knife for her to stand. "Let's go to the garage, Dr. Horton."

She stood to her feet. "Will you let me take a CD with me?" she asked.

When he nodded, she walked to the portable stereo in the corner of the kitchen. She popped open the lid of the CD player and removed the disc of Grieg's piano concerto.

She turned to him and said, "I'm ready now."

50

Seattle, Washington

Sitting beside Warmack at the podium in the Department of Health's conference room, Lopez couldn't believe the difference in how she felt. Compared to the press conference of three days earlier, the glare of the spotlights was hotter, the room more crowded, and the tension heightened. And yet Lopez was overcome by a commanding calm. She didn't know if it was her previous trial by fire or her awareness of their ace in the hole in the form of Oraloxin, but the charged up—at times hostile—crowd in front of her didn't faze her.

Again, Warmack began with a carefully crafted statement that gave an overview of the new cases and hinted at "an experimental treatment" without providing details. After he finished, Lopez spoke without notes on the MRGAS distribution along the West Coast and the CDC's attempt to contain it. She ended by saying, "We will briefly field questions—" but the rest of her sentence was instantly drowned out by the cacophony of yells and shouts erupting across the room.

Warmack waved down the din with two hands. When quiet was finally reestablished he pointed to a reporter in the front row who was waving her arm.

"Yvonne Davies, *Seattle Times*," the reporter said. "The ten-year-old girl with the pneumonia—"

"Is steadily improving." Warmack cut in reassuringly. "She will be out of the ICU soon."

"I know," Davies said impatiently. "But I heard she had never been in the hospital before. Does this mean that MR-GAS has spread into the community?"

Warmack took a quick sip of water. "She had a relative who was recently discharged from hospital, so it was a form of secondary hospital spread. But, yes, this is the first known case of community spread in Seattle."

"Will there be others?" a man yelled out from the middle of the sea of faces and hands.

"As we know of MRGAS carriers with mild or no symptoms, we have to assume there will be more community spread." Warmack flashed his most disarming smile. "Then again, if there's one lesson MRGAS has taught us so far, it's that we shouldn't assume anything. This bacteria doesn't play by the rules."

Warmack pointed to a man standing in the aisle.

"Dr. Lopez," the reporter shouted, "you talk about 'containment strategies,' but by my count there are now at least five major cities in two countries affected by this outbreak. Aren't you and the CDC trying to close the barn door after the horses have already left?"

Lopez shook her head calmly, refusing to be baited. "HIV affects seventy million people in over a hundred countries, yet we're still trying our best to contain it. You must understand, containment does not necessarily mean eradication."

"Are you saying, MRGAS might be the next HIV?" said a woman in the front row who aggressively jabbed a pen toward Lopez.

"No," Lopez replied suppressing the urge to tell the woman how stupid she considered the question. "I am saying it's possible we will not be able to eradicate MRGAS in the near future," she said evenly. "Which means we will have to focus our efforts on minimizing the further spread and damage it causes."

Warmack pointed to a man in the third row. Rising unhurriedly from his seat, the man identified himself "Adam Pearson, KOMO news."

Lopez still smarted from his inflammatory interrogation at the previous press conference. "Oh, we remember you, Mr. Pearson," Lopez said pointedly, drawing a scattering of laughter.

Pearson was unfazed by Lopez's sarcasm. "Wow. That's more than I can say for my kids at college," he said to more laughter. "Docs, I'm hearing rumors from my sources at The Unit in Harborcenter of dramatic improvements with some new wonder drug. Care to elaborate?"

Lopez glanced at Warmack who nodded once. She leaned closer to the mike. "It is way too early to classify Oraloxin as a wonder drug. Patients only began treatment less than thirty-six hours ago. The best we can say is that early results look promising."

"Why has it taken you so long to try it?" Pearson asked with an edge.

Warmack looked at Lopez warily, but she maintained her cool. "Oraloxin is still a research drug intended for a very specific use," she said. "It's not even yet approved by the FDA. One of the clinicians at a trial center was astute enough to try this drug when all others failed."

"Who?" Pearson demanded.

Lopez opted to protect Kilburn from the wolves. "A Canadian infectious-diseases specialist," she said vaguely.

Warmack swung his finger to another woman in the aisle. "You, ma'am. Last question."

"Can you tell us any more about the origins of this bug?" she asked in a voice barely audible over the room's other noises.

Warmack shook his head. "I think we covered that at the last press conference."

"Why are you so sure this is a naturally-occurring bug?" the woman persisted. "How do you know it isn't being spread like the anthrax letters were."

Lopez reached for the mike, tempted to expand upon the theory. Warmack viewed her, his eyes clouded with warning. She flashed him a smile and tapped the back of his hand once. "The CDC is working under the hypothesis that MR-GAS is a spontaneously occurring superbug like all the ones before it" she said. "However, until we've definitively established its origins, we will not discount any possibility during our investigation. Thank you very much."

More questions rained down on them, but they stood up and walked briskly for the door. Remembering Warmack's advice, Lopez sprinted for the safety of the stairwell, beating Warmack.

Joining her on the fourth-floor landing, Warmack smiled and shook a finger at her. "No yelling. No biting. And no tattling," he said. "Thank you, Cat. You behaved well in there."

She shook her head. "I lied to them."

"You didn't lie," he said. "You shared as much as was safe to share. And that's our job to do." He paused. "Let's say you're right about this Tyler/Forbes guy—"

"We *are* right, David."

"Okay, supposing you announced it to the world? What do you think would happen to him?"

Of course! Lopez thought. She viewed her older colleague with renewed respect. "He doesn't need to spread this further. It's self-propagating now. He could just disappear."

"And take his secrets with him," Warmack said, starting on the next flight of stairs.

When she reached the seventh floor, Lopez's phone rang. She waved Warmack on ahead to his office and then reached for her phone. "Lina, it's Nelson Amar," he said with usual curtness.

"How did I do, boss?" she asked.

"Do?" he said, confused. "I don't follow."

"We just held another press conference."

"I didn't see it. I've been swamped here in San Francisco. The rate of spread in the Bay Area is a disaster," he said quietly. "What's the news from Seattle?"

"Early results with Oraloxin have been astounding." She updated him on their visit to The Unit and the antibiotic responses they'd witnessed.

"Good," Amar grunted. "We've only started to get the antibiotic into patients today. With luck, we'll see a similar response by tomorrow." He paused. "We'd better."

"Nelson, there's another development," she said approaching the topic gingerly. "Regarding the spread of MRGAS—"

"You've heard?" Amar sounded surprised.

"Heard what?" she said, matching his tone.

"We have the L.A. index cases under quarantine. Not one but *two* infected addicts, a couple, who bussed from Oakland to L.A. The woman was hospitalized with early necrotizing fasciitis. But the staff took precautions. We're hoping we've caught it early enough."

Lopez sighed and switched the phone to her other ear. She wasn't surprised to hear that MRGAS had spread naturally to L.A., but she knew it would make the task of convincing her boss that much more of a challenge.

"What is it, Lina?"

"Angie Fischer, the Vancouver girl who we're assuming is responsible for the Seattle outbreak."

"What about her?" Amar asked guardedly.

"She's changed her story, Nelson. Angie admits to meeting the dark-eyed dealer and getting a free sample. She even drew a sketch of him."

"Perfect," Amar snorted. "A drawing from a teenage crystal meth addict."

"You can't discount it so easily," Lopez snapped. "This makes at least three addicts in three cities with the exact same story!" She took a deep breath and forced herself to relax. Then she told Amar about Seth Cohen and the homicide investigation that uncovered the Tyler/Forbes connection.

Bracing for another reprimand, Lopez was surprised not to hear a response immediately. Finally, Amar said: "You still haven't explained why a 'pusher' would intentionally spread MRGAS."

"That's the one piece we don't yet have," she admitted.

"Hmmm," Amar said. "Do you plan to involve the FBI?"

"Yes. Soon, anyway," Lopez said. "But Forbes doesn't know we're on to him. We might be able to learn more before bringing in the trumpeting cavalry and scare him off."

"What's your plan, Lina?"

"Sergeant Cohen is going to Philadelphia. He has a contact with the police force there. I think I should go too."

"What do you know about police work?" Amar demanded.

"Nothing," Lopez admitted. "But, Nelson, I know this bug as well as anyone. If there's a hint of it in Philadelphia, I'll pick up on it."

Another long pause followed. "I'm still not convinced, Lina. We have such an ordinary explanation for the spread of this bug," he sighed. "But I'll give you a few days in Philadelphia. If you don't dig anything up quickly, you turn over what you know to the FBI and get back to epidemiology. Am I clear?"

"Very. Thank you, Nelson." But he'd already hung up.

She looked to see Kilburn and Cohen approaching from the other end of the hallway. Kilburn held up a thumbs-up sign.

"Good job down there in that zoo, Lina," he said. "You're a natural in front of the camera. Might lead to a full-time gig for you."

"That's cruel." Lopez laughed.

Cohen showed her a slight, closed-mouth smile and nodded his approval.

Her mood had lifted at the sight of them. Especially Cohen. Since their last conversation, she felt a newfound closeness to Seth. The story of his mother had touched her. She knew he carried the same gnawing sense of loss as she did for Papa. And more and more, she'd caught herself thinking about his deep voice and intense brown eyes.

She flushed slightly and brushed back her hair. "I think I sold my soul down there."

Kilburn waved the idea away. "You handled it perfectly. Especially by keeping my name out of it. Thank you."

She smiled at Kilburn. "I won't give up the limelight that easily."

Cohen turned to Lopez. "Lina, my partner just called. He faxed Angie's sketch of Dennis Tyler/Wayne Forbes to the hotel clerk in Philadelphia. The clerk is certain he's the same man she saw in Philadelphia."

"So we have proof," she said with a frown.

"But if we go to the FBI now, they'll plaster that sketch everywhere," Cohen said.

Kilburn suggested, "Isn't that what we want?"

"A world-class pro like Forbes?" Cohen shook his head. "No, if he knows that we suspect him, I think he'd simply vanish. New name, new identity . . . a new life." He pantomimed wiping his hands clean. "Our best hope of finding him is by keeping a very low profile."

"What do we do now?" Kilburn asked.

"I'm going to Philadelphia," Cohen said matter-of-factly.

Lopez pointed a finger to her chest. "And I'm coming with you."

Cohen nodded.

"Count me in," Kilburn said. "You two can track down Forbes. I want to see Ellen Horton. Something is not right there." He glanced at the other two. "I'm concerned about her."

Cohen nodded again, then looked from Kilburn to Lopez. "Do either of you find it coincidental that Forbes has turned up twice in Philadelphia in the past six weeks?"

"Well, Forbes has been to several major cities in that time," Kilburn said, sounding somewhat doubtful.

"But all the other cities are on the West Coast. And in those places, he's been known to have spread MRGAS. No cases I know of in Philadelphia so far. But it *does* happen to be the home of the manufacturer of the only treatment for the bug he's spreading."

Lopez felt the blood drain from her face. "You think he's trying to stop the people at SeptoMed from releasing the drug?"

Cohen paused to think. "Lina, when did you learn that Oraloxin was even a potential treatment?"

"Three days ago."

"But Forbes has been in Philadelphia for at least four," Cohen said gravely.

Lopez felt her heart pounding in her throat. "How could he have possibly known before us?"

Kilburn's face paled. "Unless . . ."

51

Mt. Airy, Philadelphia, Pennsylvania

Forbes swept up the last few shards of glass into the triple-layered black garbage bag. Next, he turned his attention to the tabletop. He left the half-empty bottle of wine standing on the table, but he tipped her wine glass over beside it, allowing the few remaining drops to leak onto the table.

Forbes picked up the note and read it again. Deciding there was no harm in leaving it behind, he placed it back on the table deliberately tilting it askew so the corner of the paper absorbed the drops of wine from the overturned glass.

He noticed the pair of padded handcuffs at the bottom of the bag. Though he had put them on her inside the car while the engine was running, in retrospect he realized they weren't necessary. From what he saw, she never struggled. She had been braver than most.

Tying up the neck of the bag, he shook off any residual thoughts of her. *Look ahead,* he told himself. *Focus.* He needed to concentrate on the next stage. He had precious little time left, and the upcoming assignment might prove the trickiest challenge yet.

With the garbage bag slung over his shoulder, he headed for the door. He stopped for one last look around the staged room and allowed himself a quick self-satisfied smile.

So far, it was a textbook job.

52

Philadelphia, Pennsylvania

Even though their flight left Seattle at 5:50 A.M., with the time change they didn't arrive at the Philadelphia International Airport until 1 P.M. As he stood in the taxi line outside the terminal, Kilburn felt lightheaded in the sweltering spring heat wave that had hit the Northeast unseasonably early. Wiping sweat from his brow, Cohen looked as uncomfortable as Kilburn felt. But Lopez stood leisurely without a drop of perspiration appearing to enjoy the baking heat.

"How can this weather not get to you, Lina?" Kilburn mopped his own forehead.

"I'm from Central America, and I grew up in Arizona." She smiled. "This is the first time I haven't felt cold since I moved to the Pacific Northwest."

"Graham," Cohen pointed to the newspaper dispenser behind them. "You made the local news here too."

The headline of the *Philadelphia Inquirer* read: CANADIAN DOC USES PHILADELPHIA DRUG TO BEAT SUPERBUG. Kilburn sighed. News of MRGAS and Oraloxin dominated the front page of every newspaper he'd seen people reading on the flight. And Ellen Horton's role was no longer anonymous. The same black-and-white photo—her blank stare might have been pulled from a driver's license or passport— ran beside most of the articles. Though she was unavailable for comment and SeptoMed had not given a press release, the media had already begun the process of deifying Horton. Nobel Prize speculation was rampant for the "young genius." Kilburn's feelings were mixed. He knew it was only a matter of time before someone in the press would try to topple their new idol, and he doubted Ellen would cope well with the media scrutiny.

Kilburn dug in his pocket for his phone. He stepped away from the taxi stand and dialed Horton's direct line at work and then her home, only to hear the same stiff voicemail greeting: "You have reached the office of Dr. Ellen Horton. I'm unavailable to take your call. Please leave me a message and I will get back to you as soon as possible."

Frustrated, Kilburn turned his attention to Lopez and Cohen, who stood chatting in the queue. Kilburn recognized their growing comfort with one another. During the flight, he noticed how warm and relaxed Lopez had become with the detective, frequently touching his hand or elbow and laughing freely in his company. Cohen was less demonstrative, but his attention never left the petite epidemiologist.

Kilburn realized they made a good match. Cohen's quiet pensiveness perfectly complemented Lopez's feisty resolve. But watching their intimacy bloom only heightened Kilburn's awareness of his loneliness. An image of Michelle floated to mind. She had hardly been out of his thoughts since Louise told him she'd called. The message renewed his hope that she might be missing him, as much as he was her.

Cohen interrupted Kilburn's daydreaming with a wave. A young muscular cab driver with a buzz cut was loading their bags into the trunk of his cab. Kilburn climbed into the backseat beside Lopez, relieved to enter the cab's air-conditioned interior.

The car pulled away from the terminal. "Some hot today, huh?" the driver grunted.

"When is this heat going to let up?" Kilburn asked the cabbie.

"Dunno. Let's find out." The driver reached for his radio and turned up the volume. "Weather report ought to come on after the news."

Kilburn picked up on the female news anchor's story in mid-sentence: "—so officials are not releasing the cause of death at this hour. No one at SeptoMed Pharmaceuticals could be reached for comment. We'll have more on this story as it develops. In other news today, transit officials—"

Eyes wide, Lopez glanced from Cohen to Kilburn. "What death?"

Cohen shook his head. Kilburn leaned forward in his seat and tapped the driver on the shoulder. "Do you have any idea what that story was about?" he asked anxiously. "Whose death?"

"Dunno, but I can find out." The driver shrugged. He pressed another button. Kilburn fidgeted impatiently through the radio ad for a local car dealership and then another promising a cure for baldness, before the deep male anchor's voice finally announced it was time for "headline news."

"In breaking news," the anchor said somberly, "Philadelphia police have confirmed they've found the body of Dr. Ellen Horton in her Mt. Airy home this morning. The police are refusing to release the cause of death. Few other details are known at this hour." His tone lightened, becoming more informational. "The forty-year-old scientist is credited with developing Oraloxin, the antibiotic used during the past few days as the only treatment for MRGAS. The new superbug has caused deadly outbreaks in San Francisco, L.A., and Seattle. The treatment was—"

"Turn it back to the weather please," Kilburn said quietly, slumping back in his seat.

Lopez put a hand on his shoulder. "Oh, Graham, I'm so sorry."

Kilburn swallowed. "She was reaching out to me," he said, feeling the guilt swell. "Goddamn it! I should have told her I was coming."

"Graham," Cohen said gently, "we don't even know how she died."

"You're the detective," Kilburn spat. "What does a report like that usually mean?"

"It usually means suicide," Cohen answered evenly. He leaned forward and looked past Lopez straight into Kilburn's eyes. "But there's nothing usual about any of this."

Kilburn nodded, sorry for having snapped at Cohen. "How do we find out more, Seth?"

"I have a friend with Philadelphia PD," Cohen said. "I was planning to see him anyway. He might know something."

Kilburn turned and gazed out the window, barely noticing that the freeway had given way to the high-rises and congestion of downtown Philadelphia. His stomach churned. His temples pounded. *Ellen.* Even though their contact had lapsed, he knew their friendship had been renewed in the past week.

Their final conversation repeated in his head like a looping tape. Her labile mood and her air of desperation were painfully fresh. He flinched at the memory of how he told Ellen he was too busy to fly to Philadelphia. He had let down his friend when she needed him most. It was Toronto all over again, except this time someone died.

They stopped by their hotel only long enough to drop off their bags, after which they headed west over the Schuylkill River and past the University of Pennsylvania. The driver dropped them off in front of the Philadelphia Police Department's Sixteenth District building.

They followed the signs up the stairs to the office called "Major Crimes Unit—Homicide." Cohen gave his name to the wrinkled redhead at reception. She pointed indifferently down the hallway. "Down the corridor," she muttered. "Door at the end."

They had made it only halfway when the door opened and

a hulking figure burst out. Lieutenant Ed Franklin had short graying hair, a wide nose, and huge eyes. At least six-three and 250 pounds, the African American had a booming voice and laugh that matched his huge frame. "Yo, Kosher Cop! Well, I'll be damned."

Franklin walked up and gripped Cohen in a bear hug.

Cohen grinned. "How are you doing, Ed?" he said warmly.

"Great. Great." Franklin said. "Except, I'm a grandpa now, man. Can you believe it, Seth? I'm the same age as that no-good partner of yours and I got a grandson not much younger than his daughter!"

"Congratulations, Ed." Cohen patted the lieutenant on the shoulder. "Speaking of, Rome sends his best."

"Yeah?" Franklin chuckled. "Give him a message for me. Tell him the best part of being in Philly is no Roman Leetch."

Cohen laughed. "Ed, let me introduce my friends, Dr. Lina Lopez and Dr. Graham Kilburn. Lina's with the CDC in Seattle. Graham's an infectious-diseases specialist from Vancouver, Canada."

"A pleasure," Franklin said, pumping first Lopez's hand and then Kilburn's. He turned to Cohen with a toothy grin. "Why would doctors hang around with you?"

"We're working together on a case."

"A case?" Franklin grimaced. "Come on, we better go to my office."

They walked into his modest but warmly decorated office, the walls of which were covered by family photos and shots of the lieutenant with various civic leaders. Franklin pulled up three metal chairs to his desk and then sat down in the worn leather chair across from them.

Franklin held out his large pale palms. "Seth, how did you wind up working on a case with Doctors Without Borders here?"

"It's a little complicated, Ed," Cohen sighed.

"It's always complicated with you, KC," he whistled. "But I just *love* a good story." He folded his hands behind his head and leaned back in his seat.

Cohen summarized how his double-homicide investigation led him to the MRGAS outbreaks in Vancouver and Seattle, and Lopez and Kilburn contributed the occasional clinical clarification. Cohen told Franklin about Tyler/Forbes and how he had been sighted in Philadelphia.

"Jesus H. Christ! Thirty years in Homicide and I thought I'd seen everything." Franklin paused. "SeptoMed, huh? They've been all over the news the last twenty-four hours. Even before that scientist's suicide."

Kilburn felt another stab. "It was suicide, then?" he asked.

"Off the record, Doctor, I spoke to the CSI boys out of Thirteenth Division not half an hour ago." Franklin looked to Cohen. "If this was a homicide, it would have been ours. That's our turf."

Lopez nodded. "What happened, Ed?"

"Carbon monoxide. They found her in the garage in the front seat of her car."

Cohen rested a thumb and index finger on his chin "No doubts?"

Franklin frowned. "It looks straightforward. Doors locked inside the car and garage. And she left a note."

Kilburn's chest fluttered. "What did it say?"

Franklin stonewalled. "Haven't seen it."

Cohen pushed. "Ed, can we see it?"

Franklin flopped forward in his chair. His palms landed on the desktop with a slap. "Seth, we're on shaky ground here. Technically, it's still an active investigation."

"It could be relevant to our investigation," Cohen said flatly.

Franklin rubbed his eyes and shook his head. "Wait here." He sprang out of the chair with surprising agility and bounded out the door.

Lopez looked over to Kilburn. "You okay, Graham?" she asked softly.

He mustered a smile for her and nodded. *All I had to do was to tell her I was coming.*

Franklin returned five minutes later holding a single sheet in his hand. He sat back down in his chair and then wordlessly slid the page, a fax marking in its top corner, across the desk.

Cohen held it up, and Kilburn and Lopez read over his shoulders. Cohen cocked his head at Kilburn. "Who's Neil?"

"No idea. Ellen never mentioned him." Kilburn paused. "Come to think of it, when I spoke to her last week she was adamant that she was single."

"Maybe that was part of the problem," Lopez said. "Sounds like she regretted letting Neil go."

"I guess," Kilburn mumbled, troubled. It didn't sound anything like the Ellen he remembered.

53

Philadelphia, Pennsylvania

They separated outside the elevator on the fourteenth floor of the Hilton Hotel. Lopez headed for her room while Kilburn and Cohen turned in the opposite direction for the room they were sharing. Inside the double-queen-bed room, Cohen struggled to maintain a light conversation with the dejected Canadian physician. His heart went out to him. He had seen similar reactions in friends and family of other suicide victims; most faced a double blow, coping with the loss and the inevitable guilt of not having done more sooner.

Cohen was anxious to move the investigation forward. If Forbes was still in Philadelphia, he wasn't likely to stay. As soon as Kilburn headed for the shower, Cohen picked up the phone and dialed Roman Leetch's number.

"Homicide. Leetch." his partner barked predictably.

"Rome, it's Seth," he said. "I'm calling from Philadelphia."

"Imagine that! KC is in the City of Brotherly Love. Too bad you don't have a brother or a love." Leetch laughed. "But speaking of love, are you still with that lady doctor?"

Cohen ignored the question. "Do you have anything new on Forbes's whereabouts?"

"Nah," Leetch grumbled. "The son of a bitch isn't using his credit card. No charges since the Airport Intercon."

"I wonder if he's even still using Forbes's identity," Cohen thought aloud. "Any more background info on Wayne Forbes?"

"Oh, yeah." Leetch whistled. "Old Wayne is . . . or was . . . a real piece a work. Stock fraud was his bag. He's been banned for eternity plus a year from ever trading on the Chicago Stock Exchange and most others in the Midwest."

"Any convictions?" Cohen asked.

"Coincidentally, he was being investigated by the Feds two years ago February when he up and disappeared," Leetch said. "Funny though, Wayne fled so quickly he forgot to take his money with him. Left a couple of flush bank accounts behind."

Cohen jotted brief notes on the hotel pad by the phone as his partner spoke. "Sounds like a repeat of the Dennis Tyler story?"

"Carbon copy," Leetch grunted. "Both guys on the wrong side of the law. One day they each vanish, and then show up years later as our mystery dealer and Tara's sweetie pie."

Cohen understood Leetch's point. "Tyler and Forbes sound like white-collar criminals. Not the types to distribute tainted drugs and shoot a couple of pushers in cold blood."

"But if *our* guy knocked off the real Tyler and Forbes," Leetch said, "He probably wouldn't have huge moral issues with stealing his victims' identities."

"Yeah, why not?" Cohen said. "Sounds like no one else is looking for Tyler and Forbes."

"Hey," Leetch chuckled. "Maybe he'll do us a favor and assume Frigerator's or Mitchum's identity next. That would get him whacked in a heartbeat. Save us some trouble."

Cohen snapped his fingers, as an idea hit. "Rome, maybe we should be looking at a list of other 'disappearances' that fit the Tyler/Forbes profile. If this is his M.O., he must have helped other sketchy characters vanish. Their IDs would be up for grabs too. He might use one of their names next."

"A bit of a long shot," Leetch grumbled. "But, crap, what else have I got to do with my time?"

"And, Rome," Cohen said, ignoring the complaint, "at some point someone must have filed a missing persons report on Tyler or Forbes. If you speak to the cops involved in those investigations, we might find something useful."

"Already on it, chief," Leetch said.

"Thanks, Rome," Cohen said. "Hey, how are Sophie's birthday party plans coming?"

"Terrific." Leetch chuckled. "I think there was less fuss made over Oprah's fiftieth. And I'm sure *that* party wound up cheaper than what Sophie's is gonna cost." He paused. "But don't tell Gina I said so."

"We'll see." Cohen chuckled. "Give them both a hug for me."

By the time he hung up, Kilburn had emerged from the bathroom and Cohen, still feeling sticky from the humidity, headed in to take his turn. When he came out after his shower, Kilburn stood waiting for him by the door. "Neil Ryland," he said flatly.

"That's *the* Neil from the note?" Cohen asked, running his hands through his wet hair.

Kilburn nodded. "I just called SeptoMed. They put me through to the only Neil in Ellen's lab. He's going to meet us in half an hour at the New York Deli."

"The New York Deli?" Cohen frowned. "Isn't that the place she mentions in her note?"

"Yeah." Kilburn turned away.

Cohen threw on a short-sleeved shirt and the lightest pair of pants he had brought with him. They met Lopez in the lobby. After getting directions from the concierge, they decided to face the heat and walk the half mile to the New York Deli. By the time they reached the place, Cohen's shirt was as damp as if he hadn't toweled off after showering. Even Lopez was perspiring, and her habit of wiping her brow with the back of her thumb was, in Cohen's opinion, graceful and slightly sensual. When she caught him watching, her warm smile eased his shyness. He smiled back.

Stepping into the air-conditioned deli, Cohen spotted Ryland even before he stood up because he was the only person sitting by himself in the two-thirds-empty restaurant. Fair-skinned and slightly overweight, Ryland had disheveled blond hair, a patchy five o'clock shadow, and bloodshot eyes.

Kilburn reached Ryland first, extending his hand. "I'm Graham Kilburn." He pointed to the other two. "Dr. Lina Lopez from the CDC, and Sergeant Seth Cohen with Portland Police."

"Neil." Ryland shook hands with each of them but his expression was set in stone.

"Thanks for meeting us," Kilburn said.

Ryland shrugged and sat back down at the table. "Coffees?" he asked, reaching for his own cup and taking a sip. "The stuff is drinkable here."

"I'm leaning toward iced tea today," Lopez said. Cohen watched her again dab her brow with a thumb.

Ryland nodded to the waitress who came over and took their orders. All of them passed on food. Lopez and Cohen ordered iced teas, but Kilburn opted for water.

"I'm very sorry about Ellen," Lopez said. "We heard you two were pretty close."

Ryland cleared his throat. "Yeah, we were." He looked as if he might add more, but stopped and took another sip of his coffee.

"I don't know if she told you, Neil," Kilburn said. "But Ellen and I were friends from med school."

Ryland smiled fleetingly. "You cut up "The King" together."

"That's right." Kilburn said, surprised. "When did you first meet Ellen?"

"I joined her lab at Temple University about six years ago," Ryland said.

"Are you a physician?" Lopez asked.

Ryland shook his head. "No. Ph.D. in microbiology. Been working in antibiotic development forever. But the minute I met El, I knew . . ." He sighed. "She just had it."

Cohen wasn't sure if he meant professionally or personally but he decided not to ask. Neither did Kilburn or Lopez.

"Neil, I mean these things are . . . er . . . always a surprise," Lopez said awkwardly. "But in Dr. Horton's case, are you—"

"No," Ryland cut her off. "I'm not surprised at all." His voice cracked. "She told me exactly what she planned to do."

Lopez frowned. "*She told you?*"

"A couple of days ago." Ryland looked away and nodded slightly. "Said she felt like warming up her car an extra hour or two in the garage. But then she said it was just a tasteless joke." He paused and added in a voice not much above a whisper, "I guess I just didn't want to believe things could have gotten that bad for her."

Kilburn leaned forward and gripped the table. "She sounded awful when I spoke to her two days ago. She told me everything was wrong at SeptoMed. What was she talking about?"

"Oraloxin," Ryland said softly.

"Oraloxin?" Lopez repeated disbelievingly. "Have you seen the news?"

"The press doesn't know about the lab chimps," Ryland grunted. "Yet."

"What lab chimps, Neil?" Lopez asked.

"A couple of months ago, one of the chimps we were testing with high-dose long-term Oraloxin developed bone marrow failure," Ryland said. "We weren't too concerned. He was one of hundreds. But then two weeks later a second one developed it too."

"So it was no coincidence," Kilburn said.

"And then, a couple weeks ago, there was a third."

Lopez's expression hardened. "What were you planning to do about it?" she asked.

Cohen reached over and touched her elbow. *Go easy, Lina,* his eyes said, and she nodded her understanding.

"Nothing, at first." Ryland rubbed his eyes roughly with his palms. "These monkeys were on massive doses for much longer than intended for humans." He hung his head and sighed. "We thought . . . we hoped . . . it was a dose-and time-related reaction."

"But you didn't report it?" Lopez asked, her voice less accusatory.

Ryland shook his head. "Just over a week ago, at this very table in fact, we talked about it. Vik . . . Viktor Leschuk, the other member of our team—"

"The one who drowned last week, right?" Cohen said.

"Yeah. At Struble Lake. Ellen was devastated. They were close. We all were." Ryland cleared his throat again. "Two days before it happened, he brought El and me here after the third chimp died. Vik wanted to go to the FDA and come clean about the monkeys. He begged us to do the right thing."

"Why didn't you?" Lopez asked evenly.

Ryland pointed to Kilburn without looking at him.

Kilburn's mouth fell open in surprise. *"Me?"*

"Ellen had just heard from you, Graham. That you were testing Oraloxin on the MRGAS samples. We decided—" He interrupted himself and sighed. "To be fair, it was mainly me persuading them. Anyway, we opted to wait for those results. In case Oraloxin offered some hope where the other antibiotics didn't."

"I had no idea," Kilburn said softly.

Ryland smiled sadly. "How could you know?" he said. "Maybe it's better for the world that we *didn't* do the right thing. But to be honest, if I could go back a week I would drive Vik and El to the FDA review panel myself."

Lopez stared hard at Ryland. "How much of a risk could the aplastic anemia be to the MRGAS patients being treated with Oraloxin now?"

"It's been tested in thousands of humans in clinical trials," Ryland said.

"No bone marrow issues?" Lopez asked.

"Well . . . not until a few days ago. And that's still unconfirmed." Ryland looked down again. "Ellen heard from a Spanish investigator about a patient on Oraloxin whose white blood cell count dropped."

Lopez's eyes widened. "How could you not report that?"

Ryland held out his hands helplessly. "By the time we heard, the CDC had already found out that Oraloxin worked in the lab. We couldn't have stopped its production if we tried." He shook his head. His voice grew more self-assured. "Sixty years after its release, chloramphenicol is still one of the most widely used antibiotics in the world. It has the exact same rare side effect. If it had to be approved today, the FDA would laugh chloramphenicol out of the hearings."

"That doesn't make it right," Lopez said with a slight edge.

"I'm not trying to justify what we did," Ryland sighed. "But it seems to me that treating MRGAS victims with Oraloxin is less risky than the alternative. Besides, I think the bone marrow reaction is reversible if caught in time. The clinicians are checking patients' blood counts daily, right?"

"I think so," Lopez said in a calmer tone.

Ryland rubbed his eyes again and then looked at Kilburn. "Looking back, I think that Spanish study was the final straw for Ellen. Once the bone marrow reaction began to happen in humans . . ." His voice faded and he looked on the verge of tears.

The waitress finally arrived bearing their drinks. After she left, Cohen asked, "Neil, does anyone else at SeptoMed know about the bone marrow problem?"

He nodded. "A few of the other researchers in the lab, I'm not sure who else. I do know that Ellen told the VP of R-and-D, Luc Martineau."

Kilburn's eyes narrowed at the mention of Martineau. "What was his reaction?"

"I wasn't there. Luc and I don't exactly see eye to eye," Ryland explained. "But according to El, Martineau supported our wait-and-see approach."

Cohen nodded. "But he never spoke to you about it?"

"Just to tell me what 'important work' we were all doing on Oraloxin," Ryland snorted. "Or some other line of crap."

Cohen raised an eyebrow.

"Luc Martineau only sees what is important to Luc Martineau," Ryland muttered.

Cohen nodded. "Neil, do you think he told anyone else at SeptoMed about the reaction?"

Ryland paused for a long sip of his coffee. "I bet he did. At least Harvey Abram—the CEO—but I could never prove it. And probably Lady Andrea Byington." Ryland shrugged. "Doesn't matter to me anymore who knows. I'm through with SeptoMed. And Oraloxin. I e-mailed my resignation this morning."

Ryland lapsed into a morose silence.

Cohen considered the next step. He had no authority to show Ryland the suicide note, but he didn't want to miss the window of opportunity. He reached into his front pocket and pulled out the photocopied page. He placed it, still folded, on the table in front of Ryland. "Neil, you haven't seen Ellen's note yet, have you?"

Ryland shook his head.

Cohen pointed to the paper. "It's addressed to you."

Ryland's face crumpled. He began to fight back tears.

"You don't have to do this right now," Cohen said.

Ryland reached forward and picked the note up off the table. He took a couple of slow, deep breaths. His face smoothed. He unfolded the page slowly. Reading Horton's suicide note, he cocked his head to the side and his face wrinkled again, but this time in confusion. He put the note down and looked up at the others. "I don't understand this. Ellen and I were never romantically involved. We've always been best friends. More like brother and sister. Maybe there was a time back when we first started . . . but it never amounted to anything."

Lopez pointed to the page. "So what's all this talk of a marriage proposal?"

"I don't have a clue. Could she have been confused by the carbon monoxide or something?"

"It was found on her kitchen table. She wrote it before she got in the car. Is it possible Ellen was trying to tell you something that she wanted to keep private?"

"That kind of cloak-and-dagger stuff is nothing like Ellen. No question that it's her handwriting, though," Ryland said, pointing to the note. "Hold on!" Suddenly he shot his hand out and grabbed the letter. " 'That day at the New York Deli, . . .' " he read aloud. " 'How you wanted to let the rest of the world know how you felt . . .' " He nodded. "I bet she was referring to the day Vik tried to convince us to go to the FDA." He glanced down at the page. " 'I was scared what might happen if people found out about us.' " He paused. "I think she's talking about Oraloxin and the aplastic anemia. But the rest . . ." Ryland dropped the note on the table. "Ellen is trying to tell me something here, but I don't know what."

Cohen picked up the letter and read another passage. " 'But I didn't need to be scared of the world. The risk was all inside.' " He stared at Ryland. "What 'risk' inside?"

Ryland shook his head.

"Could this be a warning to you?" Cohen asked.

"I don't know." Then the tears he had been holding back started to roll over the rims of his eyes. "These are El's very last words to me. And I don't have a clue what she meant."

54

Philadelphia, Pennsylvania

Frustrated with the havoc the humidity wreaked on her already curly hair, Lopez spent more than fifteen minutes trying to tame it before giving up and tying it back in a bun. Then she tried on each of her five tops with both pairs of evening shoes she'd packed, before settling on a pale green sleeveless shirt, black skirt, and black pumps.

Before leaving the room, she tried Nelson Amar's cell phone but got only his voicemail.

"Nelson, it's Lina. I need to talk to you about Oraloxin. Please call me when you get a chance." She hung up and headed out the door.

Fifteen minutes late and her stomach fluttering with schoolgirl butterflies, Lopez stepped into the lobby where Cohen sat patiently waiting in a white textured short-sleeve shirt and black pants.

The temperature had cooled to a bearable level of mugginess. In the dwindling light of dusk, they walked out onto Market Street and strolled the mile down to the little Italian restaurant which the hotel concierge promised served "the best fettuccine pescatore in Philadelphia." Once they were seated inside the quaint Caffé Quattro with two glasses of Chianti in front of them, Lopez remembered about shellfish. She flushed and brought a palm to her forehead. "I'm sorry, Seth. I feel like such an idiot!"

He flashed a confused smile. "Because?"

"I've been going on about my passion for shellfish for the last half hour," she said. "And it's not kosher, right?"

Cohen frowned. "What makes you think I'm kosher?"

"You know, that nickname Lieutenant Franklin calls you—Kosher Cop."

"I don't keep kosher." His eyes lit up with amusement. "I've been living with that name since my first week on the job. One of the geniuses I worked with made that leap of an assumption because I told him I didn't like ham-and-pineapple pizza."

"And that's why they call you KC?" She giggled out of nervous relief.

He nodded, joining in on the laughter. Lopez regarded Cohen. His navy shirt accentuated his dark handsome features. She realized she was relishing the time spent with him in the restaurant's romantic ambience; it was her first chance to unwind in weeks. Only her concern for Kilburn dampened the mood and furrowed her brow.

"I feel awful for Graham." She paused, but Cohen didn't comment. "He's taken Ellen Horton's death so hard. I mean, I know they were once good friends, but . . ." She looked away, not quite knowing the best way to finish the thought.

"From what I've seen, the people who have the last contacts with a suicide victim beat themselves up, regardless of their closeness." Cohen took a sip of his wine. "I have a friend on the force who works on the crisis-intervention team. There are a lot of bridges in Portland." He sighed. "My friend has lost one or two of the jumpers he was trying to talk down. He didn't even know them, but he tells me that every death still haunts him. He can't help but assume responsibility, as if the suicide was preventable if only he'd been better at his job."

Lopez nodded. "You think that's how Graham feels?"

"I don't think it matters to Graham that he hadn't seen Ellen in the last ten years. Or that she suffered from depression. I think he believes he missed an opportunity—*the* opportunity—to intervene."

"Neil Ryland too." Lopez exhaled heavily. "She out and out told him what she planned to do. That must be quite a cross to bear."

"For sure." Cohen picked up his wineglass but instead of bringing it to his lips, he pointed to Lopez with the rim of the glass. "Lina, not that any suicide makes a lot of sense, but this one mystifies me."

"Why?" Lopez reached over and touched the back of his hand. "One of Ellen's best friends and colleagues had just drowned. And the lab chimps—she could've faced criminal charges if it got out that she had hidden those findings. At the very least, she would have been disgraced in the scientific community. Especially after that human case in Spain."

"'Would have been,' maybe." Cohen put down his wineglass. "But now that her drug has emerged as the only treatment for MRGAS. . . ." He laid his other hand on top of hers. "You're the scientist. Isn't it fair to say that in light of the impact her had drug had made, she would have been forgiven for her past sins?"

Lopez hesitated. She enjoyed the touch of her hand between his. And she realized Cohen was right. "Yeah, I suppose she would have."

Shyly, he gave her hand a slight squeeze before letting it go. "I don't understand her suicide note, either," he said. "This is the twenty-first century. If Horton wanted to tell Ryland something in confidence, she could have phoned, faxed, e-mailed, whatever. Why did she need to leave some cryptic message in a suicide note that she knew others would read?"

"Seth, if she was thinking straight at all she wouldn't have committed suicide."

"I suppose," he said. His eyes were skeptical.

Their waiter arrived with the two steaming bowls of pasta. Lopez looked from the noodles topped with the sautéed scallops and shrimps to Cohen. She bit her lip and fought back a mischievous smile. "Are you sure you're not going to rot in Jewish Hell just for trying to be polite to me?"

He grinned. "Aside from my aunt and uncle's Friday night dinners—where they still try to set me up with every girl from their synagogue, regardless of age, size, or marital status—there is no such place as Jewish Hell."

Over their dinners, which they devoured with equal enthusiasm, their conversation drifted from work to their personal lives. They discussed their childhoods, discovering they were both only children. Then they talked about the impact of their parents' deaths. Feeling safe in his company, Lopez explained how she still hadn't overcome the loss of her father. "My ex-fiancé told me I would never find another man that could fill his shoes." She hurried to clarify. "He wasn't trying to be hurtful or anything. Keith knew that for me Papa had been my family, my world. And then when Papa died so suddenly without me ever having a chance to say goodbye . . ." She swallowed, resolved not show any tears.

Cohen nodded. "How long were you and Keith engaged?"

"Eight months, but we were together for five years," she said. "Keith's a nice guy but we were at different stages in our lives. I was in my late twenties and still wanted to tackle the world. Keith was pushing forty. He wanted the instant house, four kids, and two cats."

Cohen smiled understandingly. "You didn't?"

"I'm not a cat person." She forced a laugh. "But it was more than just that I wasn't ready. I don't think we were right for one another. There wasn't enough passion, you know?" Flushing, she glanced down at her empty plate. "In my heart I have no doubt our breakup was the right thing for both of us. But in the odd moments when I'm a bit lonely, I still wonder."

Cohen nodded. "I got married when I was twenty-one. A

nice Jewish girl. She would've preferred someone with better financial prospects. We outgrew each other in a matter of months, but we lasted three years together. If she hadn't left me, I probably would have left her. But there are times to this day when I still wonder if I couldn't have done things differently to make the marriage work."

She smiled, resisting the temptation to voice how sweet she found him. Instead, she pushed her chair back from the table. "I'm stuffed!"

"Me too," he said. "Maybe we could walk off some of that fettuccine?" he exaggerated the Italian pronunciation.

"To do that, we might have to walk to Pittsburgh," she laughed.

When the bill came, Lopez reached for it but Cohen snatched it off the table. "Please," he said. "You can get breakfast."

She folded her arms across her chest. "Sergeant Cohen, that's a bit presumptuous."

"That's not what I meant," he stammered.

Lopez had never seen him redden. She found his bashfulness endearing. "I'm kidding." She reached over and gently caressed his hand. "Hurry up and pay, big spender." She winked. "It's a long walk to get to Pittsburgh by morning."

Outside on Market Street, the combination of the Chianti and Cohen's proximity emboldened Lopez. She reached over and took his hand in hers. They walked the rest of the way back to the hotel, hand in hand, chatting on subjects ranging from their favorite books to the places they most wanted to see in the world, and found out that Machu Picchu topped both of their lists.

When they reached the hotel's front door, Lopez let go of Cohen's hand. They walked together to the elevator, riding up to the fourteenth floor in silence. Cohen escorted her down the hallway to her room.

Standing outside, Lopez was overcome with fresh butterflies and a sudden shyness. "There's this, um, great fridge in my room that is loaded with free beer and wine," she said.

Cohen smiled. "I could handle a free beer."

Lopez slid her keycard into the slot and opened the door. Once inside, she turned to close the door and stepped right into him. He wrapped his arms around her, pulling her to him. Tenderly, his lips found hers.

Kissing him back, she tasted the flavor of his breath mint. She tightened her arms around him and pushed her lips harder against his. When she slipped her tongue between his lips, his tentativeness gave way to urgency. Their tongues met and his fingers dug into her back.

Flushed with excitement, she began to pull him backward toward the bed. She stopped when her foot touched the bedspread.

Cohen's eyes bore into hers. "Lina, maybe . . ."

"Maybe we should wait." She smiled and stood on her toes to kiss his forehead. "Right?"

"God, I don't want to wait." He looked down at the bed. "But this was our first date. I haven't felt like this in a long time. I don't want to mess it up."

She touched a finger to his warm lips. "Then we should wait." She smiled again. "It will make it that much better when it does happen."

55

Philadelphia, Pennsylvania

Kilburn sat at a small table in the hotel room, picking list-lessly at the spinach salad he'd ordered from room service. He reached for the cold beer and drained the last of the bottle, before giving up on the salad and wandering over to the bed.

Flopping down, he turned on the TV and flipped through the channels in search of a distraction. He stopped when the same black-and-white picture of Ellen Horton used in the newspaper filled the screen. He listened to the reporter for a minute before clicking off the TV. *Damn it, Ellen!* he thought. She had just invented the cure to the modern-day plague, why would she kill herself? Disheartened, he tossed the remote control on the floor.

Death. He'd seen too much of it over the past weeks—Thomas Mallek, Parminder Singh, and, now, Ellen. All linked by MRGAS. And Kilburn had played an inadvertent role in all of them. Another wave of guilt swept over him.

The past weeks had reinforced the cliché that life came with no guarantees and few second chances. He wondered how many regrets Mallek, Singh, and Horton had taken to their graves. Then he thought of his biggest regret. Impulsively, he reached for the phone and dialed Michelle's number.

"Hello?" she answered on the third ring in her naturally scratchy voice.

"Hi," he said.

"Graham?" Michelle asked, sounding surprised.

"Yeah," he said. "Did I catch you at a bad time?"

"Not really," she said impassively. "My caller ID says you're calling from Pennsylvania."

"I'm in Philadelphia," Kilburn said, enjoying the sound of her voice.

"Why?" she said. "Something to do with MRGAS and Oraloxin?"

"How did you know?"

"There was a story on the news tonight," she said, warmth creeping into her voice. "They said you were responsible for finding the only effective antibiotic. Is that true?"

He smiled to himself, unexpectedly grateful that his name had come to light. "That's a bit of a stretch, but I was involved," he said. "I don't know if I ever mentioned it to you, but I went to med school with Ellen Horton, the woman who created Oraloxin."

"The one who committed suicide?" Michelle asked in surprise.

"Yes," he said quietly.

"I thought the name sounded familiar," she murmured. "She was a friend of yours, eh?"

"In med school."

"I'm sorry, Graham," she said tenderly. "Do you know . . . why?"

"Not really." They shared a brief silence. Kilburn cleared his throat. "Sorry, Michelle. I didn't call you just to bring you down."

"Why did you call, Graham?" she asked.

"I was returning your call," he said. "You left a message with Louise?"

"Yeah," she said. "That can wait. I just had a question about . . . um . . . our joint account."

"Oh," he said, fighting to keep the disappointment from his tone. "How are you, Michelle?"

"I'm okay," she said neutrally. "You know, work's crazy now."

"Good crazy?" he asked.

"Yeah," she said. "A dream project. We got the contract to renovate the ninety-year-old cathedral off Seymour Street. Of course, once I saw what was behind those walls, the dream turned into a bit of a nightmare."

"You'll do wonders with it, no doubt." Kilburn smiled, remembering how intently Michelle used to pore over blueprints and plans, her eyes burning with her passion for design.

"I have a few ideas," she said modestly. "But my boss is worried I might turn it into a mosque or a synagogue."

Kilburn chuckled. "Wouldn't put it past you."

"How are Matt and Shayna doing?" Michelle asked, her voice lifting with warmth.

"They're good," he said. "Matt was asking about you the other day. Told me you were the reason why I'm not willing to sell the house."

She was a silent for a moment. "What did you tell him?" she asked cautiously.

"To finish his cornflakes." Kilburn felt suddenly less certain of himself.

"And Kyra?" Michelle asked.

"She's sober," he said, not wanting to dwell on the subject. "You know, day by day and all that."

"I feel badly for what I said about her, Graham," Michelle said softly. "I had no right to put Kyra in the middle of our problems. It wasn't fair to her . . . or you."

"Not so, Michelle. After all, Kyra—or at least the lack of

boundaries I set with her—was a huge burden on you and us," Kilburn said. "But she's doing better now. And if and when that changes, I realize now that I have to draw the line with her. Stop enabling her, as they say."

"Hmmm," Michelle said noncommittally.

"Michelle, I'm not staying much longer in Philadelphia. And when I come home"—he paused hoping for a response but got none—"I thought maybe you and I could try . . . to see if . . . maybe we could work through some things."

Her ensuing silence felt worse to him than any physical pain. "Graham, I've worked so hard to stop looking back and reliving the mistakes." She cleared her throat. "I'm thirty-two years old now. I have to move on with my life."

"You're right, Michelle," he said, stinging from her words. "I shouldn't have called you out of the blue and sprung this on you—"

"Graham, I didn't mean you. Honestly," she said gently. "I meant mistakes like blaming you for having an alcoholic sister. Like getting too comfortable with my lifestyle and not taking the next step. This is the first time in my adult life I've been on my own. I miss you, but. . . ."

"But maybe it's best, huh?" he said resignedly.

"I don't know," she said. "Maybe it's necessary."

"Okay, Michelle, it was nice hearing your voice. You take care."

"Graham," she said evenly, "when you get home, why don't you call me? We could go for dinner."

"Dinner?" he said feeling a flicker of optimism.

"Let's start with a nice dinner," she said, "then see what happens."

Feeling drained but cautiously hopeful, Kilburn said good-bye to Michelle and hung up the phone. He undressed and crawled under the covers in his underwear. He tried to sleep, but he tossed and turned, unable to shut off the stream of thoughts.

After a while, having given up on sleep, he picked up the

phone and dialed his sister's number, aware that with the three-hour time difference it was close to nine P.M. in Vancouver. His nephew answered. "Hi, Uncle Graham!"

"Hey buddy, where's mom?"

"She's out."

"Where, Matt?" Kilburn asked casually, trying to mask his concern.

"One of those meetings she always goes to. Yak, yak, yak . . ."

Kilburn knew his nephew meant an AA meeting. "So, you taking care of the family while I'm gone?" he asked.

"As if. Have you forgotten I'm only ten?"

"That's right! So much for the motorbike I was planning to bring home for you," Kilburn joked and his nephew groaned. "Your mom's okay, though?"

"I guess. She's not getting sick in the morning like before," he said, showing a glimmer of insight.

"And how's Shayna?"

"Oh, she's still all bent out of shape about that Robby Markum twerp." Then he added in disgust: "Girls!"

Kilburn chuckled. "Take it from me, they don't get any easier to understand. Hey, Matt, I'll be back in a few days. Let's get out to the rink and shoot the puck around."

"Okay," he said happily. "But I don't think you can keep up with me anymore. You're getting a bit long in the tooth, Uncle Graham."

"I have no idea where you pick up these expressions, but Matt," he warned, "I'm going to wipe the ice with you when I get home."

Kilburn remained smiling when he got off the phone. He was pleased to hear that Kyra must have stayed sober. He lay down on the bed again. Though tired, sleep wouldn't come. In his mind, he walked himself through the events from the moment he first heard of the multiresistant group-A strep growing in Thomas Mallek's sputum. He took little pride in having put MRGAS and Oraloxin together. If not him, some other clinician was bound to have made the same connection. And that realization troubled him.

He was still mentally wrestling with the chronology when he heard the click of the electronic lock. The door opened quietly. Hearing the soft padding of steps in the dark room, he reached over and turned on the lamp.

Seth Cohen stood beside his bed dressed in the same navy shirt and pants as when he left but his hair looked a little more tussled. "Sorry, Graham. Hope I didn't wake you."

Kilburn noticed that the bedside alarm clock read 2:14 A.M. "No. You were quiet. I was still awake."

"Are you doing okay?" Cohen asked.

"I'm better, thanks," Kilburn said.

"Good. Well, we better get some sleep." Cohen turned toward the bathroom.

"Seth?" Kilburn said, stopping the detective in his tracks. "Yes?"

"I've been thinking about my role in all this."

"*Your* role?" Cohen turned back to face him.

"Being the clinician to connect the bug and the antidote," Kilburn said. "Don't you find it a big coincidence that I happened to see two of the first cases of MRGAS *and* work at the same hospital running a major clinical trial of the one study drug that could treat it?"

Cohen folded his arms across his chest. "Yes, I do."

"Seems to me, someone went to a lot of trouble to spread the bug in a few specific cities," Kilburn said. "Vancouver, Seattle, Portland, and San Francisco."

Cohen's eyes narrowed. "All four cities in the Oraloxin trial. It's hard to overlook that kind of coincidence."

Kilburn stared at Cohen, chilled by his own logic. "Do you think someone wanted me or some other clinician to make the connection between MRGAS and Oraloxin?"

"Someone with a vested interest in Oraloxin?"

"Yes," Kilburn said, his heart pounding in his ears. "You heard Neil Ryland. The FDA would never approve this drug if they knew about the bone marrow complication, unless—"

"It was the only cure available for a killer disease."

"Exactly."

"I hear you," Cohen said quietly. "We need to know more about SeptoMed and the people there."

"Seth, it's a huge company."

Cohen shook his head. "The people involved had to be close to the development of this drug. You heard Ryland. Who else would have known about the bone marrow problem?"

"I suppose." Kilburn frowned. "It's odd, though. When I first tried to use the drug clinically, the VP in charge, Luc Martineau, did all he could to block my access to it."

"Maybe he's not involved." Cohen shrugged. "Or maybe he was trying not to look too eager."

"Yeah. Martineau only tried to stop me from using Oraloxin on a dying patient." Kilburn frowned, suspicions rising again. "But he had no problem with us testing it in the lab."

56

Brandywine Valley, Pennsylvania

Twenty-six miles west of Philadelphia, Forbes applied the brakes to the stolen Ford Excursion as the road wound tightly in front of him.

He'd grown so accustomed to Wayne Forbes's name that, as he drove the two-lane road, he practiced aloud introducing himself as "Nick Snider," the name that now appeared below his picture on the Delaware driver's license he carried. He wanted to ensure he didn't trip over the name when the time came to use it.

Snider's day had been a blur of activity. Rising just after four A.M., he hadn't stopped from the moment he'd shaved his head over the motel sink. Locating an appropriately sized SUV had consumed much of his morning, but he was pleased to have found the silver, nineteen-foot, 8,500-pound beast. He had to drive the car sixty miles from Allentown to get to the stretch of road that interested him. Once there, he stayed and practiced driving the same route over and over until he was convinced he could manage it virtually blind-folded. Timing would be everything.

Then he set out to find his mark. That part was easy.

Following the now familiar twisting road along the rolling hills, he considered how complex this assignment had become. So little time, so many variables. Still, Snider knew that if he executed this contract flawlessly, he would reach a new professional zenith. He knew pride now motivated him more than the substantial money.

He pushed his foot down, accelerating the truck into a gentle curve. On the other side of the turn, he again recognized the taillights of the pale blue Volvo S40 sedan in the waning dusk. With mounting annoyance, he realized he might run out of natural light. Glancing in his rearview mirror, Snider was relieved there were no cars behind him this time. He couldn't afford witnesses. Each of the previous three attempts had to be aborted because of some interloping vehicle. He knew this would be his final opportunity of the night.

He sped up and gained on the car, whose predictable speed made the timing slightly less critical. He headed into the last series of the turns, staying ten yards behind the Volvo.

His preselected spot was within 600 yards.

Confirming there were still no cars visible in his mirror, he accelerated. He pulled into the oncoming lane and brought the car even with the blue Volvo, as the next curve neared.

Snider slowed the SUV so the two cars were side by side for three or four seconds. Then, closing within a hundred feet of his chosen site, he veered to his right. He barely felt a jolt as the Excursion's passenger door slammed into the Volvo's driver's side.

For a few moments, the Volvo staved off the rightward momentum. Snider leaned a little harder into the steering wheel. The grating sound of metal and the screech of tires melded into an oddly harmonious sound.

Then the SUV rocked slightly, freed of its metallic kiss.

Snider glanced out the window and watched the Volvo slam through the low retaining wall and careen over the embankment.

Deeply satisfied, he hit the accelerator without so much as taking another glimpse in his rearview mirror.

Focus! There was so much more to do and time was running thin.

57

Philadelphia, Pennsylvania

Still half-asleep, Lopez stretched lazily in bed. The phone's third ring brought her closer to consciousness. She grabbed for her cell phone. "Morning," she said groggily, hoping to hear Cohen's voice.

"Lina, it's Nelson," Amar said.

Lopez sat up in the bed. The clock read 6:43 A.M., meaning it wasn't even 4:00 A.M. in San Francisco. She wondered if her boss ever slept. "What's up, Nelson?"

"We have more problems in the Bay Area. The response to Oraloxin has been good here, but MRGAS continues to spread rapidly in the community." His gruff voice echoed slightly in her ear. "We're up to 194 confirmed cases, but probably there are hundreds more not yet diagnosed. The labs can't keep up with the throat and skin swabs from potential cases pouring in from offices and clinics."

A jolt of adrenaline cleared away the last of her lingering cobwebs. "And Seattle?" she said.

"Far as I know, there's little change. Oraloxin is effective, but MRGAS is still spreading, although not at the same rate as in the Bay Area. Same story in Vancouver. Too early to tell in Portland and L.A." He cleared his throat. "You left a message for me last night?"

"Nelson, there's a problem with Oraloxin," she said.

A moment of dead air. "What problem?" he asked guardedly.

She told him about their meeting with Neil Ryland and his disclosure regarding the bone marrow complication. "Everyone on Oraloxin will need daily blood testing," she said.

"So we'll do the blood tests," Amar grunted. "Stopping the drug is not an option."

In the silence that followed, Lopez sensed that Amar had more news. "What is it Nelson?" she prompted.

"Lina, have you found out any more about that phony drug dealer?" he asked.

"Not yet," she said, wondering why he raised the subject he had previously avoided.

"I just heard something from our microbiology lab in Atlanta." His voice took on an uncharacteristically conspiratorial edge. "We're keeping this very hush-hush until we have confirmation."

"Nelson?"

"One of our molecular biologists has isolated the resistance genes in MRGAS. She believes the DNA has been artificially amplified." He cleared his throat. "Looks like your original hypothesis that MRGAS is man-made will pan out after all," he said grudgingly, but then his voice softened. "I'm glad you stuck with it . . . in spite of me."

Lopez swelled with quiet pride. "Thank you, Nelson."

"But we need to take this to the FBI and Homeland Security, Lina."

"I know," she said, focusing back on the issue. "But Nelson, something is going on in Philadelphia. Maybe even at SeptoMed. Our best chance of finding out what, is to approach

Forbes and the others as quietly as possible. We're getting co-operation from a lieutenant with Philadelphia Homicide. And we're meeting this morning with the SeptoMed execs."

"That's not your job, Lina," he said.

"I know." She took a slow breath. "Give us just a bit longer, Nelson. Once we find Forbes, and more importantly his employers, we'll call the big guns in."

"I don't like it, Lina." He sighed heavily. "Okay. It'll take a day or two for the CDC lab to confirm that MRGAS has been genetically tampered." His tone hardened. "The *moment* we have confirmation, we're taking it to the highest levels of law enforcement. Am I clear?"

"Crystal. Thanks." Hanging up, Lopez realized that Amar, as much as giving her leeway, was covering his own butt. He would look foolish for jumping the gun on results that were subsequently proven wrong—always a risk with early lab findings.

Feeling buzzed from Amar's grudging validation and her date with Seth, Lopez sprang out of bed. She showered, dressed, clipped back her hair, and headed for the lobby. Approaching the hotel restaurant, she noticed that Cohen and Kilburn were already seated at a table with coffees in front of them. When they saw her, Kilburn waved and Cohen smiled. As she approached, she felt unexpectedly awkward. She struggled to dismiss the thought that Cohen might have told Kilburn something of their evening together.

She sat down between them, returned Kilburn's friendly hello, and then glanced at Seth with a shy smile, relieved to recognize the glowing warmth in his eyes. Wanting to avoid fawning like a schoolgirl in front of Kilburn, she launched directly into a recap of her conversation with Amar.

Cohen frowned. "So we have less than forty-eight hours before the feds descend en masse?"

Kilburn put down his coffee. "Do you think they're the ones who *should* handle this?"

"If anyone official contacts SeptoMed, they'll know immediately that someone suspects them," said Cohen.

"Maybe that doesn't matter. Nevertheless, we're the only ones who can approach them without putting their guard up."

"Really?" Kilburn said. "What makes you think they won't be leery of us?"

Cohen pointed to Kilburn. "Because you're the champion of their wonder drug. You came to celebrate with your friend and then found out about her suicide. And Lina came to discuss the CDC's distribution plans for Oraloxin."

Lopez met Cohen's eyes. "And you, Seth?"

"That's a problem," Cohen said. "They can't know I'm a cop. And they certainly can't know that we know about Forbes." He broke into a slight grin. "One of you mind lending me a medical degree this morning? My masters in criminology won't quite cut it on this occasion."

Outside, waiting for a cab under cloudy skies, even Lopez was thankful the temperature had cooled. Their cab dropped them off at the entrance to SeptoMed's modern and massive glass edifice on Walnut Street. An armed security guard kept them waiting in the lobby before granting them clearance to take the elevator to the forty-sixth floor.

When the elevator doors opened, a tall handsome man in a stylish gray suit and open-collar blue shirt stood waiting. "Welcome, doctors," he said with a trace of a French accent and a hospitable smile. "I am Dr. Luc Martineau, the Vice President of Research and Development for SeptoMed."

They stepped into the plush bright reception area. Daylight flooded in through the floor-to-ceiling windows. Huge modern works of art lined the walls.

"Luc, I'm Lina Lopez with the CDC in Seattle." She pointed to her two companions. "This is Seth Cohen from Portland. And Graham Kilburn from Vancouver—"

"Ah, *très bien*, Graham." Martineau extended his hand and shook Kilburn's. "I owe you an apology for having been so obstructive earlier. I hope you understood my motives." His smile widened. "Besides, we are most grateful here at SeptoMed that you chose to disregard my instructions." He turned to the detective. "Dr. Cohen."

Cohen met Martineau's handshake. "Seth is fine," he said noncommittally.

Martineau pointed to a huge set of mahogany doors at the end of the reception area. "The others are waiting in the boardroom," he explained as he headed for the doors.

Following him into the room, Lopez was surprised to see that only three other people waited. The trio of execs sat in a row on the far side of the enormous conference table that could have readily seated fifty. As if on cue, they rose in unison to meet their guests. With easy charm, Martineau made the introductions.

Harvey Abram, SeptoMed's CEO, stood tall and imposing between the other two corporate members. On his left, a shorter fidgety man with a crew cut and round glasses was introduced as the company's chief in-house counsel, Fred Torrington. On his right, an attractive middle-aged woman in a gray jacket and skirt with a lacy black top smiled warmly. "I'm Andrea Byington," she said to the guests. "I'm here representing the board."

"Andrea's grandfather founded the company that eventually became SeptoMed," Martineau gushed.

Kilburn indicated for Lopez to sit between Cohen and himself, facing the SeptoMed executives. Meanwhile, Martineau walked around the table and sat in the vacant chair next to Byington.

Abram stroked his beard once between a thumb and forefinger and then showed his visitors a thin-lipped smile. "Thank you for coming, doctors." Abram turned to Kilburn. "And on behalf of the company, I would like to thank you, Dr. Kilburn. Your ingenuity has led to a crucial role for Oraloxin, one we're very proud of." The CEO paused. His smile faded. His voice deepened. "Only the tragic loss of two of our scientists has dampened the excitement felt throughout the building."

"Of course." Lopez nodded somberly. "And thank you for taking the time to meet us."

Abram shrugged as if there was never a question about the audience with him.

"Lina." Martineau held out his palms to signal a start to the discussion. "If the CDC is concerned about the supply of Oraloxin, I can assure you our manufacturing plant is operating 24/7. Fortunately, we were already planning for the drug's imminent FDA approval when MRGAS broke out."

"That is fortunate," Lopez said impassively. "So you foresee no problem getting supplies to the affected cities?"

Martineau shook his head. "Not unless the demand were to rise exponentially."

Byington ran a hand through her short gray hair. "Pardon me, Lina, but will it?"

Lopez studied the woman across from her. She suspected Byington carried far more influence than her deferential demeanor implied. "It depends where MRGAS is coming from."

Byington frowned. "You don't know?"

"Not with certainty, no." She shook her head. "But to answer your question, we're cautiously hopeful our containment measures have slowed the spread."

"That's reassuring," Abram said with a polite but detached smile.

"Who else was on the Oraloxin development team?" Lopez asked.

Martineau glanced to the ceiling. "The eighteenth-floor lab employs more than fifty staff, but Ellen Horton was the heart and soul of the drug." He sighed heavily. "Neil Ryland and Viktor Leschuk are—were—her two lieutenants."

"So only one of the senior Oraloxin scientists is still alive," Lopez said.

Martineau's gaze fell to the table. He nodded once.

"And we're told Ryland is resigning," Kilburn said.

"Neil reacted rashly." Martineau waved the idea away. "He was very close to Vik and Ellen. Once he overcomes the grief and shock, I'm sure he will reconsider."

Kilburn leaned forward in his seat. "Luc, do you think Ellen's suicide was related to the aplastic anemia seen in your lab monkeys?"

Abram's head spun over to look at Martineau. The VP

shifted in his seat. "Can you elaborate, Graham?" Martineau asked.

"The three chimps in your lab who died of bone marrow failure after exposure to Oraloxin," Kilburn said. "We understand Ellen was devastated by the complication."

"And you understand this from Neil Ryland?" Martineau's tone was chilly.

Kilburn nodded. Byington stared straight ahead, a polite smile still welded on her lips. Torrington scrawled notes on the pad in front of him. Abram's eyes never left Martineau. "Luc?" he asked evenly.

Martineau cleared his throat. "The three chimps—out of hundreds, I might add—who developed bone marrow failure were on massive doses of the drug. By the time we heard about the monkeys, the drug had already been tested in thousands of humans without seeing anything similar."

"Until Spain," Kilburn said.

Byington's smile vanished. Torrington's pen stopped. Abram's hand froze in midstroke of his beard. The brief silence that followed was flammable. "What happened in Spain?" the CEO finally asked in a slow deliberate voice.

"One Oraloxin patient's blood count plummeted in the Spanish trial last week," Kilburn said.

"I had no idea." Martineau paused momentarily. "And there is no doubt that Oraloxin was the direct cause?"

"We don't know the details," Kilburn said.

"Maybe we should find them out first," Martineau said emotionlessly, but his clouding eyes hinted at growing fury. "I don't know how to interpret your information. The Spanish investigators have not suspended their study. If they had, I would know it by now. Which leads to me to believe they're not very concerned about this supposed human case."

Torrington leaned closer to Abram, whispering in his ear as Martineau spoke.

Abram glanced uncertainly at Martineau before turning to Lopez. "I assure you, doctors, SeptoMed will launch an internal investigation immediately."

"Absolutely. We will get to the bottom of this, of course," Byington said, recovering her affable smile. "In the meantime, can you afford to have us suspend the supply of Oraloxin?"

"That's not an option," Lopez said, convinced that Byington already knew the answer.

"Luc," Cohen spoke up for the first time. "How many people at SeptoMed were aware of the bone marrow complication with Oraloxin?"

All eyes turned to Martineau. He pursed his lips. His gaze narrowed. Another electrified pause followed. *"Mais d'accord.* Several people working directly on the project on the eighteenth floor must know," he said slowly. "But I believe I was the only person informed, albeit informally, outside of the development team. I wholly trusted their judgment with respect to clinical significance, or lack thereof, of the primate findings."

"And did you share this information with anyone else in the company?" Cohen asked.

Face blank and eyes frigid, Martineau shook his head slightly.

"I think Dr. Martineau has provided a reasonable explanation for his actions hitherto," Torrington said in a voice stiff with legalese. "It is SeptoMed's written policy to report any and all adverse clinical outcomes. In this case, as Dr. Martineau clearly stated, he deferred to the researchers who felt there were no immediate clinical concerns."

Cohen nodded. "Is it fair to say that the lab findings might have influenced the FDA's review process for Oraloxin?"

"They still might, Dr. Cohen," Martineau said. "We have not yet been granted FDA approval for anything beyond the current compassionate-release status."

"Of course," Cohen said. "But now that Oraloxin is the only cure available for MRGAS, the FDA is unlikely to reject the drug."

"We didn't create this crisis," Byington said evenly.

Lopez held her breath, waiting for Cohen or Kilburn to comment, but neither did.

"Well, thank you for arranging this meeting," Abram said. The CEO rose to his feet. "I think you can appreciate how tight all our schedules are in the wake of recent events."

Lopez dug in her purse and pulled out business cards. She passed four of them across the table. "If you need to contact us while we're here, you can reach me via the cell number there."

Picking up a card, Byington asked, "How long do you plan to stay in Philadelphia?"

As long as it takes to find out which of you are involved. "At least another day or two," Lopez said.

After leaving the boardroom, they rode the elevator down to the lobby in silence. Cohen stood close enough to Lopez that their arms touched but neither made eye contact. Outside, the thin cloud cover intensified the rising humidity. Kilburn hailed a cab and all three climbed into the backseat. Lopez sat between the two men, but her leg touched only Cohen's to her right.

"What did you think?" Lopez asked as the cab pulled out into traffic.

"Martineau knows a lot more than he's telling," Kilburn said. "Not sure about the others. I found Abram and Byington very hard to read."

Looking out the window, Cohen nodded distractedly.

"Seth?" Lopez asked.

"I was just thinking about Ellen Horton," Cohen said.

"What about her?" Kilburn asked with a possessive edge.

Cohen turned from the window to look at the others, his face intense. "Do you remember what Ellen wrote in her note to Neil?" He recited from memory: " 'But I didn't need to be scared of the world. The risk was all inside.' " He thumbed back at the building now receding behind them. "Chances are the 'risk inside' was one or more of *them*."

58

Cohen felt on edge from the moment he left SeptoMed's boardroom. He had sat through too many interviews not to see through Martineau's disingenuousness. Byington was harder to gauge. Abram seemed genuinely surprised, but Cohen wasn't ready to dismiss the CEO just yet. Something niggled at the back of his mind, refusing to surface into consciousness. He sensed he was overlooking a vital link. He also struggled to ignore the pressure of Lopez's knee against his in the back of the cab. The slight contact conjured memories of their evening together. He hungered for more of her than just the touch of knees. He felt her eyes on him before she spoke.

"Seth, what's bothering you?" she asked.

Cohen turned to Lopez and Kilburn. "A freak boating accident kills an experienced fisherman. Followed by a suicide, the timing of which makes little more sense than the note left behind. Within one a week, two of the three at SeptoMed who knew the most about Oraloxin's secrets both die under circumstances that you'd have to say are, at the least, bizarre."

"Awfully convenient for Martineau or anyone else who didn't want Oraloxin's dirty laundry aired, isn't it?" Kilburn nodded. "Seth, a person could 'stage' a carbon monoxide poisoning to look like suicide that would even fool the experts, true?"

"It's been done before."

Lopez snapped her fingers. "A boating accident would be even easier to stage, right?"

"For a pro like Wayne Forbes? Oh, yes. The more I think about that suicide note, the more convinced I am it was written under duress."

Lopez laid a hand on his arm. "You mean at gunpoint, don't you?"

"Possibly," Cohen said, exquisitely aware of her touch. "But however it happened, I think it would explain why Ellen left such a cryptic warning for Neil."

Kilburn frowned. "What kind of warning is it when the recipient is oblivious to the message?"

"That's tougher to explain." Cohen's gaze drifted to the window.

The taxi pulled up in front of their hotel. Cohen leaned forward in his seat to pay the driver while the other two got out. Climbing out of the cab, he noticed that Lopez had waited for him alone. "Where's Graham?" he asked.

"He forgot his phone. He went ahead to the room to pick it up." She tilted her head and smiled tentatively. "How are you, Seth?"

"Good. In fact, great." He grinned back. "But I could've used a bit more sleep last night."

She folded her arms across her chest. "And who's fault is that?"

"I wouldn't have traded a minute of our time for twelve more hours sleep."

Her eyes shone. "Sergeant Cohen, you're very sweet."

Cohen's cell phone rang. As he brought it to his ear, the voice of Lieutenant Franklin boomed so loudly that Cohen pulled the phone a few inches away from his head.

"Ed, what's going on?"

"We just got a call from the state troopers in Brandywine Valley this morning," Franklin said matter-of-factly. "A car crashed over an embankment and toppled down a hill near Concordville."

"And?" Cohen asked, anticipating the worst.

"The car's only occupant happens to work at SeptoMed," Franklin said. "A scientist."

Cohen gripped the phone tighter. "Not Neil Ryland?"

"That's the guy," Franklin said. "The one Ellen Horton's note was addressed to."

Lopez eyed Cohen intently. "Neil Ryland was in a car crash," he said to her, cupping the phone. Then he removed his hand. "Ed, is Ryland dead?"

"No. Seems what they say about those Volvos is true." Franklin chuckled. "The car dropped about thirty feet and flipped twice on the way, but Ryland survived. His arm is broken in a couple of places, and he's pretty beaten up, but he's awake and talking. I just saw him."

"He's alive," Cohen mouthed to Lopez. "Ed, what did he tell you?"

"That someone in a silver SUV deliberately ran him off the side of the road," Franklin said.

"Did you show him the sketch of Wayne Forbes we faxed you?"

"Ryland never got a look at the driver of the SUV."

"Did he give you anything to go on?" Cohen asked.

"Not much. He's still in shock. But he wants to talk to you."

"To me?"

"Yup. Ryland mentioned you by name."

"Where is he?" Cohen asked.

"U. of Penn. emergency room." Franklin exhaled heavily. "You know, KC, short of a curse from an Egyptian tomb, luck can't be as bad as what's happened to SeptoMed's scientists over the past weeks."

"Ed, you better look very closely at Horton's suicide and Leschuk's boating accident."

"I'm ahead of you," Franklin said. "Struble Lake is a little beyond my jurisdiction, but I'm getting my boys to go over the Horton suicide scene again with a microscope." He cleared his throat. "Listen, Seth, I'm not wild about having you and the two doctors running a parallel investigation—"

"I'm not here to meddle," Cohen reassured. "I've only come to find the man who murdered two people on my turf. Maybe it's the same person as the one hunting down these scientists, maybe not. But we won't get in your way."

"Sure, KC, sure," Franklin grumbled. "And that smell that's suddenly wafting out of my phone is roses, huh?"

"We only need another day or so," Cohen said. "We have most of what we need already."

"You finish up by tomorrow, okay?" Franklin sighed. "This thing is turning ugly."

"Tomorrow," Seth promised.

"Seth, are you packing?" Franklin asked.

"With the new airline security measures, I had no time to get my gun here," Cohen said.

Franklin grunted. "Stop by my office later today, okay?"

By the time Cohen hung up, Kilburn walked toward them from the other side of the lobby. Nearing, his brow creased. "What's up?" he asked.

"Someone ran Neil Ryland's car off the road last night," Cohen said.

Kilburn's jaw fell open. "What? *Ryland*?! Did he make it?"

"Sounds like he's in stable condition," Cohen said.

Kilburn's face darkened. "Wayne Forbes?"

"Probably." Cohen summarized his conversation with Franklin.

"We better get to the hospital," Kilburn said.

Lopez glanced at her watch. "Oksana Leschuk is waiting for us now. We can visit Ryland on the way back."

They took another cab and headed north of the city to the tidy residential streets of Germantown. The driver dropped them off outside a modest white bungalow with tidy green shutters and a perfectly groomed lawn. Wearing a heavy black dress, Oksana Leschuk met them at the front door. She was a stocky woman with long black hair, blue eyes, and sharp features, but she struck Cohen as handsome. Although her eyes were dry and she smiled pleasantly, her grief was palpable, as was her apprehensiveness.

Oksana led them into a cozy living room filled with chunky furniture and knickknacks and smelling of candles. Aside from a few Russian Orthodox icons, the walls were covered with photos of their son and daughter at various stages of childhood and adolescence. Among these was a single black-and-white wedding photo depicting a young Oksana and Viktor.

They sat down on a bulky couch while Oksana rushed into the kitchen. Cohen heard the clink of china. Oksana emerged a few moments later with a large plate of home-baked cookies and a teapot on a tray with cups, spoons, a creamer, and sugar bowl. Without asking, she poured tea for each of them, and offered them cookies. "When we mourn, we bake," she said with a Ukrainian accent. "I have no room left in my cupboards. Please. Please."

Kilburn reached for a cookie. After everyone had at least one, she finally sat down in the chair next to Lopez at the end of the couch. "You have come a long way to talk about Viktor," Oksana said, folding her hands in her lap.

Lopez reached out and touched the back of Oksana's hand. "We're so sorry about your husband."

Oksana smiled tightly and nodded.

Lopez removed her hand. "Your husband was an experienced fisherman, wasn't he?"

"Ever since coming to America, Viktor loved to fish."

"Was he a good swimmer?" Lopez asked.

Oksana shook her head. "No, he could not swim."

Kilburn frowned. "And he wasn't wearing a life jacket that morning?"

"The police say he wasn't, "but Viktor always wore a life jacket."

"Didn't the police think it unusual that he wasn't wearing one then?" Kilburn asked.

"That morning when he went out was chilly, but when the sun rose it got very hot." Oksana stared at her hands. "They think Viktor was standing up to take off his coat and life jacket, when he tipped the boat . . ."

No one spoke for a moment. Finally, Cohen asked, "Did you ever fish with your husband?"

Oksana looked up at him with a sad smile. "I don't fish, but usually I kept Viktor company in the boat."

Cohen cocked his head. "Why weren't you with him that morning?"

"He asked me not to."

"Why?" Cohen said.

"Viktor worried a lot," she sighed. "Sometimes he didn't feel it was safe for me in the boat. That day, he was scared something might happen to us. To me."

Lopez sat up straighter. "Scared of what?"

"You must understand, Viktor came from the old communist system." Oksana sighed. "In the late seventies, when he graduated university, he was given a research job with a government lab in Kiev. Viktor thought he would be working on agricultural veterinary research. It was military research. He didn't want to do it but he had no choice."

"Are you talking about biological weaponry research?" Cohen asked.

Oksana closed her eyes and nodded once. "Life was not easy." Her eyes opened. "The KGB watched him at all times. He never felt safe. Even after we fled to America, Viktor never stopped looking for spies." She paused. "But the week before he died, Viktor became more afraid. He thought someone was following him."

"Did he say why?" Cohen asked.

Oksana swallowed. Her eyes fell to her hands. "Sep- toMed," she whispered.

"You mean the cover-up with the dead lab chimps?" Kilburn asked. "Was that the problem?"

Oksana looked up in wide-eyed surprise. "Viktor was tortured by those monkeys. He wanted to tell the FDA." She shook her head slowly. "But that is not why he was scared."

The other three shared a glance. "What then?" Kilburn asked.

Oksana pointed to the three of them. "That bacteria from Seattle and Vancouver."

"MRGAS?" Lopez asked, her jaw dropping.

"Yes," Oksana said. "When Viktor heard of it, he became very frightened."

Lopez grimaced. "Why would Viktor be frightened of MRGAS?"

Oksana fidgeted, appearing acutely anxious. "What is it, Oksana?" Cohen coaxed, leaning forward in his seat.

When Oksana looked up, her eyes were frantic. "Viktor worried that he had helped to create it."

59

Approaching the University of Pennsylvania emergency room in the late afternoon sunshine, Kilburn spotted the commotion at the front entrance from a block away. As they neared, he saw that two police officers, one male and the other female, stood by the doors blocking access to the flock of reporters and cameramen gathered in front of them.

Cohen pushed through the crowd and walked up to the two policemen. Lopez and Kilburn elbowed their way in after him. At the doors Cohen showed his police badge. The male cop viewed the badge and frowned. "Portland P.D.?"

Cohen pointed to the radio clipped to the man's belt. "Lieutenant Franklin from Homicide cleared us to visit the victim."

The officer reached for his radio. While he talked, Cohen turned to the female officer. "What's with all the media?"

"Something to do with SeptoMed," she said, pointing to the ER behind her. "The accident victim worked on that new drug that's been in the papers. Two of his colleagues died in the past week. Lots of rumors flying."

The other officer clipped his radio back on his belt. He nodded to Cohen. "You and your guests can go inside, Detective."

Kilburn followed Lopez and Cohen through the automatic sliding door into the bustling ER. He noticed how closely his two newfound friends moved together now without touching. Kilburn found their tentative intimacy endearing. And he thought of Michelle again.

They reached the ER trauma bays where yet another officer stood guard. The cop must have already heard from his colleagues at the door, because he waved them past, pointing to a glass-walled resuscitation room on his right. The three of them stepped into the room.

Neil Ryland's beaten body came as no surprise. With the head of the bed propped at a forty-five-degree angle, Ryland lay with his left arm wrapped in a bulky sling. His head was wrapped in so much gauze that his hair wasn't visible. On his face and neck were numerous nicks and lacerations, several of which were held together by fine blue suturing thread. His right eye was so bruised it was swollen shut. His left eye studied them groggily as they approached the bed. Kilburn assumed Ryland must have been pumped full of narcotic painkillers.

A nurse fiddled with the IV pole at the head of his bed. "And you are?" she asked warily.

"Investigators," Cohen said vaguely.

"More cops," the nurse sighed, rolled her eyes, and turned her attention back to the IV.

"Hello, Neil," Cohen said, stopping at one side of his bed while Lopez and Kilburn gathered on the other.

Ryland stared blankly back.

"Are you okay to talk?" Cohen asked.

Ryland winced, but said, "Fine. I wanted to see you."

Cohen nodded. "Lieutenant Franklin told us about your conversation. He said you didn't see the other driver."

"I didn't," Ryland said hoarsely. "Didn't even see the car until it was beside me."

"That must have been terrifying," Lopez said.

Ryland looked at her. "I didn't have time to be scared. It happened so fast." He turned to Cohen. "I think I know what Ellen was talking about in her note."

"You mean, she was warning you," Cohen prompted.

"Exactly!" Ryland nodded vigorously, bringing another flinch of pain. "I think someone killed Vik. And probably Ellen. She was trying to tell me that in her note."

"We think so too," Lopez said.

Kilburn held out hand. "Who?"

" 'The risk was all inside.' " Ryland quoted Horton's note in a slurred but urgent voice. "Had to be someone in SeptoMed! Someone well connected, too."

Cohen nodded. "Neil, we spoke to Oksana Leschuk this afternoon."

Ryland's left eye drifted over to Cohen. "She okay?"

"Yes," Cohen said. "But she told us her husband became very distressed after MRGAS surfaced."

"MRGAS?" Ryland croaked.

"Vik told his wife that you and he had engineered the bacteria."

"What?" Ryland gasped. "We didn't create MRGAS!"

"What was Oksana talking about?" Kilburn asked.

"Not MRGAS." Ryland's good eye shut slightly. "We did synthesize a multiresistant form of staph aureus. Oraloxin worked on it like a hot damn too."

"But Neil," Kilburn said, "it wouldn't have been difficult to transfer the resistance genes from your staph aureus to a group-A strep."

"True." Ryland sighed. "Are you suggesting MRGAS was created at SeptoMed?"

"Makes sense, doesn't it?" Cohen asked.

Ryland grimaced as he tried to reposition himself on the bed. "How so?"

Cohen shrugged. "SeptoMed has invested a fortune on a

drug with a fatal flaw that could come to light any day and with FDA approval looming—"

"And they also created a lethal bacteria that only their drug can treat," Ryland cut in.

"But the new bug isn't a threat outside the lab," Lopez said gravely. "Unless someone releases it."

"Oh my God!" Ryland said slowly. "It makes perfect twisted sense. The company spent hundreds of millions developing Oraloxin. If the chimp data got released it would all go out the window—*unless* the drug was made to look so essential that the FDA would be forced to overlook the side effect." He shook his head as much as his range of motion would allow. "SeptoMed's last two antibiotics were busts. I don't know if the company could survive a third hit."

"Could Ellen, Vik, and you have survived that, Neil?" Cohen asked quietly.

"A lot easier for us," Ryland snorted. "We even talked about such a failure shortly before Vik died. We could've gone back to the drawing board with a university or another drug company. I doubt SeptoMed would have that luxury."

Cohen agreed. "Who else at SeptoMed knew about the resistant bug you synthesized?"

"A couple of our senior lab techs. Two of our pharmacologists." His good eye narrowed and his voice lowered. "And Luc Martineau."

"You sure Martineau knew?" Kilburn asked.

"Yes," Ryland said. "He even visited the lab two or three times to view the culture plates himself. He was very curious about the whole process."

"Curious?" Lopez frowned. "What does Martineau know about microbiology?"

"A lot," Ryland said. "Before he became one of the suits, he was a moderately well respected researcher. He has a Ph.D. in molecular biology."

Kilburn felt his heart pound against his ribcage. "Would Martineau have enough know-how to be able to transfer the resistance genes from one type of bacteria to another?"

Ryland thought for a moment. "I think so," he said slowly. "And if not, he almost certainly would have known someone who could do it for him."

Kilburn shared a glance with Lopez and Cohen.

"I know this much," Ryland continued, his voice cracking. "Martineau could never have survived as VP of Research and Development if a third antibiotic failed."

60

Philadelphia, Pennsylvania

Outside the Sixteenth District police station, Cohen looked from Kilburn to Lopez. "I think Ed Franklin needs to know," Cohen said in a tone that sought their consent.

Lopez met his stare. "About the Martineau connection?"

Cohen nodded.

"Go tell him." Kilburn pointed at the entrance with a half smile. "We'll wait here."

Cohen followed the stairs up to Homicide. The same indifferent receptionist waved him down the hallway to Franklin's office. When he walked in, Franklin rose to his towering height, extended his hand, and grinned. "How's the rogue cop making out?"

Cohen met the handshake. "So-so."

"You seen the news, Seth?" Franklin asked, his voice somber. "The media is starting to piece it together with these dead and maimed scientists from SeptoMed. It's a feeding frenzy. I need answers in a hurry."

"Ed, we just visited Leschuk's widow and then Neil Ryland."

Franklin placed arms across his thick chest. "What did they have to say?"

Cohen recapped the interviews while Franklin listened without interruption. When he finished, Franklin sighed. "The stuff that was going on in that building . . . Sounds like we have enough to pick up this Luc Martineau."

Cohen nodded. "Ed, can I ask a favor?"

Franklin barked out a laugh. "What's the tally now, about sixty?"

"Can we be present when you question Martineau?" Cohen asked.

Franklin studied Cohen for several seconds. "Tell you what," he said. "You can. But your doctor friends have to watch through the mirror. Agreed?"

"Agreed."

Franklin pulled open his desk drawer and fished around inside. He held the gun and the holster out to Cohen. "It's hot out there. I want you to carry this. I'll take care of the paperwork."

He accepted the gun without comment and slid it out of the holster. He recognized the .357 magnum Smith & Wesson model, having trained at the academy with the same gun. He reholstered the gun, clipped it to his belt in the small of his back, and then covered it with his shirt.

Cohen thanked Franklin and returned to the waiting taxi. Climbing inside to join the two doctors, he realized that for the past few days he'd practically lived inside one Philadelphia cab or another. As he slid into the seat, he felt the holster digging into his back. It brought no sense of security.

The driver dropped them at their hotel. Walking up to the revolving door, a bellow caught Cohen's attention. "Christ, KC! Talk about milking Homicide's expense account."

Cohen turned to see Roman Leetch bounding toward him in a rumpled gray suit. His curly hair had frizzed even more in the city's humidity and his round face was pink with perspiration. He wiped at his brow. "I thought the pilot announced we landed in Philadelphia, not frigging Ethiopia."

Cohen grinned. "Wish I could say you get used to it after a few days." He turned to his two companions and introduced them to Leetch.

"Wow, I feel even less educated than usual. It's pretty intimidating when KC here is the dunce of the pack."

Lopez smiled at Leetch, before turning to Cohen. "He's exactly as you described."

"Oh, yeah?" Leetch snorted. "Wait till you hear my description of *him.*"

Inside the lobby, Lopez and Kilburn headed off to their rooms, explaining that they needed to check in with their respective offices.

"Time for the Portland taxpayers to buy me a beer!" Leetch threw an arm around Cohen's shoulder and led him to the lobby bar. "I'm thinking they'd want me to have something exotic and pricey, too. One of them Dutch beers."

As soon as they seated at a table in the bar, Cohen asked, "How was Sophie's birthday party?"

"Expensive. Excessive. Exhausting. Nothing you wouldn't expect." His lips parted in a proud smile. "She had a blast. Loved the pony rides. I got some pictures in my bag. You were missed—not by me, mind you, but by the ladies of the house."

Cohen smiled. "Did she like my present?"

Leetch nodded. "Beautiful dollhouse. Hope you don't mind if I take the month of June off to assemble the damn thing!"

"I'll help," Cohen said. "How's my dad?"

"Fine. I saw him the day before. Frankly, I don't think he misses you."

Cohen laughed. "No doubt."

Leetch clicked his tongue. "So that was *the* Dr. Lopez, huh?"

"She's okay," Cohen said evasively.

"More than okay, she's got real chutzpah, as you people

would say." Leetch winked. "Something's up with you two, huh?"

"We barely know each other."

"Yeah, sure, Seth." Leetch briefly eyed him with a disbelieving smile, but it soon faded. "KC, I haven't picked up a whiff on Forbes since the Airport Intercon. I think you might be right. He might have moved on."

"To a new identity, maybe," Cohen said, "though I'm pretty sure he's still in Philadelphia. Or at least he was last night."

"Oh?" Leetch took a long sip from his beer bottle. "What makes you so sure?"

Cohen filled Leetch in on the details of Ryland's car crash. Leetch didn't look surprised. "Yeah, I could easily see Forbes behind the wheel of that SUV. But Ryland survived, huh? See? Forbes is good, but he's far from perfect."

"He's made a few mistakes," Cohen said. "All the same, I wouldn't underestimate him."

"Maybe the pressure is getting to him. He left a trail in Portland and Philly, and now he lets his latest target get away." Leetch's bottle stopped halfway to his mouth. "Ryland might still be in danger, huh?"

"Maybe," Cohen said. "But the police have round-the-clock guards posted."

Thirty minutes later, Kilburn joined them in the bar. Lopez, stunning Cohen in a black summer dress, joined them five minutes after. They decided to move into the restaurant where, with Leetch leading by example, they ordered up a feast. They shared two bottles of wine and numerous laughs, primarily at Cohen's expense, as Leetch regaled the other two with stories of his partner's escapades.

Just before 11 P.M., they were exchanging good-nights by the elevators when Cohen's phone rang. "Seth, it's Ed," Lieutenant Franklin said in a subdued voice.

Cohen braced himself for news. "What's up?"

"Luc Martineau is missing."

61

Philadelphia, Pennsylvania

Lopez sat down on her bed. She had so thoroughly enjoyed the evening—the outstanding food, Leetch's hilarious stories, and the nearly constant contact of Cohen's hand or leg under the table—that she had forgotten about Oraloxin and MRGAS for the longest stretch of time in recent memory. Alone again in her room, however, the maliciousness of the disease and the people behind it came flooding back to her.

Standing up in her bare feet, she grabbed the television's remote control and flipped through the channels. With the news focused on the local events at SeptoMed, she could find no coverage of the disease's regional spread. She felt a pang of guilt for having spent the past days away from her post in the Pacific Northwest. She glanced at her watch and calculated that, with the three-hour time difference, it was just past 8 P.M. on the West Coast. She sat back down on the bed, reached for her phone, and dialed David Warmack's cell number.

Warmack sounded pleased to hear from her. She updated him on the Philadelphia developments, finishing with the suspicious disappearance of Luc Martineau. Warmack sighed. "I thought the one advantage to being as old as I am was that I had seen it all in epidemiology," he said. "But this . . . this is *unbelievable*."

"If it's any consolation, I think we're closing in on the index case," Lopez said. "David, what's the situation in Seattle?"

"Still more new cases," he sighed. "I'll give the psychopaths behind it credit for one thing, though. Their drug works. All of the city's 122 confirmed cases have responded to the treatment."

"Any complications seen with the drug?" Lopez asked.

"One patient—fortunately with a milder form of disease—had a drop in her white blood cell count. They've stopped the drug. They're watching her closely."

The anger ripped through her. "All this grief because of that damn side effect," she growled. "The bastard knew the drug was too dangerous to be used unless he—or they—made it indispensable!"

"They're not going to get away with it."

"Let's hope not," she said, her ire dissipating.

Warmack chuckled. "How are the two boys doing?"

"Fine," Lopez said vaguely. "They're good guys, David."

"Either one better than the other, Cat?" he asked mischievously.

"I don't know." Lopez laughed. "I guess I've seen a bit more of Seth."

"I like him," Warmack said approvingly, and she had a sudden image of Papa.

"Me too, David" she said softly.

"Listen, Cat." Warmack's tone grew protective. "Sounds like you're near some dangerous people. You be careful, right?"

"I will. Promise."

She had just hung up the phone when she heard a soft tap at her door. She walked over and opened it. In jeans and an untucked black shirt, Cohen greeted her with shining eyes and a big smile. "Hi," he said.

He looked as handsome as she'd ever seen him. Desire surged in her. Without a word, she reached out, took his hand, and pulled him into the room. He closed the door with his foot as she dragged him back to the bed. Once there, she pushed him down until he sat on the edge of the bed. She climbed onto him and straddled his legs. She leaned forward and ran her lips along his neck, drinking in the pleasant scent of his aftershave. She kissed him along the side of his neck to his chin and then up to his mouth.

He tightened his hands around her back and moaned. He reached for the hem of her dress. Removing her lips from his for only seconds, she held up her arms so that he could slip the dress up and over her head.

An hour later, still damp from sweat, she lay under the light sheet with her body pressed against his sinewy form. Lopez was startled out of her dreamy state by the ring of her cell phone. She consulted her watch, which read 12:40 A.M.

Cohen looked at her with a frown. "Who would that be?"

Naked, she slipped out of bed and strode to the desk on which her phone sat. She snatched it up and climbed back into bed beside Cohen before answering.

"Dr. Lopez?" he said urgently. "It's Luc Martineau,"

She turned to Cohen with a look of surprise. "Hello, Luc."

Cohen leaned his head close to the phone, and she tilted it so he could listen in.

"Where are you, Luc?"

"Lina, the police are looking for me."

"I know, Luc."

Cohen mouthed the words "play along."

"I didn't do this," Martineau said.

"Okay." She forced herself to speak with calm deliberateness. "Why don't you turn yourself in, so you can sort it out with the authorities?"

"They won't believe me," he said in a robotic voice. "I need your help."

"How can I help you, Luc?" she asked as supportively as she could muster.

"I need you and the other two doctors to meet me at Ellen's lab," he said. "I can show you her notes. Everything is explained. As scientists, you'll understand. Then you can help sort this out."

"Understand what?" Lopez demanded.

"Meet me in half an hour at SeptoMed," Martineau said. "The Oraloxin lab on the eighteenth floor. You'll see."

"Luc, it's after midnight."

"Half an hour," he snapped. "I'll leave the keycards in the planter by the door. I'll distract the security guards."

"Luc, we can't—"

"Lina, I'll be watching," Martineau cut her off. "If the police show, I will disappear. And so will Ellen's notes and the answers you're looking for."

The line went dead.

62

Philadelphia, Pennsylvania

The cab dropped them off two blocks from the SeptoMed building. As he stood on the corner with Lopez, Cohen, and Leetch, Kilburn had never felt more out of his element. Still, he experienced a similar nervous exhilaration when working the ICU trauma room.

Cohen appeared to share none of his rush. His face was creased with concern as he turned to his partner. "Rome, we don't know what's waiting for us up there."

"Only one way to find out," Leetch sighed. "Anyway, I'll have your back."

"Rome's right," Lopez whispered. "You heard how scared Martineau sounded." She touched Cohen above the elbow. "If we call in the police, he's not going to stick around."

Cohen looked to Kilburn. "Graham?" he asked.

Kilburn shrugged. "I don't think we have a choice, Seth."

Cohen nodded and then turned back to Leetch. "Five minutes, right?"

Leetch held up his watch. "No problem. It's Swiss," he said with a forced laugh.

They hurried down Walnut Street. As they approached the SeptoMed building, Kilburn saw the scattered glow from a few lit offices and a row of red beacon lights along the top floor of the otherwise dark tower. Reaching the entrance, only Cohen and Lopez stood beside him. Kilburn looked over his shoulder, but Leetch was nowhere to be seen.

A dim fluorescence played over the security desk in the center of the lobby. None of the overhead lights were on. Kilburn rubbed his damp palms together as he scanned the lobby. No security guard in sight.

They exchanged a nod. Cohen stepped over to the large planter by the door. His hand patted around the pebbles at the base before pulling something out. He returned to the door holding a keycard in his hand. He slid it into the slot by the door. The indicator turned from red to green. It buzzed and Cohen pulled the door open.

Kilburn took a deep breath and stepped into the dim lobby first. Lopez and Cohen followed. Cohen pulled out a small clear plastic ruler from his jacket pocket. He dropped to his knees and wedged the ruler into the crack of the door. Standing up, he tested the door to make sure it would open. With a satisfied nod, he turned toward the elevators.

Three banks of elevators divided the floors: two to fifteen, sixteen to thirty-one, and thirty-two to the roof. They headed for the middle one. Cohen slid the keycard into the slot above the call button, and the button lit up. Kilburn kept expecting to see a guard stroll by but none did; his apprehension heightened.

The elevator doors opened, and they stepped inside. Cohen slid the keycard again into the slot and pressed "18." Then he reached forward and tossed the card on the carpet outside the closing elevator doors.

Kilburn's stomach dropped as the elevator ascended. It stopped abruptly but smoothly just before the doors opened on the eighteenth-floor. The hallway was no better lit than the lobby. Kilburn glanced at Lopez, who nodded back, her eyes sharp with vigilance. Brow creased, Cohen nodded once and then stepped out of the elevator.

Once the hum of the elevator died away, they stood in the absolute silence of the hallway. Cohen pointed to his right to the opaque glass double-doors at the end of the short corridor. As they approached, Kilburn saw that the doors were ajar. A brighter light escaped from within the crack.

Kilburn looked over and saw Cohen digging under his jacket and into his waistband. Temples pounding, he realized the detective was unclipping his gun.

Etched in the glass, the door read: R&D LABORATORY. DR. E. HORTON. Cohen looked from Lopez to Kilburn. "Okay?" he whispered.

Kilburn rubbed his palms roughly together and nodded. Lopez looked less certain. Cohen reached out and touched her shoulder gently.

"Go," she whispered with a thin smile.

Cohen reached for the doors and pulled them apart. He hesitated a moment and then stepped into the small reception area where an unmanned desk was positioned near the back. To the right was another hallway. Kilburn saw the door to the first of several offices that he assumed lined the far wall. Beyond the reception area was another opaque glass door, also backlit.

Cohen pointed toward the wall of offices. They started for them, when a voice called out. "Lina, Graham, Seth, I'm here in the lab," Martineau's unmistakably French-tinged accent called from behind the glass door.

"Coming," Cohen replied.

Martineau's voice startled Kilburn. The weight of the malice that sprung from within the walls of the lab came back to him. He remembered Annie Mallek's quiet tears and Gurdev Singh's despondent wails. Anger gripped him.

A drop of sweat ran down his forehead and past his pounding temples as Kilburn stepped forward and grabbed for the door handle.

63

Nick Snider scratched his bald head, still unaccustomed to his prickly scalp. Alone in Ellen Horton's spacious office behind the main body of the lab, he had a flashback to the last time he'd seen the scientist. Cuffed to the steering wheel, Horton had sat motionless in the running car, her expression calm, her faraway eyes refusing to make contact with his.

Bored with the memory, Snider peered out through the cracks between the horizontal blinds. Though the office was dark, the rest of the lab was illuminated by overhead fluorescent lights. Through the gap between the blinds, he surveyed the space again.

The size of a gym, the lab was about forty feet square. Uniformly white and smelling of disinfectant, the area was broken up by four rows of chest-high workbenches running from front to back. A fifteen-foot-long enclosed workbench ran along the side of the room against the building's outer wall. The countertops held computers, microscopes, and centrifuges. Other complex machinery Snider didn't recognize stood on the laminate floors between benches.

The etched glass door swung open. A man took an aggressive couple of strides into the room but faltered when he reached the row of workbenches at the very back of the room. Graham Kilburn snapped his head from side to side, searching.

From his employer's description, Snider recognized the next man as Seth Cohen. Lina Lopez followed, as pretty and petite as described. As Snider anticipated, they clustered by the back row of workbenches. The two doctors flanked Cohen—Kilburn to the left and blocking the glass door, Lopez to the right within arm's reach of Cohen.

"Luc?" Lopez called out.

Snider stayed put.

"Martineau?" Kilburn snapped.

Snider didn't budge.

Cohen reached behind his back and pulled out a gun. He held it out in front of him. "No more games, Luc," he said evenly. "Come out now."

Snider recognized his cue. He casually stepped out of the office and into the light of the open lab. Cohen's arm swung around. From thirty-five feet away, the barrel of the .357 magnum locked onto his chest. Snider smiled. "Dr. Martineau sends his regrets."

The two doctors froze, but Cohen showed little surprise. "Hands above your head, Forbes," he said calmly. "Now."

Snider was floored by the Forbes reference. *Focus!* he commanded himself. He shook his head slowly. "Wayne Forbes is gone," he said evenly.

"Hands up," Cohen raised his voice and wagged the gun in his hand.

Snider shook his head again. "It's not going to happen like that Sergeant Cohen."

"Yes, it is, Forbes or Tyler or whoever you are today." Cohen steadied his aim with his other hand.

The reference to his other alias momentarily rocked

Snider, but he shook it off. "Sergeant, look at my right hand," he said.

Cohen glanced at Snyder's right hand, which held a remote control the size of a car key fob. Understanding settled in the detective's face, but his aim held firm.

"Now look under the counter of that workbench in front of you," Snider said.

The doctors' eyes dropped to the underside of the countertop to view the cantaloupe-sized glob of putty with the central flashing red light while Cohen's gaze remained fixed on Snider. "What is it?" Cohen asked.

"Three kilos of Semtex," Snider said, raising the remote in his hand slowly up to chest level. "In my opinion, still the best plastic explosive in the business."

Cohen's arms wavered. He looked down under the countertop and saw the explosive.

"Detective, that much Semtex has at least a fifteen-foot lethal blast radius. I think you know as well as I that none of you would survive detonation." Snider brought his hand closer to his chest, enjoying the exchange.

Ten stalemated seconds passed, before Cohen's arms buckled and then his hand dropped to his side.

"Drop the gun in front of you, Sergeant," Snider said.

Lopez looked over to him. "Seth, don't!"

"He knows what to do, Dr. Lopez," Snider said and then turned to Cohen. "Don't you?"

Cohen let the gun drop on the hard floor. It landed with a metallic clatter by his foot.

"Where's Martineau?" Kilburn snarled. "We heard him calling."

With his left hand, Snider dug behind his back and pulled out his gun, a Glock 9mm. Aiming the gun at Cohen, he gently placed the remote control to the explosive down on the counter beside him. Finally, he reached into his jacket and pulled out the mini-recorder. He hit the PLAY button and Martineau's voice called out: "Lina, Graham, Seth, I'm here in the lab."

Snider fought off another smile. "Dr. Martineau couldn't make it, but he did send me ahead with this recording."

"You son of a bitch," Kilburn muttered.

Snider shrugged indifferently and then took three steps closer to them. He pointed the gun at Kilburn's head. "Dr. Kilburn, please move in beside the others."

Snider had full faith in the Semtex, but he wanted to herd them closer to the center of the countertop where the plastique was attached.

Kilburn didn't move. "How will you explain away this one?" he asked.

"That's not my job. But from what I understand, industrial espionage is a growing problem among major corporations. Even the drug companies aren't immune to it."

"You're not serious," Lopez spat.

"I am. And I'm running out of time." He steadied his aim directly at Lopez's face. "Dr. Kilburn, you have three seconds to join them or I will put a bullet between Dr. Lopez's eyes," he hissed. "One . . . two . . ."

Defeat clouding his features, Kilburn began to shuffle toward the others and out of the way of the opaque glass door.

Snider caught the blur of gray moving behind it.

64

Philadelphia, Pennsylvania

Cohen heard a deafening crash. For a moment, he thought the bomb had detonated. Then he realized that the etched glass door behind him had erupted from Snider's single gun blast.

Two shots from outside the lab answered back.

Cohen saw Snider duck to his left behind the cover of a waist-high enclosed workspace in the far corner of the lab. Cohen glanced over his shoulder and saw his partner diving in through the door and sliding through the shattered glass. Leetch rolled awkwardly to his left and almost slammed into Kilburn.

"Rome!" Cohen snapped and pointed to the counter directly in front of them. *"A bomb!* Remote control on the counter up front! Six feet to his right. Don't let him get there!"

"Got it," Leetch yelled and fired off a shot at the workstation sheltering Snider.

Cohen dropped to his knees and patted for his gun. His hand met Lopez's. She thrust the cold handle into his palm. Without taking his eyes off Snider's corner, he barked: "Lina, Graham, to the elevators on three. *Got it?!?*"

"Yes," they said in unison.

"One . . . two . . . three—"

Cohen sprang from his crouch and fired off three shots in Snider's direction. The powerful recoil of the magnum jerked his hand back with each noisy blast. Out of the corner of his eye, he saw Lopez and Kilburn scramble for the gaping doorway and heard their footsteps crunch and grind on the door's broken glass.

Snider popped up to fire a shot but sank back down as quickly when Leetch unloaded two rounds at him. A computer monitor exploded in the corner of the room and more glass rained on the floor.

"Keep me covered," Cohen yelled to his partner. He dropped to the floor and crawled to his left. He heard a whistle and then the thud of a bullet smashing into the desk behind him. Leetch's reply came with two roaring bangs.

Cohen lunged the rest of the three feet to the workstation lining the far wall. He landed painfully on his left wrist and then scrambled behind the floor-to-counter unit. Roughly twelve feet long, he figured the unit would provide some cover to nearly halfway down the length of the room.

He crawled on hands and knees along the length of it. Just as he reached the far end, Leetch yelled, "Seth, he's moving!" Leetch fired two more shots. *"The remote!"*

In horror, Cohen looked around the corner just in time to see Snider's hand reach over the central desk and pat the tabletop for the bomb's remote. *"Get out, Rome!"* Cohen screamed. He fired two desperate shots at Snider's groping hand. Then he saw the fingers grasp the small fob.

Cohen leapt to his feet and sprinted for the front desk, dodging the rows of workspaces and firing his gun wildly.

He made it to within six feet of the desk when he felt a

force hurl him forward in the air. A brilliant orange-red flash filled the room. The explosion sounded like a firecracker detonating in both ears. He slammed onto the floor shoulder first. The building shook. Smoke and dust filled the air. The smell of sulphur and burnt almonds overpowered him. Water rained down from the ceiling sprinklers.

Cohen lay on the ground stunned and gasping for air. As soon as his lungs filled, he climbed shakily to his knees. He couldn't hear a thing except the ringing of the explosion in his ears. Blood dripped onto the ground in front of him, but he had no idea where it came from.

Cohen scanned the desk area in front of him where the remote had sat but saw no sign of movement in the smoke. The windows in Horton's office were blown out and the blinds splayed apart, but he couldn't see Snider inside. He glanced over his shoulder. The back desk and other workstations—including the one he had just crawled along—had been replaced by a heap of twisted debris. Part of the lab's back wall was missing, exposing the hallway beyond. And the Philadelphia sky poured in through the gaping four-foot hole torn through the outer wall.

He forced himself to his feet. He staggered back toward the shattered door, stumbling over objects, unable to see the ground for the lingering smoke. A head appeared in the doorway. Cohen's gun-laden hand shot up. But he held his fire when he saw it was his partner.

"Seth! Down!" Leetch cried.

The ringing in his ears had subsided enough for Cohen to make out his own name. Leetch waved his gun frantically at the floor.

Instinctively, Cohen fell to his knees. At the same moment, he saw Leetch's muzzle flash twice but heard only a couple of dull thuds. He spun around. A hand with a gun stuck through the space where Horton's window had been.

Cohen rolled toward Leetch. Agony shot through his wrist and shoulder with each turn. A bullet ricocheted close by. He crawled painfully over the rest of the glass and rubble until he reached the blown-out doorway. The two men both crawled backward along the burnt hallway carpet to get out of Snider's line of fire.

"He's holed up in Horton's office," Leetch said. "He's got nowhere to go."

Cohen nodded. As the echo in his ears lessened, he heard the wails of approaching fire trucks, police cruisers, and ambulances. "All we have to do is pin him in," he said.

They steadied their guns on the office.

A minute passed.

"Don't shoot," Snider yelled. "I'm coming out."

Leetch glanced to Cohen, his face contorted in anger. "Don't know if I can help myself," he growled.

Cohen saw a gun sail through the missing window of Horton's office and land in the middle of the room with a clank. Cohen and Leetch crawled closer back into the destroyed lab. Two hands rose slowly above Horton's office window followed by sleeved arms.

A knot formed in Cohen's stomach. He had a flashback to the Portland alley where Frige and Jimmy lay, but he couldn't make the connection.

Snider's baldpate appeared, followed by the dead eyes and blank face that Angie Fischer had captured perfectly in her sketch of him. Soon he was standing, hands above his head, the view of body cropped from the waist up by the empty window frame.

With guns held rigidly in front of them, Cohen and Leetch both rose to their feet. "Listen, you son of a bitch!" Leetch snarled. "I'm begging you to give me a reason to shoot! One tiny twitch—"

"I'm not moving," Snider said calmly.

They tread gingerly over the rubble and approached Snider slowly.

Though Snider stood stock-still, sudden foreboding overwhelmed Cohen. *Portland . . . Portland. . . .* Then it hit him! Forbes had gotten the drop on the already armed Frigerator. His eyes darted to his partner. "Rome! He's got a hidden gun!"

The moment that the words left his mouth, Cohen saw a glint of black snap into Snider's hand. In an instant Snider's right hand dropped down and fired.

Leetch toppled backward with a loud groan.

Snider's arm flicked to Cohen.

Cohen squeezed the trigger and the magnum buckled in his hand.

Snider's head jerked back.

Snider collapsed below the lower edge of the window frame, but Cohen kept firing until the chamber was empty and the gun clicked harmlessly.

65

Kilburn experienced a sense of déjà vu as Lopez and he followed Cohen into the U. of Penn.'s glass-walled postoperative recovery room.

Stepping inside, Kilburn saw that Leetch's eyes were open. Surrounded by monitors, he lay back on the bed with his head propped up slightly. A red bag hung from an IV pole and transfused blood into Leetch's right arm. Bandages covered most of the left side of his chest, from which stuck a hoselike chest tube that drained blood and air from around his left lung into the negative-pressure chamber at the foot of his bed.

Leetch's complexion was sallow. Oxygen tubing ran under his nose. But Kilburn could see that his eyes were as bright as ever. Leetch turned to Cohen with a weak grin. "Hey, KC, next time remind me to send a card instead of visiting you, huh?" He coughed a laugh.

Cohen raised his own bandaged left hand out of the sling in which it had been placed and rubbed the dressing covering the deep laceration over his eye. "I promise. I'll remember." His smile dimmed. "Are you in pain, Rome?"

Leetch shook his head. "They got me good and drugged. I don't even feel where they made the cut. Some kind of epidural freezing or something." He reached over to pat the bandages on his chest.

"The surgeon says the bullet missed your heart by an inch," Cohen said.

Leetch sputtered another chuckle. "I told you my tiny heart would come in handy one day."

"Nothing tiny about it." Lopez stepped up to the side of the bed, leaned forward, and kissed him lightly on the cheek.

"Hey, I'm a married man." He raised an eyebrow at Lopez. "What was that for, anyway?"

"For saving our lives," Lopez smiled. "You were amazing last night."

"I want to thank you, too, Rome." Kilburn grinned. "But no kisses from me."

"There's a crushing disappointment, Doctor," Leetch grumbled. He looked over to Cohen. "Forbes is dead, right?"

"Yeah," said Cohen. "Of course, he never was Forbes, Tyler, or Nick Snider, as his most recent ID claimed. When they ran his prints against the national database, they got a match. Murray Adamwell from Cleveland. Shot his grandfather on a hunting trip when he was fourteen. Did four years of juvenile for manslaughter. Never had an adult record, though."

"Trained to be a hit man in reform school, I guess," Leetch grunted and broke into another paroxysm of coughs. "So he had a gun up his sleeve the whole time, huh?"

"Yeah," Cohen said. "A Jacob's ladder–type device with a spring release. When Snider tugged on the string looped around his finger, it popped a little three-inch Black Widow revolver into his palm. No doubt it was how he surprised Frigerator."

"Resourceful bastard, huh?" Leetch sighed.

Cohen nodded. "Snider went to a lot of trouble to rig that

explosion in the lab. Cops found two murdered security guards in the stairwell. But he didn't touch their keycards. Seems he had all the access he needed to enter the building."

"Martineau!" Leetch snapped. "Where is he?"

Lopez shook her head. "No one knows."

"Homicide traced the call he made to Lina last night," Cohen said. "Came from his cell phone. He was a couple of miles from SeptoMed at the time. Somewhere at the foot of Chestnut Street near the Schuylkill."

A tall nurse in scrubs walked into the room. "Sorry to break up the party, but we need to change Mr. Leetch's dressing," she said authoritatively. "You'll have to come back later."

"And next time, it wouldn't kill you to bring some flowers!" Leetch grunted.

"Rome, I spoke to Gina earlier," Cohen said. "She and Sophie will be here this afternoon."

"I know." Leetch's voice cracked. "Thanks, partner."

They said their good-byes and headed for the door. "KC!" Leetch called after him. "You keep me in the loop, okay?"

Walking down the hall toward the elevator, Cohen said. "Too bad Neil Ryland was already discharged. I'd like to talk to him again."

Lopez grabbed Cohen's elbow. "And how about Andrea Byington and Harvey Abram?"

Cohen nodded. "Let's start with Byington. Ed is bringing her in to the station now."

"Good," Lopez said. "Byington and Martineau seemed a little too cozy when we interviewed them."

"And if her family founded that company, she must own a sizable chunk," Kilburn pointed out. "You heard what Ryland told us about SeptoMed being unable to survive a third failed antibiotic? Byington's financial viability might even hinge on Oraloxin's success."

"True," Cohen said. He looked from Kilburn to Lopez. "You two have already gone above and beyond the call. If you need to head back home . . ."

Kilburn shrugged. "I'm going to stick around for Ellen's funeral." Then he added quietly, "She doesn't have much in the way of family."

Lopez smiled at Cohen. She reached over and touched the bandages above his eye tenderly. "I'm not going anywhere, Seth."

66

Philadelphia, Pennsylvania

Stepping into Ed Franklin's second-floor Homicide office, Lopez noticed the chill in the lieutenant's greeting. But Franklin saved most of his wrath for Cohen. Franklin listed the points with his fingers, and said, "I got two murdered security guards, a hole in the side of a skyscraper, two injured Portland detectives, a very dead hit man, and a whole damn city up in arms." Franklin stared hard at Cohen. "What I don't have is the person responsible for it all."

"Ed, we had no choice but to follow Martineau's instructions," Lopez spoke up in Cohen's defense.

"Lina is right," Kilburn said. "Martineau painted us into a corner."

"Doctors," Franklin snapped. "Sergeant Cohen knows a thing or two about police procedure. He knows we're capable of responding discreetly in these situations."

"You're right, Ed," Cohen said. "I knew better. I'm sorry."

Lopez admired the way Cohen made no effort to deflect the blame. Franklin responded well to the apology: After a deep sigh, his expression lightened. "We just heard from Martineau's bank. Apparently, he moved a considerable amount of money—or at least tried to—last night."

Cohen tilted his head. "How so?"

"He put in an electronic sell order for two hundred thousand SeptoMed shares, but as trading was halted on the stock this morning, the order wasn't filled. However, he did manage to move about three quarters of a million dollars in cash to an offshore account."

"He's padding a nest for himself somewhere, isn't he, Ed?" Lopez asked.

"Looks that way," Franklin agreed with another sigh.

"Where did he get that kind of money?" Kilburn asked. "Has he been dumping SeptoMed stock all along?"

Franklin shook his big head. "Not according to his bank records. The money came in from some private numbered Cayman Island account the day before."

Cohen nodded. "Ed, do you know where he placed these electronic transactions from?"

"The tech boys traced the order back to a wireless laptop. Somewhere in Greater Philadelphia," Franklin sighed. "I don't understand all the mumbo jumbo—something to do with WiFi and IP addresses—but apparently they can't pinpoint it any better."

"What time?" Cohen asked.

"About 1:30 A.M."

"So Martineau was still around after the explosion," Kilburn said.

Franklin shrugged.

"Maybe he's still in the city," Lopez suggested.

"Wouldn't count on it," Franklin said. "But he's going to have a tough time moving about. His photo is everywhere."

Lopez knew Franklin wasn't exaggerating. Every newspaper or TV screen she had passed in the last twelve hours was broadcasting Martineau's face to the world.

The phone's harsh metallic ring startled Lopez. Franklin reached for it. He listened for a moment and then said,

"Okay, we're on our way." He hung up and rose to his full, intimidating height. "Andrea Byington is here."

They followed the lieutenant out of his office and down a gray corridor, stopping at two sets of doors. The first opened onto a small, darkly lit room where two rows of chairs faced a large two-way mirror that looked into the room next door. That room was empty except for a long wooden table with three chairs on either side. Two middle-aged men sitting in the first row turned away from the mirror to view the newcomers. They both waved their coffee cups in a toast of greeting.

"This is your stop, doctors." Franklin pointed to the men. "Dr. Lopez and Dr. Kilburn, meet Detectives Granger and Cunningham." He stared at the taller, of the two detectives, the one with the beak of a nose and mischievous smile. "Behave, Granger, okay?"

"Wouldn't have it any other way, Ed," Granger said.

Lopez led Kilburn over to the front row of seats. She sat beside the squat, bearded Detective Cunningham, who shook her hand and showed her a friendly smile. No sooner had the introductions been made than the door to the room on the other side of the mirror opened.

Byington walked in, followed by Franklin and Cohen. Franklin led her to the chair facing the mirror. Then he sat down beside Cohen on the near side of the table, their backs to the viewing gallery.

Lopez recognized the same confident poise in Byington's manner as the day before, but her makeup didn't hide the bags under her eyes or the deeper lines at the edge of her lips.

Franklin leaned forward. "Ms. Byington . . . ," the speaker crackled in the observation room.

She interrupted with a wave of her small hand. "It's doctor, actually. But I prefer Andrea, please."

"Thanks for coming in, Andrea," Franklin said. "I believe you've met Sergeant Cohen."

"Of course," Byington smiled benignly. "Though, when we met yesterday, the sergeant didn't have the war wounds."

She pointed to his wrapped arm and face with a sweep of her hand. "And at the time, he was said to be a physician."

Cohen shrugged. "We thought it important to conceal the reason for my involvement."

"I understand, Sergeant," she said. Her tone sounded even more clipped to Lopez over the room's tinny speaker. "Of course, that's no longer an issue."

Franklin leaned back in his seat. "You've heard, then?"

"Lieutenant, the entire world has heard," she said.

"Not good for SeptoMed," Franklin pointed out.

"No," Byington sighed. "But the worries of SeptoMed and its shareholders are probably not your overriding concern."

Franklin leaned forward in his seat. "Andrea, do you know where Luc Martineau is?"

She shook her head.

"When did you last see him?" Franklin asked.

"Yesterday morning after our interview with the doctors, we discussed the developments for another few minutes. Then Luc left. I haven't seen him since."

"How would you characterize that private meeting?" Cohen asked.

Byington viewed him with a semi-amused smile. "I think you can imagine that our CEO was less than pleased to hear about the bone marrow complications of a SeptoMed drug from three West Coast doctors." She paused. "Harvey had a few pointed words for Luc."

"And you?" Cohen asked.

She frowned. *"Me?"*

Cohen nodded. "How did you feel about hearing of the drug's side effect that way?"

Byington's eyes narrowed slightly, but she didn't shed her smile. "I'm a board member, and I have a substantial financial interest in the company," she said, "but I'm not responsible for operations like Harvey is."

Cohen nodded. "Have you known Martineau for long?"

"Three years or so."

"Do you know him well?" Cohen asked.

Byington considered the question. "I suppose," she said. "We've been lovers on and off since we met."

Kilburn nudged Lopez in surprise, and the two detectives beside her exchanged whispers.

"Are you on or off these days?" Cohen asked.

"If you consider last week 'these days', then I suppose we're on," Byington said.

Cohen put his good arm on the table, palm down. "Do you think Luc Martineau is capable of this?"

"You mean killing three of our own scientists?" Byington asked.

"And deliberately releasing a deadly bacteria," Cohen added.

Byington stared at Cohen for several seconds, and sighed. "Luc is the most wildly ambitious and selfish man I have ever met. He has shown more than the occasional flash of corporate ruthlessness. I've often thought there was nothing he wouldn't do to advance his own career." Then her voice lowered. "But *this*? No, I don't think even he is capable of this."

Franklin folded his arms across his chest. "Then maybe you can explain why he tried to sell two hundred thousand shares of stock and move three quarters of a million dollars into an offshore account an hour after the explosion at SeptoMed?"

Byington's eyes grew large. *"He did?"*

"Would you expect Luc to have that kind of money in cash?" Cohen asked.

Byington's eyes dropped to the table. She shook her head slightly.

"Can you think of where he might have gotten it?" Cohen asked.

Byington was quiet for a long time. "That son of a bitch," she muttered.

"Andrea?" Cohen said.

When she looked up, her aristocratic smile was gone. Lopez was shocked by the change. Her tired face looked much older. But her eyes blazed with rage. "I trusted him," she spat. "That miserable son of a bitch!"

"Trusted him with what?" Cohen asked.

"Two months ago, when we first heard about the aplastic anemia in the chimps," she said, contradicting her earlier statement. "Luc got an e-mail. The sender said he would go to the FDA with proof of the side effect unless we paid him off."

"How much did he want?" Cohen asked.

"Two million."

"Two million!" Franklin whistled.

"That was nothing compared to what it would have cost us—cost *me*—if the FDA rejected Oraloxin," she grumbled.

"So you paid the blackmailer?" Cohen asked.

"I supplied the money." Byington looked defeated and sounded defeated. "Luc took care of the arrangements . . . or so he told me."

Franklin tapped the table in front of him. "You think Martineau was the blackmailer all along?"

Byington laughed coldly. "I trusted him," she hissed.

67

West Chester, Pennsylvania

Sitting in the pew beside Lopez and Cohen, Kilburn tried to focus on the Reverend's words, but his mind drifted in too many directions. He was heartened to see how packed Third Presbyterian Church was, even though Ellen Horton was survived by no immediate family. Friends, colleagues, and former students crowded into the small church. SeptoMed had sent ahead a huge floral bouquet that bloomed in front of the dais.

The media and police had also shown up in large numbers, the latter primarily to contain the former. Both held out the faint hope that Luc Martineau might make a surprise appearance.

Kilburn knew better.

Though his apprehension prevented him from concentrating on the service, it didn't lessen his sense of melancholy. With her casket on display and her photo on the front of the service's programs, the senselessness of Ellen's death sunk in.

Outside the church after the service, Kilburn noticed that the weather had finally changed. He thought it sadly apt that the clouds that had gathered all morning had finally erupted. He huddled under one umbrella with Lopez and Cohen on the church's steps as the rain pelted down.

Holding an umbrella in his right hand, Neil Ryland limped down the steps to greet them. He wore a black trench coat slung over his gray suit and the sling supporting his broken left arm. His right eye was open now, but the bruising had turned yellowy-black and extended from his forehead to his chin. His other eye looked as bloodshot as the injured one.

"Beats the humidity, I guess," Ryland said with a forced smile and tipped his umbrella to let the rain run off.

Lopez nodded. "How are you, Neil?"

He shrugged. "Lot of funerals these days."

"Too many," Kilburn said.

"No sign of Martineau?" Ryland asked.

"Not recently," Cohen said.

Ryland shook his head.

"Neil, can we give you a ride home?" Cohen asked.

Ryland gestured at Cohen's sling that matched his own. "You don't look in much better shape to drive than I am."

"I'm at the wheel," Kilburn said.

"Ed Franklin lent us a car to drive out for Ellen's funeral," Lopez said.

"I live outside of Glen Mills," Ryland said. "It's not exactly on your way. I was just going to grab a cab."

"It's no big deal," Kilburn said.

"Okay. Sure. Thanks." Ryland raised his umbrella. "I've got a bottle of Chivas I was planning to open back at home. If you like, we could have a commiseration toast." He swallowed. "To Ellen and Vik."

In the near-blinding rain, the quaint historic roads presented more of a challenge to navigate than they had on the way out. Driving with a carefully constant speed, Kilburn focused on the roads while Cohen and Ryland provided most of the small talk on the ride to Glen Mills.

Kilburn pulled up in front of Ryland's modest but attractive Cape Cod home with its neat front hedge. They trudged through the rain and into Ryland's front entrance. He led them through the tidy but sparsely furnished living room and into the fifties-style kitchen. With linoleum floors and cork cabinets, the kitchen was square and open. It bordered onto a small nook. The other three stood in the center while Ryland headed for the cabinets.

"You haven't reconsidered your resignation?" Cohen asked.

"Too many bad memories." Ryland opened a cupboard door. "I couldn't go back there now after"—he cleared his throat—"what happened to my friends."

"What's going to become of the company?" Lopez asked.

"I think SeptoMed will be just fine," Ryland said with a tired chuckle. "Martineau might have initiated the MRGAS crisis but it looks like it will be with us for a long time. And since there is no other treatment option besides Oraloxin, SeptoMed will be with us too."

"In spite of all the suffering he caused, Martineau probably saved SeptoMed," Kilburn said ruefully.

"Not worth saving at that cost." Ryland reached into the open cupboard, bringing down a sealed bottle of Chivas.

"Can I help?" Lopez asked, walking up to Ryland's side.

"Please. If you could open the bottle, I'll get some more glasses."

"What are you going to do now, Neil?" Cohen asked, as Ryland reached up with his good arm and pulled four highball glasses down one at a time.

"Wait for my arm to recover, I guess. After that, I don't know. Maybe go to another company. I'm even thinking about going back to university life. Doesn't pay as well, but it's a hell of a lot safer." He forced a chuckle.

"What about in the meantime?" Cohen asked, his tone more prying. "I hope you have some bonuses or stock options from SeptoMed."

Without turning, Ryland pulled open the drawer and stuck

a hand inside. "Far as I know, they don't give you bonuses for quitting," he said. "But I shouldn't complain, I made out better than my colleagues on the project."

Kilburn swallowed. "Sounds like you're putting a positive spin on a bad situation."

"Not really. I'm still alive. That's more than I can say for my friends. And unless Martineau escapes to some exotic island—"

"That's not going to happen, Neil," Cohen said emphatically.

"I wish I was as convinced," Ryland said, pulling his hand back. "He's an oily bastard, that one."

"Neil," Cohen snapped. Ryland's hand stilled. Even Lopez stopped pouring the fourth drink. "You and I both know that Luc Martineau is dead."

68

Glen Mills, Pennsylvania

Intense silence permeated the room. Lopez felt the weight of the Chivas bottle in her hand. She heard the sound of her own breathing.

"What makes you so sure?" Ryland asked.

"A couple of things," Cohen said.

"Such as?" Ryland queried without turning around.

"For starters, how would Snider know I was a cop?" Cohen touched his lip. "Martineau and the others thought I was a doctor. You were the only one at SeptoMed who knew otherwise."

"Wouldn't be hard for him to find out," Ryland said, his back still turned.

"Then there's the expertise involved in synthesizing and packaging MRGAS into street drugs," Cohen said slowly. "We checked. Martineau's background didn't extend to the kind of complex microbiology involved. That was your specialty."

Ryland moved his head back and forth. "At least three others at SeptoMed knew enough to do the same."

"And Snider's 'attempt' on your life?" Cohen said.

Ryland raised his broken arm like a wing. "What about it?"

"Volvo or not, he was far too professional to screw that up."

Another pause. "It's all just wild speculation, Seth," Ryland said.

"Ah, Neil, but the money," Cohen said with an edge. "You can never hide the money."

"What money?"

"The two million dollars. The FBI cracked your shell-game accounting," Cohen bluffed. "We know you were the one blackmailing Martineau and Byington."

Ryland didn't respond.

Silence consumed the room again.

"Neil?" Cohen prodded.

Ryland struck so quickly that Lopez felt the fiberglass cast hit her in the ribs before she even registered the blur of movement. In the next instant the cast pulled her backward into his body, pinning her against him. Lopez struggled to free herself but froze the moment she felt the sharp blade pressing against her neck.

"Don't!" Ryland yelled. Kilburn and Cohen stopped dead, halfway to her. "If you think after all this that I would even hesitate to . . ." Ryland let the unfinished threat dangle in the supercharged air.

Her heart pounding, Lopez felt a scratch as the blade dug into the skin of her neck. Ryland's hot breath blew on her ear. A drop of blood trickled down her neck.

"It's done now, Neil," Cohen said calmly. His eyes locked on Lopez's. "Let Lina go."

"I don't think so," Ryland grunted through gritted teeth. "Back up. Now!"

Kilburn glanced at Cohen. They both backed up four steps to the far side of the kitchen.

"What now?" Cohen asked.

Lopez felt Ryland's cheek brush against hers as he looked from side to side. "I'll need your car keys."

"Why, Neil?" Kilburn growled, his face flushing. "You were supposed to have been Ellen's friend."

"Why? *Why?*" Ryland cried. "You're supposed to be a goddamned doctor. Can't you even see it?"

Kilburn's lip twitched. "See what?"

"Open your eyes. *The bugs are winning!*" he snapped. "The bloody post-antibiotic era has dawned."

"Only because of you," Lopez whispered.

"*Me?*" Ryland's arm tightened around her ribs to the point where breathing became difficult. "Remember your own press conference, Lina? All that antibiotic abuse you railed against? The demanding patients, the lazy doctors, the greedy drug companies and cattle ranchers. You were right. Nature *is* striking back. MRGAS and other even more resistant bacteria *are* on their way with or without my help."

Completely still, Cohen stared at Lopez with reassuring eyes. He nodded to her.

"And finally a drug with real promise like Oraloxin comes along," Ryland said. "But those idiots at the FDA can't see the forest for the trees. A couple of dead lab chimps is enough to make them give up on one of the last hopes against the onslaught of bacterial resistance."

"So we should thank you for introducing MRGAS?" Kilburn said, his cheeks red with rage.

"Yes!" Ryland snapped. "I showed the world a tiny taste of what's coming in the near future. *I helped prepare us.* And I'm not sorry that a couple of junkies had to die to do it."

"Good people died," Kilburn murmured.

"Have you heard of the greater good, Doctor?" Ryland grunted.

"You were trying to save the world. Right, Neil?" Cohen said coolly.

"Not just that," Ryland said. "Take a look around at this shitty little house of mine."

Lopez felt his grip loosen a little on her chest but the blade was still held firm to her neck.

"I wasn't about to start all over with nothing but a ruined reputation," Ryland said. "Not after helping to create one of the greatest drugs of the past fifty years. *No way!* So I did what I had to do. I extorted some money from that slimeball Martineau and his filthy-rich slut Byington. Then I hired Snider or Forbes, or whatever you call him to do the legwork of disseminating MRGAS."

Kilburn's eyes were fire. "And Ellen?"

Ryland hesitated. "Don't talk to me about her. I loved her. Vik and Ellen were my best friends."

Kilburn snorted. "So, naturally, you had to kill them."

"There was no choice!" Ryland yelled. "Vik was on the verge of going to the FDA. And Ellen had figured out where MRGAS came from. They were both too principled and too narrow-minded to have ever listened to reason. . . ." He paused again. When he resumed speaking, his tone was frigid. "But that weasel Martineau . . . that was easy."

Lopez slid a foot over, but stopped when she felt the cast tighten around her chest.

"So you had Snider fake an attempt on your life to deflect suspicion from you," Cohen said. "Then you kidnapped Martineau and forced him to set us up."

"Snider kidnapped Martineau," Ryland said.

Cohen nodded. "And killed him. Meanwhile you moved the money into and out of Martineau's account to frame him for paying Snider's bills."

"Those 'bills' consumed most of the two million," Ryland grunted.

"A pittance of what you stood to gain from Oraloxin—"

"Enough!" Ryland said. "We're done with the history talk."

He pushed Lopez forward a step. "Give me your damn car keys!" he snarled at Kilburn.

Kilburn reached in his pocket and pulled out the keys.

"Put them on the countertop," Ryland instructed. Kilburn stepped over to the counter and placed the keys on it.

"Now, you two are going to go down the stairs and lock yourself in the basement," Ryland told the men.

Concentrating, Lopez held her breath.

"And you?" Cohen asked.

"Lina is going to give me a ride out of here," Ryland said. "Then we can all get on with our separate lives."

"And we should trust you the way Ellen and Vik did?" Kilburn said.

"The stairs are behind you," Ryland said, ignoring the question. "Move now! Or Lina dies."

Now! Lina thought. The moment Cohen turned for the stairs, Lopez drove her elbow down as hard as she could into Ryland's groin. At the same moment, she shot her other hand up and grabbed his wrist.

Ryland screamed in surprise. The knife scratched the front of Lina's neck, just as she caught his hand and wriggled free of the blade. She struggled to pull completely free but felt a burning pain as the knife dug deeply into her shoulder. She winced and then looked up to see the blade coming at her again.

Before the knife made contact, Kilburn's hand grabbed Ryland's arm. Under Kilburn's weight, they all slammed into the cupboards. When they made contact with the cabinets, Lopez sprang free of the tangle and staggered back a step. Stunned, she watched Kilburn and Ryland wrestle against the wall.

After Kilburn smashed Ryland's hand twice into a cabinet, the knife dropped to the ground with a thud. Kilburn punched wildly, missing with his left fist but smashing his right into Ryland's nose, from which blood spurted on contact. Ryland screamed again. Ryland swung his casted arm like a bat, hitting Kilburn in the head and knocking him off balance.

Ryland dove for the knife, but Cohen lunged for his waist

and tackled him with his free arm before Ryland could reach it.

Kilburn recovered his footing and jumped over the other two bodies to grab the knife. He spun and kneeled over Ryland, raising the blade above his head like a dagger. "You monster," he growled. His hand twitched.

Cohen rose to his feet. With his good hand, he gently grabbed Kilburn's extended wrist.

Lopez stared down at Kilburn. "Graham, he's not worth it," she urged.

The knife held firm for a moment, but then Cohen let go and Kilburn's arm dropped to his side.

The back door to the kitchen exploded off the hinges.

Uniformed men armed with assault rifles stormed in through the door. Moments later more men flooded in from the living room, until the FBI assault team filled the kitchen.

All guns trained on the bleeding Ryland.

69

Sitting at the round table in Caffé Quattro, a one-handed Cohen struggled with the plate of fettuccine pescatore in front of him. To his right, Lopez was faring no better with her pasta.

Kilburn raised his wineglass and laughed. "Look at the pair of you. Even your disabilities match." He pointed from Cohen's wrapped left wrist to Lopez's right shoulder where the bulky bandages, covering the deep laceration made by Ryland's knife, poked out from underneath one side of her shirt. "I've never felt more like a third wheel in my life."

Lopez grinned playfully. "Graham, if it will make you feel more at home, we're perfectly willing to break your arm."

"Thanks. I'm doing all right with this." Kilburn rubbed the golf ball–sized bruise at the angle of his jaw where Ryland had hit him with his cast.

Cohen looked at Lopez with exasperated admiration. "Lina, I still don't understand why you had to fight," he said. "With the FBI surrounding the house, Ryland wasn't going anywhere. They would've taken him down before you got three steps out of the house."

Lopez shrugged. "I just couldn't listen to any more of that self-righteous psychopath." She grinned and bit her lip. Her eyes danced. "Besides, how many other chances will I ever get to elbow him where I did?"

They shared a laugh. "According to Ed Franklin, Ryland has clammed up in custody," Cohen said.

"Good thing the FBI taped our conversation," Kilburn pointed out.

"Yeah," Cohen said. "Silence won't help him much after that confession."

Kilburn shook his head in disgust. "Ryland got *two million* in blackmail money out of Byington. Why wasn't that enough? Why did he have to cause so much heartache and death?"

"He wanted it all." Cohen rubbed his thumbs against his index fingers. "The money *and* the fame and adulation of having helped create a wonder drug. Plus, with his SeptoMed stock options and bonuses, he stood to make tens of millions off the success of Oraloxin."

Lopez nodded. "And he figured his reputation would've been destroyed if the FDA rejected Oraloxin and published the chimp findings." She put down her fork. "Besides, he knew people would soon figure out who was behind the blackmail if he was the only one to walk away from a drug development failure with money in his pocket."

Kilburn turned to Cohen. "So they found Martineau's body, huh?"

"Yes, just this morning. At the bottom of the Schuylkill River with a bullet through his forehead and cement blocks tied to his feet. Took them two days."

"Can't say I liked what I saw of Martineau," Lopez said, "but he ended up getting a bum rap. Ryland killed him and nearly got away with vilifying him forever."

"Martineau conspired to hide a potentially lethal side effect from the rest of the company and the world." Kilburn thought of Mallek and Singh with sadness. "People a lot more innocent than him ended up paying just as heavy a price."

Cohen glanced from Kilburn to Lopez. "What happens to MRGAS now?"

"I don't know if it's going anywhere," Lopez sighed. "There are still new cases in Seattle and Portland. And it continues to spread—although much more slowly—in the Bay Area."

"Lina's right," Kilburn sighed. "We've yet to successfully eradicate any bacterial infection. I think MRGAS will be around for a long time."

Cohen took another sip of wine. "Meaning, so will Oraloxin."

"Until something safer comes along," Kilburn said.

Lopez reached over and touched Cohen on the back of his good hand. "Seth, the irony is that Oraloxin isn't that bad a drug after all," she said. "The only two patients, out of thousands, who developed the bone marrow complication both recovered as soon as the drug was stopped."

Cohen frowned. "So Ryland had a point?"

"He's a self-serving sociopath," Lopez snorted. "But some of his arguments weren't too far off. With people's inadvertent and shortsighted help, nature will keep producing resistant bacteria. And to some degree, we've handcuffed the researchers who are trying to find new cures."

Kilburn lifted the bottle out of the ice bucket and drained the rest of the wine into the three glasses on the table. "This might sound strange for an infectious-disease specialist to say, but I wouldn't mind if I didn't hear the words 'bacterial resistance' or 'antibiotics' again anytime soon."

"How about 'pandemic flu'?" Lopez asked with a mischievous smile.

"Not that one either," he laughed.

Cohen asked, "What do you plan to do now, Graham?"

"I'm flying back to Vancouver in the morning. Then?" Kilburn shrugged. "Catch up with my latest family crisis.

Clean up the mess that my practice must be in. Have a strip torn off me by Louise." He broke into a grin. "Come to think of it, it'll be like any other week." Graham knew there would be one difference, but he didn't share it with the others. The past weeks had given him a new appreciation of life's fragility. He was determined not to continue living with regret. He would try his best to mend his relationship with Michelle.

Flushing slightly, Kilburn asked the other two of their plans.

They shared a shy smile. With Cohen's functional right hand, he reached over and clasped her left hand. "We have a little sick time on our *hands*," Cohen said.

Lopez squeezed Cohen's fingers. "We're planning a trip," she said.

"Maybe the Oregon coast," suggested Cohen.

"Or maybe Machu Picchu?" Lopez leaned over and kissed Cohen on the lips.

Cohen beamed. "Okay, Peru it is."

Kilburn laughed. "I can just see you two in ten years."

Lopez cocked her head. "In Portland or Seattle?" she asked.

"Don't know that part." Kilburn winked at her. "But I see a brood of little Lopez-Cohens following you around. Brilliant, tireless, and headstrong, every last one of them!"

Lopez chuckled, but Kilburn thought he noticed a slight blush in her cheeks.

Cohen smiled warmly at Lopez. "First, we've got to survive Peru."

Kilburn glanced at the two of them and appreciated that, despite the harrowing circumstances of their meeting, he'd made a pair of lifelong friends. And with a hint of pride, he realized they had helped to stem the spread of a dangerous pathogen and contain its malicious source. That didn't bring back Thomas Mallek, Parminder Singh, Viktor Leschuk, Ellen Horton, or any of the others, but it made their deaths seem a little less meaningless.

Kilburn's nagging guilt dissipated. He thought of Michelle again. He was ready to move forward with his life too.

Look for Daniel Kalla's next novel

RAGE THERAPY
0-765-31225-5

Available in
hardcover,
October 2006,
from Tom Doherty Associates.

Turn the page for a preview . . .

Chapter 1

"Why psychiatry?" I've heard the same question posed in different forms by friends, family, and even complete strangers. As often as not, implicit in their tone is the insinuation that something must be a little off kilter in my own head for me to have wound up a psychiatrist. I used to shrug off the suggestion with varying degrees of politeness. But standing under the shower's lukewarm spray, I realized I wasn't sure anymore. My psychological closets were full to the point of bursting. And the same was true of more than a few of my colleagues.

The ringing phone jolted me from my introspection. I considered ignoring it but then it occurred to me that I'd been in the shower for over half an hour. Even my obsessive-compulsive patients would have to concede that by now I was clean. So I stepped out of the stall and slid out of the bathroom.

I reached the phone on its fifth ring. One too late. I waited until the voicemail light flashed on my phone and then I played back the message. "Doc, it's Dev," said Homicide Sergeant Ethan Devonshire in his unmistakable low-pitched

Southern drawl. "Not the best way to tell you this, but Stanley Kolberg was found dead in his office. He was shot in the neck, and uh . . ." he left the word-picture unfinished. "Anyway, we're at the scene now. We could use your input. Can you call me on my cell as soon as you get this?" He paused. "Sorry."

Still damp, I sat on the edge of my bed, forgetting my towel. Conflicting thoughts and emotions swam in my head, but I forced myself to focus on the prospect of joining Dev at Stanley's office—an office I'd once shared with the victim. It made no sense for me to become professionally involved in his murder investigation. But call it shock, or maybe just morbid curiosity, I wanted to go to the crime scene. I needed to see what fate worse than a bullet to the neck had befallen Stanley and stopped Dev's description in mid-sentence.

I rose from the bed and wandered over to my dresser. When I reached for the top drawer, the photo on top caught my eye. I picked up the five-by-seven frame. Stanley had taken the action shot of Loren and me on the 30-foot sailboat. Life jackets on, we had struggled to keep straight faces and look nautical, but we ended up just looking goofy. And happy. I looked from the photograph to the mirror in front of me. Still no gray hairs, and the lines had only slightly deepened at the corners of my mouth and eyes. But the mirror didn't tell the whole story. I felt as if I'd aged a lifetime in the five years since Stanley had snapped the photo. If she were still alive, I doubt Lor would have aged a day in the interim. Then again, maybe I wouldn't have either. God, I missed her.

After positioning the frame back in its spot, I threw on a pair of khakis and a shirt that dampened on contact, not necessarily from the shower, and then headed out the door to my garage. I climbed into my car and said my little prayer. It worked. The engine of the silver 88' Honda Accord coughed a few times, sputtered, and finally lapsed into its familiar unhealthy rumble. Tomorrow I'm going replace this piece of crap, I promised myself. That promise was becoming a mantra.

I pulled into the underground parking lot of my old office building, which still had no gate despite multiple complaints from the tenants. Using the key I hadn't bothered returning when I quit the practice, I let myself in through the basement door. More than a few drug addicts had let themselves in through the same door with the aid of a crowbar. Medical buildings and their promised cache of drugs and syringes draw junkies like pollen does bees; thus the complaints.

Even before the elevator doors opened to the third floor, I could hear the commotion emanating from Stanley's office. I walked out into the fluorescent-lit sterile hallway, passing a dental office and two family practices. At the end of the corridor, a door was ajar. The two shingles on the door read: "Stanley Kolberg, MD" and "Calvin Nichol, MD". Beneath them the paint was faded in a shape and size matching the other two placards. That was where my name, "Joel Ashman, MD", used to hang.

I pushed the door open and walked into the waiting room where I saw the first of the "bunny men". Crime scene investigators from the Seattle's Medical Examiner's Office wear white overalls, gloves, and foot covers to all crime scenes, but it is their white hats, worn with goggles and sometimes earphones, which make them look like mutant rabbits.

I watched the bunny men scour the walls and floors, using their infrared and violet blues and God-knows-what other equipment. To me, it looked like an Easter egg hunt gone awry. But I knew what the CSI guys were looking for—residues, fibers, and, most of all, a blood corpuscle or hair follicle or single sperm cell or any tantalizing scrap of DNA that under a microscope might divulge a social security number or Zip Code. They didn't acknowledge me, but I wasn't surprised; I'd long ago decided that the bunny men didn't have much time for bodies above room temperature.

Following the din, I rounded the corner and almost slammed into Dev coming the other way. Ethan Devonshire—'Dev' to everyone but his wife—was tall with broad shoulders and a slight paunch. Below his unruly salt-and-pepper hair, he had a round face with deep laugh lines, shallow acne scars, and perpetually amused gray eyes. This evening, he'd worn jeans with a collared pullover. As always, Dev had erred on the casual side, but in his defense, it was after midnight.

His weathered face broke into a sympathetic smile. "Sorry about your friend."

I nodded my thanks. "Can I see him?"

Dev reached over and patted me on the shoulder. I turned for Stanley's office and took another step down the hallway. "But Doc—" Dev's voice stopped me—"It's kind of grisly. Sure you want to see it?"

With a nod, I began to trudge toward Stanley's interview room at the end of the hallway, stopping only when I reached the wide-open door.

I had walked onto worse crime scenes, but I froze in the doorway. This time, the victim wasn't a stranger.

The sheer volume of blood astonished me. No surface was spared, but the floor bore the brunt. Near the center of the room, the green carpet had blackened in a ring encircling Stanley Kolberg's barely recognizable corpse.

Stanley lay in a heap in front of his desk. Of all the distorted anatomy, his arms were the most jarring sight. Twisted above his head and obviously fractured at the wrist, his right hand appeared to have hold of its own forearm. Though not as deformed, his left arm shot out unnaturally above his head, hand turned over, as if trying to pat down the carpet with its bloated fingers.

I took in the other details with growing nausea. Stanley's face was a battered pulp. With all the tissue that oozed down from his forehead, I couldn't tell whether his eyes were open. His nose deviated badly to the right, Picasso-like. His lips were swollen to the width of bananas. Crusted blood matted his hair and stuck to his beard.

In one of those bizarre reflex-associations, I wondered again why so many of my male colleagues wore those Freudian beards. It was Stanley—no one ever shortened it to

Stan—who'd once explained: "All other physicians have uniforms. O.R. scrubs, white coats, stethoscopes, and what have you. Helps sell the whole shtick to the public. But what do we psychiatrists have? Nothing. So we grow beards like Sigmund's." Then he smiled and winked conspiratorially. "Besides, most of us shrinks are a wee bit fucked in the head. No?" Stanley was as academic as they came, but when he wanted to emphasize a point, he'd slip into a folksy idiom and pepper it with expletives.

An excited voice pulled me back to the moment. "You get a load of that, Joel?"

I looked over to my right to see the chief CSI investigator, Nate Schiff, now stood beside me. Schiff was one worked up bunny. He jabbed a finger at the hemorrhagic wall inside the room. "Check out the wall!"

I glanced at the red streak that arched across the wall like a lost band of a rainbow.

"A real pumper," Schiff exhaled. "Only one thing gives you a spurt like that. An arterial bleed. And a big one, to boot!" He whistled appreciatively. Schiff wasn't morbid the way some people who work around the dead were, but he had a scientist's appreciation for the mechanics of his study, which happened to be murder scenes.

I viewed Stanley, but I couldn't spot a wound through the layers of blood and tissue. Reading the uncertainty on my face, Schiff brought two fingers up to his own neck as if checking his pulse. "The carotid. The second biggest artery in the body, after the aorta." Having been through medical school this wasn't exactly news to me, but I didn't interrupt Schiff; he was on a roll. "A fresh cut carotid will spray close to ten feet. Drain a gallon or two in less than a minute. Like slicing open a garden hose!" He pursed his lips and made an unnecessary whooshing noise.

Schiff stepped into the interview room. I took a breath and followed him. Avoiding the dark patches on the carpet, we kept moving until we reached the victim's feet. From up close Stanley looked less like road kill and more like the man I knew, which made the whole tableau that much more disturbing. To distract myself, I concentrated on forensic details. "Only one shot?"

"Only one that hit him." Schiff shrugged. "But our guy fired another. The stray up in the wall." He pointed at a small crater in the drywall above the door behind us. "Don't have a clue what that was all about. No one's that bad a shot from in so close."

"Stanley was standing when he was shot?"

"You can see exactly how he went down . . ." Schiff swept a hand over the room, looking more like an interior decorator pitching colors than a CSI technician describing an execution. "The victim is standing right in front of his desk. Bam!" He fired an imaginary shot from his fingertip. "He takes it off the side of his neck, reels, and spins to his left. Now blood's spurting out at a mean pressure of 120 mm of mercury. Just follow the spray. See how the blood trails down the wall, over the chair, and onto the carpet?" Schiff pantomimed Stanley's collapse. "The victim's dropping as he spins."

"And the other injuries? Obviously, they're not just from his fall."

"Not unless he fell from an airplane." Schiff chuckled. Then he cleared his throat and looked away, remembering, I assume, that the deceased and I were friends. "I figure once he's on the ground, our perp gives him a real nasty workover."

"With what?"

"Dunno. Something blunt. A pipe? Maybe heavier. Not a pistol-whipping." He shrugged. "The pathologist should be able to fill in the rest."

"Was he beaten before or after he died?"

"Can't tell. Autopsy should help there, too."

Schiff shifted from foot to foot. I could see he was getting antsy. There was more to find in this goldmine of physical evidence, and he probably didn't want to miss a strike chatting with me. I asked him for a moment alone. And with a quick nod, he was gone.

I stood and stared at the remains of the man who had influenced my life more than almost any other. A man who had come to remind me so much of my father that at times I had confused him for the role. I saw past the mutilation and visualized Stanley's youthful face—not handsome, but distinguished—with bushy eyebrows, hazel-brown eyes, long nose, and a beard that was darker than his uniformly gray hair. His face commanded respect, but could still convey sympathy, understanding, and trust. Especially trust. Many, many people over the years had willingly put their lives in those hands that now lay mangled above his head.

A familiar voice broke the silence. "Doc?"

I looked over to see that Dev had joined me. Beside him, stood a woman almost his height but lacking any trace of his paunch. Her tawny blond hair was clipped back away from her face. With a strong chin, her face was on the narrow side, but her milk-and-honey complexion and scattering of freckles set off her high cheekbones and intense green eyes. The soft lines etched in her forehead and at the edges of her lips suggested she was more experienced and older than the twenty-something rookie she first appeared. She glanced at me with a brief nod before turning her impassive gaze back to the victim.

Dev regarded me with uncharacteristic somberness. "You okay?"

"Could be worse." I cleared my throat and shrugged, fighting off the torrent of emotions. "It could have been me."

Dev chuckled softly, but I thought I caught a disapproving glance from his colleague.

As if to get out of Stanley's earshot we stepped out of the room and talked in the hallway, but the door remained open, leaving a clear view of the body. "Dr. Ashman, meet my new partner, Detective Claire Shepherd." Dev pointed from me to her. "Claire's just joined Homicide."

I stretched my hand out to her. "It's Joel."

"Nice to meet you, Joel." Claire met my hand with a firm handshake, but maybe because of my earlier remark, she didn't reciprocate my smile.

"Doc consults for Homicide," Dev explained in a southern twang that more than twenty-five year of living in the Pacific Northwest hadn't masked. "Does our psychological profiling. Once in a while, he's useful."

"Stop gushing, Dev. You're embarrassing me."

Dev's smile faded. "Joel and the victim were friends," he said to Claire. "They used to share a practice."

Claire frowned and her green eyes widened sympathetically. "Oh, Joel, that's awful."

"Yeah," I said, breaking off eye contact.

"Hate to drag you down here so late." Dev cleared his throat. "I thought you could might give us an early lead on the investigation."

"I was up anyway," I said noncommittally.

The businesslike squint creasing Dev's forehead told me that we'd just moved beyond condolences. "Doc, what's your take on this?" He pointed at the carnage in the room.

I tried to focus—the crime scene is the chassis on which all psychological profiles are built—but the mix of feelings and memories clouded my assessment. All I could muster was: "It doesn't look like the work of someone who stumbled across Stanley while pulling a B- and -E."

"No shit," Dev grunted.

"So how did he get in?" I asked, stalling.

"Smashed the glass by the entrance," Dev said. "Wasn't even the good stuff. This building has no alarm. Security around here is a joke."

"You don't know the half of it." I told them about the overly accessible garage, and the trouble we'd had with previous break-ins. Then I got back to his initial question. "The killer shot Stanley in the neck, and then went to the trouble of beating him badly enough to kill him twice over . . ."

Claire nodded without taking her eyes off the cadaver. "Overkill."

"Exactly," I said. "Pure rage! And I don't think we're talking about a jealous spouse or cheated business associate. It's even more irrational than that."

Dev nodded. "You talking about one of his nut-job patients, aren't you?"

I wasn't in the mood to take issue with Dev's politically incorrect choice of terms. "You've got to consider his patients. Stanley worked with all comers."

Claire cocked her head. "How so?"

"Nowadays, most psychiatrists sub-specialize. Private practice, geriatrics, the institutionalized, forensic psychiatry, and so on. Not Stanley, he did it all. The man is—he was—a giant in the psychiatric community."

"Nobody jumps to mind, huh, Doc?" Dev asked.

I hesitated.

Dev picked up on my indecision. "Doc?"

I needed more time to sort it out in my head, so I said: "Divorced for years. No children. Did well, financially. And for the most part, he was well-liked."

Eyes narrowed, Claire viewed me quizzically. "'For the most part?'"

"His colleagues respected him," I said. "His patients could be another story."

"Oh?" Dev chewed his lip. "Why's that?"

"Stanley was interested in anger management. In fact, he was a pioneer in the field."

Dev thumbed at Stanley's pummeled corpse. "I think it's possible our killer has anger management issues," he said dryly.

"And Stanley use to consult at Western State Hospital." I turned to Claire: "Where they keep violent offenders with psychiatric diagnoses. The so-called forensic psych patients."

Claire nodded politely, but it struck me that she would've known about Western State. I mentally kicked myself for coming across as condescending, and then wondered why I cared how I came across to her on this of all nights. "I used to work with those forensic patients, too," I said. "Believe me, you wouldn't want some of them bearing a grudge against you."

"We ought to find out if any of them have been released lately," Dev said.

Claire pointed at the violent tangle of Stanley's arms. "Joel, what about his hands and wrists?" she said. "What's the significance of that?"

"Sometimes you see bizarre positioning like that with ritual murders." I shrugged. "But the rest of the scene doesn't fit with ritual homicide."

Staring at Stanley's fractured wrists and crushed fingers, we lapsed into a brief silence. "I hope our perp left an easy trail," Dev finally sighed. "I can tell you already, we're looking at a long suspect list."

I gazed at the splatter on the wall that traced the path of Stanley's final tumble.

"You two were close, huh?" Dev rested his hand on my shoulder again.

Without taking my eyes off the wall, I nodded. "Over the years, we shared an office, a partnership, and a close friendship."

What I hadn't figured out how to tell them, yet, was that we'd once shared a patient. Technically, she was Stanley's patient first. Then she became mine. And remained so, up until the moment she plunged off the Aurora Bridge.

I first laid eyes on Angela Connor a year, almost to the day, before Stanley's murder. The night I met her, I was working my regular on-call shift at Swedish Hospital's Emergency Psychiatric Unit.

Watching the security guard unlock the door to Angela's Quiet Room, I wondered what awaited me on the other side. More often than not, people locked inside Quiet Rooms (desolate little spaces, designed to safely hold patients at risk to themselves or others) are anything but quiet. But when the guard opened the heavy door, I found Angela sitting silently on the mattress atop the bench built into the wall with her knees drawn and a blanket wrapped around her from the neck down. She didn't look at me as I approached. Even when I sat down at her feet at the edge of the bench, she stared straight ahead and rocked gently, as if still alone.

"Angela?"

No reply.

"Angela, I'm Dr. Ashman."

Still nothing.

"I'm a psychiatrist."

She grunted a laugh, but showed no sign of acknowledging me.

One of the wonderfully simple rules of the psychiatric interview is: if you have nothing useful to say, keep your mouth shut. I took advantage of the silence and studied my new patient, while she continued to ignore me.

Angela's short hair stood in disarray on her head. Her tired face bore no makeup, and her lips were cracked and bloody. In spite of her unkempt appearance, I could see she had striking features: high cheekbones, upturned nose, full mouth, blue-gray eyes, and short, jet-black hair. From her chart, I knew that she was twenty-five, but if I hadn't, I would have guessed younger.

After a couple of silent minutes, Angela finally blinked. "When can I leave?" *she asked in a voice that was hoarse from having had an endotracheal tube of a ventilator recently pass through her vocal cords.*

"Angela, do you understand what it means to be held here for evaluation?" *I asked.*

She shrugged. "Doesn't mean I have talk to you."

True. According to state law, we can involuntarily hold anyone for 72 hours who we deem a potential danger to themselves or others. In that time, we can restrain, drug, force-feed, or even subject them to electroconvulsive therapy, but we can't force them to talk.

"Tell me, Angela, why amitriptyline? You're not even prescribed that."

Another shrug.

"Why not just swallow your prescription's worth of Fluquil?"

"Have you ever seen anyone die of a Fluquil overdose?" she asked.

"No."

She bundled the blanket tighter around her.

"But you're not dead," I pointed out.

"Not this time," she said. "They told me I came close."

"Very close," I agreed. If not for an astute ER physician, a ventilator, and an intravenous drip of sodium bicarbonate and potassium, no question, she would have died. But aside from a deep burn on her upper back—attributed to passing out too close to an electric baseboard heater—she'd survived her overdose physically unscathed.

"Do you plan to take another crack at it?" I asked.

Angela dropped her head into the blanket and sighed.

"What would you try the next time?"

"A gun? A rope? Carbon monoxide? What does it matter?"

"As you pointed out, some methods aren't that successful."

"I don't make two mistakes in a row," she said without looking up.

"What other mistakes have you made?"

"What a typical shrink's question!" She shook her head. Then, for the first time in fifteen minutes, she lifted her face to me, and her eyes challenged mine. "If you have to know, my last big mistake was talking to one of you."

Mentally filing the provocative comment to address later, when and if I could establish trust, I changed subjects. "Angela, where did you grow up?" Interview rule number two: when in doubt, go for the childhood.

"Here we go." She groaned and broke off the eye contact. "Let me make this easy for you. I grew up here in town, in an upper middle class, stable family. Daddy was a successful lawyer, mom a housewife. Two siblings—an older sister and a younger brother. All in all, I was a happy, well-loved little girl." She paused, then added as if an afterthought: "Okay, Dad was fucking me from eleven on, which didn't help, but hey, no one's got the perfect childhood. Right?"

Accusations of incest don't shock me anymore, but I don't ever remember one being couched in the same context. I managed to keep the surprise off my face, sensing that no reaction was my best approach.

"High school was a breeze," she continued, as if she'd been describing a tediously routine upbringing. "No eating disorder. No drug or alcohol issues. Never date-raped or anything. I went to college back east, Queens, on a scholarship. Needed a break from the old man, you understand." Again, she looked up and challenged with her eyes. "Graduated summa cum laude. With my marks and Daddy's connections, I could've gone to law school anywhere, but I chose not to."

"How come?"

She dropped her eyes back to the blanket. "You're thinking it was because I didn't want to validate Daddy by following in his footsteps, right?"

"You don't know what I'm thinking."

She ran a hand through her short hair. "Chances are, you're thinking what a great fuck I would be."

This time I couldn't hide the surprise. "Where did that come from?"

"It's my life story. Men always want me." She shrugged. "Truth be told, it's a blessing most of the time."

"What happened after college?" I asked, grabbing for a semblance of rapport.

Ignoring my question, she broke into a half-smile. "I don't mind you thinking about me like that. You're very cute in that intellectual way." Then the smile disappeared, and she added in a smaller voice: "Just don't hurt me, okay? I couldn't deal with that again."

With warning bells blaring inside my head, I rose from the bench. "Angela, I think it's best if I find you a female psychiatrist."

She said nothing until I reached the door. "I don't want another shrink."

"The fact is, Angela, you have to talk to someone."

"I want to talk to you . . . Please, Dr. Ashman."

There was nothing special in the words, but something in her voice—a glimmer of vulnerability that I hadn't heard up to that point—struck me. I felt a sudden pang of sympathy for her. Or maybe, subconsciously I'd already noticed the glaring similarities between Angela and a girl from my childhood. Whatever the reason, I turned and walked back to her bed. "You've got to understand that my concerns for you are strictly on a professional level." I met her stare. "Am I clear?"

"Crystal." She nodded. "No more nasty talk."

"Okay, after college . . ."

"Oh, God," She rubbed her face in her hands. "Odd jobs. A couple of short-term relationships. One with a girl. But much as I like the concept of lesbianism, I'm just not wired that way . . ."

And so it went. Salvo. And counter-salvo. I left the one-hour interview frustrated and exhausted, and not much further ahead for my effort. By the time I reached the back desk, Angela's old chart awaited me. She had only two previous psychiatric admissions; her most recent was a year earlier for a month-long stay at University Hospital. The faxed records reiterated what Angela had told me, but the University team had never found anyone to corroborate her incest story. Her discharge diagnosis read: "Major Depression with suicidal ideation and probable B.P.D." I sighed when I read the initials that stood for Borderline Personality Disorder. Exemplified by patients with unstable relationships, frequent suicide gestures, and hopeless responses to therapy, those three letters, 'B-P-D', have the power to send a chill up a psychiatrist's spine. Mine, anyway.

Mulling over the interview as I scribbled notes, I realized Angela wasn't a typical suicidal patient. Putting aside the attention-seeking and psychotic, people seen immediately *following a genuine suicide attempt act remarkably similar. Most are either regretful about, or indifferent to, the failure of their attempt. The depressed are easy to spot, because their mood is contagious; after five minutes with them, you begin to feel like stepping in front of a train.*

But Angela exhibited neither the despair nor the indifference typical of the depressed. Even at the time of the interview, I had the feeling she was assessing me—deliberately baiting me and then judging my reactions—as much as I was her. I didn't have a handle on Angela, and that troubled me.

Much about Angela troubled me. As frank as she had been for a first interview, I knew I was just scratching the surface. But I already was convinced that Angela was a tortured soul. And it wasn't merely my professional opinion. From the moment I met her, Angela reminded me of Suzie, the girl who had inadvertently cut short my childhood.

I fought off a chill. And I wrote off the visceral sense of unease as simply the remnant of a sad memory.

I was so wrong.